SECRET
KEEPERS

ALSO BY MINDY FRIDDLE

The Garden Angel

SECRET
KEEPERS

Mindy Friddle

St. Martin's Press
New York

SECRET KEEPERS. Copyright 2009 by Mindy Friddle. All rights reserved. Printed in the United States of America. For information, address St. Martin's Press, 175 Fifth Avenue, New York, N.Y. 10010.

www.stmartins.com

Library of Congress Cataloging-in-Publication Data

Friddle, Mindy.
    Secret keepers / Mindy Friddle. — 1st ed.
        p. cm.
    ISBN-13: 978-0-312-53702-9
    ISBN-10: 0-312-53702-6
    1. Older women—Fiction.   2. Parent and adult child—Fiction.   3. Mothers and sons—Fiction.   4. Mothers and daughters—Fiction.   5. Family secrets—Fiction.   6. City and town life—South Carolina—Fiction.   7. South Carolina—Fiction.   8. Southern States—Fiction.   9. Domestic fiction.   I. Title.
    PS3606.R49S43 2009
    813'.6—dc22

                                            2008043928

First Edition: May 2009

10   9   8   7   6   5   4   3   2   1

For Saga

ACKNOWLEDGMENTS

I'm grateful to my friend and former teacher Wilton Barnhardt for providing valuable feedback early on. Special thanks to my editor, George Witte, for his close reading and insight, and hats off to Terra Gerstner and all the talented folks at St. Martin's. Judith Weber, my agent *extraordinaire*, provided sure-footed guidance, tireless readings of many drafts, and powerful encouragement. Thanks also to Nat Sobel and all the readers at Sobel Weber. And love to Mike for his steadfast support and unfailing sense of humor.

How hard it is to escape from places. However carefully one goes they hold you—you leave little bits of yourself fluttering on the fences—little rags and shreds of your very life.

—KATHERINE MANSFIELD

PART I

am a ranth (AM-ah-ranth) n.

1. *Any of various annuals of the genus* Amaranthus *having dense green or reddish clusters of tiny flowers and including several weeds, ornamentals, and food plants. Also called pigweed.*

2. *An imaginary flower that never fades.*

ONE

The town had moved the Confederate Monument from the square to the gates of Springforth Cemetery some twenty years after the War of Northern Aggression, and General Robert E. Lee—who stood atop the mossy marble with a scowl—had never quite recovered. The general was listing, slowly sinking in the boggy soil, his finger pointing no longer at the ghostly Union brigade ahead, but just down and to the left, toward the new Ideal Laundry Factory, as if to demand extra starch. The stony glare of the good general was the last thing Emma Hanley's grandfather saw as he sat at his mahogany desk in his office, pondering a lost factory—foreclosure by some outfit up North was imminent—and an astonishing sweep of bad investments. As he swallowed the muzzle of a Colt .45, William McCann peered at the general, who seemed to look back at him approvingly, a kinship that comes from being beaten down by Yankees.

William McCann's self-inflicted gunshot on that brilliant spring day in 1908 made a mess of things. But then, he never did have a head for business. In those days, a man was born with his fortune, and occasionally he increased it, but he never lost it. And McCann, who'd never quite cottoned to the textile industry, had managed to lose everything, as his widow, Josephine, quickly discovered. The tree-lined estate in town went first, the family's seasonal residences next—the seaside place in Charleston, the summer bungalow in the Blue Ridge Mountains—everything inside them auctioned off, crated, and shipped *down to the pickle forks and finger bowls, how could they?*

They could; they did. The wealthy in Palmetto had little sympathy for downfall brought about by a gentleman's folly. Travel lust, for example. Seduced by the lure of far-flung jungles, perilous crags, and shimmering deserts, McCann had, for some time, been obsessed by exotic botanicals. He fancied himself a plant hunter—ignoring his failing business and leaving behind his wife, Josephine, for months at a time, appeasing her with promises of civilized travel fit for a woman upon his return.

A pity, many in the town noted, that shortly before her husband's unfortunate firearm accident—for that is what the family thereafter referred to it as, an *accident*, a man simply cleaning his gun—Josephine McCann had already sent a steamer trunk to Paris, in preparation for a season with her daughter, Angeline, on the Continent. That voyage was canceled, the trunk recalled. Without means, the McCann women found themselves stuck in Palmetto, South Carolina.

The financial snarl untangled, the fortune unspooled, and the McCann women's property shrank to a dot on the map, to a single address: Amaranth—a staid Victorian at the edge of town, built on a whim a decade previously, on land McCann had purchased purely for its rich, well-drained soil, fierce fecundity, and eastern light.

At Amaranth, the widow Josephine insisted decorum remain. Linen napkins, yellowed as old teeth, were used at all meals, as well as a few remaining pieces of silverware, the handles heavy as guns. In time, daughter Angeline—who had not been a debutante, having lost that privilege along with other trappings—settled for a young soldier as a husband, a doughboy. The poor soul lost his mind on the battlefields of France and never found it again. Angeline moved from her brief newlywed venture back into Amaranth with her mother. Six months later, Emma arrived, born into a household of women pining for escape, who continued to insist they were trapped in a decidedly lower station in life, a station from which there was no leaving the town, at least not in any sort of civilized fashion.

But that was going to change, finally. For on this unseasonably warm April morning nearly eight decades after her grandfather's firearm mishap, Emma Hanley, seventy-two, found herself just days away from embarking on a journey of a lifetime. The Trip, as her husband, Harold, referred to it—often while rolling his eyes— a cruise to Europe.

That was the year spring rushed through the town, barely stopping. By April, a morning stroll produced clammy sweat at the nape of one's neck—a sure sign of an approaching brutal summer. But this harbinger of a merciless season did not overly concern the people of Palmetto, as it would have years before, back when a cruel season made airless lint-filled mills suffocating, left crops dead, farmers unpaid, and children unfed. Now, there was central air, office jobs, and grocery stores. Cable television brought news all day and all night—reports that the Berlin Wall might soon fall, rumors the Japanese were buying up Hawaii, hotel by hotel. There was a rosy-cheeked president well into his seventh decade for whom Emma Hanley did not much care, though she did find some use for him: When Harold protested that Emma and he were too old to take the Trip, she reminded her husband that the Leader of the Free World—a man for whom Harold had twice voted—was even older.

That was the spring when Emma's life took a dramatically new course, and it all started that Saturday morning in April 1987, a day when Emma was happier than she'd been in years— studying her itinerary, wondering about comfortable shoes and all-weather cloaks, peering at her husband across the stack of maps and Fodor's Guides on the dining room table, nodding pleasantly as he announced he would soon be heading to the Biscuit Basket for his daily coffee klatch. For in the last few weeks, travel plans had brought to the Hanley marriage an unexpected spirit of compromise. Nowadays, when Harold sucked his teeth or stayed too long at his breakfasts, all Emma had to do was think of the Trip, and a thrill like harp strings would thrum inside her, and she would be happy again.

"Look here at this mess," Harold said now, holding up the morning newspaper. "No respect for the dead." Emma glanced up from the brochure she was reading on converting foreign currency. CEMETERY VANDALS STRIKE AGAIN! the headline on the front page of the *Palmetto News* screamed, and there was a picture of the general himself—festooned with toilet paper and what appeared to be Hawaiian leis, looking, appropriately enough, drunk and rakish. Behind the statue, streamers drooped over the rusty iron spires of Springforth. Harold studied the article. When he read silently, his lips moved. "Says here, kids done it," he said. "Teenagers and their parties." He shook his head.

"Perhaps someone at town hall will remember now to fix the memorial," Emma said cheerfully. There had been talk about repairing the Confederate Monument for years, and restoring the cemetery, and doing something with the old mill and all the rest, but then the town would forget, and nothing happened. It was as if the people of Palmetto just stopped seeing the statues, the shuttered cotton mills, the vandalized graveyards. They drove right by, sealed behind their tinted car windows, sipping their travel mugs, nodding their heads to music. Even the McCann saga had apparently been wiped from the town's memory. Although the old cotton factory—with the McCann name fading on the brick—remained, and there was still a McCann side street and, for a short time, a shopping center with the name, no one except Emma herself and her friends Miss Gibble and Lila Day associated the McCann name with lost fortune or with penniless women lamenting their strangled fate. Come to think of it, Emma reflected now, perhaps the town's collective amnesia wasn't such a bad thing after all.

"Gonna be a hot one today," Harold said, reading aloud now

the detailed weather forecast—complete with humidity levels and wind directions—in that halting way that set Emma's teeth on edge. *The Trip,* she thought, *the Trip.*

She smiled. "Good, it will be nice to get away. They say that London is cool this time of year."

Harold grunted in agreement. He remained a reluctant traveler. Now that they had a little savings and an abundance of time, he had finally agreed to venture overseas because, as Emma reminded him, he owed her this favor. He owed her because decades of installing appliances meant Harold had spent years in women's kitchens, which led to having coffee with them, or iced tea and a slice of pound cake, accompanied by long talks and she didn't know what all. She didn't care to speculate. Oh, Harold had cultivated himself quite a following in Palmetto, all right, though Emma had never put her foot down. Well, perhaps a few times, many years before: knock-down drag-outs that ended with seething anger, threats of leaving, a violent clashing, damp sheets, and, nine months later, a child. Three of these battles had names: Will, Dora, and Bobby.

"More coffee?" she asked.

"I'll get some Sanka later." He put on his jacket. "Sure you're not coming?"

"Not with all the things I've got left to do."

It was part of the Hanleys' new unspoken agreement: He would pretend to demand Emma come along to his morning coffee klatch with all those adoring widow women as vigorously as she would decline. With the Trip on the horizon, Emma was perfectly happy to send him off to the Biscuit Basket, and he knew it. Her interests remained elsewhere: across the Atlantic, where, according to their itinerary, they would be within a week at *the dazzling Dutch Capital of Amsterdam with its quaint, cobbled streets, steeply gabled merchants' houses, and famous museums and galleries.* Yes, thought Emma, after thirty-seven years of marriage, she and Harold were enjoying some well-earned equilibrium, at least temporarily. A regular cease-fire. For what was marriage but a treaty between two warring little nations, a congress of conflicting desires and wills?

"There is one little thing, before you go," she said.

"What's that?" He stood at the door in the black jogging pants he'd taken to wearing these days. His tan Windbreaker was zipped, the baseball cap pulled down, hiding his eyes. He was waiting to be dismissed. It was twenty after eight. In ten minutes, he'd be out the door. You could set your watch by him. Emma's husband was a man who'd established times for everything—bedtimes, meals, and bowel movements. Daylight saving time presented a quandary every six months in the Hanley household, until Harold, with a shot of prune juice and a stack of *Reader's Digests*, reset himself. Try to drag a man like *that* across the ocean and to a different time zone.

"Could you help get my old trunk down from the attic?" she asked.

Ah, the travel trunk. One of the few possessions Emma had brought to her marriage.

When she'd met Harold, Emma had still been living at Amaranth. It was a rooming house by then, run by Mrs. Leonard Anderson, a jowly and coarse woman whose meaty arms waggled as she beat eggs; she was glad to have a fine lady like Emma as a tenant, quiet and minding her own business among the cacophony of boisterous, drunken fools who swarmed the place.

While there were respectable rooming houses in the town for maiden ladies in 1950, Amaranth wasn't one of them. But how could Emma leave? That place was a kind of purgatory, a parallel world that both tortured and flattered her with memories of better times. The chandelier in the foyer, stripped of its crystals, blinked dimly and swung in crooked, precarious arcs. The strips of torn cabbage rose wallpaper in the hallway waved vaguely in the drafts of cold air. The red carpet, trod upon by steel-toed work boots, offered a pink threadbare path up the stairs.

Emma had been teaching the lower grades for nearly a decade

by then. Her grandmother was long gone, her mother, with whom she'd shared one drafty room on the second floor, had been dead all of six weeks, and Emma found some comfort in going through her grandmother's travel trunk daily, sorting her grandfather's botanical sketches. She'd kept the trunk since she was a young thing, cherishing it like a hope chest. Instead of putting away linens and finery for an impending marriage—prospects were too dim for that—Emma had stuffed the steamer with magazines, a crumpled atlas or two, and a bundle of vintage postcards from Rome, Paris, and London that she'd happened upon once at a flea market. And there was also the small, sad worn wad of money that her grandmother had stashed there for an emergency, an occasion that, Emma reflected, not only had arrived, but also, for a very long time, never stopped.

In those weeks after her mother died, Emma checked the train schedules every Tuesday, taking along her emergency fund, zipped in the side pocket of her satin-lined pocketbook. A one-way ticket could take her very far, indeed. Once, she even approached the station ticket window, close enough to see the bearded, weary man there talking on the black phone while eating his lunch, close enough to see the nervous, timid red-headed woman reflected back in the glass.

And then came the morning Emma heard an awful clatter from downstairs, and Mrs. Anderson's hearty laughter, too. Emma closed the trunk, locked her door, and ventured downstairs to the kitchen to find out what all the racket was about, the clanging and shouts. There was a new stove being put in. *The other one just upped and quit on me*, Mrs. Anderson told her, *no telling how old.* The previous stove, white enamel, heavy as God, sat upended in the corner, its doors and pipes amputated and discarded in a pile, and it hurt Emma to look at it, to remember the legions of Christmas turkeys and Easter hams her grandmother had once cooked in it. Then, from behind the new stove, Harold Hanley stood up, plaster dust smeared across one cheek, a sheen of sweat glistening on his forehead, HAL stitched over one pocket of his

tight dun-colored work shirt. His gaze fell on Emma, and he nodded politely, but he left those yellow eyes on her face, the heat of
him shone on her and she was so alone, like freezing to death,
numb and half-dead for so long—she hadn't realized how lonely!
And scared? Lord, she was scared, her mother not cold in her
grave, and Emma herself hibernating. There were combed
grooves in his black hair. Hair oil! Only the lower-class men wore
hair oil, only the workers. The room spun and left her weak-
kneed, till Mrs. Anderson hobbled over with a dinette chair and
said, *You sit down here. Girl, you look right peaked.*

And so it was that Emma found herself courted, quite suddenly
engaged, and scolded by Miss Gibble, her supervising teacher, who
taught the upper grades. Upon news of Emma's unlikely suitor and
imminent betrothal, Miss Gibble pulled Emma aside. "You'll be
bored to tears, with your mind," Miss Gibble warned. "What on
earth will you talk about with that man?"

Talk? Talk didn't have much to do with it. Instead, Emma's
impending marriage had to do with the certain spot on the nape
of her neck that Harold Hanley had discovered. Yes, there were
those who said she was marrying beneath her, settling for an un-
schooled appliance repairman who did not even have his high
school diploma. But there were those who thought the reverse,
too, that Harold Hanley was marrying an old maid teacher when
he could have had a levelheaded girl better at doing things like
pickling peaches or ironing sheets and scrubbing the kitchen floor
with Old Dutch.

"You're not settling down. You're just settling," Miss Gibble
chided, before she turned to clap the erasers over a trash can.
"Now you'll never leave this town."

*And what does ol' dried-up Eleanor Gibble know about loving
anyway?* Harold had asked later, after Emma had shared her best
friend's misgivings with him. Back when Emma still shared such
thoughts with Harold. *What does that one know about loving?*

Miss Gibble did indeed know about loving, since she'd lost
her fiancé, a pilot from Mississippi, when he was shot down over

Germany in the war. He'd been a blond, handsome man with enormous red protruding ears, whose smiling photograph and lock of hair stayed in a heavy gold locket tucked behind the starched white muslin of Miss Gibble's blouse. Occasionally, Miss Gibble would open the locket and gaze down at the diminutive grinning face there before slowly closing the cover again, as if it were the lid of a tiny coffin. *I shall always be a miss,* insisted Miss Gibble to the teaching faculty after the funeral. *None of this silly talk about how there will be others. For there will be no one else.*

Shortly after her marriage, Emma used the emergency fund from her travel trunk to finance a used 1949 Chevy pickup, officially launching Hanley's Appliance Repair. She and Harold moved into their '50s split-level that was all the rage then, a spec house that went cheap when the builder went broke. By then, Emma was expecting, and couldn't lift anything heavier than a teacup. They'd hardly had any furniture anyway. As for the travel trunk, it was relegated to the attic, until this day, when Emma persuaded Harold to finally lug it down.

The trunk, battered and filthy, sat now in the sunny corner of their kitchen like a mysterious stranger soaking up warmth and company.

Harold looked warily at it from the corner of his eye while he drank a glass of water at the sink, as if he still didn't believe her claims that, no, she didn't plan to *take that old thing on the Trip.* What Emma had in mind was finding her grandmother's travel journal. She was certain it was in there somewhere, and wouldn't that be something? To take it along on the Trip. But she kept that wish to herself. There was no use appealing to Harold's nostalgic side, for Emma suspected her husband did not have one. The past did not much concern a man who was content to live in the present, whose retirement days offered him so much fun.

"Maybe I should make Bobby get out a little this morning," Harold said now from behind her. "On the Trip, he's going to have to get used to doing things he don't like."

"Well, you can try, I suppose," she said, playing along. By pretending to insist their son accompany him, Harold was clearly assuaging his own guilt about escaping to the Biscuit Basket.

"Bobby?" he called. "You sure you don't feel like a walk?"

There was no reply from the living room, just the antic whirs and *boing boing* sounds of morning cartoons and the smoke from Bobby's unfiltered Camels.

"Son?"

"No," came the groggy response.

Harold met her eyes, then shook his head, sadder than usual. "Well, I tried."

"Don't worry," Emma said now. "He's going to have to get out with us this afternoon." After a beat, she said, "Shoe shopping, Harold. Don't tell me you forgot?"

Puzzlement did a funny little dance across his features, until resignation took hold. "No. No, I didn't forget. Guess I'll pick up the medicine at the drugstore on the way back this morning. Reckon you better call and check to make sure they got it ready?"

"All right."

"The extra, too," he said.

The medicine for the trip is what he meant. Bobby's pills. The extra dose to help Bobby calm down and sleep. Was it a rebuke, Harold's reminder about Bobby's need for extra medicine? Perhaps. Taking Bobby along on the Trip wouldn't be easy. But they couldn't very well leave him behind with Dora.

Dora would *insist* on taking Bobby to that new church over at the Crossroads shopping center. All that talk of demons fleeing, saints suffering, and Jesus appearing just ignited Bobby's own delusions. For days after his last visit, when Emma asked Bobby to do something as simple as taking out the garbage, she found herself competing with the voices of John the Baptist and Saint Paul. And the saints always won out.

"Yes, I'll call the pharmacy." Emma said. "I'll see to it they have the extras ready. You're walking?"

Silly question. Harold always walked to his breakfasts. Somehow, even in sweatpants and Windbreaker and cap, he was fine-looking. Yes, she'd have to give him that. He was slim, without the paunch most men his age acquired. And he had his own teeth and drove at night. Quite a commodity.

"I suppose Betty will be at breakfast?" she couldn't resist asking. "And the McCormick sisters?"

"Yeah, I reckon Betty and them will be there."

"I believe she mentioned that last night. When I ran into her at Winn-Dixie. Funny—Betty didn't know about the Trip. I promised we'd send her a postcard."

Harold adjusted his cap in the hall mirror.

The evening before, when Emma had encountered Betty Snodgrass hovering over the cucumbers in the produce aisle, Betty had practically purred, *Oh, your husband, that Hal Hanley, he just tickles me no end!* And Betty, whose arthritic hip gave her a gimpy sway like a drunken dancer, and whose thin lips shone like cellophane—lip gloss at her age!—whispered, in her smoker's rasp, *He keeps us in stitches. Just a darling.* Emma chuckled in a way she hoped resembled fondness before reminding Betty in an offhand way that she was *just frantic* planning their *golden honeymoon*, as Harold liked to call it. Emma had made that part up, of course. Harold would never call their impending trip a *golden honeymoon*, but a little lie like that was worth it just to see Betty's crestfallen expression.

The truth was, Emma now lacked the patience to converse with Betty or Velma Scranton or the McCormick twins about double-coupon days and the senior citizen booth at the flea market. The McCormick sisters still dressed as if they were young things, rouged and clad in polka dots and heels, sopping up sausage biscuits and milk gravy, their dentures clacking. Velma claimed she was retired from the textile industry, though Emma knew she'd spent thirty years sewing the crotch seam in dungarees. Not one of them was interested in the Eiffel Tower or Stonehenge or the Royal Tulip Garden; they had made that perfectly clear. Hal's Gals, people called them.

"I guess I better get a move on," Harold said now. The stove clock read eight thirty.

"You go on," Emma said, thereby releasing him. *To the Biscuit Basket and your fans*, she stopped herself from adding. "I'm sure they'll be waiting."

He stepped out on the front porch and turned to close the door behind him, not bothering to hide the delight and anticipation on his face as he finally headed out.

It never occurred to Emma he might not return.

TWO

The first temperature-controlled shopping center dazzled the fickle town like a mistress. From the moment it opened in 1968, McCann Square's long passages of indoor shops and artificial lighting, the narrow escalator and tiny skylight, the acres of asphalt parking, left the town smitten. Suddenly, downtown Palmetto, with its paved-over trolley tracks, old-fashioned tattered awnings, and stand-alone three-story brick buildings, seemed shopworn and tired, and a little embarrassing. Who wanted to brave the elements anymore for a pair of socks?

The land for the new shopping center had come about years before from an impressive strip of wilderness property lost in the fog of bankruptcy after William McCann's fateful gun accident. McCann had hoped he might one day bequeath the town a botanical wonderland—an arboretum, a garden of exotica, plucked by his own hands from Amazonian bogs, Himalayan steppes, Andes wilds. It was not to be.

By 1970, the temptress, McCann Square, lured shops away from downtown at an alarming rate. Rows of Palmetto stores were abandoned. Downtown was officially discarded—faithful and solid to the end, but dowdy and heartbroken, lied to, and a good deal poorer, like an ex-wife after a bitter divorce.

And then, inevitably, the town's passion for the shopping center cooled. By 1985, a sleek new two-story mall on greener pastures—outlying land once known as "way out yonder near the airport"—replaced McCann Square as the town's favorite. Despite a face-lift and a new electronic sign, the lonely, dated corridors of the shopping center reeked of desperation.

McCann Square's signs of age and shabbiness troubled many in the town and saddened Dora Quattlebaum. Dora suspected that many townspeople who drove daily by such an eyesore wondered what they'd ever seen in such a place. The blond brick was stained, the magnolias unpruned, the parking lot cracked and scarred, the weed-choked islands deserted in the vast emptiness of the parking lot. What would become of such a monstrosity now? Dora was troubled to think this downtrodden shopping center might not survive, for she harbored a secret fondness for the place. After all, it was Dora's great-grandfather who once owned this parcel of land.

And then, crisis.

Dora was among the first to hear about the rumored Neeple's Gentlemen's Club opening at McCann Square, right where Belk's department store once stood. Dora penned a letter for her husband, Donny, to send to the editor of the *Palmetto News*, titled NO SODOM SQUARE FOR PALMETTO! reminding readers that Neeple's had for years been located near the railroad tracks and shuttered mills, where such unsavory places should stay. With a strip club as an anchor, could a billiard hall, liquor store, and hourly hotel rooms be far behind? The next zoning hearing was packed, as was the town council meeting. Dora and her husband, Donny, along with Pastor Pete, attended both, and added their voices to the chorus of angry townspeople. By then, even the *Palmetto News* had voiced its outrage with a devastating editorial:

> Perhaps the shopping center developers in danger of selling out for their thirty pieces of silver should remember that they live in the very buckle of the Bible Belt, *not* below it.

The shameful business in danger of rearing its ugly head now should remain zippered, ignored, and out of sight, as the traditional town of Palmetto demands, and certainly not exposed at McCann Square.

How delighted Dora was when the situation was quietly defused, as behind-the-scenes discussions lead to a public announcement: McCann Square would not be sold into the clutches of greedy, sinful sleaze buckets with pinkie rings but purchased by Christian Crossroads Incorporated, a new center for faith-based commerce. The town fathers breathed a sigh of relief and decided to ignore the tenuous shady financing and considerable finagling this new development had wrought. Christian Crossroads Church would anchor one end, and at the other end of the complex, a number of vendors had already committed to moving in: Holy Smoke Cigar and Pipes, Pray and Pay Title Loans, and Hole in the Sole Shoe Repair.

After McCann Square was rescued from the clutches of degradation, Dora felt more bound to the place than ever. Not only had the land once been family owned, but the new Crossroads Shopping Center had also been delivered from sin and redeemed by faith-based commerce, just as she herself had been. Lately, Dora was pleased to see the place looking better. The magnolias were trimmed, the brick power-washed, and the parking lot weeded. The same furnishings, garments, scents and textures, knickknacks and what-nots that now filled Crossroads also filled Dora's own life with a dizzying sense of gratification.

Today, however, as Dora pulled into the entrance of Christian Crossroads, her usual pleasure at arriving for morning shopping had been deflated—tamped down by her husband's single sentence directed to her from across the breakfast table, just as she'd been shredding cheese over a steaming bowl of grits for Kyle and Sandy. *No shopping today, Dora.*

Which was absurd. They went to church at Crossroads several times a week. Not only that, Dora's aerobics class met Saturday mornings here at Crossroads. She could hardly avoid the shops. Donny knew that.

Dora walked across the empty parking lot, relieved to find she still had enough time to warm up and test the sound system on-stage. Inside the shopping center, the double doors echoed with a lonely clang behind her. Dora headed to the center of Cross-roads, stepped up on the stage, and set down her purse by the boom box and stack of cassettes. She took a deep breath, exhaled slowly, stretched her arms.

Dora took pride in keeping herself up. It was one of the reasons she'd been selected to head up the Firm Believers, a weekly Christ-centered weight-loss program at Crossroads. She also had—at one time, anyway—infectious enthusiasm. The clubs, councils, parties, and antiwar protests she once organized in her youth had been re-placed by PTA, prayer circles, pro-life rallies, and Firm Believers. Dora liked it out here in the middle of the shopping center, not stuffed in that empty store the Firm Believers started in, the place over there by the restrooms that used to be This Little Light of Mine Candle Shop and still smelled like melting crayons. That aw-ful room, with its low ceiling and abandoned cash register, had about suffocated her, so she'd insisted the Firm Believers move out here under the skylight and on the little stage area, where she could breathe, and that's when half the Firm Believers quit, since they were convinced the shoppers walking by were staring at them.

The corridors began to echo with footsteps and conversation as more shoppers straggled into Paws for Prayer Pet Grooming and Testamints & Candies. Crossroads began to sound busy. Not so busy as McCann Square had been in its heyday, certainly. No one could top that. Dora began stretching with some knee bends. She would start the group with the usual warm-ups.

The clouds moved across the domed skylight overhead, un-hurried, with tantalizing serenity. Two sparrows fluttered near the ceiling, twittering. Were they trapped, or had they taken up residency?

A few members of the Firm Believers arrived. Flossie West

and Garnet Stewart wore skirts. They claimed the leotards were too hot, and since they were going through the Change of Life, they were both tormented by hot flashes, and stopped constantly to fan themselves and each other midway through the routine. Jill Cuttler waved to Dora and began head rolls and knee bends. Dora's arms suddenly felt heavy. Was this really *her*, up on the stage, head of the Firm Believers, moving expertly through these crunches and lunges? More and more, she felt as if she were just going through the motions.

Betty Snodgrass trotted up, the McCormick sisters right behind her. They had on matching Firm Believer outfits—white leotards and terry cloth headbands with the little silver crosses embossed in front, although Betty was wearing hers all wrong. The skirt was pulled up too high, and the headband was around her neck, of all places, like a turtleneck. They all looked up at Dora, who stood on the stage, her hands at her waist, twisting.

"I thought for sure I was running late," Betty Snodgrass said, looking around. "Don't we start at noon?"

"Let's just wait a few minutes," Dora said, peering down at them. "You know how hectic Saturday mornings are. It's hard to get everyone here on time."

There was a murmur of agreement, and the McCormick sisters lay down on their mats and made flapping motions, but Betty continued to stand and look at her watch. People called them Hal's Gals, Dora had heard. She supposed she should be grateful for the three women coming to the Firm Believers, even if it was just to curry favor with her. Dora had found herself in an uneasy alliance with the women. They'd told her what a delight her father was, how desperately he would be missed on that trip he was taking, and what a shame it was that such a charming man couldn't get out more among friends. "Your daddy was in fine form this morning," Betty said, giggling.

"But that trip he is so worried about," one of the McCormick twins piped in. "He is just tore up about being dragged off halfway around the world. The poor man is in torment."

"Let's continue to warm up," Dora said. "Stretch, ladies! Reach for heaven!"

The Firm Believers had begun with such great hope, but Dora looked out now with bitter disappointment. The group had dwindled from two dozen eager women to a handful. All the young mothers had dropped out first, claiming it was just too hard to arrange babysitting, which was a silly excuse when you thought about it, because Suffer the Little Children Day Care was just down the hall. Others claimed that they were making spectacles of themselves smack-dab in the middle of Crossroads with shoppers walking by, staring. Well, but no one wanted to do the actual exercising; that was the problem. The group loved the opening prayers and the doughnuts and coffee afterwards, but no one really liked the hard work in between. Yes, this was a sorry bunch, surely not at all what Pastor Pete had planned when he'd told Dora the Firm Believers could be an excellent recruiting tool for Crossroads. They could have really been something.

Dora should have cared more about such a failure, but as hard as she tried, she couldn't. Not now. Not while Donny kept her so secretly penniless, and not when Kyle was sneaking out of his bedroom at night and acting up so badly that Donny told him no son of his would run wild in high school, and reminded him there would be no further warning—there would be action. The bad part was that Donny didn't even know about those other times Dora had caught Kyle sneaking out, those times she'd scolded Kyle and was beside herself with worry. She was keeping the knowledge to herself until she worked up the nerve to tell Donny.

Yes, Dora thought, as she continued stretching up onstage, going through the motions was all she could manage anymore, and even that was getting testy. Lately, memories flooded her mind without mercy, saturating her dreams and wrecking her concentration. Her prayers seemed staticky and distant, as if the Lord had tuned her out. She was beginning to feel forsaken, and that, she knew, was a dangerous thing.

"Dora, honey, shouldn't we start?" Betty asked now. "It's almost ten after."

And to punish Betty—who had the impudence to remind Dora to start at ten after twelve, when Dora was holding out for more members, for surely more women would be coming today, surely this wasn't all!—to put Betty in her place, Dora asked her to lead the group prayer.

"Oh, dear," Betty said, shrinking in nervousness, "I hadn't planned on—"

Dora turned on the microphone up onstage and glared down at Betty. "And now Miss Betty will lead us in prayer," Dora's voice echoed through the corridors. She handed the microphone down, which screamed with feedback and drowned out Betty's words. The women held their ears and grimaced.

". . . in Christ's name we pray . . . ," Betty finished.

Dora took back the microphone. She felt foolish standing on stage in front of six women, but if she came down off the stage to lead the class, how would that look? Like failure, that's what. The Firm Believers were shrinking drastically, all right, but not in hip measurements.

"Well, I've got a real treat for us this week." Dora turned on the tape player behind her. Rock music wasn't allowed at Crossroads, unless it was Christian rock. But Dora had bought a new cassette tape from A Joyful Noise that promised faith-based music with a beat. *Your favorite pop tunes . . . remade with Christ-centered lyrics!* She popped in a tape from George Thoroughlygood.

A guitar riff poured from the speakers of the boom box on stage. Drums. Dora began the routine with two small kicks. Betty frowned and adjusted her hearing aid. The singer began. *I'm washed clean in the blood of the lamb . . . I'm good to the bone. Good to the bone, yeah! G-g-g-g-goood. Goood to the bone.*

For a few minutes, with her heart pounding, her hands clapping, a sheen of perspiration on her lip, Dora felt as if she were dancing to the hi-fi in the barn again. The barn! How could she forget it? It had been Will's idea to fix up the old place at the back of their parents' property. He'd found a roll of green shag rug somewhere and strung up some lights. Dora added candles and lawn furniture. And a cot, of course.

Goood to the bone . . . She was dancing faster now, fast fast fast. The Firm Believers were leaning on each other and grunting.

"Dora? Honey, I'm about to burn up," someone said.

"Let's start the cooling down," Dora said, and began a head roll. She looked up again at the skylight. The wind had picked up. Big clots of cotton were skittering past playfully.

But the Firm Believers had already stopped and were packing up.

A few shoppers straggled by, averting their eyes.

What, Dora wondered, was she doing here?

Afterwards, the Firm Believers headed to Grounds for Faith for their usual doughnuts and coffee. Dora had already made up her mind to stay behind.

"I'm sure there will be more people next time," Jill whispered to her.

Dora tried to look busy packing up her cassette tapes.

"Let's get coffee with the others."

"You go ahead," Dora said. "I don't trust myself there."

"Oh, come on, Dora. You can afford the calories."

Little did Jill know, but it wasn't the calories that Dora couldn't afford. Dora had just twenty-four dollars for the rest of the week, and she still had to pick up some things for supper. Even a buck for a cup of coffee might cause another big fight. Ever since Donny had insisted she turn over all her receipts to him every week, he scrutinized her every expense before he doled out her weekly household allowance. How on earth was she supposed to feed a family this way?

"Let's skip it, then, and go to Agape," Jill said as Dora came down from the stage. Jill had sweated off most of her makeup, except for her red lipstick. She was cheerful and petite, with the quick movements of a finch, and beside her Dora felt ungainly and dour, flightless as an emu, one of those birds raised on ranches now, like cattle. "Did you hear? They're having a big sale."

"Oh, no, I don't think so. Donny would kill me."

"Honey, that's what credit cards are for."

"Well, I don't know." She did have the extra Visa in that secret flap in her wallet, the one that hadn't yet been maxed out, the one for emergencies.

"Think of all the money we'll save on a sale like this. And you know everything will get picked over tomorrow."

Dora let herself be led down the hall and past the coffee shop and right up to the entrance of Agape. The gift shop already had a line at the cash register. "See? What did I tell you? You just have to see the twelve apostles candelabra. It is to die for."

"Next time, maybe."

"Oh, Dora, you are so good. You put me to shame."

But she wasn't good. Not at all. Dora's inner peace was gone; that was the problem. And Crossroads made it worse. The place was packed with memories. Try as she might, she would always see McCann Square winking at her behind the veil of Crossroads. Even now, as she walked through the corridor, Dora found herself thinking of McCann Square's grand opening on June 12, 1968—the same day she had lost her virginity. Both events featured high expectations and too little planning. Yet, McCann Square's grand opening was deemed a success, while Dora's fumbling deflowering was both unremarkable and indelible. The day of the grand opening, when Dora's parents—when all the parents in the town, it seemed—had been walking around the shopping center in awe, that afternoon she'd let Ernie Teek come over to her parentless house, sneak into her room, and have his way with her. She just hadn't bothered to stop him, or perhaps she hadn't tried hard enough, but surely she *had* tried. The memory of that afternoon floated up to her now—how she'd been amused at the contrast of Ernie's long blue-jeaned legs sprawled alongside her pale, freshly shaved ones on the white eyelet of her bedspread.

Dora was certain then, at sixteen, that she was in love—not with the smitten Ernie Teek, whose father owned Teek Chevrolet and who made up for tongue-tied conversation and limp, bad hair by driving a convertible—but with Jim Morrison. For propped on her bureau, across from her bed, sat the Doors album she'd pilfered from her brother Will's room, the album that her brother and she had fought bitterly about just that morning when he'd accused Dora of wearing it out by playing it so much and swearing then to get a freakin' lock for his room if she couldn't keep her greedy little fingers off his things. It was the sullen pout of Jim Morrison on the cover of the Doors album that held Dora that day; it was into Jim Morrison's perilous eyes that Dora peered over the pimply shoulder of Ernie Teek; it was to the voice crooning "Love Me Two Times" that she directed her breathy moans. Before Dora knew it, Ernie was kissing her, and after a furtive thrusting, it was all over, and she hadn't even gotten a good look at the mechanics of the act. But when Ernie peered down at her with a stunned expression—grateful and a little in awe—that kind of power was like jet fuel for Dora, launching her life into a new orbit.

She and Ernie had arrived at the crowded McCann Square grand opening late, disheveled, with a glazed look in their red-rimmed eyes, which was more a result of the marijuana cigarette Ernie had introduced Dora to on the way there in his convertible than carnal bliss.

Will had spotted her in front of Ivey's Department Store, where she stood giggling with Ernie. Will had known, somehow. He'd come over and gripped her elbow. "Dora, what happened?" he asked.

Wanda Wilson hung back behind him and looked at Dora with pity. Wanda, her best friend since second grade, who, just a few summers before, helped Dora build frog houses with flower-pots and mud and who'd laughed when Dora drew constellations on her freckled back with a ballpoint pen—Wanda had the nerve to fall in love with Will, and since then, the two had become practically inseparable, and Dora a third wheel.

"Dora?" Will's grip tightened on her arm, and she'd grinned and looked away. By then Ernie had taken off, Will's glare on his back like a laser. Yes, it was always Will who knew Dora best, who could clamp down on her like no one else, who'd tried his best to deadhead the wild bloom of her foolish spirit.

By the time Jake Cary came along her junior year, Will was just happy Dora had a steady. Of course, Jake did not so much stem the gushing stream of Dora's lustful acts and growing skill as focus them. Dora had dragged the cot out of the barn on sunny days and then lay there smoking a joint in her bikini, getting tanned as an Indian, waiting for Jake to get off work. There was this thing Jake used to do to wake her up: mix vodka in an Icee and pour frozen glops of it in the hollows of her collarbones and belly, or behind her knees and . . . her face reddened now at the memories. And lately the pictures just didn't stop; that was the problem. Just didn't leave her alone. She even thought she saw Jake Cary at a filling station last week, and that was just crazy, a sure sign she was losing it.

It was hard to believe she'd been Kyle's age when the happiest craziest days of her life began. It was frightening to think just how carefree she'd been. And then there was the summer before Will was in country, before Bobby theorized about hidden microphones in spiderwebs, or Jake got his draft notice. Before it all collapsed. The war compressed their summer, wrung out the sweetness. That was the beginning of a very bad time in her life. Oh, Lord, why? Why was she thinking of those things now? Her mind flew around, never landing, like one of those trapped sparrows in the skylight.

In truth, Dora missed her old church, Palmetto First Baptist, where she and Donny were married and where Dora was baptized. She would never admit that to Donny, of course. They'd stopped attending First Baptist last year and joined Crossroads because Donny said it was a must for business. And now he was treasurer of Crossroads, for goodness' sake. Besides, Crossroads had saved McCann Square. And it had the biggest youth program around. But still.

Back when Dora was born again, she believed she'd be a new person, and it had felt like that. For a while. Long enough to marry a man like Donny and have two children, long enough to feel redeemed. She could never have managed to have her family, a husband like Donny and two children, and a normal life without her redemption. Of course, her husband had always assumed her youth was filled with loose morals, just garden-variety hedonism, and even he didn't suspect just how dark her sin was. And never would! What she would love right now was to confess to a man of the cloth, someone who could assure her that she was truly absolved from her darkest, most vile sin, the betrayal that haunted her most. Like the Catholics did.

It hadn't helped matters when Kyle announced last week at dinner that his grandmother said he resembled his uncle Will and, oh, how Donny flinched when Kyle bragged about that, since he'd always hoped Kyle took after the Quattlebaum side. Dora, herself, had been taken aback and unsettled. It was true. Her mother was right. How could Dora have missed seeing the resemblance, just in the last year? The lanky build, of course, but the thin upper lip, the deep-set gray eyes, too, and the way Kyle's eyebrows were so much lighter than his hair. Like Will. That was the night Dora's prayers, more desperate than ever, became stilted and lifeless.

Oh, but it really wouldn't hurt, would it? A little window shopping? As Dora sat in her car, her fears melted away in the heat, and she regretted her decision to leave without at least taking a look at the sale items in Agape. Just browse. Check the sale items. Look. Touch. Maybe just . . . hold things.

In Agape, breathing hard from her brisk trot, Dora looked for Jill, but she'd already gone. The twelve apostles candelabra was there, however. Dora found herself fondling the ceramic figures of Peter and Matthew. Each head had a little hole for the candle. Even Judas dazzled with his hand-painted bearded scowl. Dora found the price sticker under Luke's sandled foot. Her heart sank. Reduced, and she still couldn't afford this. Who was she kidding, anyway? Donny still wouldn't approve of spending such a sum on décor. Even Christ-centered décor.

"Isn't that precious?" the salesclerk said from behind her. "Just think of the table setting you could have with this candelabra. What a centerpiece!"

At the cash register, Dora handed over her Visa, her heart thumping hard, as if she'd just had a good run. She chatted cheerfully with the salesclerk, her mood soaring, away and up, beyond herself. Surely this was her soul feathery and free; surely this was how the Lord wanted her to feel. She glanced at the receipt. AGAPE: PROFIT FOR PROPHETS! it said in purple, along with a sum that made her gasp. She folded it carefully. She would remember, this time, to throw it away.

THREE

The travel trunk—when Emma opened it—smelled musty and dry, like the inside of a clock. By the time she sifted through her grandfather's sketches, studied her grandparent's stern wedding portrait, and discovered her grandmother's leather-bound travel journal—the moldering pages still blank—by then, Emma had lost the morning, and was shocked to see it was noon.

"Bobby," she called to the living room, "Lunchtime. How about a toasted cheese sandwich?"

Silence.

"Honey?" she called. "You there?"

The living room chair was empty, the television blaring. She should have checked on him before now. She never knew when Bobby would get the notion to take off somewhere. One day, last year, he'd wandered off and got all the way to Belton. The memories of that night still terrified Emma. The police officers called them to come pick him up—confused but not hurt, thank goodness.

Bobby wasn't in his room. The narrow twin bed was empty, the musty sheets rumpled, pillows scattered. A breeze wafted through the window, softly rattling the hundreds of sheets of lined paper tacked to the wall, all those sketches of furred tentacles, dark maws, googly eyes. The squeaks of the hamster wheel rose from Sugar's cage in the corner before the inexhaustible creature paused to peer at Emma and flick its whiskers. The rolltop desk in the corner held bird nests, dried husks of hydrangeas, a bookshelf of insect guides, and an almost complete set—they never could find the *T* volume—of the *World Book Encyclopedia*, jumbled haphazardly. On the floor beside the bed, a misshapen clay ashtray—pottery from summer camp years ago—overflowed with cigarette butts. Only the bulletin board was empty. Once a social worker had come and posted a schedule and calendar for Bobby there, noting the need for structure in his life. (*You know, a job might be good for him?* this blond, bossy child of twenty-two had told Emma.)

Sounds from the highway drifted through the open window—distant screams of braking tractor-trailers. Bobby knew better than to go that far. Didn't he? Oh, she'd been too caught up with all those plans and maps. The Hanleys' driveway sloped and meandered like a river down to the highway. She tried not to think about the melons that tumbled off a produce truck last summer, oval greenness marred in an instant, gashed into scarlet seed-speckled clots that spread across four lanes and a median.

Had Bobby changed his mind about going with Harold and taken off in pursuit?

Outside, Emma walked around to the backyard, down the worn path in the grass.

"Bobby? Come out this instant! Bobby?" Her voice broke.

Around the side of the house, the hydrangeas were starting to bloom. It was dark and damp and a little mossy, and the heavy blue lace caps, as big as her head, wept with leftover rain. Bobby was there, peering closely at something on the leaves.

"Bobby," she said, gasping. "Thank goodness you're here."

He didn't look up.

"Honey, what is it?" she asked.

"Arachnid. Charlotte with fangs. It's harmless, I think." He breathed heavily. He studied the thing closely now, his nose touching the leaf.

"Not too close."

The brown spider crouched. It waved its front legs, whether from alarm or greeting, she couldn't begin to guess. Bobby's face must appear like an enormous pink planet to that creature, she thought, blocking out the sky, the trees, the sun.

"This one doesn't jump," he said.

"No?"

"Nope. This one crawls."

Emma stepped closer, brushed away the silver thread of a web.

"The wires, Mom."

She cleared her throat. "Son, it's noon. Dad will be back any minute. Let's have some lunch."

"They'll *catch* you."

Sometimes it was easier just to go along. "No, I got away. The wires didn't catch me. I'm safe."

Bobby looked back at the little spider. "Look, her mandibles are moving." His father's lanky good looks were still there sometimes. Tantalizing glimmers of handsomeness in Bobby that still occasionally drew the stares of cashiers or nurses.

Emma reached up and straightened Bobby's foil hat. He looked noticeably calmer, then. He'd forgotten he had it on, his crowned talisman. The shine would deflect the rays, the wires; that was his theory, anyway.

"Why don't you take a nice warm bath," she said, "while I make some soup."

Bobby emerged from the steamy bathroom, a towel around his waist, and headed to his room. His damp back was soft and meaty, mottled as canned ham. Hard to believe those same slumped shoulders collected freckles when Bobby started scooping up tadpoles down by the pond. Emma could just see him like it was yesterday, in first grade, snaggletoothed and serious, carting home jars of pollywogs and water bugs, his frail shoulders sun blistered. He'd been a gifted science student once. When he won the school district's science fair, the newspaper had come out and taken his picture.

But then came the day sixteen years ago when the school nurse had phoned, and Emma had been forced to rouse herself from the itchy comfort on the sofa, where she'd been, in truth, all day. Will had been dead for nine months then, and it was a horrid time, a reverse gestation that seemed to suck the life right out of her. No, Bobby wasn't hurt or anything like that, Emma recalled the tinny, serious voice on the line say, he was . . . Well, she should better just come on down to the school where they could talk in person.

Upon arriving at the school nurse's office, Emma's apology spewed out of her like a sickness. "I know I look like a wreck," she said. The nurse stood there, a grim-faced figure in white. Beside her, Coach Weathers, the football coach, appeared to be holding Bobby down in a chair.

"They're going to kill me." Bobby told her. He was rocking in the chair, his eyes wide with terror.

The nurse told Emma her son appeared to be delusional.

The coach, a chubby man in shorts, breathless from holding Bobby, glared at the nurse. "No kidding. Why don't you just give him a damn nerve pill, Nurse Berns," he snapped, "and be done with it?"

The nurse looked at Emma and continued calmly. "Mrs. Hanley, Bobby is convinced the lunchroom ladies tried to poison him."

"He may have a point," the coach said.

"For God's sake, Tom," Nurse Berns said. Her pockmarked cheeks flushed. "You're not making this any easier."

Coach Weathers's loyalty warmed Emma, for Will, quite an athlete, had been a favorite of his. Of course, Bobby had shown no such interest in sports, sticking to the chess club and science labs, but the coach's tenderness for Will's brother gave Emma courage.

"Bobby, please. Come along with me." Emma said, "Let's go home."

The nurse fixed her take-charge stare back on Emma and told her Bobby had been plucking hairs from the heads of females students and keeping them in his locker. "He says he is weaving a web," she said.

"Bobby?" Emma whispered.

"They came in over the intercom and warned me this morning," Bobby told her.

"We've all been recovering from Will's passing," Emma managed to utter then, with great effort. "All of our family. In our own ways." *Dora's gone,* she thought, *and we haven't heard from her in weeks, and Mr. Hanley's away all day, Lord knows, in some woman's kitchen, and I'm laying on the couch all day, sometimes I don't even change out of my robe.* "We're just trying to make it day to day."

"Will's coming for me," Bobby blurted. "The spider told me, up here." He tapped his forehead. "She's curled up there with a web, ready."

Behind the nurse, metal shelves in the little room were filled with tongue depressors, cotton balls, rolls of gauze. And on the back of the door was a poster warning of head lice and flu. Those were the kinds of afflictions for which a school nurse was expected to call in a mother, Emma thought. Oh, the innocence of those warnings! How Emma yearned for such curable inconveniences. *Yes, give Bobby pneumonia, lice infestation, skin rashes. Give him crabs, give him mono. Give him anything,* she thought, *anything but this.*

"I don't know where your father is," Emma told Bobby now, looking at her watch. "He should have been here by now." She set down the toasted pimento cheese sandwich and tomato soup in front of him. "Why don't you go ahead and eat."

From the corner of the kitchen, Emma squinted at Bobby—in his bathrobe, swaddled like a toddler—until he looked smallish and faraway. A secret, guilty pleasure: She could pretend he was a child again, and she was younger. That all her children were younger: Dora and Will and Bobby. And they could all start over again. Dora could be a devoted daughter, Bobby could be a gifted scientist, and Will—Will could be alive.

"When your father gets home, we're all going to the store to get new shoes," she said. "We'll be doing a lot of walking on the Trip."

Bobby nodded sleepily. Emma shook paprika over a platter of deviled eggs and set it in front of him.

There was the crunch of gravel on the drive then, and a car door slamming.

"Oh, there he is now. I suppose he got a ride home."

But it was just the mailman bringing bills, catalogs, and— what was this?—a new *Travel for Seniors* magazine.

Harold was dreadfully late now. Really, there was no excuse for this.

Of course, he did have the drugstore errand. And, face it, those breakfasts could last a while. But it was two o'clock! Was he on one of those long walks he'd taken to lately?

At three thirty, Emma called the drugstore. Bobby's medicine still hadn't been picked up.

The Biscuit Basket was closed.

Emma paced in the kitchen, down the hall, on the front porch. She walked across the yard, the grasshoppers clicking and fleeing in panicked arcs. Harold remained a stickler for schedules and promptness, all right—as long as they were *his* schedules!

The street was quiet. Insolent in its silence. No cars, no bikers, no walkers. No Harold.

FOUR

Emma didn't recall phoning Dora, but someone must have, because shortly after Emma and Bobby arrived at the emergency room, Dora was there, too, with wet hair and an inside-out oversized sweatshirt that showed one freckled shoulder. "I was in the shower," she said. "I would have come sooner."

Then the young man wearing a stethoscope and a wisp of a goatee—surely too young to be a real doctor—sat them down in a "family consulting room" and began to gently relate how Harold must have been dead for an hour or more by the time the teenagers on skateboards discovered him and called an ambulance. As usual, Bobby, slouching in his seat, showed little emotion, and didn't appear to quite follow the conversation, focusing instead on a heating vent in the ceiling. Dora, on the other hand, sobbed great wet coughs. Emma sat in a daze between them.

Harold had drowned in the Biscuit Basket's retention pond.

He just lost his footing somehow, the youth in pale green scrubs said. As he glanced down at his clipboard and droned on, speculating, theorizing, hardly meeting her eyes, Emma's numb shock began to wear away, as if she were a patient emerging from the funk of anesthesia. She began to picture Harold's last minutes of life, a grim newsreel that would, for days, loop endlessly in her mind: how Harold, who'd incorporated those long walks into his fitness routine since retiring, had almost certainly been preening from his breakfast at the Biscuit Basket with Hal's Gals and, puffed up and smirking from a morning of flirtation, had commenced jogging across the parking lot, his gaggle of septuagenarian female admirers waving farewell, and then, out of sight, he'd stumbled past the concrete barriers and rolled down the steep ditch, hit his head, and plunged into that fetid pool where he was found, hours later, floating facedown among the cattails, ketchup packets, and Styrofoam cups.

Emma did not care to share grief. She was not an animal who ran howling and nipping in packs. She was, she thought stubbornly, like a sick, old dog that preferred to tremble alone in a box by the stove. Yet, when she and Bobby came home that evening from the emergency room, it was to a horde of casserole-carrying do-gooders. Apparently, Dora's prayer group had been dispatched quicker than any EMS unit. "He's been called home, honey," one of Dora's friends cried out, followed by a loud chorus of "Rejoice!" Emma could take only so much of that. Why, those Crossroads people didn't know her husband at all! Then, to make matters worse, Hal's Gals arrived—the honking and sobbing of the Mc-Cormick sisters, right there in front of goodness knows how many neighbors and all those busybodies milling around Emma's dining room. Such hysterics shut Emma down, packed her own blistering emotions in ice.

Emma made her way through her noisy living room and up the stairs. She glanced down from the top of the staircase to see Dora below—surrounded, hovered over, sung to, and prayed for—like the star of a choreographed dance troupe. By then, Emma's feet were lead blocks, her head a raw, pulpy ache, but she summoned her strength and headed to her bedroom for some quietness. But first Bobby would have to be seen to. Didn't Dora realize all this confusion and loudness would take its toll on him? Emma walked down the hall, and there was Bobby in his room, calmly playing checkers with Will.

Will? Oh, Lord, it was Will! The dry sob that Emma had clamped tightly all day swelled like a wet sponge, filling her lungs.

"Grandma? You okay?" The shadowy silhouette spoke.

"*Kyle.* My word."

"You need to sit down?" Her grandson sprang up to offer his chair. Bobby, fixated on the checker game, didn't even look up.

"No. No—I'm fine. I was just a little startled to see you there, is all. I mean, well, to tell you the truth, you looked a lot like your uncle Will there with Bobby."

"I did?" Kyle smiled crookedly, and Emma saw he was pleased. "I mean, I do?"

"Will Two." Bobby held up two fingers. "Will Two," he said again softly, pointing to Kyle. "That's who we have here."

"Yes," Emma said. "I can see that." Kyle, fourteen, looked mature for his age. He was tall, for one thing. And so . . . solemn. And he did look a little like Will, didn't he? Or was Emma losing her mind? She realized she was leaning limply on the door frame, and made an effort to stand erect. "I'm so relieved you are here . . . with Bobby. You just don't know how happy that makes me."

The sounds of clapping erupted from downstairs, ribbons of singsong prayers arose. The doorbell rang.

"I'd rather be up here with Uncle Bobby, anyway," Kyle said.

"Your sister?"

"She's in the kitchen polishing off the mac and cheese."

"Bobby, did you eat?" she asked.

"We ate," Kyle said.

"Are you tired?"

"Sometimes," Bobby said.

So far, he was holding his own. She would have to talk to Bobby tomorrow, explain more. When she had the strength.

"After this game, we'll call it a night," Kyle said. "Uncle B, that okay with you?" Emma could have hugged him in appreciation.

"Maybe I will go lie down, then," she said.

"Sure. But sleeping through this?" Kyle pointed down. "It's only going to get louder when Pastor Pete comes."

"Are you all still going to that church at the shopping center?" Emma could not stop herself from asking.

"Crossroads. Yeah." Kyle was poker-faced. What a challenge to be a stoic in Dora's family now. Emma could only imagine.

"You're still liking Palmetto High?"

"That den of iniquity?" he flashed a wry smile.

"I see." Although, of course, she didn't. Dora herself had gone to Palmetto High; all of Emma's children had. And yet Dora and her husband had threatened to take Kyle out and send him to that fly-by-night private school at Crossroads Christian Shopping Center, or whatever they called it now. It had all gotten out of hand. As if Kyle were into trouble, when anyone could see he was a perfectly normal young man. So far, Emma noted proudly, Kyle remained unflappable in the face of it all.

"Crown me, man," Kyle told his uncle. "I jumped you."

Yes, indeed, Kyle had inherited a vein of stoicism that ran in Emma's own family, she thought. Thank goodness. And yet—the men in Emma's family failed to thrive. They were cut down in their prime or, like Harold, perished without warning. None of their men died old and worn out and in the comfort of their own beds. Not one. That realization squeezed Emma's chest with the meanness of a heart attack. Staring at her grandson now—his loosened tie, white starched shirt cuffs shoved up his arms, his new angular face, his knobby wrist holding a checker—suddenly left Emma terrified. "Kyle?" she said loudly. They both looked up, startled, these men of hers—one newer to the world, one removed from it. She squeezed Kyle's shoulder, strong and warm under his white starched shirt. "You'll tell me if you need something?"

"Yes, Grandma." He gave a little laugh. "Don't worry. Really. Go to bed."

"I mean, any day. Anytime, sweetie. You'll come here if you need . . . anything? You promise?"

He nodded, looked at his uncle, then shrugged. "Sure," he said, more quietly.

"I didn't mean to bother you. I just—go back to your game. I'll be right down the hall."

And then Emma left them to their quiet game of checkers and retired to her own room, only to discover that, yes, Kyle was right. The hubbub from downstairs only increased. How odd to go to bed and leave a house full of guests rumbling downstairs! But she was a widow now, Emma reminded herself, and she deserved to retreat, to gather her strength. Her son-in-law, Donny Quattlebaum, had already mentioned that he would be handling the details of the funeral arrangements, and Emma couldn't have that.

Oh, where was her purse? She must have left it downstairs in the kitchen. She thought of Harold's watch—in the sealed plastic bag, just the way the hospital had returned it—tucked in the side pocket of her purse, ticking down there even now, like a heart. She crawled into bed, still in her clothes. The sheets offered the faint scent of Harold's Old Spice and Right Guard, and Emma wondered just how long it would be before she found the courage to wash them.

As it turned out, she would need her courage for something else. The next morning, Emma managed to extricate herself from her house full of strange relations and related strangers long enough to drive over to Palmetto Mortuary and meet with the funeral director to tell him what she woke up knowing. She and Harold were not so organized as to have "pre-need" funeral arrangements, perhaps because they did not take to big funerals. Burying a son had burdened them with more than enough ceremonial grief to last a lifetime. The funeral director had raised his brows slightly when Emma firmly announced what she'd decided, but she warned him her mind was made up.

And then, back at home, inside her crowded kitchen, over platters of crustless chicken salad sandwiches and pickled peaches, Emma announced that Harold would be cremated, with a private memorial service on Wednesday.

Dora was incredulous. "You *what*? Daddy without a proper burial?"

Trussed like a chicken, drained, and pumped with fluid—what was so good about *that*, Emma wanted to argue. Something about the Rapture, she supposed, as if the Lord couldn't reconstitute ashes into flesh and blood, better than new, like that space show Bobby used to watch where they just *beamed you up* from spaceship to planet.

"You don't want people to think he had something to hide, now, do you Emma?" Donny whispered to her in the living room, away from the hordes in the kitchen. Of course, her son-in-law immediately set about trying to reverse what he called Emma's grief-stricken lapse in judgment, but he failed to move her. Indeed, with his practiced charm and hand-patting, and his beseeching divine guidance to look down mercifully on her soul and to open her eyes to the truth and give her husband the funeral he deserved—well, it all had the opposite effect on Emma. She dug in her heels.

"You don't want people to think that your husband—Dora's father—wasn't a Christian and beloved by all of us?" Donny had a habit of pursing his lips before his firmest announcements.

"I don't care what they think, Donny," she said. And if he was frustrated, he didn't show it. Not yet, anyway. His calm reply tamped down any signs of temper. He was, Emma realized, still confident he could change her mind.

"A funeral is for everyone," he said, "to honor the deceased and celebrate his journey home to the Lord."

"Maybe we should all visit the mortuary together," Dora said as she sat beside Emma on the sofa then, "and talk to them about . . . other arrangements."

Emma thought she could hear a trace of defeat in Dora's murmured statement, and grew encouraged. Perhaps she and Dora could come to an agreement—surely her own daughter understood Emma's distaste for pageantry and public grief. She reached for Dora's small fine-boned hand. Dora got those delicate hands from

Emma's own mother, who, with great pride, wore child-sized gloves all her life. Then Dora exchanged a look with her husband and sighed and said, "Just let Donny handle everything, Mother."

"We'll have the funeral services at Crossroads in the new sanctuary, and Pastor Pete will give the eulogy," Donny said. "I've already talked to him"—he held up his hand as Emma tried to speak—"I've already explained everything about Mr. Hanley. You all haven't been churchgoing for a while, but Harold was baptized, and you're family. All you and Dora need to do is select the hymns. I'll take care of it."

"No thank you, Donny," Emma said. "I've made up my mind." She was not in the habit of blindly giving her burdens over to anyone, human or divine, and she wasn't about to start now, at seventy-two. She was certainly not going to permit some long, loud, drawn-out affair at that Crossroads place, and then find herself surrounded by Hal's Gals—all those silly old women boohooing over Harold's open casket. She just couldn't face that kind of carrying on.

Emma's son-in-law looked, for an instant, bewildered. Doubt—finding a hostile countenance—veered away, replaced by indignation, which settled right in. Donny's lips tightened. He glanced away briefly before presenting her with a new calm gaze—irked scowl ironed away with resolve. She held her hands in her lap, determined to conceal her own secret inkling of satisfaction. For all his concern about sending off Harold in style to his heavenly rewards, Donny had more ambitious motives: to publicly save Emma and Bobby from the clutches of heathenry, for one thing. Emma was not a churchgoer, and she'd never hidden that fact. It did not look good for Donny—deacon and pillar of that Crossroads outfit—to have family out of the fold and squarely in the camp of the unchurched.

"Think what Harold would have done for your funeral," he said. "You know he would have spared no expense."

And it was true. Had Harold been sitting here on the sofa with Dora and her husband planning Emma's funeral, he would have

no doubt acquiesced and let them give Emma a grand send-off.
White coffin, gold trim, and red velvet lining—it hurt to imagine
it. He would have handed the reins over to Donny, for Harold had
liked Donny well enough. Or perhaps not exactly liked him—but
was grateful to him. Harold had often reminded Emma, when she
dared complain about their son-in-law, about the terrifying weeks
all those years ago when the Hanleys thought they'd lost Dora for
good and how, in the end, it was Donny Quattlebaum who rescued her.

It was Donny who'd plucked Dora from that burbling de-
spair after Will's death. Dora had disappeared, unheard from for
weeks, until Donny brought her pale and weak and placid as a
newborn thing to their doorstep. Saved her. Or perhaps ensnared
her, Emma couldn't tell, though Harold would have none of it.
He's a good provider, ain't he? Harold's reminder had boiled
down to that one point over the years, leaving Emma alone in
wondering if their headstrong, volatile daughter wasn't still
missing. Was this really Dora? With hair curly and thick as a
privet, hair she had once rolled at night with bobby pins and
empty orange juice cans until it fell to her waist in a silky wall of
amber? That was back when Dora didn't want to stand out as a
small-town girl, when she strived to look the part of the sacrific-
ing protester; back when she went with that crowd down to the
statehouse and pushed down police barricades and squinted
through tear gas, and raised her voice and hand-painted signs to
end the war.

Now, the closest Dora got to protest was her bumper sticker:
IN CASE OF RAPTURE, THIS CAR WILL BE EMPTY. These days,
Dora said it wasn't this life that mattered much; only the afterlife
counted. Emma never liked that. Aftertaste, afterthoughts, after-
birth, nothing good came from afterthings. What a waste of a
perfectly good life!

Donny cleared his throat, leaned forward, lowered his voice.
"Cremation? You don't really want that. There needs to be a
gravesite to visit."

"I don't go to the cemetery anymore, Donny. It doesn't seem to help."

"You should bury Daddy beside Will, Mama," Dora said.

"Think of them together there," Donny said. "Waiting for you."

"Waiting? For me?" Emma said. "Why, that's a horrible thought."

"There has to be some kind of church service," Donny said, impatience creeping into his tone again. "A *private* funeral? I tell you, it's a disgrace."

"There is something to be said about dignity and quiet and grieving with family," Emma said.

Donny looked at her now with frank suspicion. Honestly! Did they think Emma planned to scatter Harold's ashes right in that sunny corner at the Biscuit Basket where he'd sat surrounded by his smitten flock of widow women? No doubt there were those who suspected Emma would fling those ashes around the greasy vinyl booths and plastic molded seats where Harold's dusty remains might very well be swept or hosed down out of the restaurant, ending up right back in the Biscuit Basket's retention pond.

"No respect," Donny said, shaking his head. "To cremate someone who never planned on it."

"Harold certainly never planned on having his coffin paraded around where Sears used to be, either."

"People will want to pay their respects to Mr. Hanley in a normal way, at his grave."

Those who wanted some of Mr. Hanley for themselves, Emma thought, were certainly welcome to their share. In an urn. For no matter what kind of ceremony or coffin or *container* everyone else might want for Harold, Emma would always think of her husband's final resting place in the gully below the parking lot of the Biscuit Basket. Consequently, Emma planned on keeping her husband close: on the fireplace mantel in the living room.

FIVE

utted, legally abandoned, Amaranth was, nevertheless, now home to a clutch of struggling souls. Previously a prim Victorian, the house lingered for years with a patient elegance until it buckled from dry rot, drooped, and leaned to the west in a casual sort of swagger. It appeared now to be shrugging off shingles and shutters, discarding gingerbread and spindles, as if peeling away ruined finery—setting aside cuff links, shedding gloves and starched collars—in a sort of weary resignation. The grounds were no better: Where once a wide shady spot provided a tranquil oasis for afternoon croquet, an unpruned, ragged lushness now mutinied against the last remnants of a lawn.

Some said it was arrogance that led William McCann to have a homestead constructed so far down the avenue—aloof, apart from the cluster of elegant abodes just two blocks away—as if inaccessibility and mystery were somehow correlated with wealth and power. In fact, McCann built Amaranth at the turn of the century as a refuge from social constructs—back when the surrounding land at the end the avenue still offered tranquillity and rich loam.

By the time the house was sold out from under Josephine McCann, it was too close to the swelling community of Freetown, where the coloreds lived, and too near to the textile mill to ever thrive. Any hope of rescue, of tender refurbishment, was quashed when Amaranth served as Mrs. Anderson's Rooming House. In any case, the magic wand of gentrification in the town had stopped waving some two blocks away.

Amaranth now sat between the Hot Spot convenience store and a vacant lot, a flophouse that provided sanctuary to, among others, one Gordon Johns, who had recently set himself up on the second floor. The house could be a dangerous place, and Gordon—who'd already put out a fire, stopped two fights, and slept with a steak knife tucked in his bedroll—claimed (though he couldn't know it) William McCann's former study for his very own, hanging a shower curtain where the French doors once stood. On the occasions when his headaches, trembling, and sour gut did not distract him, he began to take great pleasure gazing out the window frames and onto McCann's once splendid grounds. Gordon himself knew a little about the attraction of flora and fauna on exotic lands, and remembered the vines thick as his wrist in far-flung jungles of the Mekong Delta before Agent Orange stripped the land and took away even that small pleasure.

On this beautiful day, Gordon felt particularly fine, and stood at the window with the spring sun warming his face, scratching the ears of his dog, Sweet. Gordon was admiring an overgrown gardenia shrub in the front yard, bent with scented blooms—the very shrub from which Harold Hanley had, years ago, plucked a fragrant waxy bloom he later tucked behind the ear of Emma in the parlor below—the very shrub beside which Jake Cary stood now, calling for his friend Gordon to come out and settle a bet.

Gordon descended into the bowels of Amaranth and emerged from the doorless entrance, walked across the rotting porch planks with Sweet beside him, and stood squinting out into the bright day.

"Lord have mercy."

"You're not a easy fellow to find," Jake said.

"Depends on who's looking." Gordon said. A gold tooth winked when he smiled. He'd shrunk down a little over the years; the thick neck and wide knotty shoulders had worn away like soap. Only his weepy eyes, slightly yellowed, betrayed his straining liver.

"Ed McMahon and the Prize Patrol, maybe."

Gordon Johns and Jake Cary had spent their childhoods together, until the razor-sharp blade of Separate but Equal sliced them apart during schooldays. After high school—Sterling, the black school for Gordon; Palmetto, the white school for Jake—fate grabbed them by the scruffs of their necks and threw both into a pit called Khe Sanh.

"Who told you where I was?" Gordon still squinted in the light.

"Roselle." Roselle had answered the door that morning and told Jake that Gordon had left because the father of her children had finally come home, and so Gordon had not only moved out of her place, but jumped off the wagon, too, and now he was having one of his drinking spells again. *We all have our demons, I reckon,* Jake's mother used to say. "Said you were here. At Amaranth."

Jake looked back at the place. The collapsing porch, sagging in the middle like a smile, the weather-warped siding, the pitched roof, the mossy, curled shingles. Ruin. Rich white people used to live there. And then it was a rooming house, and now it was nothing at all.

"Thought you was up North for good," Gordon said. "Thought you wasn't ever coming back."

"My old man finally did something right."

"Yeah?"

"Died. Died and left a piece of land and a place to stay that the good state of South Carolina has finally found fit to hand over to me."

Gordon's khaki shirt was slightly starched, a faded oval where a name badge used to be. Roselle told Jake she was still doing Gordon's laundry on the sly, and he pumped gas sometimes at the Hot Spot when they needed him, which wasn't much. Nobody needed full service at a gas station anymore. "Which leads me to you." He handed a flyer to Gordon, who took out a pair of glasses from his pocket. Jake laughed. "Jesus, you're getting old. Glasses?"

"You might need 'em, too, if you ever read." He snapped the yellow sheet and commenced to read it. The dog sat on its haunches beside Gordon, its curled tail wagging.

"I'm here to collect," Jake said, allowing himself to smile now. "That bet we had, remember? Whoever stopped working for the man and got himself his own place of business, then the other one helps out. Well, I'm starting a business. And I need some help."

Gordon looked up from the flyer. "You moving back here, then?"

"Got somewhere to stay here, at Daddy's place over there near the river. Long growing season here, and I know the land. It's a whole different game up there near Pittsburgh. But I'm gonna need help. My back's still wrecked."

Gordon laughed. "You trying to tell me I'm the only tower of strength you know?"

"Some of these folks are going to want me to hook up their watering, sprays and sprinklers and you wouldn't believe the mess. I don't have a clue."

"You got that right."

Gordon had once rigged a contraption to catch rainwater in the jungle—the whole unbathed filthy platoon had lined up for it, for just a splatter of that sun-warmed shower in the middle of a jungle, and it felt like the Ritz-Carlton. When it came to water, the man had talent.

"I was thinking about your brother, too. Little JJ."

"He don't do yardwork," Gordon said.

"Man, I *know* that. I heard he's up at the bank."

"Robbing it, probably," Gordon shook his head and laughed. But the sudden bitter tone, like a false note, was not lost on Jake.

"Y'all have some falling out again?"

Gordon shrugged. "You think Little JJ gonna give you money, you got a surprise coming."

"I heard he's running the bank over there on South Main. He's a vice president, or something like that."

"Something like that."

"It's some sorry-ass landscaping they got there for a place with columns. He might give us a shot at doing the grounds for the bank."

"You think Little JJ going to give you a job just because you bring me along?" Laughing then coughing then laughing again so hard he had to sit down on the stoop. "A lot of things changed around here," Gordon said finally, then wiped his mouth with the back of his hand. "You got woman?"

"Women," Jake said.

"I hear you." Cackling now. The old Gordon.

Jake felt eyes, and glanced back at the house again. "How many in that place with you?"

Gordon shrugged. "I ain't the innkeeper."

"I'm lining up some more yards today. I'm aiming to start tomorrow. Try it for just a week if you want. I'll pay in cash. Off the books." Both of them staring straight ahead now, across the way, as if the Hot Spot were the most interesting place on earth.

"Only if I can bring Sweet." Gordon reached down to scratch the dog's ear.

"Aw, now, you can't bring a dog—"

"Not going without Sweet."

The dog looked right at Jake with his tongue out, laughing at him.

Jake sighed. "I can pick you up in the morning."

And then, from the corner of his eye, Jake saw the nearly imperceptible nod.

"So you'll do it?"

"For a week."

The fact that Lila Day and Miss Gibble, two spinsters Emma had known since her youth, remained, all these years later, her closest associates seemed both terrible and amusing. One would think

Emma might have seen some of the world and—yes! she often imagined it—held forth regularly among a wide circle of mysterious friends with foreign accents. But, no. No, Lila Day and Miss Gibble remained the heart of Emma's social network, two souls whose lives appeared even more atrophied than her own. Emma supposed she just hadn't been the type to branch out much. The town of Palmetto didn't offer much room for branching.

"You've got to stay busy, Emma, that's my advice. I suppose you're still feeling numb about it all, aren't you?" Lila Day told her now.

In fact, since Harold's passing, Emma felt the opposite of numb. Her body seemed, overnight, more finite and fragile, riddled with new aches. Well, but at her age, Emma should be accustomed to the idea of life winding down. Yet the certainty of death on the horizon still shocked her. She hadn't done enough! She'd always been so stuck.

"There's always the Wednesday Lunch and Learns at the Senior Center, you know," Lila said. "*That's* something to look forward to." Emma nodded absently, resisting the urge to decline Lila's firm insistence she attend. Emma simply didn't have the energy, much less the interest in the luncheons, but her one attempt to beg off over the telephone had been met with her friend's arctic silence. Lila had recently been elected president of the Lunch and Learn's steering committee, and had resolved to revive interest in the weekly event with a roster of lectures on "pragmatic" topics. Emma pointed out to her friend one had only to glance at the obituary pages these days to grasp the reason for the anemic attendance, but Lila would have none of it. "We're going to have a full house again, you'll see. No more arcane speeches on Mormon architecture or Chinese foot binding. Our speakers will address *practical* matters." Thrifty Dinners for One, she said, and How to Burglarproof Your Home. "*That* ought to pack the house," Emma muttered, but only after she'd hung up with her friend.

"We're making some progress," Lila said, standing back to admire her handiwork. Plates and dishes were labeled, alphabetically, with names; bowls nested in descending sizes. After a career as a school librarian, Lila had certainly cultivated a zeal for categories and a talent for shelved order. If she could have found a way to employ the Dewey decimal system here in Emma's kitchen, she would have done so.

"Thank you, Lila. You've been a big help."

"Well, for goodness' sake, Emma, you're one of my oldest friends. That's just what I told Miss Gibble this morning, you know. I said, 'Emma Hanley is our oldest friend, and she could use some cheering up,' and so I checked out Miss Gibble from Monaghan for another outing and we just happened to come by for a visit."

Happened to come by? Emma didn't believe that for a minute. Lila never attempted anything without a plan, and the roll of masking tape, markers, and handwritten list that she'd plucked from her purse confirmed this was no leisurely visit. It was a mission. Apparently, there was a widow's grace period for hoarding do-gooders' dishes, and Emma had exceeded it.

Lila's cheerful humming stopped when she began to examine a stack of wobbly plates. "How odd. Whose dishes are these?"

"My word, where did they find those?" Emma asked. "My hand-painted china." Stashed in the back of the pantry, no doubt. After the paper plates and all the china were used for the heaps of food arriving daily in the long horrid days after Harold died, someone had apparently resorted to scavenging the dark recesses of Emma's kitchen cabinets for more dishes. And to think her hand-painted china remained buried under the borrowed serving dishes and plasticware for all these weeks, as if hunkered down, trying to sneak out of the Hanley house undercover. "I haven't laid eyes on them for years," Emma said.

"Hmmm," Lila said, peering at them with an appraiser's eye.

"I know they're awful, Lila. It was just a hobby." Emma had even fashioned a little studio space for herself years ago in the barn. For a while, she'd tried to believe she might be an artist, or perhaps just *artistic*. But the blooms and vines she envisioned came out extravagant and frightening—plump petals in oranges and pinks and purples, thorny stalks, and prickly ferns with furry fronds—designs that either mystified people or left them feeling itchy. She turned over her space to the children, who as teenage marauders redecorated the barn for their own raucous pleasures.

"Oh, dear. And here's another dish without a name." Lila shook her head and held up a casserole dish.

Emma shrugged. "I'm afraid I have no idea."

"It's a disgrace how many aren't labeled," Lila said. "I suppose it never occurs to some people just how *burdensome* it is for a widow to sort out a mountain of dishes after a funeral." Lila's pale green eyes grew wide in damp bewilderment behind her thick glasses. She continued to chatter happily in Emma's kitchen as if losing one's husband were something unfortunate, unpleasant, unavoidable, but fixable—like a bad transmission or a faulty heat pump. You patched things up and carried on. Perhaps for Lila, a woman who'd never had a husband to lose. But for Emma? Nearly four decades of marriage—turbulent at times, far from perfect, certainly—had ended just three Saturdays ago, and Emma surprised herself by missing her husband more than she ever could have imagined.

"This is the only one left without a name," Lila said, holding up a large plate. "The Last Supper platter."

"Oh, that's from one of Dora's bunch."

Lila was quiet and studied the dish. She'd heard, no doubt, about the falling out between Emma and Dora over Harold's funeral arrangements.

"Have you been over there to the Crossroads?" Lila asked.

"Once." And, she wanted to add, she would certainly not return. Emma had never liked the idea of the first awful shopping center, McCann Square, being built at that tranquil spot all those years ago. That land had once belonged to her grandfather McCann, and it had seemed such a shame to ruin it.

"It could have been worse, you know. McCann Square was going down fast. No one shopped there anymore. They say it was going to be turned into one of those awful places before that Crossroads outfit rescued it. Would you rather have dancers over there who bare their bosoms and do their dirty business?"

"Of course not." Though Emma was curious about exactly what Lila, who had not had a suitor for nearly four decades, might consider "dirty business" at a shopping center.

"I declare," Lila said with a sigh. She submerged the Last Supper platter in a sink of soapy water. "This town is harder and harder to recognize. Have you been down Lavinia Avenue lately?"

Emma shook her head.

"Well, don't. It will break your heart. Amaranth is full of bums. It's a disgrace."

Thanks to her friend's industry, Emma's small kitchen gleamed with order and shine. The effect, unfortunately, only emphasized the work left to do in the rest of the place. Mail and newspapers had piled up in the hall, and there was Harold's closet to clean out. The whole place needed a good dusting. It was as if Lila Day had scrawled WASH ME! over Emma's neglected, grimy household. "I believe I'll dart outside and check on Bobby and Miss Gibble," Emma said to the back of Lila Day's neck.

"By all means," Lila said with enthusiasm, as if suddenly recalling her duty to cheer her friend. "Sally forth. I'll be right out."

Emma walked through the living room, which was still full of death: fading floral arrangements and stacks of sympathy cards. A bouquet sent from an appliance distributor, a large burst of red tulips, dwarfed the coffee table. The tight red-petaled lips arrived lascivious and vibrant, but had turned to soft black fists. She really should throw the thing away, but she just couldn't. Not yet. By now, she and Harold and Bobby would have been on the Trip, and she'd often imagined the three of them wading through a field of Amsterdam's tulips. Instead, Emma was sorting Tupperware and writing thank-you notes for meat platters.

Outside, Emma squeezed past the boxwoods.

"Miss Gibble?" she called. Why was it that she and Lila always addressed their friend by her surname? Perhaps it was simply due to Miss Gibble's air of authority. For she had a mythic quality about her—like an oracle in a Greek tragedy. It had been Miss Gibble, after all, who'd once rather pointedly warned Emma not to marry Harold, not to settle for a common man and a life of boredom. *You're just settling. You'll never leave this town.*

"Emma, is that you?" Miss Gibble bleated now from the bench where she blinked sleepily. Bobby sat nearby, petting the neighbor's cat curled in his lap. "Let's have ourselves a nice talk out here," she added, patting the seat beside her.

"Look at us, Emma," Miss Gibble said. "You and I—two ancients with nothing, no one at all, about to leave the world as empty-handed as when we entered it."

Emma bristled. Oh, Miss Gibble's grand pronouncements of doom! With her straggly silver hair, her cane gripped like a scepter, her milky-white eyes fixed on Emma, Miss Gibble really did resemble a prophetess now.

"Why, Miss Gibble," she said indignantly, for she, Emma Hanley, did indeed have a family, and was not a spinster living at Monaghan Nursing Home with *nothing and no one at all.*

And yet . . . where *had* Emma's family gone? Will shipped home from Vietnam in a flag-draped coffin. And Dora, soon after her brother's death had traded in her flowing, gauze garments and macramé purses for dowdy A-line skirts and pearl-clasped handbags and become a different person altogether, one who did not care to converse with her mother. And Bobby, her sweet Bobby, who'd once held such promise, a child prodigy in science, even while disease was secretly corroding his mind, gnawing at his synapses like squirrels on power lines. That boy had vanished, too, hidden in Bobby's hefty, lumbering body, in his scattered thoughts. Her children—gone. And Harold in the retention pond.

They sat in silence until Lila approached, balancing a tray of teacups chattering like teeth. "I thought we could have ourselves a little tea party," Lila chirped, sitting the tray on the patio table. "Just like old times." She looked around Emma's garden, her expression darkening. "Oh, you're going to need some help around

here, Emma. A yardman. And let me tell you, these days it's hard
to find a good one."

"We'll manage," Emma said. She had already thwarted
Donny's offer to mow the lawn. Indeed, her son-in-law had not
even asked, but had come over unannounced on one occasion
with his own mower and trimmer and hacked her forsythia to
pieces. Her firm request that he cease was met with more ill will.
She supposed he thought her overgrown yard now was a rebuke,
a poor reflection on him. But help was not something Emma was
prepared to consider just yet. She had an overdeveloped sense of
privacy. Certainly, hired help always blabbered, no matter whom
you trusted. If they penetrated the shell of your life, like a worm,
everyone would know there was a nut in there.

"And speaking of help, perhaps you can have someone stay
with Bobby so you can plan another trip," Lila whispered.

The Trip. Emma still did not want to talk about the Trip.

Jake drove up the curved tree-canopied driveway of the Hanley
place with some trepidation. He'd had the fortunate—or perhaps unfortunate—experience of running into Miss Day, the
retired school librarian, the day before at the Lo-Buy. Miss
Day, who had hushed, scolded, and hissed at Jake more times in
his life than he cared to remember, had somehow managed to
hold on to her uncanny ability of plucking out an errant individual from a crowd with her predatory gaze. And so it was
yesterday, as Jake stood in the congested express lane, when
Miss Day, two lines over, selected him with a sure nod, like a
witness identifying a perp. He waited for her in the parking lot,
feeling sheepish and chastened, as if he were a twelve-year-old
again.

She'd already heard he was back in town, and what he was up
to. Word traveled fast, of course, especially among the blue-hairs.
That was okay, he mostly got a kick out of them, and face it,
that's where half his business was. Widows Weeds; Jake Cary,
Owner. Had a good ring to it.

Miss Day told him about Mr. Hanley dying like he did and the place was looking rough, and good luck to him because Mrs. Hanley didn't take kindly to help. But then, Jake knew the Hanleys, didn't he? Went to school with the Hanley children? That would certainly help matters, she said. Jake considered going over to Mrs. Hanley's place just to pay his respects then and maybe offer to mow the lawn for free once or twice just to help her out, and well, if she wanted to hire him, then fine and dandy. But that didn't seem the right thing to do, either. Too pushy.

Now, sitting for a minute in the quietness of Emma Hanley's driveway, Jake tried to work up his nerve. Probably Mrs. Hanley would say no. No, she didn't need landscape services; no, she didn't want to spend the money; no, she didn't know him from Adam. And chances were she wouldn't remember him, not after all these years, and that wasn't necessarily a bad thing. Jake smiled grimly and ran a hand through his black hair. He should have gotten a haircut. Six bucks down at Cutting Edge; he saw the sign yesterday. He put on his cap, then took it off—he should get some caps with his landscaping company's name soon. Whenever he decided on a name. God almighty, there was just so much to do all at once.

This wasn't a cold call. No need to get so nervous. It was business, and he needed every customer he could get. Sign up just one more today, and he would be in good shape. *Whatever you do, don't let her know I sent you,* Miss Day had told him. *Pride, you know.*

The gravel crunched beneath his steel-toed boots as he got out of his truck. He stomped each foot once and shook out the pain, then gingerly loosened his back brace. Riding around town for an hour had just about done him in. He slipped off the back brace, grimaced, and threw it into the back of the truck. People wouldn't hire a landscaper with a bad back. He laid a hand on the hood, as if patting the flank of a horse, and the pleasure of a new 1987 GMC S15 pickup (paid in full!) dulled his pain a little.

There were fifteen bales of pine needles and eight bags of compost in Jake's truck bed, all of it purchased the day before and arranged carefully, stacked like props in a store window display. He stretched, and tried not to grimace, heard his spine pop. He was summer swarthy, with narrow black eyes he'd inherited from his Cherokee grandfather, but people were forever trying out Spanish on him, like he was a Mex. He stood at six feet, lanky but solid, limping by lunchtime. Nevertheless, he'd cultivated an air of robust confidence that disguised his spells of pain. Who would have thought Jake Cary would have a truck paid in full, his own business? And all because six months before, some lady rushing to her tennis lesson had rammed her Benz into his ancient Datsun, pleated it like a paper fan, sent Jake to the ER with a ruptured disk and a crushed shoulder. All that on top of his cobbled-together war wound from seventeen years before. Still, his lawyer finessed a sweet settlement, based on his not being able to work again at the plant. Enough pain and suffering compensation to buy a new truck and start his own business. And then Jake's father died and left a little piece of land, enough to come home to Palmetto for, anyway.

Jake walked up to the front porch. He could leave a flyer, but he probably wouldn't hear anything back. The older ladies had to be dealt with face-to-face. They had to look into your eyes. The steps squawked as he navigated past a stack of yellowed newspapers. Jake stood at the front door and stared down at a trail of his footprints in the chartreuse pollen dust. When it got like this, the old folks were desperate to keep up appearances, or else embarrassed relatives were talking them into selling the places, and there was a frantic need for landscaping, or just a mowing once a week. He took another quick look around behind him, drew encouragement from the overgrown, weedy yard, the unpruned pines, and voracious English ivy. And that was just the front yard. He knew all about the back—the thicket of woods. And that barn. Oh, Lord, yes. He knew about that.

He knocked gently. After a minute, he sensed somebody's presence, then heard heavy footsteps thudding away. The door finally swung open, and Emma Hanley peered up at him, her hair, pure silver, neatly pinned back, a clod of soap there on her hand, which clutched her yellow sweater. A damp apron. He'd interrupted her dish-washing. "Hello, Mrs. Hanley?" He began to lurch through his spiel. "I'm, uh, well, I'm handling a lot of yards in your area. Everything from mowing lawns to drawing up landscape plans. I can do as little or as much as you need. I just thought you might be interested." He swallowed nervously. He hadn't gotten it down right, yet, but hell, he was in landscaping, not speechmaking. He handed Emma Hanley his business card. And then he said it. "I'm Jake Cary, by the way."

"Well, I declare," she said, squinting at the card. "Why, I know *you*." She was staring at him now with eyes pale and icy as a husky's. "You . . . Jake . . . my goodness." The statement came out like an accusation, yet she seemed warmed by the realization. "You and . . . ," she said, letting the sentence fade unfinished.

"Yes, ma'am."

"Well, isn't that something. Where have you been keeping yourself these many years, Jake?" She glanced at the card, then met his eyes. "I mean, Mr. Cary?"

"Oh, you can call me Jake."

"Nonsense. You're a professional now, Mr. Cary. A business-man. Insist on Mister. Insist on a last name. I used to tell my husband the same thing." She sighed. "Not that he listened. He insisted people call him Hal."

"I was real sorry to hear about . . . Mr. Hanley."

She looked away, nodding.

Jake stared down at his feet. "I'm uh—" He cleared his throat. "I'm just getting started. Came back home not long ago. I got a place now over at the base of the mountain. Just a piece up the road."

"I see," she said, with something like resignation in her voice, "and what do you recommend for such a mess as this?" She looked beyond him, her eyes skipping like flat stones on water, past the ivy-swallowed stump, the patchy lawn, the overgrown beds.

"I'd start with a good weekly mowing. Maybe aerate the soil, fertilize a little. You got crabgrass and broad leaf taking over. The usual suspects. Then, we could move on to—"

"Mr. Cary, did Miss Lila Day put you up to this?"

"Who?"

"Did Miss Day or anyone else send you here?"

"I did hear you were a widow, Mrs. Hanley. I was sorry to hear that. But like I said, I've got some clients in the area—"

"Did anyone from that Crosswind place send you?"

"Cross what?"

"Crossword . . . Crosswalk . . . Crossroads. *Crossroads.*"

"No, ma'am."

"Did my daughter send you?"

"Dora?" Too late to hide the look of startled amusement on his face. "Why, I haven't spoken to Dora in years, Mrs. Hanley. I didn't even know she was still living in town." Oh, but he'd heard.

She looked at him. Crossed her arms and just looked.

"Mrs. Hanley, no offense, but it looks like you need some help. I mean, yeah, I heard about Mr. Hanley and all, but—"

"Your proposal sounds just fine," she said, with a dismissive wave of her hand. "Start as soon as you're able."

"I'll work up an estimate and get it to you."

"No need," she said. "You're an honest man, aren't you?"

"Yes, ma'am. But if I weren't, I'd still tell you I was."

This brought a smile. "Just drop by your estimate anytime."

He patted his shirt pockets. "I got a price list here somewhere."

"Why don't you come in for a glass of tea. Get out of this terrible heat."

"Oh, I need to get cleaned up, Mrs. Hanley. Got my work boots on. You don't want me tracking in this red clay, anyhow."

He handed her the price list. The pain in his back was subsiding now, a manageable throb. She again insisted he come in. Why, she would be insulted if he didn't. He found himself following her into the coffin-dimness of the living room, through a vague beam of sunlight that squeezed through the closed blinds.

A console television with four squat feet like a god sat in the corner of the airless living room, and in front of it, a big man—blond hair thinning, jeans, and a baggy black T-shirt—sprawled in a stained tweed recliner, a slumped supplicant. Lord God, if it wasn't Bobby Hanley. Cigarette smoke drifted from the ashtray on his knee. "Bobby? We have a guest. Do you remember Mr. Cary here? He was a friend of Will and Dora's." Bobby looked over at Jake with hooded eyes. Jake felt the lie in his gut. Will Hanley a friend? Oh, sure, they were in school together, and there for a while, they were in country at the same time, too. And he knew how it had ended for Will. He and Will knew each other real well, all right, mostly through Will's good-natured but steely reminders to Jake to keep his hands off his sister. But friends? And as far as Dora—well, he wouldn't exactly call what he and Dora had all those years ago a friendship.

"Have a seat and I'll bring you a glass of tea, Mr. Cary," Emma said now.

Jake sat on the crushed velvet couch.

"Sorry to hear about your dad," Jake said.

Bobby got up, turned up the volume on the television, sat back down without so much as a glance Jake's way. Rock music blasted.

Emma appeared with a glass of iced tea. Jake thought he heard her sigh flutter among the screaming guitars. "Mr. Cary, why don't we move to the kitchen?"

Where was Dora? That was the question begging to be asked. Where was Dora in all this mess—the overgrown yard, Bobby on the edge, Mrs. Hanley a helpless widow—well, no. No, that wasn't quite right. Mrs. Hanley wasn't helpless at all. She was, Jake thought, one of those ladies who could take care of herself just fine, thank you very much. He sat down at the dinette set and drank his tea in two gulps. Wiped his mouth with the back of his hand before he remembered his manners.

Emma looked pleased. "There's more."

"Thank you. I guess I didn't realize just how thirsty I was."

"Oh, you have to watch that in your line of work. Dehydration can kill. Why, it was just on the news last night. Some poor man waving an orange flag for the highway keeled right over from dehydration. The steamroller just missed him. It's the electrolytes, you know. Your body shuts down. And suddenly there's poor skin turgor and collapsed capillaries and shock and . . . that's that. The human body is very fragile."

"I'll keep that in mind." Dehydration, Jake mused, was the least of his worries.

Guitars screamed from the other room. The Stones. *Just a kiss away, just a kiss away.* Was he getting one of his headaches? He pretended not to hear. The music clamped down on his head like a helmet. Emma Hanley's mouth moved soundlessly. "Got yourself a little kitchen garden out there, do you?" he asked, looking beyond her through the window. He rose slowly from the chair and he was up then, standing, his back cooperating, his legs as sturdy as a ladder, and he was okay. He found the back door.

Outside, in the sweet, holy quiet of the yard, Jake admired the promise of Emma Hanley's hard green tomatoes. "Do all this yourself?" he asked when he sensed she stood behind him. "What you got here? Tomatoes, crooked neck squash, peppers?"

"Oh, lately I manage to do it myself. Bobby helps."

"All this. Just y'all?"

The land beyond Emma's garden was wildly overgrown, worse than he'd thought. And the barn was gone.

Emma watched his face. "Mr. Cary, it's all ruined back there. Gone to seed. And this vicious spring heat beats anything I've ever seen. Look at that kudzu—you can almost see it bolt. Why, in just these weeks since Mr. Hanley has been gone . . ." Her hand fluttered to her breast in a girlish gesture. "Well, I'm just in a quandary about staving it off before it swallows Bobby and me whole."

"Oh, now."

She held a hand over her eyes as she looked out into the woods. "Do you use poisons?" Emma asked him now, brushing a caterpillar from her tomato vine.

"Oh, we might when things get real bad. But I don't make it a habit."

"I was never one to use poisons, myself. But Mr. Hanley used to fill an old sock with Sevin and dust everything in creation. It was the bagworms on the junipers that drove him to fits." Emma crushed a twig of rosemary and held it to her nose. "I just never could stand to do something so . . . mean. It just seems like too much power, even over these creatures that nibble my vegetables."

"I'll instruct my crew not to use insecticide, then."

His crew. That was a good one. Jake looked beyond the garden again, past the ivy-swallowed courtyard, where the kudzu and scrub pines were thick. "And what about . . . out there? You want us to see after that? Clear it out some?"

"Why, yes, Mr. Cary. I suppose it is necessary, don't you?"

"I'm afraid so."

"Mr. Hanley had the barn bulldozed down last year. The roof caved in. It had become . . . a hazard. I suppose it served its purpose. Oh, Will and Dora and those barn parties! Honestly. But you're only young once, that's what I always say. Do you remember all your youthful indiscretions, Mr. Cary?"

The scent of baby oil on sunburned skin, and those Hendrix guitar riffs shorting on and off from a cheap-ass turntable, the taste of vodka and grape Kool-Aid, the slippery, willing mouth of Dora Hanley. Jake smiled. "The problem is forgetting them." He stamped his right boot, shook out the mischievous twinge that flared down his thigh before it ignited in pain. "I guess I better get going."

"Well, I'm sure glad you stopped by."

"I'll be coming back around in the next couple of days. The first time, you being widowed and all? I won't charge you."

She shielded her eyes with a hand. She looked away, but her profile seemed to sharpen in the harsh afternoon sun, her half smile frozen, and when she looked at him again, her eyes were piercing. "That's no way to run a business. No way at all."

"Uh, well, if—," he stammered, off guard.

"If I decide your services are unsatisfactory, I'll certainly inform you."

Jake swallowed. This one had some steel. She came at you sideways, her pincers nipping.

"You just stop by anytime and get started," she said. She glanced downward and managed to look shy.

Jake cleared his throat. "No need to show me out, Mrs. Hanley. I'll just walk through the side yard back to my truck."

Emma didn't appear to hear him. Instead, she was focused on her roses. "Look at that!" She said, "Japanese beetles. They really try my patience. On my New Dawn!"

"They'll bore through the buds, all right."

"Don't I know it! The way they lace the leaves. Voracious, greedy, *vile* things." She shook her head.

Jake dug out two of the shiny green beetles, their spurred legs clasped together in insect ecstasy. Curling themselves up in the pink petals, like sultans in silk. He should have dropped them on the patio, ground them like a cigarette butt until they crunched and oozed, but he flung them—still stunned with pleasure—out into the grass. A useless gesture, but cathartic, nevertheless.

SIX

When Kyle slipped into the front seat of the waiting car, his mother gave him the silent treatment. After four blocks, she said, "I don't appreciate being kept waiting, especially when we are running late."

"Sor-*ry*."

His mother had dropped him off to deliver a gift basket to his grandmother's front door while she drove all the way back home to get something she'd *supposedly* forgotten. And the deal was he was supposed to be waiting for her by his grandmother's mailbox. His mother was always running late anyway; he had three tardies at school and lunch detention because she could never seem to get him there on time. So, on Sundays, Kyle just tuned out her flurry, because, hey, what did he have to lose? They didn't give you detention at Sunday school for being late. Not yet, anyway. When she'd dropped him off and told him to hurry, and *be standing at the end of the drive ready in five minutes, I mean it,* he hadn't. Instead, he'd followed his grandmother inside to her living room, handing over the basket.

She took out the loaf of banana bread and read the card inviting her and Bobby to Crossroads that night for the evening service.

His grandmother had chuckled and shook her head. "She just never gives up, does she?"

His uncle was watching television and—was that Bon Jovi?

"Grandma? You've got cable now?"

"Yes, I thought we'd give it a try. Your uncle loves the MTV." Even his grandmother had cable! Everyone in the world had cable television now except for Kyle. *What are you, like, Amish?* Julie asked when he admitted to the fact last week. And he'd laughed, but not really.

His grandmother handed him a plate of chocolate cream pie. He sat down. Bon Jovi, he wasn't about to miss that.

And then a car horn bleeped twice, and there she was, his mother, out there waiting in the Dodge minivan with the engine running.

"From the way you smell," his mother said now, "I'd say your uncle Bobby is still smoking like a fiend." She shook her head. "Which is dangerous. Did your grandmother get her card?"

"She asked me to convey her regrets."

"Is that what she said? *Convey my regrets?*"

"Something like that."

"What about dinner later? Did she mention anything about that?"

"Why don't *you* ask her?"

He was shocked at how flip his answer sounded, but he was sincere. Why *didn't* his mother ask her own mother about such things? What was he? Some kind of translator?

"*Excuse* me, young man?" She braked at the intersection. The tires screeched. Kyle put a hand on the dashboard and looked at his mother with astonishment. He'd just visited his grandmother, for crying out loud, but his mother acted like he'd penetrated a force field, a toxic, dangerous place, and he needed to be decontaminated. He braced himself for the scrub. His mother pulled to the side of the road. She took a deep breath, closed her eyes, and bowed her head. "Let me have your hand," she said. She squeezed Kyle's fingers and murmured a prayer, something about strength in the face of disrespect. Kyle pretended to close his eyes. His mother's eyelids were shiny with violet powder. "Amen." She looked at him then, her gaze distant and strange, as if she were peering out from a mask.

"There, now." She tried to smile.

"Mom, I just mean—," he continued.

"Your grandmother can be very set in her ways. It's sad she's not bringing Bobby tonight. Your father will be real disappointed."

He shrugged. Since his grandfather had died, Kyle learned just how precarious it was to navigate through the dark gulf between his parents and his grandmother.

"You know, we're going to keep inviting her to Crossroads with us, her and Bobby." His mother looked at herself in the rearview mirror, adjusted the knotted silk scarf at her neck. On her lapel, she still wore the orchid corsage they'd given out to the Firm Believers at church that morning, a freckled, curlicued, waxy thing that appeared to study Kyle now with an inscrutable expression. For a minute, Kyle understood how his uncle Bobby felt when he talked about being watched all the time, when the secret keepers peered at him from drains and cracks in the wall, threatening to punish him.

His mother pulled back onto the road. Staring straight ahead, she said, "Five demerits for your insolence, honey. I'm sorry, but that's the rule."

"Fine. I never get to go anywhere anyway," Kyle said, and instantly regretted it. He was, somehow, still in his mother's good graces, even if she pretended to give him a hard time. He didn't need to blow it. He stared out the window, fixed his gaze on an overturned traffic cone.

"Why are you so . . . disobedient today?" His mother asked calmly. She did not bring up *the incident*. The night last week when she caught him sneaking back into his bedroom. He'd claimed he'd just gone outside to smoke one cigarette. Just to try it. And she'd believed him. Or didn't. He wasn't sure. She wanted to believe him—his claims that it was a mistake that wouldn't happen again. She was scared not to believe him. He knew that, and didn't know exactly how he knew it, but he did. And, most important, his mother didn't tell his father. It was, Kyle reflected now, as if the incident never happened, as if he hadn't eased into his bedroom window (again) last Thursday at two in the morning, reeking of beer (six, at least) and cigarettes (not his) and perfume (Julie's) and seen his mother sitting there in her baby blue robe *on his bed* with this freaked-out look on her face that wasn't fury so much as fear. And then his mother had a silent conniption like she was a crazy mime or something. Whispering threats and pantomiming fists. The next day, in the stultifying boredom of Spanish class, thinking about the soundless but wildly physical panic of his mother the night before, like she was Lucille Ball on speed, he surprised himself by grinning. It wasn't funny, but it cracked him up. Still, the incident was off the family radar for some mysterious reason, for some kind of logic only his mother understood. For that, he was both puzzled and grateful.

He gnawed on his thumbnail.

"You shouldn't sulk, honey. We're almost there."

Was he imagining that his mother sounded some kind of warning again, reminding him to get unsulky before his father saw him? Maybe not. Probably not, Kyle thought as they pulled into the Crossroads parking lot and his mother arranged her own features into an expression approaching cheerfulness.

His father tapped his watch now and approached the car as Kyle and his mother got out. He had on a dark blue suit and pale yellow tie, even though the other fathers wore golf shirts and button-downs. Didn't he know the Sunday-night service was supposed to be less formal than the mornings? His family was always overdressed, Kyle thought, but his father insisted that a man in a suit always had an edge. Something about the real estate business, probably. One of those sales classes he was always taking to find out why he could never make sales. Kyle loosened his own tie. His sister, Sandy, stared down at her new black patent leather shoes.

"Is everything all right?" his father asked, striding over to his mother.

All around them, people scurried inside what used to be Belk's department store. Their church was inside the shopping center, and his mother was proud that Kyle's father had been on the committee to start up Crossroads. But the place sort of creeped Kyle out. The congregation sat in rows of metal folding chairs, under the dusty skylight, in front of a stage that had once been used for modeling contests and Santa Land. The mall fountain, which burbled weakly, was now used for baptisms; you could still see a layer of green pennies under the yellow foam.

"Well, we were waylaid a little," his mother said breathlessly, dropping her voice and gaze. Kyle didn't flinch. "Kyle managed to get himself four demerits." As if being late and talking back were the worst things he was capable of, facts that seemed to comfort her. As if she weren't blind to his off-the-radar stunts, as if, by citing his demerits, his father could trust her to keep an eye on him.

"Five demerits, you mean," Kyle said cheerfully, watching his mother's face darken.

"Five demerits?" his father asked too loudly. He gripped Kyle's arm. "I believe we're going to have ourselves a little chat, young man, after church." *Oh, please,* Kyle thought, *young man?* Who says that anymore to a fourteen-year-old? His father shook his elbow before letting it drop. Two kids from Kyle's Sunday school class looked over and whispered.

Kyle dutifully headed to the Crossroads Christian youth hall, now located in the defunct food court. Dozens of tables and chairs were bolted to the cracked-tile floor, and several abandoned fast-food stands were shuttered. Kyle stood in front of the empty Bubba's Burger kiosk. There was hardly anyone around he wanted to talk to, except maybe Sam Jenkins, his lab partner in Biology.

Pastor Pat-Rick, the youth minister, started with a prayer, then announced it was the last day to turn in Summer Saving Souls Goals. "People, listen up. Souls Goals. Remember? We're in the business of what?" He clapped.

"Saving souls," the crowd murmured.

"I can't hear you."

"Saving souls!"

"That's better." Pastor Pat-Rick's blond curly hair was buzzed short, wiry but tamed. His real name was Olipat Richard Keene, but he told them—warned them—to call him Pat-Rick for short, like John-Paul or Billy-Bob. *Not* Patrick, he said, because *if you call me Patrick and not Pat-Rick, it might definitely get you off on the wrong foot.* He had a springy step and he clapped his hands and snapped his fingers a lot when he spoke to them. He was a college cheerleader and stood on an orange crate ("my soapbox") to talk to them.

At first, Kyle didn't like him, because he didn't much trust cheerful people, but when he saw Pastor Pat-Rick's girlfriend, his opinion changed. She was a fox. Thick gobs of dark hair and wicked green eyes. Kyle saw Pastor Pat-Rick grab her ass in the parking lot when he thought no one was watching. Another time, Kyle heard Pastor Pat-Rick listening to Styx on the car radio, blasting it from his Triumph convertible at a red light, with his girlfriend right there beside him. The time Kyle got demerits at home for listening to Guns N' Roses in his room, cranking it up, really getting the air guitar going, when he thought his parents were out shopping, that night he came close to asking his father about why, if Pastor Pat-Rick listened to rock music, *if the freaking youth minister at Crossroads jammed regularly to music,* music that normal people listened to, how could it be so bad? But he stopped himself because he didn't want to get Pastor Pat-Rick fired. His father said, "Kyle, one thing leads to another. It's the lifestyle I'm talking about." Sex, drugs and drinking, violence and evil—yeah, he knew the drill. No R-rated movies or cable television, and no rock 'n' roll. Not while he was under their roof.

"Okay, my shepherds. Gather around. This is how it works." Pastor Pat-Rick stood on his orange crate and snapped his fingers. "There are sign-up sheets on the wall for Mission Possible, Neighborhood Witness, or Day Care Angels. If you don't do one of those, you need to turn in your individual plan and goals for witnessing to me tonight."

Kyle hated Mission Possible—all that hammering and putting up drywall with a bunch of football players. If you weren't a jock, forget it. You got all the sissified, crappy tasks, like sorting nails or handing out water bottles. Last year, his father wouldn't let him do Neighborhood Witness, where you went around in groups to the really bad neighborhoods and read Scripture to the crackheads or basically anyone who would listen. That left Day Care Angels, which was definitely out. Being trapped in a room that smelled like paste with a bunch of brats who made pipe cleaner crucifixes all day was Kyle's idea of hell. Still, he had to do something for Souls Goals. It was required. If you didn't do it, they called in your parents.

Kyle sidled up to Pastor Pat-Rick over by the punch bowl.

"Hey, uh, Pastor Pat-Rick?" Kyle enunciated carefully. Pat. Rick. "How do you do an individual plan?"

"Hey, there, buddy." Pastor Pat-Rick clapped a meaty paw on Kyle's shoulder. Pastor Pat-Rick probably didn't remember Kyle's name, but Kyle preferred it that way, especially when it came to Saving Souls Goals. "What did you have in mind?" he asked.

Up close, Kyle saw how freckled Pastor Pat-Rick was, covered in tiny flecks of brown like he was paint-splattered, all up and down his arms and across his nose and forehead. The undersides of his thick arms were white and firm, like a fish belly. He bounced on the balls of his feet as he looked down at Kyle.

"Uh. Yeah, well, I thought, there's these two people that I know that could use some help around the house." Pastor Pat-Rick already looked distracted, and he curled his lip like a horse reaching for a carrot.

"These two people," Kyle continued, "one of them is elderly

and the other is sick. Real sick. And neither of them have been to church in like, fifty years or something." Pastor Pat-Rick looked interested again. "I'm pretty sure they're not Christians anymore," Kyle added.

"Wow," Pastor Pat-Rick said, shaking his head. A soft, breathy whistle escaped his lips. Even his hazel eyes were splattered with brown specks. "That will be quite a challenge. Are you ready for that level of witnessing this summer, buddy?"

Kyle thought of his grandmother and his uncle Bobby, and he thought of cable television and MTV and maybe even a little free time to see Julie. "Yes, sir," Kyle said. "I'm ready."

"Okay, what you do is fill this out." Pastor Pat-Rick handed Kyle a form. "And I'll sign it."

Kyle looked down at the form. *Document your Individualized Witness Plan's goals with dates and times, if possible. How will you lead others to Christ? How will you accomplish your Souls Goals for the summer? Be specific.*

I will visit these two people frequently, Kyle wrote, *like probably every day. Reading Scripture to them and helping them out with stuff like groceries and cutting the grass. Listening to them, and applying biblical principles to their problems.*

Kyle handed the form to Pastor Pat-Rick, who scanned it without moving his eyes. "Sounds like a plan, my man," he said, then clapped Kyle on the shoulder again.

Dinner at the Quattlebaums that night was a disaster, and his sister started it.

"Mom?" Sandy asked. "Are these new?" She held up the salt and pepper shakers. They all stared at the little robed figurines. "What are they, anyway?"

Oh, crap. Here it comes. You didn't bring that stuff up! His sister hadn't caught on yet.

"They are apostles," his mother said. "Luke and John."

His father squinted and stopped chewing. "New?" he asked in a controlled voice. "Bought when?"

"Oh, a while ago," his mother whispered, staring down at her meat loaf. "Agape had a sale. On place settings."

"Is Mary the sugar bowl?" Kyle asked.

Sandy snickered.

"I just—it was such a savings. Forty percent off."

His father glared at his mother, and Kyle felt something move between them, stinging and slippery as an eel. "What were you doing in Agape?"

"I just stopped in after the Firm Believers. Jill told me about the sale and . . ." His mother's words faded.

Kyle said, "Hey, too much Luke in these potatoes. But the meat loaf could use a little Luke and John."

Sandy laughed.

"Kyle!" His father pounded a fist on the table. "That's enough."

"That was uncalled for, Kyle," his mother said quietly.

"Demerits for that," his father said. "In fact, I think it would be a good idea for you to go to your room for a few minutes and think about respect."

His mother stared at Kyle, even Sandy looked serious, and gazed at him with pity. In a matter of seconds, the storm shifted, the hot fury blew on him now, his parents like ferocious apple-cheeked clouds on ancient maps. As usual, his demerits refocused their ire from each other and onto him.

"Think about respect," his father said as Kyle stood.

"Respect?" Kyle met his father's eyes.

"Don't ever, *ever*, make light of our Lord or his apostles. Scripture is holy, do you understand that, Kyle? Holy."

Kyle turned away from the table. *Make light? Of the apostles? You gotta be kidding me. I'm not the one buying salt and pepper Luke and Johns.* He sauntered coolly to his room, but his knees felt wobbly and his throat hurt. He felt his mother's concern sweep over his back like searchlights. He shut his bedroom door and sat down on the bed. He wouldn't go back there, even when his father called him to come out. His mother would save him left-overs. He heard them now, back to eating—someone scraping a serving bowl, his father's request for more butter please, his sister's "What's for dessert?"

At least this time his father hadn't threatened to take Kyle out of Palmetto High and send him to the military school or to Crossroads Academy, a warning that always scared Kyle. The worst part was when Kyle got blamed for things he didn't even do. Like that time a bunch of Palmetto High students were caught painting SUCK ME, SANTA! across the water tower on Christmas Eve. And those reports in the newspaper of a water condom fight at a big party that got out of hand after the Homecoming game. (*Homecumming,* they called it. But not in the paper.) Kyle's only hope now was the money thing. Surely, his parents couldn't afford to send him to private school, even a crap school like Crossroads. He'd heard the collectors call every night, and his father's barks of anger when the bills came in, his mother's weeping. (*It's the mortgage or the car payment, Dora. It's come to this.*)

Kyle stretched out across his bed, but there were just way too many cushions, and he shoved them onto the floor and then stretched out on the new, stiff bedspread, which still smelled like a polyester factory, and wasn't comfortable at all. He missed the ratty, soft quilt he used to have. He came home from school one day to find this red bedspread with football motifs all over it. Like he was a jock or something. The pillows were shaped like baseballs and basketballs and footballs and soccer balls, and his mother bought them last month because they were *just perfect* for a boy's room. *Her* idea of a boy's room.

It was too crowded in here; that was the problem. He couldn't think with all this stuff. His dresser was so crammed with undershirts—which he never wore anyway—he could hardly close the drawers. His bedside table was crowded with Daniel and the Lion's Den action figures which he was *way* too old for, though his mother ignored his protests and kept buying them for him anyway at Agape. The Job figure (with boils!) was still in shrink-wrap. He'd given up using the desk in the corner for studying. It was loaded down with stacks of spare spiral notebooks, a bin of markers, and packs of orange pencils stacked like cordwood. He kept his textbooks under his bed. He didn't want all this stuff. He didn't need any of it. But did his mother listen? No.

For so long now, the Visa and MasterCard envelopes arrived monthly, growing fatter. And then there were the letters and rude phone calls from collectors that made his father holler and demand why. Why? And, in turn, his mother's weepy confessions, *I don't know why, don't you see?*

There was a soft knock on the door. "Kyle?" His mother opened the door. "Come finish your dinner."

"No thanks. I'm not hungry," he lied.

"Are you sure?"

"I'm sorta tired. I got tons of homework."

At that, she barged over, and felt his forehead. "Are you sick?"

"Nope." He yawned for effect. "I'm beat."

"Well . . . ," she said, scrutinizing him in that complicated way she did lately. She'd cut him some slack. He knew it. After all, he'd waved the red flag for her at dinner, hadn't he? Got her out of his dad's crosshairs for a while, anyway. "I'll bring you a plate."

Later, Kyle took out his collection of magazine pictures from behind a loose tile in his closet. His favorite was a model kneeling in a forest, her face hidden by a wall of dark shiny hair, her body bent gently like a stem. You could see the corded nape of her neck. She held a pinkie under the ankle strap of her sandal, her legs long and slender and cool, her neck perfumed—Kyle just knew it—sweet-smelling like the fragrant clouds that billowed around Pastor Pat-Rick's girlfriend, or like Julie's tingly flowery scent, which he could sometimes, almost, conjure up at will. Kyle folded the picture. It wasn't even porn, really. Just a picture that was nice to look at, and that happened to include a naked woman. Not like the wild stuff from some of the magazines that Tee and the other guys at school had shown him. Things you could order. Now that would be serious demerits. Hello, Crossroads Academy.

Abusing yourself. That's the term his father used when he

talked to Kyle about the dangers of *self-gratification*. It all started last year when his mother had found the *Penthouse* in his room, before he got smart about hiding stuff. Kyle endured a lecture from his father about how *bad habits now will be hard to break later*. Okay, Kyle wanted to say, okay, *just what am I supposed to do, explode or something?* No one knew what a freak he was, how he wondered what people looked like under their clothes. Everyone. Even at church, all he saw were naked people sitting there with their legs crossed and the sex parts of them hidden, moist, covered up under their dresses and inside their pants like small furry animals that everyone shielded and looked at and took care of in private. Like pets they carried around in secret.

"An undisciplined body is an undisciplined mind and spirit," his father told him. "Job 31. Look it up, Kyle. Memorize it." And if his father wanted to ensure those words were seared in his brain, it worked, because Kyle was both blessed and cursed with an excellent memory: "I made a covenant with my eyes not to look with lust upon a girl. I know full well that the Almighty God sends calamity on those who do."

Now, as the recliner thumped closed, the late-night news on the television turned off, and the quiet settled on everything like snow, Kyle put away his pictures and slowly opened his door to take a peek. The coast was clear. He locked his bedroom door from the inside, opened his bedroom window, and popped out the screen. He crawled outside and found his sister's bike propped beside the air-conditioning unit, just where he'd left it that afternoon. He headed for the woods, pedaled down the main road of his flat, treeless subdivision under the buzzing streetlights. The windows of the houses flickered with late television, purplish and shadowy, like bruises.

Kyle's knees stuck out awkwardly from the bike. It really was painfully small. And humiliating, too, with the My Little Pony stickers, the purple and pink handlebar streamers. His own bike had been stolen a year before, as he swam in the neighborhood pool. Why hadn't he used the bike lock? his father wanted to know. Didn't he realize the dangers out there in the world? The mandate came down: Kyle would have to earn his own money to buy another bike, or go without, and after some halfhearted lawn mowing for several neighbors and a disastrous day of car washing, Kyle grew disgusted and discouraged and decided, much to his parents' dismay, to go without a bike. Hence, the glittery banana seat beneath him now, the lavender Barbie basket on the handlebars.

Anyway, his sister never rode her bike. She wouldn't miss it. Kyle crossed over the highway and stashed the bike under the first overpass, beneath some overgrown juniper bushes. No one could see it from the road. It would be safe here. The bike would save him time on those days he had to get to his grandmother's. After his mother dropped him off at Crossroads for Saving Souls, Kyle would sneak out the back way and then walk here up to the highway, and ride the bike the rest of the way to his grandmother's.

Kyle looked at his watch. The cemetery party was just cranking up now. He could make it there in ten minutes. Julie might be there already. He broke into a run, his sneakers slapping the sidewalk with a tempo—Julie Julie Julie—and even after his breath grew ragged, he didn't slow down. He ran uphill toward the gates of Springforth, past the statue of the general in the gloomy shadows, and when a muscle spasm gripped his ribs, Kyle bent over in a loose self-hug, gulping air, willing the pain to stop.

SEVEN

L et's see what the mice left us," Emma said, "up there." She pulled down the creaky, narrow foldaway stairs, and Kyle ascended. Emma had meant to go through the attic for years, of course, but Harold would have none of it. "Out of sight, out of mind," he'd told her, a philosophy he'd adopted and applied universally to all manner of problems—social, financial, and marital. And so the years of accumulation, both precious and unremarkable, had collected in the attic, out in the barn, in every room in the house, like barnacles on a hull. And it was time to scrape, thought Emma. It was time to winnow. And now that Kyle was coming by regularly and had asked to help out, Emma was forced to invent a project like this one. Cleaning out the attic. For she'd drawn his rapt attention when she casually mentioned his uncle Will's old record albums were somewhere up in the attic.

"There should be a stack of boxes over there by the window," Emma called up to him. "You see them, honey? You can start there." She strained to hear him.

"Do you want me to bring down all three of them?" he asked, peering down.

"Yes, but take your time. Hand them down to us. Careful."

Bobby held up his hands, and Kyle dropped a box. With an *oof,* Bobby put it down.

Emma herself had stood there at the top of the attic stairs years ago, looking down at her own children. Back then, she'd escape to the attic after putting Will and Dora down for their naps. She'd set herself up a little reading area under the eaves. There was an old rug, a lawn chair, and a pile of *Life* magazines, *National Geographics*, and her old dog-eared books from her previous life: Shakespeare, Whitman, Dickinson. She'd felt guilty about it, as if she were doing something terrible, like nipping whiskey, when all she wanted was to go away, just for a while. But try telling that to children, especially ones who refused to nap. She would hear them down here carrying on something awful and Will, at four, trying his best to entertain Dora. As she got older, Dora became more demanding, stationing herself at the base of the stairs, baby blanket around her shoulders like a mantle, stomping her foot, like a tiny queen. "Mama. Down. Right now. *Right now.*"

"You don't have to do chores all the time," Emma told Kyle after they had closed the attic stairs and turned their attention to sifting through the boxes. "You can watch the MTV with your uncle or use the telephone anytime." There! The color rose in his cheeks. "If you want privacy, just use the phone in my bedroom to call that young lady from the other day. What is her name?"

"Grandma, you promised no more questions."

"So I did."

He managed to look absorbed in the task at hand: sorting through a stack of record albums. "Cream. The Doors. Hendrix. Oh, man. These are excellent."

"You can have them."

"Are you serious? Grandma, I can't take these," he said.

Bobby drifted into the living room, back to his chair and cigarettes. Kyle continued to comb through the clutter—record albums, yearbooks, jeans and T-shirts she couldn't bear to give away.

"I'm not a fool, you know," Emma said then. "Did your mother send you to help me?"

"She doesn't know."

"She doesn't want me to *think* she knows, or she really doesn't know?"

He looked bewildered. "I promise. She doesn't know."

"Where on earth does she think you are when you visit us?"

"I told you. They just think I'm doing this thing. At church? Saving Souls. You sign up to—you know—help people? And I decided to, um, spend my time here helping you and Uncle Bobby."

For some reason, this explanation left Emma feeling deflated. And she had been sure Dora had been behind these visits. But, no. No. She and Bobby were just Bible school projects for Kyle.

"I got special permission, because I really wanted to spend the summer here with you and Uncle B." There was a smear of grime on his cheek, and his hairline was damp with perspiration. Bless him, Kyle knew how to redeem himself.

"But you do plan on telling them you're here doing this Saving Spirits with your uncle and me?"

"Saving *Souls*. Yeah. I'll tell them . . . when the time is right."

Emma poked around in some other boxes and found a string of old Christmas lights, a bolt of faded gingham fabric, three cans of paint, and a plastic doll—naked, missing arms, with helpless eyes.

"Maybe cleaning out the attic isn't such a good idea after all," she said.

"Why not?" Kyle said.

"Well, it just dredges up things. I think your grandfather was right." And who cared about what happened to all this after she was gone? Why did she worry about who would poke through these piles or who might buy her china at an estate sale?

Emma pulled out a large framed photograph. It was the Hanley family portrait that she'd insisted on all those years ago for posterity. And posterity had arrived. There they were, chafing in their pressed collars and stiff shoes. Will—hulking and stern, his Adam's apple squeezed above the collar and wide, hideous tie, his black hair parted in the middle, falling to his shoulders, just as the boys wore it back then. He was fourteen in the photograph, the seams of his jacket straining against his shoulders and biceps, which just that summer had risen and plumped, like bread in the oven. There was a little of his father in the beakish profile, the blustering expression. He had missed basketball practice for this? his eyes seemed to say. Dora sat in front of Will, her silky tan hair shoved behind her ears, bangs in her eyes. Emma had forbidden the white lipstick and false eyelashes Dora had insisted every other thirteen-year-old girl in the world was allowed to wear. Consequently, Dora glowered up at the camera from a crouch, like a furious elf. She'd been told by the frustrated photographer to *sit up straight, young lady, please, shoulders back!* but, in typical rebellious fashion, done the opposite, until, by the end of the session, she was hunched, arms wrapped around her legs, as if taking part in a tornado drill. And there was Bobby—a towhead, the only family member looking even slightly amused. A few years later, his expressions would disappear altogether. His high school photographs would show the same blank appearance as he looked into the camera's eye. Blunted facial expression, a negative symptom. She can still hear the doctor's recitation of that horrible matter-of-fact checklist.

Stationed like sentinels on either side of their children in the portrait were Harold—ravenlike, brooding, with yellow eyes and a slightly cocked head—and Emma herself, redheaded (out of a bottle by then), pale and stiff, with a slash of scarlet lipstick and a Peter Pan collar. No one in the Hanley family was smiling. Not one of them.

"These record albums," Kyle said. "Could I keep them . . . here?"

"Here? Don't you want to play them at home?"

"Well, I don't have a stereo player in my room. Maybe I could use the one here."

"Take it, too, if you want."

"I think it's better if I keep it all here." He held up an album. THE DOORS it said, with PROPERTY OF WILL HANLEY! DO NOT

TOUCH! written across it. "I guess Uncle Will really liked putting his name on his stuff?"

"That was for your mother's benefit. They were always squabbling about those records. Your mother took them without asking him. He had a summer job, and he could buy all the records he wanted. Then Will moved the hi-fi out to the barn and that solved things. They could share the music. And they did—for miles around, whether you wanted to hear it or not."

Kyle looked doubtful. "That doesn't sound like my mom."

"Oh, no?"

"No. The reason why I can't take those albums of Uncle Will's is—they wouldn't let me play them at home, anyway."

Emma sighed. "Well, perhaps if you start gradually, with one that's . . . easy listening." She looked at the albums, cascading across the floor. "Here—" She held one up. "A woman singer."

"Grandma," he said. He closed his eyes, sighed, and looked, suddenly, like a little adult. "Janis Joplin is not easy listening— never mind. It would never work anyway. You know how they are. They're so strict. They're *freaks* about stuff. My friends can't even understand. It's my dad. He grew up that way."

"Perhaps. But your mother didn't."

"I *know*. That's what's so nuts."

"Your mother was always busy at school or at some meeting or other. And those parties! Barn bashes, they called them. She and Will, both. But your mother was the one who was always starting up things."

"My dad said that's what almost ruined her. She was in the wilderness of sin when he met my mom, he said. And she was lost because she was brought up wrong." This confession wounded Emma, but she was certainly not transparent enough to let such terrible nonsense provoke her into an angry response by a grandson who, though dear, was desperate for her to take sides.

"That is the most ridiculous prattle I've ever heard," Emma heard herself say. Yes, apparently she *was* transparent, and manipulated quite handily. Her face burned. "Judgmental hogwash.

Your mother—" Surely, Emma reminded herself, surely she would
not allow herself to be lured into this fray, to enter this squabble
and lose Dora for good, not to mention Kyle and Sandy. She must
keep a cool head. "Your mother is more lost than ever, if you
want to know my opinion," she said, and found herself in cahoots
with Kyle after all. Ah, well.

Emma took a breath and collected herself. "That's no excuse
for sneaking over here," she said. "You need to tell your mother
about your visits soon—"

"Grandma. Please."

"This is all getting a bit complicated, I'm afraid."

"But then I'd have to tell her about Saving Souls and how I
sort of misled her and she'd never . . . It's hopeless," he said.

Yes, Emma thought, the situation did seem that way. It gave
her a horrible headache just dwelling on it. An awful piercing on
the right side that she'd read the other day could be a symptom of
a stroke. Right now, her blood could be pooling against a single
weakened blood vessel, frayed and leaky as an old garden hose.
Oh, you could be here one minute, flat-out dead on the linoleum
the next.

"I can start coming every day now that school is out," he said.
"For a while, anyway." He searched her face for approval. "Please."

Of course not. Emma hugged him to soften the blow. Of
course she couldn't consent to such a thing. Not until Kyle told
his mother. Emma breathed in the scent of Kyle's neck—soap, a
little sweat and dust, a whiff of smoke and something else, something boyish and budding, tickly as pollen. He smelled delicious.

"All right," she said.

He arrived most days in the early afternoon, riding that ridiculous pink bicycle. Today, Emma watched for her grandson at the
kitchen window, her pocketbook hanging in the crook of her elbow. Her toes were crunched in her high heels, her pantyhose
tight and itchy.

She had an important appointment. She'd been ready for hours.

Emma walked down the hall, knocked on the bathroom door. "Bobby? Are you all right in there?"

"Yes."

"Kyle is here." There were splashing sounds, the drain's gurgling.

"I'm ready."

Bobby whispered then, but she couldn't make out what he was saying. Sometimes he talked about Will, told her things Will said. Harold had warned her not to encourage Bobby when he got out of his head like that. "It ain't real, Emma," her husband had once whispered, gripping her hand. "So stop talking to him like it is."

Kyle opened the front door. He had a key now.

"I think you've grown an inch just since yesterday." Emma told him now, laughing. "You're shooting up faster than corn."

"Hey, Uncle B."

"Will Two! You're here." Bobby stood in his robe, still dripping.

Her son really loved Kyle's visits, Emma thought now. Hanging on his every word. Why, Bobby's face moved with some emotion today, and that was a rare pleasure to see. And Kyle had such an easy manner with his uncle, not acting afraid like most everyone else, or ignoring him, like the mailman or the gas meter readers did when they spotted Bobby on the porch.

"Kyle, I've got an errand. I thought you two could just . . . visit together while I'm gone."

He shrugged. "Sure."

"Would you like to pull the car around?" Emma asked. "Right up here to the front door. Just leave it idling."

"But Grandma, I don't even have my permit. I can't drive alone for, like, another year."

"My, things *have* changed. When Will was your age, he was already driving."

"Driving? At fourteen?"

"Carting kids around the whole county."

"I took driver's ed at school, but I've got a lot of practicing to do."

"Will drove everywhere." Emma said wistfully, "Will and your mother and Wanda. They were always heading somewhere."

"Wanda?"

"Wanda was Will's girl. His first love." And his last, a thought Emma usually managed to avoid.

Kyle stood now, fidgeting with the car keys, looking away, awkward as a suitor. "But what if I wreck it?"

"You won't."

"Bobby?" she asked when Kyle went outside. He was dressed now. Dressed and clean and she'd only had to remind him twice. "You'll keep Kyle company? When I'm away?"

"Where are we going?" The car cranking from the back garage startled him.

"Nowhere. That's just Kyle, bringing the car around for me." She kissed her son, then rubbed off the scarlet stain above his brow. "You be good now." Sometimes, she couldn't help it, Emma thought about how much easier it would be not to always be tethered to this large, sweating, lump of confusion, this boy-man whom she loved so fiercely. Fear always managed to pierce her weariness. If not her—who, then? Who would take care of Bobby?

There was the squeal of brakes, a scraping. Kyle veered off the driveway and lightly swiped a fence post. "Oh, dear," she said. Her little beige Impala lurched and hiccupped, innocent and helpless. Kyle put the car in reverse, and got it back on the driveway. On the front porch, Emma dug around in her purse for her compact. She powdered her nose, then reapplied her lipstick, Crimson as Sin. She'd gotten the lipstick years ago, at Lawson's Pharmacy. It probably wasn't even safe to wear anymore. Could lipstick expire, she wondered? Could it harbor colonies of bacteria? *E. coli*? Botulism? Digging around some more at the bottom of her purse, amidst crumbs, wadded tissues, and old receipts, she found her summer gloves and three linty Lifesavers in a slender peel of wax wrapper.

Kyle got out of the car looking frantic. "I, uh, I think I sort of scraped it a little. Right back here, by the back fender."

"Where? I don't see a thing. You did just fine. Now, you'll keep an eye on Bobby?"

"Oh, yeah—sure, Grandma. Don't worry."

"I'm not worried in the least." She adjusted the rearview mirror.

"Uh, I just, you know—I sorta need to be back at the church today no later than four."

Emma nodded. "I'll be back in plenty of time."

Bobby dug holes in the back garden, and Kyle couldn't stop him.

"Uncle B? That's not helping."

He looked up at Kyle, sweating, hunched, a little desperate. "It is helping."

"Grandma wouldn't like it."

"Will told me to."

Jeez, how could you argue with that?

Bobby stood up, hands caked with red mud. He pointed across the garden with one filthy finger, gesturing wildly like a symphony conductor. "Past there, then down some and under. Way under."

Whatever. Kyle, bare-chested, tugged at the lawn mower cord again, and the mower finally sputtered to life, coughing sickly, spewing fumes. Boy, would his grandmother be surprised when she came back to find her lawn mowed. That was supposed to be the kind of thing he promised to do for Saving Souls, anyway.

After his grandmother left, he and Bobby plundered the shed in back, finding the ancient rusty mower under a tarp. That it had any gas in it all was a wonder; that it started, nothing short of a miracle.

How in the heck had his grandfather ever used this thing? Kyle thought, as he mowed. Oh, it was a dirty job, the dust and heat and sweat stuck to him. His Saving Souls T-shirt was getting grimy. He wiped his face with it, anyway.

"Uncle B? Maybe you could rake up the clippings and sticks and stuff?" But his uncle was sidetracked by something there in the grass. Kyle walked over and knelt down beside him. A praying mantis was perched on a stick. Its hammerhead swiveled and gazed back at them with cool detachment.

"*Tenodera sinensis*," his uncle said. "She'll shed her skin twelve times until she's fully grown and then lay three hundred eggs."

"Really?" Kyle wondered if this was just more wild talk, but his uncle was focused on the insect with a kind of confident delight.

"Her front legs are like knives. Very sharp," his uncle whispered.

"What's she doing?"

"Praying for prey."

He stayed crouched, watching the thing while Kyle worked, but whenever the mower choked on Kyle, his uncle walked over and pulled the cord, and the engine sputtered another few feet or so. In this fashion, Kyle and his uncle spent the afternoon mowing half the side yard.

There was a boy cutting the grass when Jake arrived at the Hanley place. Damn, wouldn't you know it? With the old ladies, you just never knew. Emma Hanley had probably forgotten she'd even hired Jake or maybe she just found a kid who'd do it on the cheap. Oh, but this one wasn't having an easy time of it. Bare-chested, pushing a sorry-ass old mower that choked, blades dull as church.

Jake got out of his truck and went to the front door. No one answered his knocks.

The boy came around front. "Um, can I help you?"

"She here? Mrs. Hanley?"

"No, sir."

Shambling back down Emma Hanley's creaking steps, Jake should have paid attention to the embers of pain that kicked up along his spine: the buzz saw was cranking, heading for his back. He should have stood there for a moment, and taken a breath, and looked around the front yard like he was taking it all in, and he should have steeled himself for what he knew was coming, but he instead he swaggered back to his truck like a landscaper should, and lifted a bag of topsoil. He'd start on Emma Hanley's yard, all right, before she changed her mind about hiring him. He nudged a bag of soil conditioner with his foot, like he was poking a log in the fireplace, and right then the sciatica seared like a hot wire down his spine, through his leg, all the way to his big toe. Oh, Christ, like someone flipped on a neon sign inside him, crackling and sizzling and zapping, killing him, *killing him*. His back, dear God, his back. His eyes watered. The buzz saw was screaming.

"Maybe I should come back," he managed. After a moment, he said, "I guess you're the yardman, now?"

"I'm the grandson."

The pain, my God, the pain. Jake took a deep breath, released it slowly. "You're Bobby's boy?" he asked. Will hadn't had a kid; he knew that much.

"No, sir. Bobby is my uncle."

The pain was receding now, wasn't it? Yes, mercifully the twinge was fading. He checked the kid, to make sure he hadn't noticed. Bobby Hanley was standing there, too. The boy, skinny as a greyhound, and Bobby, his face with as much emotion as a loaf of bread. What a pair. But the boy was a sharp one. Unfortunately.

"Are you . . . okay?"

Jake had already skipped one lawn that day, bowing out with an excuse about how he was running short on fertilizer. And he should have gotten to Emma Hanley's yard yesterday. In truth, his back was bad today. Real bad. "I woke up with a crick in my neck this morning. That's all." And if he could shrug it off, Jake would have. But he could hardly shrug at all.

"We'll unload the mower and stuff for you," the boy said, as he and Bobby Hanley moved to the back of Jake's truck.

"No," Jake protested weakly. "No, thanks. There's no need for that." By then the boy had jumped up on the truck bed and Bobby unloaded the mower with one grunt.

"What's next?" the boy said, wiping his hands.

"Well, that's mighty nice of you, but what's next is both of you need to git. I got work to do."

The boy looked so crushed, Jake regretted the sharp words.

"Look. What if your grandma came home and saw you and your uncle out here doing all this? What kind of yardman would I be, then, having clients do my work?"

"Oh," the boy said. "Okay."

"You all got things to do inside, don't you?" The boy nodded. His eyes, that slanted gaze! "Wait a minute," Jake said. "Wait—" Lord, he should've known. "Don't tell me—you're not Dora's boy?"

He nodded, surprised. "Yessir. I'm Kyle Quattlebaum."

"Well, I'll be damned." Jake shook his head slowly.

"You know my mom?"

"Oh, yeah. We were in school together at Palmetto High. Had some good times."

"Really?" His voice cracked with surprise.

Jake laughed. "Is it that hard to believe?"

Kyle blushed and looked away, and there was Dora's profile again.

"I go to Palmetto High."

"No kidding? God, I feel old," Jake said. He threw his cap in the back of the truck. "Well, I guess you could put back that sorry-ass lawn mower you were using. I'll get started."

"Oh, yeah. Sure. Uh, if you need help, tell us. I'm sort of supposed to, you know, help with things around here. For my grandma." The boy looked over at Bobby, who stood smoking.

"If I got any questions, I'll be sure and let you know," Jake said. Still, just getting that mower down off the truck had helped more than they could know. Come tomorrow, it would be good to have Gordon along again. Not that he'd be totally reliable. He wouldn't. Today he said he felt poorly, but at least he showed up to tell it. Claimed he had jungle rot starting up, from back in the day. *Like a big ol' wedge of soft cheese,* Gordon said, *that's what I feel like. Remember that?*

Jake stopped the mower a minute to mark the borders of Emma Hanley's perennial garden. It needed some weeding like most of her yard, but he could make out the stubborn green knobs of daylilies coming up, the coneflowers and black-eyed Susans muscling through, the hydrangeas' purple bursting. Everything was early this year; it was the heat. He bent down (watch the back!) and hand-weeded. He'd mulch it after mowing. The confederate jasmine's perfume wafted over to him, and he stood up a happy man. He would never work under fluorescent lights, or drive a forklift, or work an assembly line again. Never.

Emma lay naked in Lucinda Hayworth's bedroom. She peered up at the ceiling.

"Could you scooch down just a little for me, Mrs. Hanley?"

Emma scooched.

"Dr. Ghati will be back in just a sec."

The blond woman smiled down at Emma. They didn't wear white uniforms anymore, the nurses. They wore blouses with cartoon characters or flowers or bubbles. Cheerful, smiling things.

Until Emma had arrived here at Palmetto Ob-Gyn—late as it turned out, having gotten herself lost and flustered—until she'd walked up the curved brick walk past the PALMETTO OB-GYN sign and onto the porch where she and Lucinda Hayworth had once, sixty years before, played jacks and gulped lemonade, until then, she'd had no idea this doctor's office was in the old Hayworth place. Once inside, Emma found herself in the Hayworths' parlor; only now it was a waiting room. The entire street was turning into offices; she'd known that. But somehow she thought the Hayworth home would never give in.

Emma shivered in the chill of the examining room. It had once been Lucinda Hayworth's bedroom and had always been drafty, and that was why the Hayworths' maid, Della, had kept the coal fireplace over in the corner stoked all winter and into spring. Now, modern overzealous air-conditioning kept the room frigid. The mantel, she noticed, was painted mint green, and above, where Lucinda's portrait (in white eyelet holding Muff, the terrier) used to hang, were diplomas. SHIVANNI GHATI, MEDICAL DOCTOR.

Emma laid a trembling hand on her chest, over the thrum of

her heart, her finger instinctively brushing across her left breast, seeking out the lump she'd discovered last week in the course of donning her underthings. The door swung open, and suddenly the doctor was in. Dr. Ghati stared down at her. A foreigner. A woman from India.

"Are we ready?"

Emma never expected a doctor like this one: spiked black hair, longer in back, with a row of earrings in one ear, a tiny diamond stud at the side of her nose, hidden like a secret. All Emma knew of India was from Rudyard Kipling. *The Jungle Book.* Mowgli and Kaa. That sort of thing.

"Take a deep breath for me, Mrs. Hanley."

The light fixture that Lucinda's mother had ordered from Ireland was centered in the ceiling, like a simply set jewel. Pink frosted glass, fluted. And there was the same ghostly water stain by the window, bleeding out from under a layer of paint. She had always thought that stain was shaped like Mongolia. Was that country even on maps anymore? Were there Mongolians? There were Mongoloids, that was for certain. Lucinda's own sister was a Mongoloid who'd slept downstairs with Della in the maid's quarters. A cheerful, stout girl who Della managed to keep in crinolines and knee socks. A girl whose squat, stubby brazenness and need for affection frightened Emma so, Della had to keep her shut away in the kitchen when Emma visited. *You gonna make biscuits with me, now, and leave them little girls be.* Emma could hear Della as if it were yesterday. She felt for her, all these years later, Della's patient, unwavering protectiveness of her charge. Emma knew a little about that herself now.

And then, the doctor's smooth, cool hands moved over Emma. She closed her eyes. Lucinda Hayworth had been her classmate in sixth grade. It was here, in Lucinda's room, that Emma and Lucinda had conjugated French verbs; here, the two of them had memorized the European capitals.

There was the snap of latex gloves, and Emma tensed. Oh, this part was dreadful, the worst! The nurse—her name was Glo, she'd explained, short for Gloria—placed Emma's feet in the stirrups. "Just relax, Mrs. Hanley. I'll proceed with a thorough examination. It shouldn't take long."

Lucinda was a meek, bespectacled girl, easy to order around. On nights when Emma stayed over and they slept in Lucinda's softly sagging bed, Emma demanded Lucinda brush Emma's long unbraided hair, the girl's fingers lighting on her like butterflies. Lucinda's glasses would turn moist, her eyes hidden, her mouth held in a line of determination or stoicism, Emma could never tell. Afterwards, drowsy and ashamed, Emma would feign sleep, never once returning the favor.

"There, now, that wasn't so bad, was it?" Nurse Glo said. Emma's eyes fluttered open.

"Mrs. Hanley?" The doctor said. "Please get dressed and I will be back in to talk with you."

And then they were gone, Nurse Glo and Dr. Ghati, they were gone and Emma was alone with the lump, hard and round as a spring pea.

Kyle studied the driveway, waiting for a glint of metal, the sound of tires, the sight of his grandmother's car. It was three thirty and she still wasn't back. Even the cheerful commentary of Martha Quinn, VJ on MTV, could no longer lure Kyle's eyes from the driveway. *Oh my gosh, where is she?*

Outside, the sounds of the yardman's lawn mower hummed rhythmically. The man, Jake, was tanned dark as copper, with a profile like an Indian-head penny. His hair was too long. It hit his shoulders like a girl's. He claimed to know Kyle's mother, but Kyle was pretty sure he was lying. Or maybe just exaggerating. He didn't look like the kind of friend his mother would ever have.

From behind Kyle, on the couch, there was the sound of his uncle shaking out a cigarette and crinkling up the cellophane wrapper. Without turning, Kyle said, "Uncle B, you shouldn't smoke so much." His uncle's restlessness, his occasional yearning to escape, reminded Kyle of a stray cat he'd once held, flat-eared, tail twitching, allowing itself to be petted while patiently waiting to spring. *Don't let your uncle out of your sight,* his grandmother had told him.

If his grandmother wasn't here in seven minutes, he would have to leave Bobby—3:37 was the absolute latest he could stay and still make it to church by four. His mother would be waiting, and if he was late, then she might go talk to the other mothers or even Pastor Pat-Rick, and then she would find out Kyle wasn't doing Mission Possible or Day Care Angels this year at all. But he couldn't leave Uncle Bobby. Could he? He turned to look at his uncle, who was hunched over in his chair smoking, staring at the television, an empty bag of Doritos at his feet.

Emma was lost. Somehow she got herself turned around in a town where she'd spent the better part of a century. The streets were changing. There were traffic cones everywhere and construction men (and women!) flagging motorists. The houses had been painted new colors. (The Hollinger house was purple now—oh, Etta must be turning over in her grave!) Taking out trees, adding lanes and medians, putting up fences. After she'd left the doctor's office, Emma wandered a street over to where she'd parked. Where she *thought* she'd parked. Perhaps it was a block in the other direction, on McBee. She'd been so distracted when she'd left the doctor's office, she could hardly recall exactly where she'd left the car.

The card in her hand grew damp. Radiologist. Appointment. Arrive fifteen minutes early. She tucked it inside her purse, beside the Lifesavers. They wanted a picture of her insides. They would call her, they said, and she must go there. *Not today,* she told them. *Not today, I have to get back home.* One afternoon when Kyle could stay with Bobby again. Maybe then she could arrange it. This business would have been so much easier if Harold were still around.

She walked across Lavinia Avenue, down past the post office, those streets that had been left alone. No MEN AT WORK signs here. The only changes were appointed by nature itself. Rot and peel and warp. Emma's old street. Her feet were numb now; she wasn't accustomed to these pumps with their little heels, their sweet buttons. She should have just worn her tennis shoes. How foolish—an old woman dressed up to go to the doctor.

And then—Amaranth. The shutters had long disappeared, two windows were broken, wisteria was devouring one side whole. Several men sat out on the porch, swigging from their brown bags, squinting at her. She looked back at them accusingly.

This ramshackle place had once been her home. Only the crescent-shaped stained-glass window at the top of the vestibule remained intact. A jewel-colored peacock lay hidden in that glass, handmade in Germany at the turn of century, ordered by Emma's grandfather. The peacock's tail—violet, garnet, and golden flecks— once glimmered in the eastern morning light. Now filth saved that precious thing, grime and dust and inaccessibility.

One of the men leaned over a half-rotted porch railing and spit.

She was afraid to look at her watch, but she did, and she gasped. It was after four, and didn't Kyle say he had to be back by then? He had to be somewhere by four. She had to find her car! Emma stumbled past Amaranth and turned a corner. There it was parked at the curb, her Impala with the new scrape on the back bumper. She had walked in a circle.

When she fastened her seat belt, Emma's hand found its way back to her left breast, a secretive salute. When the nurse chided her for having stopped her annual checkups, Emma told her the only doctor she'd had in her adult life—Dr. Beasley, who'd done everything from delivering her children to taking off moles—had died several years back. And she had never gotten around to finding a new one. Until now.

What she didn't say was that in the wake of Harold's death— his sudden, shocking, *senseless* death—Emma had become convinced her own life was in peril. It was as if she'd been a drowsy passenger on a train, lulled so long by the sight of the landscape going by—distant, flat, blurred—it was startling to finally pull into the station. Wake up. Time to disembark.

And this dimple of darkness she'd discovered? Well, in a way it was . . . expected. The doctor told her the tests would tell them more, and rule out anything serious. *Before it spreads,* Emma can't help but think now. Optimism never was her strength. Driving home, she remembered other things that had grown inside her— her children—rising in her body like moons.

PART II

Anything will give up its secrets if you love it enough.
—George Washington Carver

EIGHT

Dora dreaded the pool party all morning. It was for Bethany Henderson, one of Sandy's friends, but all the mothers would be there, including, of course, Barbara Henderson. Or Barb, as Dora privately thought of her, because the woman sure knew how to draw blood. Dora parked down the street from the balloon-festooned mailbox, letting the van idle while she worked up her nerve.

Barb Henderson had an uncanny talent for probing tender spots and weaknesses, and took pride in eliciting public confessions, but, so far, Dora had managed to be the last holdout. *There, there you just let it all out,* Barb would declare to her victims, folding them into her bosomy embrace, patting backs. *You poor, poor thing, we are all going to pray on this.* In this fashion, Barb had managed to draw out quite a few of the Crossroads mothers' secrets: Gracie's first botched marriage; LeaAnne's brief fling with Baha'i, *a cult. A dangerous cult! You could have been killed!* Vickie's mysterious outbreak of herpes, *I bet it was all those public toilets, all those rest stops!* Gigi's strangled admission about her brother, lost in the homosexual lifestyle down in New Orleans, *You can't make sinners do right, honey. You can just pray they repent.* Barb soothed, patted, and tsk-tsked, while the tears and stories spewed.

Even Dora had to admit the weekly spectacles of late at Tuesday Night Prayer Circle certainly bumped up attendance, as if Barb were performing some ancient purification ritual.

The Hendersons' neighborhood, a new one, crammed with vinyl-sided Cape Cods and narrow sodded lawns, was not so different from her own. Just a little more expensive. Twenty grand more for a half bath and bonus room. Who needed that? Dora got out and walked up the Hendersons' driveway, her heels clacking like hammers. She wore a navy skirt and pale blue blouse—inappropriate for a pool party, which was precisely the point. She wouldn't stay long.

The earsplitting squeals of a dozen girls in the pool greeted her as she headed to the backyard. In fact, there wasn't much of a yard left at all. It was mostly chlorinated water—bordered by three narrow strips of pea gravel. There was, Dora noted as she opened the gate, hardly a sprig of grass in the whole place. Lance Henderson was a swimming pool salesman, so of course the Hendersons had the largest pool in the neighborhood, with a water slide and a diving board.

The mothers, in the far corner, hunkered around the patio table, which was littered with juice boxes and baby monitors. Dora saw with some relief it was a small group—Gracie, LeaAnne, Vickie and . . . where was Barb? Dora closed the gate behind her, turned around, and nearly gasped. Barb stood inches away, as if she'd been conjured.

"Oh," Dora said. "My goodness. I didn't see you."

"I'm glad you could make it, Dora. We've been waiting." Barb showed her teeth.

"I'm sorry—I had to pick up a few things and . . . errands," Dora said. "You know how it is."

"Well, come join us. We've got a ton of food."

Dora spotted Sandy sitting alone at the shallow end of the pool. The other girls splashed and giggled in the deep end. Dora's heart sank. Maybe it was the swimsuit—a flabby one-piece with a cruel little skirt. "You're long-waisted like me," Dora told Sandy yesterday when they'd had trouble finding a swimsuit that fit her, but the saleswoman had steered them away from the pastel lacy confections to the drab, dark bathing suits in the Big Girrrrl! section. Sandy was, face it, running to plump.

"Dora's here," Barb warbled as she took her seat at the head of the table.

"Take a load off, hon." Gracie Vaughn patted the space beside her, and Dora reluctantly perched. Dora knew Gracie back from their days on student council at Palmetto High. She'd been Gracie Farr then, perpetually tanned with hair black as a tire, who had a penchant for rum and coke, and basketball players. Gracie had attended more than a few of Dora's barn bashes and had, Dora felt sure, once harbored a secret crush on Will. Not that they ever rehashed those days. On the contrary, she and Gracie had fallen into a kind of mutual forgetfulness, as if they weren't connected at all by their own feral pasts. They were mothers now, they were *Crossroads* mothers. They'd acquired different last names, new habits and identities, and repressed memories, as if they were in witness protection. That Barb had managed to tease out Gracie's past marriage and hush-hush divorce was a testament to Barb's ability for spearing the most slippery of secrets. The only time Dora glimpsed the young Gracie anymore was in her lanky, gum-smacking, smart-alecky daughter, Sue Ellen, a nine-year-old who, at this moment, defied her mother by somersaulting off the diving board.

"Sue Ellen!" Gracie pointed when Sue Ellen's dark head, slick as an otter's, appeared in the deep end. "Didn't I tell you to stop that?"

"Your timing is perfect, Dora." This from LeaAnne, mother of Erica and twin infant boys. "The babies are all napping, at the same time, if you can believe it." The mothers looked down proudly at their baby monitors, buzzing pleasantly with white noise.

"Yep, I just checked," Barb said. "They're all out."

"For some reason, Zack hasn't been sleeping well lately," Vickie—mother of a six-month-old—said. "I can't believe he's even taking a nap."

"Sometimes they get overtired," Barb said. "You have to enforce a sleep schedule."

Dora did not have a baby anymore, and didn't plan on having another. Her sleep deprivation now was of a different kind, but she would never discuss with the mothers Kyle's sneaking out at night. Not with Barb Henderson lying in wait. No wonder Dora's closest friend these days was childless. Hardly a day went by that Jill Cuttler didn't call Dora, crying. *I'm barren barren barren* and all Dora had to do was listen.

Barb smeared a cocktail napkin with coconut butter and basted one thick red upper arm until it shone like a glazed ham. Barb had the broad, top-heavy body of an opera singer, and was, in fact, a frequent soloist in the Crossroads choir. That such a stunningly beautiful soprano voice could emerge from the likes of Barb Henderson was, to Dora's mind, nothing short of a miracle. Last Sunday, as Barb sang "Nearer My God to Thee," Dora had imagined every ethereal note fleeing the rib cage, escaping the throat, floating from the poisonous lips of Barb, ascending heavenward, like souls sprung from hell.

"How's your mother?" Barb asked Dora as she began varnishing the other arm.

"She's . . . fine," Dora stammered. "She's actually doing . . . as well as can be expected. I—"

"I'm still praying for her," Barb said, cutting Dora off. A chorus of yeses arose from the mothers. "I just know one of these Sundays she'll come to Crossroads."

Barb knew all about Dora's frustration with her mother, of course. Knew about Emma's stubborn refusal to allow Donny to handle the funeral business, and all the rest. No telling what else Barb knew. Donny blabbed everything to the husbands at the Thursday Men's Prayer Breakfast, and Lance Henderson brought it all home.

"You know," Barb said, meeting Dora's eyes, "I just hate to see your mother suffer . . . alone."

"Well, she's right here in town," Dora said. "So I can drop by any time to check on her."

"No, I mean *alone* . . . in eternity. Without the comfort of . . . Christ."

The monitors crackled with the sounds of a baby's cries, and the mothers startled.

"Oh, that's my Zack," Vickie said, standing up.

Barb held up her hand like a traffic cop. "Wait. Let him cry for a minute. He'll go back to sleep."

Vickie sat back down with a chastened look. The baby monitor sputtered, crackling like some fried thing.

"Dora, have a brownie," Gracie said, holding out a platter. "We're trying out recipes for *Cooking at Crossroads.*"

Dora herself had failed to muster the interest and courage it would take to contribute recipes for the cookbook, perhaps because she regularly concocted family meals from recipes off soup can labels and sauce jars.

"It's delicious," Dora said as she finished the brownie.

"How do you do it?" LeaAnne asked her. "I just look at that brownie and gain three pounds. You scarf up things and don't gain an ounce." LeaAnne's blue eyes, which had all the depth of a kiddie pool, grew wider as she realized she'd waded into an awkward subject. She bit her lip. The other mothers looked down and away. Because they knew how Dora did it. Firm Believer dropouts, all of them. Except for Barb, of course, who'd never joined in the first place. "It would wreck my voice," Barb had said by way of explanation.

Dora's gaze strayed to her daughter, who was, evidently, content to watch the world more than participate in it, and who sat with a look of drowsy contentment on her round face, like a little Buddha.

"Your Sandy is an angel," Barb said. Dora tensed. "So quiet and sweet and . . . easy. Just sits there, no trouble at all. Hardly says a word."

Dora stood. "I hate to eat and run, but we have to go. Sandy's piano lesson got moved up an hour."

"Bethany!" Barb stood up and positioned herself beside Dora. "Bethany Ann Henderson."

"Yes, ma'am." Bethany splatted across the cement and stood dripping and squinting up at her mother. "What did I tell you about not leaving Sandy out?" Barb hissed.

Dora's cheeks burned. She couldn't tell if Sandy heard, but behind her, the mothers had fallen silent.

"We're *not*, Mommy."

"How would you like to be just sitting all alone feeling like no one likes you?"

"But . . . Sandy *likes* to just . . . watch. She told us."

"You know, Sandy hasn't been feeling well," Dora said quietly. "One of those . . . virus things."

"Are you sure?" Barb asked. "She's been eating all right." Barb turned and clapped. "Girls! Who wants to dive for moolah?" Barb tossed a handful of quarters into the water. The laughter and shrieks stopped, replaced by a dozen pairs of puckered feet waving in the air. Sandy roused herself and reached behind her for a cupcake, sat back down cross-legged, and licked off the green icing. She studied the antics of the swimmers with bemusement, as if she were observing the seal exhibit at the zoo.

Barb shrugged. "Well, I tried." She smiled, her eyes black and round as a shark's.

"I hear your poor husband is busier than ever," Dora said, her heart racing. "Donny said Lance is on the road so much, he can't even find time to fix the baptismal font at Crossroads."

"My Lance works hard."

"Too hard, I bet," Dora said. It was pure instinct, but Dora had felt Lance Henderson's greasy gaze slide over her, and linger. He zeroed in on well-turned ankles, and frankly appraised chests and rear ends with all the discretion of a mannequin dresser. "I hear he was in Vegas last month? What with all those hot tub conventions and pool parties . . . I bet Lance is working himself silly."

Barb narrowed her eyes, before she recovered enough to slip on a look of pleasant distraction. But Dora saw the struggle, and she recognized the effort. Dora hadn't even realized she'd been saving this arrow in her quiver until now. How frustrating she'd let Barb goad her into using it! Clearly, she'd wounded Barb, although it was just a warning shot. And yet, Dora didn't feel triumphant at all. She felt alone, and more than a little sad. Spent. And now her quiver was empty.

When they arrived at Crossroads to pick up Kyle, he wasn't waiting out front with the other kids. Dora was on time for once, and wouldn't you know it? Kyle was late. Or maybe he was inside, away from this sweltering heat. Wasn't that Pastor Pat-Rick over there, heading into Crossroads? Dora parked, and she and Sandy walked inside the echoing emptiness of the shopping center where it was cool, dim, and—more and more—unsettling. The silver banner overhead announced HEAVENLY SHOPPING! but something about the ornate script and glittery stars reminded her of prom night, and she thought of going to McCann Square all those years ago, in search of a dress.

She and her mother had fought about that, just as they fought about most things then. Emma had always preferred downtown, and had never warmed to McCann Square, since the shopping center reminded Emma of her grandfather's firearm misadventure, and her family's lost fortune and missed opportunities. Dora had reminded her mother that all the girls were buying their prom dresses at McCann Square, but Emma wouldn't hear of it, and took her to Miss Edna Greenbow's Wedding and Formal Shoppe on Main Street, a musty, dim place crammed with debutante dresses and candlelit taffeta wedding gowns with high collars and seed pearls. Mrs. Greenbow had served them iced tea with sprigs of mint and lemon cookies and summoned her seamstress with a little hand bell. The ancient woman, gnarled and brown as a root, half a dozen straight pins gripped in her puckered lips, shuffled out from behind some curtains like a creature from a fairy tale.

Nothing would fit, no pattern suited, no dress would do. Crinolines were hopelessly out, anyway, as Dora informed her mother, as well as those silly gloves, and so they'd ended up at McCann Square after all, Dora and her mother both snarling and crying by then, hardly speaking. In the end, Dora's father had been sent for, in order to mend the quarrel, and Dora got what she wanted: a devastatingly bare-shouldered crepe sheath in mint green purchased for her by her father at Ivey's Department Store, not twenty feet away from where Dora now stood. Oh, she missed her father. She really did.

"Why are you sad, Mom?" Sandy asked.

"I'm just . . . thinking of Grandpa."

"Oh." Sandy frowned, and Dora felt a pang of guilt. Was her own funk contagious?

"And . . . I was remembering a fancy dress I had a long time ago."

Her daughter perked up. "Did you wear a crown with it?"

"No. No crown."

"When I grow up, I'm going to wear crowns with all my fancy dresses."

"I bet you will," Dora said.

Dora couldn't imagine ever bickering with her own daughter over a prom dress. Of course, Dora realized now that she and her mother had quibbled about a silly thing like a dress because the whole world had been falling apart and they were both fit to be tied, each in her own way. It was 1970, and Will had just been drafted. Will drafted! Dora's mother had fallen into a dreamy sadness for weeks, writing Senator Strom Thurmond and reminding him that Will was from the McCann people, good Southern stock—as if that mattered—and begging for a delay until her eldest son might have a taste of university life. That was a laugh, as Will didn't care one whit about college, and was perfectly content to work with their father in the appliance repair business and make plans to marry Wanda, and do his duty to fight the communists. Dora went the other direction entirely—joining the antiwar protests that had, by then, even found their way to South Carolina. In May, three weeks after the prom, she convinced Jake to drive her down to some big demonstration at the university in Columbia. She'd rounded up a bunch of people from the high school, and they drove in a caravan the whole two hours there. Everyone but Wanda, of course, who would never do such a thing and was sure Will, over there fighting in the jungle for their country, wouldn't approve. And, plus, didn't Dora know those things could get out of hand?

They got out of hand fast. Dora returned from the protest with her eyes still burning from tear gas. Jake's car was nearly ruined from the raw eggs. Jane Fonda had been there, and the Guard had even been called in. Oh, but the energy! The weed, the wine, the ecstatic anger. The idea something big and awful like a war could be stopped, that you could change things.

Things changed, all right.

Nowadays, Hanoi Jane was busy with the whole aerobics craze. The new enemies were processed sugar and sloth. Trade your sit-ins for sit-ups. Go for the burn.

HEAVENLY SHOPPING! The banner flapped and tittered above Dora every time someone opened the doors and came into Crossroads. Something like that could get on your last nerve fast. She was beginning to hate it in here. She couldn't wait to quit the Firm Believers. Let someone else lead it. She didn't have the heart.

"Let's wait outside," she told Sandy. The blistering heat in the parking lot would be better than this.

And then she saw him.

Saving Souls was over and Kyle was late. His mother was not. She was waiting for him in the parking lot, her face scrunched in fury. Kyle tried to get his excuse right. After stashing the bike beside the overpass and running here in a panic, it was hard to appear calm. And he was worried now, worried that he'd done the wrong thing by leaving Uncle Bobby. The yardman was there, but he hadn't liked it one bit when Kyle told him his grandmother was on her way back, could he just keep an eye on his uncle for a few minutes? *Now, just come back here. Don't you leave me with*—But by then Kyle was pedaling his sister's bike furiously down the drive and managed to call over his shoulder, *She'll be here any minute!*

His mother leaned against their van, shielded her eyes with a hand.

"I was—uh, I had to go. To the restroom. Couldn't wait—," he managed.

She was squinting in the sun, not glaring with anger at him after all. "Hop in. Sandy has piano."

Relief flooded through him; his knees went weak. He was so grateful not to be found out, he didn't even make Sandy move to the backseat.

"So, how was Saving Souls today?"

"Boring," Kyle said, "as usual." Somehow, he would have to call his grandmother, the minute they got home. His stomach cramped with concern. What if something had happened to her? Maybe her car broke down. Maybe Bobby threw down a cigarette on the rug and the whole house was in flames. Maybe the yardman got fed up and left, and Bobby was there alone.

"You need socks, don't you?" his mother asked.

"No."

"Yes, you do. There was a sale today. . . . I picked up a few more pairs. They're back there somewhere."

He looked in the shopping bag beside him. "Oh. There's, like, gobs of socks in here," he said.

"Tube socks," his mother said. "You can never have enough."

"Apparently."

After her sprees, his mother was happy. Then his father went nuts, and his mother would cry. *I just want to make sure the kids have everything they need.*

"They're your favorite, aren't they?" his mother asked. "That kind?"

"Yeah. Fortunately. Thanks. I'd say my sock needs have been met through, like, middle age." Three dozen pairs of tube socks? That was messed up.

"I got some for you, too," she told his sister, "while you were at the pool party."

"*What?* You mean these teensy-weensy precious pink things aren't for *moi?*" Kyle asked, holding up a pair of lacy socks.

"Kyle! Give those to me," Sandy said, turning around in her seat.

"Jesus, Sand. It's a joke."

"Language," his mother said, her eyes meeting his in the rearview mirror.

Kyle's mother grew quiet, the buzz from buying all those socks gone now. When they pulled into Mrs. Cuttler's house, where his sister took piano lessons, she turned off the ignition. And sighed. Weird. His mother usually chatted it up with Mrs. Cuttler. Usually these visits took forever because Mrs. Cuttler was his mother's best friend or something, and now his mother looked like she dreaded going in.

Kyle thought again of the yardman, Jake. *We had some good times,* he said about his mother. And for a tempting instant, Kyle imagined asking his mother about him. *Hey, Mom, you know this guy named Jake? He mows the lawn with his shirt off and he needs a haircut and he says he knows you. He says you had some good times and the way he says it . . .*

"Can I please stay in the car?"

"Kyle," his mother said through clenched teeth. They got out.

The way he says it, somehow I don't think he's talking about Beta Club or History class, you know?

They walked into Mrs. Cuttler's ranch house, where in no time, his sister began banging out a painfully bad rendition of "My Favorite Things." Kyle restrained himself from holding his hands over his ears, because he knew there'd be hell to pay for that. Serious demerits. Mrs. Cuttler, diminutive and clad in pink, stood by the piano, then motioned them over.

"Just listen to this marvelous improvement!" she said.

Sandy stopped banging the keys and began spinning on the piano stool.

"Hey, kids. Care for a lemon square?" Mrs. Cuttler held out a plate that dwarfed her short arm. She couldn't be five feet. She had a rubbery, lipsticked smile. Sandy grabbed two lemon squares, and Kyle took one for himself. Then Mrs. Cuttler and his mother disappeared in the kitchen for one of their whispered talks. This was going to take forever.

"Where are you going?" Sandy asked Kyle from the piano stool.

"Mind if I take a leak?" Maybe he could use the phone in the back bedroom to call his grandmother. But, no. No. Too many eyes and ears around here. Sandy, quiet, watched.

"You used an ugly word."

"Aren't you supposed to be doing your scales or something?"

"I'm going to tell."

"If you really want to torture me," he said, "start playing."

Kyle headed down the sea-foam green carpeted hallway to the bathroom. His tone-deaf sister was using up money for her private piano lessons, when it was he, Kyle, who had the musical talent in the family. He could play a decent guitar, which he'd taught himself back in seventh grade—thank you very much—with his friend Corey's guitar. His father put his foot down on that one when he found out. He could start out playing a band instrument like the stupid-ass clarinet, if he wanted music.

He closed the bathroom door behind him. He didn't have to go, but he was bored. He opened the medicine cabinet, then closed it. Nothing seemed to change in Mrs. Cuttler's bathroom. There was the pale blue toilet paper, the framed cross-stitched message— WHEN THINGS LOOK DOWN, LOOK UP—over the guest towels. And in the cabinet under the sink, women's stuff—Tampax and a dusty Summer's Eve Springtime douche box. Mrs. Cuttler and her husband couldn't have children. Once, Kyle heard Mrs. Cuttler crying in her kitchen, talking to his mother, saying how for years they'd been *trying and trying* to have a baby. Her husband, Buck, was a big, meaty man who drove an eighteen-wheeler up and down the East Coast. In church, he was beet-faced and miserable, his thick neck squeezing a lip of fat over his collar.

Kyle stepped out of the bathroom and caught a glimpse of the master bedroom, a quilted lavender bedspread, lacy cushions, and a teddy bear. It was hard to imagine the Cuttlers *trying and trying* without imagining wee Mrs. Cuttler suffocating underneath her sweating, huffing and puffing, hideous husband. It was sort of gross. And funny, too.

The ivory phone on the bedside table beckoned to him, and, despite the risk, he picked it up and dialed his grandmother's number. It rang. Rang and rang, but no one answered.

"Kyle? Let's go," his mother said from the other room.

Kyle quietly hung up. He felt worse than ever.

His mother and Mrs. Cuttler stood at the end of the hallway, Sandy behind them.

"My goodness, look how he's grown, Dora," Mrs. Cuttler said. "Every week he changes. Oh, he favors your side, doesn't he?"

"He's looking more like Donny's side, really. If you look at the pictures." His mother's voice trailed off.

"No, I can't believe it."

"They grow up so fast," his mother said. "I just can't believe it sometimes. The high chair one minute, high school the next."

Mrs. Cuttler sniffed. "I know it. I'm running out of time. I'll never . . ."

His mother said, "Don't you worry. Keep praying."

There were tears in Mrs. Cuttler's eyes. "Oh, I will, Dora. You're so strong. Just a rock." It was always Kyle's mother who gave out advice, and never asked for help. So strong. Perfect life. Yeah, right.

The man's face trembled in pain. The mouth opened and made little squawks, like a bird. The two eyeballs rolled back and forth under their moist thin lids. Bobby sat in the chair across from the couch and reminded himself not to move. He'd promised Kyle to stay put. Then the man came in and drank a glass of water at the sink and sat on the couch and pretended to watch television. "Mind if I catch the Braves?" he asked. When he'd fallen asleep, Bobby had turned off the television and watched him dream.

The mouth was moving, it was whimpering now, but the eyeballs still paced under their lids like caged animals, back and forth, back and forth. Sometimes the features on people's faces did not connect or work together. Like the way this mouth kept jumping around, as if it were trying to get away from the nose's two dark, tiny caverns. Bobby thought of the time he'd tried to take a chemistry class at Palmetto Tech, and how he'd known that first night of class he shouldn't be there. He knew because the teacher's eyes told him to leave. The mouth told him to sit down, please; the mouth smiled. But the eyes screamed at Bobby to get out. Then, from the poster on the back wall, the periodic table of elements started laughing at him, Helium chirping first like a cricket (He He He), Manganese clanging like a gong, and Tungsten joining in—*Get up! Get out!* It all got so loud, Bobby stood up from his desk and held his hands over his ears. He'd run into the hall, where he'd called his father from the pay phone to pick him up. When he'd gotten home, he'd calmed down by taking a warm bath.

Wake him up. Will stood behind the couch, looking down at the man. *Tell him to leave. You're the man of the house now, right? Tell him to get his sorry ass out of here.* Will was dressed in his army clothes today. His hair was short. He looked like the photograph that had been in the newspaper. The picture that had started talking to Bobby when everyone else in the kitchen was crying.

Bobby leaned in closer and studied the man's eyelashes, looking for a demodicid. Mrs. Wilson, his Biology teacher, had once said there were mites that lived in everyone's eyelashes, demodicids that were too little to see with the naked eye. Even now, he can remember that day in tenth grade when the mites became real to him. He'd felt them crawl over him, and he could see the bacteria teeming in his blood, the electrons swirling in atoms, the mitochondria mewling and squirming, trapped in cytoplasm. Everything swarmed. Nothing was still, or solid. That was the day he'd realized you could put your fist right through people, you could pass through walls if you wanted.

Who is he? Now Will was bare-chested, in mud-splattered combat pants.

Bobby shrugged.

I know him. Will pointed his finger at the sleeping man. *I know who you are.*

"Don't," Bobby said. His own voice rang out in the room. "Don't wake him up." Sometimes it was hard to tell his own voice from the other ones. But Will's voice always broke through, loudest of all. It was hard to ignore Will, though his doctor told him it wasn't really Will; it was Bobby's own mind that made the voices. When Bobby tried to explain, his doctor called it a flight of ideas.

Wake him up.

Bobby shook his head.

Don't you remember? This guy with Dora?

"No."

C'mon. He was there, remember? That night with Dora and Wanda right out back, the night—

"Stop. Don't say it."

You remember, don't you, Bobby?

The secret keepers began their deep thrumming, like bullfrogs at dusk.

"Oh, no. Stop them."

There's nothing I can do.

And now Will was sad. His hair was long again and he was holding a basketball.

"Will, make them stop."

The man's mouth was sad now. It was yelling. The eyes were trapped in their pink covers. Bobby saw the glint of a wire move across the man.

Mom's home, Will said, then stepped back into the shadows and disappeared.

While his life drained away, Jake listened for the thrumming of the chopper, the beating of propellers like faraway drums, and looking up, through the quivering stalks and fronds that seemed to titter foolishly above him, watched the metallic underbelly approach, felt the unmistakable *wap wap wap*, the hot sting of rushed air. He must have lost his helmet. Something on his head now, something bad . . .

Get it off me. Get it off. He clawed at his head.

"Mr. Cary?"

He stomped it. Killed it.

"Mr. Cary, are you all right?"

It was Emma Hanley's pale blue gaze that yanked him back from the clammy, reeking depths of his dream. Only the dream wouldn't let him go. It was cruel as a garrote. Warm blood burbling up busily, soaking his back. The canned peaches from the mess tent he'd devoured that morning were ready to gush in a sour stream

"Oh, good Lord," Jake said. He was sprawled out, more on the floor than on the plaid sofa. "I must have nodded off."

"We were worried about you, Mr. Cary," Emma said. Bobby stood behind her, peering at him over her shoulder.

"Don't be," he said. "I must have had one of my dreams. It's nothing." He stood slowly, fought the pain shooting up his spine, and stepped on something, a wad of tinfoil under his feet.

Mrs. Hanley gazed at him steadily. "My grandson? Bobby said he left?"

"Yes, ma'am. You just missed him. He seemed to be in a hurry. He said you'd be along directly and I—" Jake searched for the right terms. Surely it wasn't good for a man like Bobby to know he had to have a babysitter. But he didn't want Emma to think he was a lazy bum who took naps on the job. "I said I'd come in and keep Bobby company until you got home."

That seemed to satisfy her. In fact, she seemed cheered. "Yes, I understand." She smiled. "I'm glad you and Bobby had a nice visit."

"I'm sorry about nodding off—"

"Don't be silly."

"I don't know what got into me."

"Nightmares?"

No use to deny it, though he was tempted. Surely, Emma Hanley knew quite a bit about battling one's demons. "I have them sometimes. It's war stuff. The same dream over and over." He didn't add that what brought it all on today was being in this place, with Will Hanley's picture up there on the mantel staring at him even now. He'd heard about Will Hanley dying like he did. How he'd volunteered to check out a tunnel. But Jake knew how those things worked—you drew straws or else it was just flat-out your turn—and while Will's lieutenant held his backpack and four other grunts took a smoking break, Will strapped on his flak jacket and had wormed down that spider hole where the VC down there blew him up.

"Could I offer you some iced tea?" Emma Hanley asked.

"You could, but I'd have to decline." From a corner table, Dora peered at him beneath a wedding veil, her stare fixed into the distance, her mouth set, her chin raised. Not a blushing bride, maybe, but a determined one.

Jake bent down to pick up the mess of foil around his feet, and there it was, his old friend, the twinge of pain shooting from his back, down his leg. It was always worse after the dreams, as if his body were remembering.

"Just leave that, Mr. Cary. We save the foil crowns to make new ones."

He nodded, as if that made sense. "Well, I guess I'll be heading out, then."

As he gathered up his trimmer and gas can, he thought about how he could have ended up like Will, easy, down a spider hole. But when his last day in battle came, just a month in country, Jake had managed to hit the dirt right before that AK-47 sniper round hit. It was looking up that had saved him. Instinct. At first, the doctors didn't know if Jake would walk again, much less piss straight. And children? It probably wasn't in the cards, the doctor said, with a tight smile. The army nurse was more forthcoming. *Siring your own? It ain't never going to happen, baby.*

But it could have been worse. Like what happened to Will Hanley. *Where is Wanda?* That's what everyone wondered after the funeral. The hero dead, the sweetheart AWOL. That fueled the rumor mill, all right. Not that any of it had mattered much to Jake by then. Back in Palmetto, he'd been ensconced in the warm haze of painkillers, just days off a morphine drip, and he gloried in the land of sweet indifference, not thinking about Dora, or her last letter. Thanks to Percodan, Jake had been removed, plucked and bloody like an extracted tooth, embedded in soft cotton, tucked away in his own little box.

Now, as Jake turned to load his mower on the trailer, Mrs. Hanley watched from the porch. Bobby approached him, fidgeting, hardly meeting his eyes.

"Listen," Jake told him, "don't worry about it. I'm just going to roll it up the ramp back on the trailer." But Bobby ignored him and with a squat and heave, loaded the mower. "Jesus. You got some strength," Jake muttered, and wondered how much Bobby understood. It's not like he was slow. There was a time when he was a genius. An image floated up to him of Bobby as a kid, Dora's hand on the back of his pale, narrow neck, guiding him through the halls of Palmetto High. Bobby was still a little kid then; for some reason he'd gotten special permission to take a high school class.

"Well, thanks again for your help and all." Jake opened the truck door.

Bobby stepped closer. "Will wanted to wake you up, but I didn't let him." Jake decided to ignore that.

"You have wires. I saw them. When you were on the couch." Mrs. Hanley was still on the front porch. She hadn't heard. Or pretended not to. "That was a dream," Jake said. "I had a bad dream."

Bobby looked at Jake—toward him—somewhere beyond Jake's right shoulder. Jesus, where had all those smarts gone? Talk about life being unfair. *Damn,* Jake thought, shaking his head. *I mean, damn.*

"Hey," Jake said. "That time you talked to our class back in high school, you remember that?"

But if he did, Bobby did not acknowledge the memory.

"You were what, ten or something? Some biology thing you got an award for, and they had you come talk to the high school science classes? Dora brought you. You were a puny little thing with a flat top and a clip-on tie. Remember?"

For the first time all day, Bobby met his eyes. "Sometimes I have flying ideas," he said.

Jake imagined a sudden fluttering, a great winged migration from trees, the land shrinking below.

Emma approached him. "You did an excellent job out here, Mr. Cary. My yard hasn't looked so well tended for years."

"Well, I appreciate the business. And tell your grandson thanks for me, too. He and Bobby helped me unload. Nice kid."

"Oh, I will." She cocked her head, as if she'd just remembered something. And then the secretly pleased look came back on her face, the same expression she'd had when Jake stammered around and said he'd been keeping Bobby company. "Wait just a moment."

When she came back out of the house, she handed him a check.

"Mrs. Hanley," he said, looking at the amount, trying not to look too happy, "this is way too much."

"That's for today and for next time. And . . . for a proposition I have for you."

"Proposition?" He didn't like the sound of that. Not that he couldn't use the money. None of his customers paid him up front, but Mrs. Hanley insisted she always would. And in cash, if he preferred. Hallelujah. "What," he asked, "did you have in mind?"

NINE

"Dora, I've got the cancer." That's exactly how she would tell it. Emma had already imagined just how the scene would play out: She would receive confirmation of her grim diagnosis, and immediately call Dora with the news. Only it didn't happen that way at all.

Instead, when the doctor phoned with the results of her tests, Emma, standing there in the kitchen with a spatula in one hand, the phone in the other, had to sit down for the longest time. The cyst they had expatiated was benign. It was the best-case scenario, Dr. Ghati told her. "It is a pleasure to give patients good news," she said in her singsong lilt. "You must be very happy. Have you any questions?"

Yes, Emma wanted to ask, why didn't she *feel* happy? Of course, she was relieved. Of course. But she had been so sure. She had already glimpsed her deathbed that day she'd felt that lump. Perhaps they had made a mistake. It happened, didn't it? You couldn't pick up the newspaper these days without reading about how some hospital sent the wrong patient down to the morgue where the poor soul woke up hours later on a gurney, toe-tagged and half frozen. Or else a surgeon left a clamp in the innards of some unsuspecting patient, or took out the wrong kidney. Mix-ups happened all the time.

It had already played out in Emma's mind: how she would call Dora with her shocking announcement and Dora would be beside herself and drive right over and there'd be no more arguing about Harold's funeral or why Emma was downright heathen. And Lila Day would be summoned to help Emma get her affairs in order. Emma would have all her photographs labeled, her grandfather's papers preserved, her last will and testament finalized, and her own funeral arrangements—cremation, no service!—planned down to the last detail. And Emma would finally make those decisions about Bobby. She would figure out just how he was going to be taken care of after she was gone, and then . . . Well, she hadn't thought of what happened next, but it had to do with a few months of blissful remission, when her health held up just long enough for Emma to take a little trip somewhere. Not *the* Trip, just *a* Trip. To a place with a balcony and gauzy curtains that fluttered in the breeze and a plate of mangoes and melon, the strumming, drumming mariachi music rising from the street below.

Emma took a plate of pancakes out to Bobby in the living room and set up a TV tray. He was transfixed by a detective show. A blond tanned man in a white blazer, pretty as a girl, was flashing a badge and kicking in a door. "Kyle will be here soon," Emma said, patting her son's thick helpless hand. A blister— angry but healing—puckered on his thumb, and that pleased her. A workingman's hands. There was no shame in that.

The jig is up! the pink-shirted lawman on television yelled, pointing a gun.

Yes, thought Emma, one day she would either wither away or depart this life suddenly, like Harold, but it certainly would be nice to have a little warning.

"There's something I need to tell you," Kyle announced, biting his lip. "About my visits?"

"Oh . . . dear," Emma said.

"Don't worry," he said, seeing her stricken expression. "It's not a big deal or anything. I'm still going to come over as usual."

"You don't like working afternoons with Mr. Cary, is that it? It's too much to look after your uncle on that job. I should have known."

Now it was Kyle who looked wounded. "No, Grandma. No, it's not that—I like working. I mean, we both do, Bobby and me. And getting paid? Definitely don't want to mess with the job thing."

Good, then. Emma's secret arrangement with Jake Cary seemed to be working. The last three afternoons, he'd come by in his truck with his friend, a black man who, in Emma's opinion, appeared too frail to be out in the sun outside all day anyway, and then Kyle and Bobby would join them and work on yards for a few hours. The first day, Bobby and Kyle had returned sunburned and dirty and sore—their pale hands rubbed raw. But by yesterday, the two of them appeared a little more tanned and callused. Her tender men, toughened. Primed a little more, she hoped, for the world out there.

"It's just . . . you should know that, um, maybe . . . there will be a preacher coming around to check on things."

"A preacher?" Emma asked. "Here?"

"He's not the main preacher or anything. He's just the youth minister. . . ."

Kyle's voice trailed off, he began to look forlorn, and if Emma wasn't a little miffed about this surprise guest who would apparently be arriving unannounced and, to her mind, uninvited, she would have hugged Kyle and let him off the hook. "So he's, you know, sort of in charge of . . ."

"The youth?" Emma finished.

"Yeah. And Saving Souls. That program I told you about. So he could pop in anytime . . . one day . . . in the next couple of weeks."

"Anytime? No warning?"

He shook his head.

"What should we do?"

"Well," Kyle said, sheepishly, "when he comes, you could just verify I've been here helping you and Uncle B—"

"Of course."

"And . . ."

Poor dear, even his ears were scarlet with shame.

She let him hem and haw for a minute while she folded clean towels. The sad little pile of socks she saved for Bobby to sort, a chore he'd done for years.

"And?" she asked.

"And, well, can you maybe not let on that I'm, uh, related to you and Uncle B?"

She laughed. She dropped the sheet she was folding and sat down. "You're teasing!"

"No."

"You want your uncle and me to pretend you are a stranger—"

"Not a stranger. Just a kid who helps. A volunteer. Like what I'm doing. Just not, you know, *family*. It's real important, Grandma. I can't get credit without it, and if they find out, then they'll call in my mom and dad. My visits will have to stop," he added, as if that settled everything, and of course, for both of them, it did.

"And this preacher man won't know who I am? That I'm your grandmother?"

"Pastor Pat-Rick won't, I'm sure. He's new. And he's in charge of a lot of kids."

"I'm beginning to see the gravity of this situation, although," she sighed, "I hope you don't miss the irony."

"Irony?"

"This is supposed to be a church program, and you have found yourself in a nest of falsehoods because of it." There, that did it. Her duty to needle him for not being forthright. Of course, she would do her part to keep him, and she was, she realized with an odd sense of self-disapproval, entirely too flattered that he trusted her. "So this preacher will arrive—"

"Youth minister. Pastor Pat-Rick."

"Pastor Patrick."

"Pat. Rick."

"—and check us off his clipboard and be off on his merry way? Is he a pleasant sort? Or one of those Dimmesdale sourpusses?"

"Oh, don't worry, he's real nice. Like I said, I didn't know anything about it until yesterday when he told me at the last minute. Because I have a special deal, I guess. An individualized program or whatever."

"I see, so this is an audit. Let's hope it's the briefest sort and your Pastor Patrick is a sloppy bookkeeper."

He nodded, chewing his lip.

"Well, let's get started on the rest of those attic boxes, shall we?" she asked. "I found some pictures last night and, oh, just wait until you—"

There was still something bothering Kyle, a niggling around the eyes.

"I'll be on my best behavior with that preacher," Emma said, "if that's what you're worried about. And I suppose if you and Bobby are out with Mr. Cary, I'll just . . . stall or something. What's wrong?"

He swallowed. "If he—if he asks about church or anything? Tell him that you're thinking about starting up again. That you're thinking about Crossroads."

Dear Lord, Emma thought, realizing it was her own kind of prayer, released like a helium balloon.

"It's part of the program, Grandma. Talking about, you know, church stuff with you."

"Now you're asking for real acting."

"It's . . . real important. Talking about the Crossroads part, I mean."

"Yes," she said, sighing. "I'm beginning to see that."

The photograph showed his uncle Will surrounded by a bunch of rowdy-looking people mugging for the camera. Will's hair was buzzed, army-ready, and he was trying his best to smile for the camera, but couldn't quite pull it off. There was a girl wedged under Will's arm, a freckly girl in jeans and a yellow halter top, burrowing her face into Will's chest. Her hair was too orange. Everyone had major red-eye. All the colors in the picture were off—brash and hard—apparently, color film was just getting started back then.

"It was taken at a big party they threw for him. Out in the backyard. In the barn," Kyle's grandmother said. "Before . . ."

Standing beside his uncle Will, in a red bikini, with hair hanging to her waist, hands on her hips, yelling something at whoever was taking the picture—yelling and laughing at the same time— was Kyle's mother. His mother! Kyle's grandmother said it was the last picture she had of Will. *Before . . .* and her voice drifted off again with that word. And then his grandmother ran her cool, dry hand over Kyle's temple and forehead and said, *You look like him there, right there.*

Sometimes, when Kyle arrived at his grandmother's house, he found her sitting on the sofa with his uncle Bobby in the dim quiet of the living room, the two of them looking straight ahead, like strangers waiting for a train. Their faces lit up when they saw him. It occurred to Kyle that they waited for him like that every day, a thought so dismal, he chased it from his mind.

"Are you *sure* that's her?" Kyle asked, studying the photograph.

"It's your mother, all right. Running the party as usual."

His mother in that skimpy bikini looked—face it—a little wasted and stoned. Maybe that explained all the red eyes.

"It was winter, but they decorated the barn back there like it was the tropics. I don't remember why. I guess it's what your uncle Will wanted for his bon voyage." His grandmother fixed her pearly blue gaze on Kyle. "You go to parties, don't you?"

"Parties? Not really."

"No?" His grandmother put the picture down. She tugged at her collar, lost in thought, her fidgety hand resting finally, at her throat. "That must be lonely," she said.

"There's these things at the cemetery sometimes. I guess you could call them parties."

"Oh, you go to those? Didn't I read something about that in the paper?"

"Yeah, one time it got out of hand. But mostly it's just a bunch of high school kids partying. This guy Tee Garrett heads it up."

"Garrett?" his grandmother asked. Too late, Kyle realized he should've kept the name to himself. How stupid was that? The Garrett family's reputation was well established: You could usually find them behind bars or sitting at them. Kyle waited for the reprimand, but his grandmother surprised him with a dreamy look. "You know, I bet that cemetery is perfect for summer parties," she said. "All that open space, with the sweet smell of lily bouquets in the air, and sad cement angels in the moonlight. It sounds . . . romantic."

It wasn't exactly romantic. There were cans of warm beer hidden among the headstones like Easter eggs. Tee saw to that. And a bottle of Jack at the foot of the general's statue. Sometimes, if Kyle was lucky, there were a few minutes alone with Julie.

"So that's what young people are doing for entertainment these days?" his grandmother asked. "Sneaking out at night to the cemetery?"

He shrugged. "There's concerts. I'm saving up for one."

"Concerts?"

"Bands. Rock bands. They play at the auditorium."

Three more afternoons of work with Jake, and Kyle could afford to buy two tickets to Van Halen. Julie had already said yes. They could catch a ride with Tee. He didn't know exactly how he was going to pull it off, what excuse he could use to cover himself at home the night of the concert, but he'd figure it out. Next month. His first official concert. With Julie. Oh yeah, he was going.

"I saved this picture for last," his grandmother said, handing him a framed photograph. She might as well have handed him a cattle prod.

"No way," he said.

His grandmother nodded; her smile twitched with mischief.

"No *way*. That's not—"

"That's Mr. Cary. Isn't that the funniest thing? I forgot all about . . . this picture."

Jake! Wearing a hideous lime green tuxedo, gripping the waist of his mother. "You mean—they went to the *prom* together?"

"Yes. It's coming back to me now. That prom business. It took forever to get the right outfit." Emma shook her head.

Kyle ran a hand through his hair nervously. "For some reason, this sort of freaks me out."

"Don't they look young there? Yes, so very young."

"Different. She looks . . . different."

"Mmm. Yes."

Jake Cary didn't look all that different, though, Kyle thought. In the photograph, his hair fell to his shoulders in a straight black sheet, the way he still wore it. Somebody should tell him how uncool it was to keep the same haircut from high school all these years later.

"Maybe we ought to show this picture to Mr. Cary when he gets here," she said. "I'm sure he'll have some stories." But Kyle didn't think that was a good idea at all. It was best to keep all these different worlds apart—his mother, Kyle's secret visits here, Julie, his job with Jake—each one spinning on its separate axis. He was having enough trouble keeping all the balls in the air. He didn't need any more complications. Just yesterday, he'd discovered the yard he and Uncle B were edging and mulching belonged to Miss Dewberry, his English teacher. That was a shocker. Especially because, until yesterday, Kyle had been under the impression Miss Dewberry was not the type you could joke around with. Despite her high voice, her delicate frame, Miss Dewberry had managed to intimidate plenty of students in Freshman English, Kyle included. She was, she told them, a self-appointed guardian of the language. She did not suffer fools. "You're quite welcome to my garden of words," she'd announced to her students, "but step delicately, people. I do not like to see poetry trampled underfoot." Miss Dewberry's left arm was shrunken, her hand a knotty pink fist. On the first day of class, by way of introduction, she'd written *thalidomide* on the blackboard.

"My mother ingested this substance when I was a fetus inside her," she'd told them, "and my atrophied limb is the result. That is all I am going to say about it."

How weird then to see Miss Dewberry yesterday in her own yard, in front of her ordinary brick ranch, pale as an egg, in shorts and a T-shirt, greeting Kyle pleasantly when he'd finally got the nerve to stammer out a greeting. Before they left, Jake had presented Miss Dewberry with a flower from the truck bed, broken off from one of the shrubs. "It's a gardenia. Reminded me of you. Real white. Delicate-like." Kyle wondered if Miss Dewberry knew that Jake Cary was flirting with her just for her business. She couldn't be that stupid. But then Miss Dewberry had laughed with Jake and spouted poetry—*The desire of the moth for a star . . . that's Shelley*—and offered to go inside and bring out some beers for Jake and his men. Kyle did his best to look like he wasn't listening. It just didn't seem natural to see his English teacher, *the guardian of the language*, hooting it up with the yardman and offering him a brew.

"Well. Look at the time, would you? Mr. Cary will be here any minute to pick you both up for work. I'll pack some sandwiches for you to take." His grandmother took the prom picture and tucked it back into the box with the other photographs, much to Kyle's relief. She dashed to her room and came out wearing pearls and lipstick.

"How many do you suppose there will be with Mr. Cary today?" she asked. She tilted her head, putting on an earring.

"I'm not sure." He shrugged. "I think it's whoever shows up to work." There was a man named Gordon, which was confusing at first, since the curled name patches on his shirts said TED or MITCH. Yesterday, there'd been a guy who told Kyle he danced at a bar up near Charlotte on weekends, whatever that meant. And Gordon's dog, Sweet, who always got a sandwich slipped to him. "Three, maybe?"

"I better make extras just in case," she said. His grandmother tied on an apron and fluttered around the kitchen, humming.

She'd started making lunch for everyone a week ago. The first day, there was just a plate of crustless pimento cheese sandwiches, and today there was going to be a whole basket of stuff. And even after Jake told her she was going to spoil them all if she didn't stop, his grandmother acted pleased and kept right on, bringing out a tray to the porch and pitchers of tea, or packing a basket for them to stick in the cooler. Now, as she scraped out a jar of mayonnaise, two bright spots of pink on her cheeks, Kyle thought of Miss Dewberry in her yard yesterday, and how she'd liked it plenty when Jake teased her, too.

"Kyle? Are you listening?" his grandmother said now.

"Um . . . what was that?"

"I said, would you mind putting that box away?"

But before he put the box back in the attic, Kyle found himself sneaking a handful of the pictures. His grandmother said he was welcome to anything, so he didn't know why he felt so sneaky, but he did. He just wanted to study a few of them in private; that was all. He shoved them in the back pocket of his Levi's, along with a postcard that showed a Holiday Inn on the front, postmarked June 6, 1970, and on the back just a scrawled sentence: *Oh, Dora, I'm dead inside.* He'd put them back in the box in a few days. He might even show them to Jake. Maybe. Just see what he had to say.

"Shall I pick you up?" Lila chirped by way of greeting when Emma answered the phone. Emma had her feeble excuse ready for skipping the day's Lunch and Learn—a headache—but for some reason Lila's phone call caught her off guard.

"Lila? Is that you?"

"My goodness, Emma. *Of course* it's me. Were you napping?"

"No. I was just . . . relaxing."

Her friend must have sensed Emma's reluctance, for she suddenly took another tack. "It *has* worked out with the yardman, hasn't it?"

"Why, yes. It certainly has. Very well."

There was silence on the other end.

"So it *was* you who sent Mr. Cary," Emma said.

"Oh, I just put a bug in his ear about . . . your needing a yard-man, that's all." Lila sniffed. "And I'm glad I did."

Emma was glad, too. She felt a twinge of guilt. "Thank you, Lila. That was . . . good of you."

Her friend cleared her throat. "I imagine having Bobby work afternoons has given you more free time lately?"

"A few hours here and there."

She did not tell Lila about the lunches she'd been providing Mr. Cary and his crew. Or about the basketball she'd bought over the weekend to give Bobby and Kyle something to do while she fixed all those lunches. Between doctor appointments and meal preparation, Emma didn't have much time for anything else, and that actually suited her just fine for now. Her friend, however, would surely chastise Emma for "not getting out more," and the conversation topic would lead right back to the Lunch and Learn.

"Did I tell you I saw your boy working the other day?"

Emma felt her face grow warm with pride. "Did you?"

"Yes, he was out with your grandboy watering someone's yard. The whole group was there. They are a rather strange lot, aren't they? All of them together, I mean. What do they call them-selves? The Blooming Idiots? But I tell you, Jake Cary seems to be doing just fine. I heard he's going to do Monaghan Nursing now, and one of the banks, too."

"Really?" Emma said. "I had no idea. He just said . . . they were busy. They must be doing good work."

"In this awful, oppressive summer heat, too," Lila said. "That's saying something. Nothing seems to thrive in my yard. I lost every single Boston fern on my porch. My petunias are pitiful. Shall I drive?" she asked again, without missing a beat.

"Yes," Emma found herself saying. "That would fine."

"I'll be right over."

"What did you say today's topic was?" Emma asked, wonder-ing if it would be terribly rude to bring a book and sit in the back.

"Didn't I tell you? It's 'The World of Orchids.' Some plants-man from over near Clemson that the Master Gardeners recommended is going to talk and let us in on the secret."

"Oh," Emma said, relieved. "At least that sounds interesting."

"Well, I hope it proves instructive. How many times have you bought one of those things and it never blooms again? Orchids are not cheap, either. I brought mine home from the store, and the blossoms fell right off. On purpose! I tell you, they are the most stubborn, sneaky houseplants. I've been watering a clump of leaves for years, waiting, and not a sign of a flower. I'm ready to pitch the thing out."

At the Senior Center, Emma sat at the head table with Lila, who was in charge of introducing the speaker. Lila had taken pains to prepare for her task by noting her remarks on a single index card, which she had insisted on reading aloud to Emma while driving them to the Lunch and Learn. Lila did not speed, far from it, but during her verbal rehearsal—with Emma growing increasingly queasy with unease beside her—Lila's ancient Lincoln twice hit the curb and once sailed through a red light with the authority, and speed, of a parade float. The experience had left Emma with her heart in her throat, but at least, she told herself now, the adrenaline would keep her awake.

"What is all this?" Lila accosted the speaker as soon as he arrived. He was unpacking what appeared to be a slide projector, which Lila told him in no uncertain terms they were not equipped for. He was an older man—Emma seemed to remember Lila reciting something in the car about his being a retired professor of botany. Or was it biology? That was right before Lila had driven off the shoulder of the road the first time, so Emma hadn't absorbed the facts. He was shiny-bald and bearded, and wore a tie and a dark blue suit a trifle too big, but in which he nevertheless appeared to chafe. He had a gimpy shuffle, but there was a remnant of nimbleness in the way he unrolled the orange extension cord and searched for an outlet, and a glimpse of merriness when he nodded but ignored Lila's fretting and fluttering and calmly continued to set up his slide carousel despite her protests. Emma hoped the man wouldn't be disappointed by the sparsely attended luncheon. But she needn't have worried, for the speaker—Dr. Burnside was his name—seemed absorbed by the task at hand. He clicked on the first slide, adjusted it on the flyspecked white screen, and was soon clearly caught up in relating one rapturous tale after another. He began by showing a lady slipper, an indigenous orchid that grew wild in the area, and then they were off to Madagascar.

Midway through the presentation—just as they got to the tongue orchids of Australia—Lila nudged Emma and hissed in her ear, "This won't do. This has nothing to do with caring for your orchids." Emma was too caught up in the speaker's description of the brazen ruses of orchids to lure pollinators to hiss anything back, and silently shushed her friend.

And then, all too soon, there was a smattering of applause as the lights went up, and a handful of Emma's lifelong neighbors and acquaintance blinked like pale creatures from under a log. Dr. Burnside stood behind the podium and announced he would take questions. Emma was thankful Frank Looper—one of the few men in attendance—raised his hand to ask whether the speaker had a favorite orchid.

"I couldn't begin to choose," Dr. Burnside said. "They are all so fierce and clever. You've never seen such commitment to living . . . to multiplying. It never ceases to amaze me the shows they put on. All that finery to entice pollinators. Flowers are scented, glowing, *magnificent* reproductive organs."

Lila wore a strangled look. She stood at once and strode over to the podium, where she thanked the speaker and announced there was simply no more time for questions. She walked back to the table, Dr. Burnside at her heels. Emma looked down at her untouched lunch—a wet ball of tuna salad on a limp lettuce leaf, a canned pear topped by a greasy gobbet of mayonnaise and a whisker of shaved cheese. Shoddy sustenance for such an esteemed guest, but the speaker again put her mind at ease by appearing not to notice, and indeed, seemed to consume the meager lunch with gusto.

Lila—sufficiently recovered from the shock of hearing the terms *magnificent reproductive organs* emerge from the mouth of a Lunch and Learn speaker—reluctantly resumed her hostess duties. "Dr. Burnside—I understand you're just passing through our area?" she asked. "What brings you here?"

Dr. Burnside explained he was staying temporarily with his niece and her family near Clemson. His visit to the area was a happy coincidence, he said, brought on by the need for hip-replacement surgery, from which he was recovering. The health issue was seized upon at once—with Frank, Lila, and several others around the table eagerly chattering all at once about orthopedists, co-pays, and recovery time.

"I highly recommend staying busy," Dr. Burnside said quietly. "It's why I signed up with the gardening speakers' bureau."

Emma met his eyes. No one else appeared to be listening. She smiled politely. "We're glad you did. Your talk was wonderful. I felt . . . *transported.*"

And now there were murmurs of agreement around the table. Except for Lila, who said the slides were all well and good, but she still had no idea what to do with her own orchid at home, which hadn't bloomed for years.

"Maybe your orchid needs pollinating," Frank said, mischief burning through his rheumy eyes. Lila did not acknowledge the remark. Indeed, after five decades of ignoring Frank Looper, Lila had long ago learned how to remain unflappable in the face of her old friend's coarse teasing. It was newcomers who gave Lila fits.

"I imagine you're eager to move on," Lila told Dr. Burnside. "And go far from here."

"Actually, I may have to curtail my traveling. Not by choice—exactly." He shrugged, a gesture that managed to appear both friendly and sad. "At my age, maybe it's time I finally settled down. It's something I never learned to do." He looked up at Emma and the others. "Maybe you can let me in on the secret."

"Oh, settling down is no secret," Emma said. "It's a mystery. And the mystery is *why*." The speaker laughed—a loud laugh for a diminutive man, a clap of thunder—then dabbed politely at his mouth with the thin paper napkin, as if squelching his own mirth.

Lila cleared her throat. "Dr. Burnside, *my orchid*. I'm not clear about fertilizer. It's all so confusing. What should I feed it?"

"They eat the sun," he said, sitting back in his chair. He crossed his arms and looked into the distance. "They all do."

"They . . . eat what?" Lila said.

"Autotrophs. Plants. They make their own food," he said. "That's always struck me as remarkable. Oxygen is their by-product. And we suck it up. We're parasites."

"Parasites!" Lila asked.

"Why," Emma whispered, "I never thought of it that way."

"That's because we're not parasites," Lila said.

"The perfume, the nectar, the colors, the mimicry, the trickery. I've seen lips on orchids that resemble a wasp's mate." Dr. Burnside's eye danced. "Petals that are landing pads for insects. Exploding seedpods. I've seen pleated downy petals fragrant as a woman's—"

There was the scraping sound of a chair as Lila stood abruptly and fled. The metal chair fell over behind her, cracking like a shot.

Emma managed to mumble an apology for Lila, and left to seek out her friend. But down the hall, when Emma rounded the corner, Lila, spry as ever, grabbed Emma's wrist, her eyes wide with outrage. "Emma? Emma, you must do me this favor. In my stead, would you please escort that *Rumpelstilskin* out to the parking lot? I've had quite enough for one day."

To hear Gordon tell it, there were ghosts in the garden.

"Spirits," he told Jake. It was barely dawn, no promise of a breeze, already too hot for coffee. Gordon had been waiting for

Jake as usual in front of Amaranth, and they stood now, leaning against the truck, finishing off the egg biscuits Jake brought along. Gordon squinted into the distance. "Spirits, more like. That's what I'm talking about."

"There's spirits, all right," Jake said, laughing. Gordon's front shirt pocket bulged with its usual contents: one flat amber-filled glass bottle, lying in wait.

"Naw, man. You know what I'm saying."

"Usually people want to leave haunted places," Jake said. "Not spend the night in them." Sometimes when Jake picked up Gordon in front of Amaranth, he repeated his offer—didn't Gordon want to stay with him? At least for a while? But Gordon would have none of it. Even if he did occasionally go to Jake's for showers and to watch TV, he never stayed overnight. "There's things up in there I got to tend to," he'd say, tilting his head toward the wildly unkempt grounds beyond the Amaranth place. And Jake knew enough about Gordon—how he could set his mind on something—not to push it.

That was the mistake JJ made, Gordon's little brother over at the bank. JJ always pressed issues with Gordon, nagged him to pieces, always had, but now the two brothers were having one of their spats, not talking, and Jake was smack in the middle of it. ("You? In *business*? Got my brother working for you?" JJ had asked yesterday at Palmetto Bank, laughing skeptically behind his wide paper-stacked desk. "Like I said, he's working with me near about every day," Jake said, emphasizing the *with*. JJ nodded, eyes narrowed, smile gone cynical, before finally giving Jake his answer. "We're going to try you out here landscaping at the bank, Jake, and I'll get other businesses coming your way, too, but—" There was always a *but* where JJ was concerned. "—you got to make sure my brother stops flopping and gets sober as a judge." And Jake said, "Let's get something straight"—chuckling to warm the statement—"I'm not your brother's keeper." JJ, raising his chin, cinching his tie, standing up—meeting over—said, "Oh, really? I thought that was the deal.")

"What's taking the others so long?" Jake asked Gordon now. He looked at his watch. Starting time was beginning to be a problem.

"No telling." Gordon shrugged.

Somehow Jake had assembled himself a crew. Terrell, a man with a stiff braid and eyes gold as corn oil, who said he worked nights in "entertainment," and who practiced his singing as he mowed or trimmed hedges. He was flopping in Amaranth, the newest resident, but Jake didn't pry. In fact, with Terrell, it was best to change the subject when he got around to explaining his life story—once he started, you couldn't shut him up. When the man wasn't singing, he was talking. And his songs were better. Sometimes two Mexicans showed up for a day's pay, but neither could speak a lick of English. Afternoons, there was Bobby Hanley and the boy. That part of the crew was even subsidized by Mrs. Hanley, but Jake wouldn't take her money after today. He had agreed to do the favor at first because he thought for sure those two would wilt in the heat and not last the day, but they surprised him. In fact, by the time Jake and the rest of the crew swung by Mrs. Hanley's to pick them up at noon, Bobby Hanley and the boy were a fresh second shift.

Now, with Palmetto Bank a new client, with more work coming in, and everything everywhere needing to be planted, trimmed, watered and mulched all at once, Jake finally found himself with a good problem: he needed all the help he could get.

"You sure you didn't see Terrell or anyone around?" Jake asked Gordon now. "Besides your ghost, I mean."

"Spirit," Gordon said, "Pan Sa came to me as a spirit."

"Pan who?"

"A Yard. He came to me last night." Gordon pointed with a thumb, meaning back *there*, in those woods beyond the house.

"A Yard?"

"Man, you remember the Yards, don't you? You ever saw them in Nam? Spears and arrows like Indians? Best trackers around."

"I heard something about it."

"This one Yard, Pan Sa? He saved my *ass*."

Jake crumpled up the empty breakfast bag. The dog had gotten the last biscuit as usual. Jake had even started ordering an extra. If he didn't, Gordon tore his own biscuit in half and fed it to the dog. "That was a long time ago."

"So? That don't mean I'm gonna forget."

"Maybe you should try," Jake said. "Drives you crazy if you think about that stuff all the time."

"Naw, what wears you out is trying to forget," Gordon said. "You ain't figured that out yet?" He glanced sideways at Jake with the same deep-set onyx eyes he shared with JJ, eyes that could look calculating on one brother, brooding on the other.

"When Pan Sa came to me last night, I'm telling you, it brought all the pictures back. I got myself on water detail that day he saved me—switched at the last minute with this dude, O'Shaunnesy. I started filling canteens but then I looked up and saw Pan Sa standing there. He used to come by the mess tent sometimes, and I'd give him a beer, or a can of peaches. But that day he looked different. Serious. See, what it was, he was warning me. I dropped flat, right there in the paddy, don't even know why. Just did. Next thing I know, a sniper hits, and O'Shaunnesy is calling for his mama. Bled to death waiting for the medic." Gordon shook his head. "Never saw Pan Sa again. Until last night."

"You had a dream is all."

"No dream." Gordon laughed. "I talked to him, man."

Lord help, Jake thought. Between Gordon's ghosts and Bobby Hanley's voices and Terrell's singing, this crew was going to get itself a reputation. Jake's Blooming Idiots. "So, did you two catch up, or what?"

"I told him I was glad he came around 'cause I never did thank him for what he did. And then he stared at me—" Gordon stopped, looked back at the woods. "Looked at me like . . ."

"Like what?" Jake asked.

"Like he was trying to . . . man, I don't know." Gordon took out a blue bandanna from his back pocket, mopped his forehead, lost in thought. "You know what? Hold on. Hold on!" He whistled, and the dog came over. "I forgot something. Be right back."

"Forgot? Forgot what? Listen, we're running late," Jake said.

"I hear you," Gordon said, not looking back. He started down past the house, behind him, the dog's white-tipped tail waving above the tall grass like a flag.

Oh, hell. So much for trying to get an early start. In a few hours, they'd feel the full brunt of this pitiless sun, and here Jake was, everything ready, jobs set up all day, a schedule to keep, and no help in sight.

Jake walked over to the porch, what was left of it. "Terrell?" he yelled into the doorless, dark place. "You in there?" Nothing. He knew better than to go searching. It wouldn't do to let his truck out of his sight—not with every piece of equipment he owned loaded in the back. Not on this street. He tromped through the ivy, over to the edge of the woods. "Hey? Gordon? Man, we gotta get a move on." The greedy green thicket that had gulped up Gordon and the dog swallowed Jake's words, too.

What in the world could be so important to Gordon? What besides his bottle and that dog? Maybe the heat really was getting to him—the sun, the drinking, the sleeping outdoors. Bringing it all back. Those demons from in country. There was that day last week when Gordon swore he had jungle rot again and then that wild story of seeing a Yard last night. You couldn't let the memories take over. Gordon knew that, surely he did.

"Hey! Anyone?" Jake called. *Anyone . . . one . . . one . . ."* His voice echoed against the rotting planks of Amaranth, mocking him. "I'm leaving," he said quietly. He went to sit in his truck. He scanned the radio, looking for weather. Between bursts of white noise, the voices all said the same thing: brutal heat wave. The catchwords of the season. Like a song lyric running over and over in your head. And yes, things were dying—petunias, impatiens, crape myrtles, some of the succulents—shriveling, shrinking in the *brutal heat wave.* Jake had seen some landscapers around town replanting entire beds after everything they'd put out died. But Jake had the best waterman around. Gordon could hook up soaker hoses like IVs. Figure out just where the water needed to go to keep loam damp but not soggy. It was a talent, like playing the harmonica, and Gordon had the gift.

Jake started up the truck. He was going to have to be a hard-ass about it and just leave. Teach them all a lesson. Gordon, Terrell, the Mexicans. My way or the highway. This was a business. There was a schedule. He gunned the engine, once, twice. Then he turned off the ignition and listened to the engine's soft ticking. Who was he kidding? Jake was no hard-ass. It was, he thought, likely to be his ruin.

Sweet growled now, but Gordon shushed him. "Don't raise a ruckus." He could hear Jake calling him, telling him not to dawdle. Never mind—once he saw what Gordon was going to bring him, Jake would stop looking so worried all the time. Because standing out there with Jake, swigging bitter coffee, talking about Pan Sa, the strangest thing had happened. A pinpoint of light flickered in Gordon's fogged morning thoughts: the thing that Pan Sa had been trying to tell him last night. And now, as he and Sweet plunged through the briars and dense shrubs, Gordon knew what it was.

He came to the clearing where Pan Sa had appeared to him last night, wearing his usual loincloth and sports jacket, the crossbow hanging from his shoulder like a broken wing. That goiter on his neck, too, big as a plum. "You ain't changed a bit," Gordon had told him. In Pan Sa's country, Gordon had been living under a poncho in the elephant grass, and it was not so different from where he camped now—under a tent and a refrigerator box, among the clumps of long, soft leaves, tawny as baby hair. "I guess I ain't so different either," Gordon had said, and Pan Sa's face—flat, dark, deep as a lake—moved with the faintest of smiles. "You like my place?" Gordon asked him, looking around. "You like it here?" In Pan Sa's land, death and beauty had gotten all

mixed together. In country, you'd come across a slipper flower—
fragrant, radiant, angel-innocent—right next to a human jaw-
bone sparkling with flies. The greedy sauna heat, wet and cloying
as a whore, stole your sweat and your will to go on.

"Drink?" Gordon had offered Pan Sa a swig of his wine bottle
then, and they'd finished it off, neither of them saying anything.
Pan Sa couldn't understand English anyway, but that never bothered Gordon. There was something to be said for holding both
sides of a conversation.

And then, before he'd disappeared, Pan Sa stood, watchful as
always, his back against a small gnarled tree, his face lit up, as if
he had something he wanted to say. Kneeling at that spot now, at
the very place where Pan Sa's bare feet had been planted, Gordon
gently cleared away a wet blanket of leaves. His fingers met a tan-
gle of shoots, and a single delicate damp knob the size of his fist,
and then another, and another. He sat back on his heels and took
it in. A bed of ruby-ridged buds had pushed through the clotted
rich soil, swelling, opening, baby-bird greedy, a whole mess of
them. Flowering damp blooms. What they were, he had no idea.
But he'd let them loose.

That's what Pan Sa was trying to tell him. Let them loose.

TEN

The Blooming Idiots made short work of Emma's crustless egg salad sandwiches. They ate leaning against the truck or squatting in the grass. They tossed back lemonade in Dixie cups like shots of whiskey. They did not bother to use the napkins she'd set out on the picnic table, or the paper plates. The tablecloth and plastic forks remained untouched, alongside the sprigs of mint and sliced lemons. Kyle wondered why his grandmother bothered to set a table at all. It was for show, these props. The same, every day. As if his grandmother really believed they were having an elegant picnic.

"I've got cookies to bring out," his grandmother told Jake. "I'll just be a minute."

"Oh, now, Mrs. Hanley, that's really not—"

"Don't be silly, Mr. Cary. You have to keep up your strength, all of you. Not another word about it."

Jake sighed and gave Kyle a sidelong glance. "You got some hardheaded women in your family," he said.

Women. The image of his mother's prom picture floated up to Kyle—blurry at first, then sharpening—like a print in fixative. Jake gripping her thin bare shoulders, as if he were used to touching her. The way Kyle liked to hold Julie sometimes, on the good nights at the cemetery parties. He felt the flat, thin stash of photographs in his pocket now, hidden as memories.

"All right," Jake said. "Break's about over. Let's wrap it up." He leaned back against the truck, winced, stood again.

"Uncle B? You want water?" Kyle asked.

But his uncle was busy giving out cigarettes to Gordon and the others, much to their delight. Uncle B watched under hooded eyes—with a Greek statue's faint hint of stony pleasure—as the cigarettes he offered were plucked from the pack. The crew today included Gordon, Terrell, Pedro, and Manuel, along with a strange-looking woman who called herself Lay Down Sally. She started out wide—a puff of yellow hair like a troll doll's, big pillowy bosom, thick waist—then tapered like a carrot, her scrawny legs emerging from a pair of men's khaki shorts, cinched with a rope. They all leaned against the truck now, lighters clicking, smoke trailing up, except for Jake, who stood under the shade tree, and who kept glancing at his watch and at his grandmother's front door. The lunches put them behind schedule, but Jake never said anything.

"What's next, boss?" Gordon asked Jake. He had a deep, rumbling voice he seemed too thin for.

"Like you don't know," Jake said.

Gordon laughed—a cackle that dissolved into coughing.

"Might as well get started," Jake said. Gordon nodded and headed for the back of truck.

Jake stomped his right heel, and winced. He took off his shirt, wiped his face with it, and threw it on the floorboard of the truck cab. An ugly scar, thick as a snake, curved across his back, down one side.

"Does that hurt?" Kyle asked when Jake turned around.

"Does what hurt?" Jake took out a clean T-shirt from under the driver's seat, pulled it on.

"On your back. It looks really . . . bad." Like he'd been busted into pieces, thought Kyle. Like they'd stuck him back together.

"Nah. Happened a long time ago." He pulled up his shirt, exposing the scar, ridged like a seam, then grabbed a handful of skin.

"See? It's numb now." When Kyle cringed, Jake laughed. "You look like you've seen a ghost." Kyle turned away. "Look, I'm not laughing at you," Jake said after a minute.

"I know," Kyle said with a shrug.

"It's just—the way you looked all of a sudden, so serious." Jake smiled again, and then his eyes seemed to darken and he wasn't smiling at all.

Kyle bent down, buried his face in the thick damp fur of the dog, Sweet. The pictures in his pocket shifted, he could feel them protruding. With one hand, he shoved them back in place. He might show them to Jake later, away from his grandmother's house. Or maybe . . . next week. After he'd had time to think about it. Over at the truck, Terrell was trying to talk Spanish to Manuel and Pedro. *Dónde está la playa?* he kept asking, each time louder. They shrugged.

Gordon, who was unloading something from the truck, said, "What you trying to tell them, Terrell?"

"I'm not telling them nothing, man. I'm asking them something."

"Where is the beach," Kyle said, standing.

"What now?" Terrell asked, arching an eyebrow that was, Kyle noticed, thin and sort of . . . penciled.

"*Dónde está la playa.* That means 'where's the beach,'" Kyle said, then added, "I think." He didn't want to sound like a know-it-all and make Terrell angry, because Terrell seemed sort of hyper. Plus he wore earrings.

Gordon chuckled. "I guess they don't know how to tell you it's two hundred miles east."

"I thought it meant something different," Terrell said. "I thought it was like, where you hang out?"

"Aww, cut it out," Jake said. "It's time, anyway," he said, stretching, like he did a lot, one hand at the back of his neck. "Let's get the show on the road."

"Lord, you just reminded me. My show!" Terrell said. "I need a ride to the dry cleaners today. For my outfit."

"What you think this is? An errand service?" Jake said.

"It's on the way," Terrell said.

"Yeah, okay," Jake said. "Jesus." He looked into the distance, at a wisp of clouds. "It might just rain tonight," he said.

"Naw." Gordon said, squinting up. He cradled a cardboard box. "Gonna be Sunday at least."

"We ready?" Jake asked. Gordon nodded. "All right," Jake said, "Everyone, listen up. We gotta little job here before we go."

The screen door slammed. "Cookies," Kyle's grandmother announced in her singsong hostess voice. She walked toward them, balancing a platter. "Peanut butter. I hope that's okay. I hope no one has peanut allergies."

"Mrs. Hanley, you're spoiling the Blooming Idiots rotten," Jake said, just as he did every day. "But today, we're gonna spruce up your yard a little and add a little something special, and be on our way."

"Why, there's no need for that." She put the plate down on the picnic table. "My yard looks perfectly fine from the last time. I'm sure you all have customers to see to this afternoon."

"You *are* a customer, Mrs. Hanley," Jake said. Kyle's grandmother drew herself taller. She nodded to Jake, oddly formal, and looked as if she might say something, her hand nervously fingering her collar. She gazed over at Bobby, who was struggling to put on a pair of work gloves.

"And we got a lot of jobs coming in," Jake continued, his voice so low that Kyle had to step closer to listen, "so if Bobby and Kyle want the work, I'd sure be glad to have them for a few weeks, maybe the summer. They're a good team. I can pay cash, fifty cents over minimum wage."

"Mr. Cary, that sounds just wonderful," she said, her voice cracking, or had Kyle imagined it? "You don't know . . . how wonderful."

Jake cleared his throat, addressed Kyle. "You and Bobby think you can spread some fresh pine straw around your grandmother's flower bed over there?" he asked.

Kyle nodded. He had a job! For the summer! Not even sixteen, and he had some cash and a job his friends would give their left nuts for. He'd just have to work out the timing, is all. Stretch out the Saving Souls alibi. But he'd do it, somehow.

His uncle put on the gloves and held them up, two big paws. Jake turned to Terrell and the others, who hovered over the plate of cookies. "All right, everyone grab a shovel. Follow Gordon to Mrs. Hanley's flower bed."

"Come look at the Secret Keepers outside," Bobby said.

Emma sat up in bed. "My goodness," she said. "You scared me to death." She looked over at the alarm clock and thought of Harold's face as well, the way he cocked his head as he'd set it nightly. The clock's hands glowed in the darkness, with the wrong time now, of course, since the thing hadn't been wound for . . . weeks. "It's still dark outside. Go back to bed."

"They have arrived."

"What . . . do you mean?"

"The Secret Keepers have been born."

"Bobby," Emma said, sighing. "Can't this wait?"

"They won't wait."

"They?"

"Flower power."

This was her fault. Yes, she'd cut back on Bobby's pills, just a little. He'd been doing so well, and he'd had more energy and been more alert in the afternoons working with Kyle, and then yesterday, when Jake Cary offered to hire them on, she'd been so encouraged. Well, but perhaps she'd been wrong to try to taper off, for now Bobby was clearly out of sorts, talking about his conversations with flowers. And she'd had such hopes . . . that he might just . . . flourish . . . that her son might finally have the tiniest, most meager kind of life—with a schedule and a pay stub. Now she'd have to take Bobby to see Dr. Babbitt first thing Monday morning, before Kyle arrived.

"Don't pace, honey," she told Bobby now as he walked to her

bureau and back. His calves and bare feet were stippled with grass clippings. "You've been outside alone?"

"I wasn't alone."

A chill ran through her. He stood by the window and cast a longing glance outside. "If I go with you and have a look," she said, "then you must promise to go to bed and get some sleep."

Emma donned her robe and slippers, and followed Bobby outside, out into the gilded chamber of dawn. She'd forgotten just how *busy* daybreak was. The rising sun winked on window-panes, the songbirds began their ruthless calls to rise. Emma had never been an early riser and felt a pang of regret. She'd missed the frenzied preparations of so many new days! She walked over to where Bobby kneeled, steadying herself with one hand on his shoulder. There was nothing, really, in the lumps of pine needles, not that she expected anything. An insect, probably, is what had Bobby excited. She moved her hand to the back of his creased, whiskery neck, soft as chamois. And then she saw it—what Bobby pointed to, a scarlet knob poking up from the soil, a bud—slick and innocent, crowning like a newborn.

"The fragrance will come from essential oils produced when an acid and an alcohol are combined," Bobby pronounced. "Phero-mones are how they communicate."

"It's very strange and . . . lovely. What kind of flower is it?"

He shrugged.

"So these are what you planted yesterday with Mr. Cary's crew?"

"Shhhh." Bobby put a finger to his lips, "It's a secret." And he seemed calm then. Calm and a trifle smug. He returned to bed without an argument, sleeping until noon.

Emma, on the other hand, was the one left agitated. It was that strange plant. It bothered her. She'd seen it before. After a cup of tea—jasmine, her most exotic—she opened up the travel trunk and, in no time at all, found it: sketched right there on the third sheaf of bundled papers: the thick, pointy leaves, the hint of a scarlet bloom—the paint brown as dried blood now. Underneath, the slanted, spindly writing of her grandfather: *Figure 1. I will christen this one upon my return to Amaranth. Whether the fragile roots will survive in such dratted piedmont clay remains to be seen.* On the other side of the page, there was another drawing of the flower in bloom, petals splayed like a pinwheel: *Figure 2. Actual size. The hand of Tulu, holding first bloom. I await the aromatic headiness.*

As she pored over her grandfather's scrawled notes, the piece-meal chronicle of his sad fate left her more disturbed than usual. But try as she might, she couldn't tear herself away from his diary. *I am as sun-blistered as a common laborer, my tongue is thick as a prickly pear,* her grandfather had written, not three weeks before he died. *Yes, even now as Tulu clacks and hums a blessing in that strange tongue, I offer up my own, for who knows if my beauties will take root? Who knows when the Great Blooming begins.* And then the last entry, which Emma kept returning to: *I shall book passage, I must. The torment of such visions! One day, I will have the beauty here. I have hunted, marshaled, carried, sown. It is folly, they say, but the great blooming will be revealed.* He'd been quite mad, her grandfather McCann. For some reason, Emma hadn't realized that until now.

Kyle was up to something, Dora just knew it. Even if he had been in good spirits lately, obedient and helpful, coming back sun-burned and cheerful from his work with Saving Souls. *Especially* because he was in good spirits. At breakfast yesterday, when he'd volunteered to spend his Saturday helping his father clean out the garage, Dora had to stop herself from slamming down the milk carton and asking him point blank: *Just what is going on?* Instead, she'd stood and stationed herself behind Donny, glaring at her son, letting him know she was on to his act, even if his father wasn't. He shrugged innocently—*What, Mom?*—but she'd spotted the tiniest glint of a smirk. Donny, however, fell for it. Sucked it up like the ten-attachment Hoover deluxe, still in the box, which he and Kyle found later that afternoon under the carpet remnants in the garage. Yes, according to Donny, Kyle was finally a Good Son, and Dora could only pretend to agree, since she could hardly confess that she'd caught Kyle sneaking back into his room at ungodly hours on more than one occasion, from goodness knew where, and that his laundry these days smelled of smoke and drink, and that she'd kept that information to herself.

If Donny ever caught Kyle—well. He wouldn't have patience with that kind of behavior. Not one bit. Especially if he realized the Good Son had tricked him. He would send Kyle away to that military academy for high school boys in Camden, which would break Dora's heart, or else enroll him at Crossroads, which was getting a high school program started, and Kyle would hate that. He wouldn't do it, Kyle just wouldn't, and it scared her to death to think about such a confrontation. When it came to infractions and second chances, Donny was like a cop with a nightstick, wielding Proverbs without mercy. *Thou shalt beat him with the rod, and shalt deliver his soul from hell.*

And if she brought up how he was too hard on Kyle, then he would remind her: *Folly is bound up in the heart of a child, but the rod of discipline drives it far from him.* It wouldn't help to point out that as a teenager, Dora herself had sneaked out of her bedroom a few times, before she realized her father snored like a troll and couldn't hear her even if she were to bound down the stairs with a pogo stick. Her mother had caught Dora once, tiptoeing down the hall past the kitchen, holding her shoes in her hands. And her mother, standing there in her nightgown like a specter with a cup of tea, sighed and said, "It's your life, Dora. You can make a mess of it or not. I'm going back to bed."

If Donny even suspected that Kyle was *lost in the wilderness of sin*, as Dora had been, he would remind her of the wages of wickedness—Will was dead, Bobby had lost his mind, and worse . . . that always worked.

Starting tonight, Dora was not going to let her guard down. Not for one minute. She would listen for the sound of Kyle's bedroom window opening. She would make silent rounds. The tricky part was keeping the vigil without Donny suspecting, without waking him as she slipped out to check on Kyle.

She turned down the covers now and slid into bed, angling the clock radio on Donny's bedside table so she could see it.

The toilet flushed. The sink faucet sputtered and complained. Teeth were brushed. Donny stepped into the master bathroom in pajamas, his damp ginger hair combed back from his high gleaming forehead.

"I've got an early day tomorrow," he said.

"A meeting?"

He began to select his clothes. His best blue suit. An olive tie. At last month's sales seminar, he'd learned that people were more likely to trust a man whose tie matched his eye color. All the sales guys knew that little trick, he told her. They'd picked it up from the trial lawyers.

"It's . . . a presentation," he mumbled, lips pressed.

"Oh." She'd once seen the aftermath of such a meeting when she'd dropped by Donny's office. Flip charts scrawled with furious arrows that looked more like a weatherman's nightly forecasts about pressure systems and tropical depressions than like sales goals.

"It's important."

"You didn't mention anything about it before. I could have had your suit cleaned." *Or bought more green ties.* Maybe that's what she'd do tomorrow. Go in search of more green ties for Donny, in the exact shade of his eyes, so he could wear a new one every day this week. Stripes, solid silk, a nice sea foam knit. He'd be miffed that she'd shopped again, but he'd be secretly pleased, especially when it helped nudge a deal or two. He'd have to give her credit for helping him, even if Dora remained unclear about what "deals" Donny worked on and with whom. He was downright stingy with the details, and defensive if she asked, as if she questioned his ability to be the family's breadwinner, which she did not. Not at all. She never had. Only, back when he was manager of the paint department at the hardware store, at least then he'd been full of stories about picky customers and mismatched paint chips. But now: Responsibilities. Presentations. Sales goals. Sighs. A lot of pressure. That was as far as he got. *Do you ever wonder if taking that job was a mistake?* She swallowed that burning question, as she had for many nights. It wouldn't do to rile up Donny in the evenings. He'd never get to sleep. And she already knew his answer, anyway. It was no accident that he and Gus met at that Profit for Prophets seminar just when Donny was getting his real estate license, was it? Just in time for Donny to help Gus out with the Crossroads development, just in time for Gus to hire Donny on as an associate. Did she doubt Donny's abilities? Hadn't Gus said a man like Donny would have no trouble in sales, that he had a talent for talking to folks? They needed cold callers, and Donny didn't mind that a bit. He enjoyed talking to strangers. In fact, sometimes Dora wondered if Donny wasn't better at conversing with strangers than with his own family. He preferred blank slates. Steering around touchy points with loved ones was another talent altogether, one he didn't take to.

"Good night." He reached over to kiss her cheek. A whiff of aftershave muscled through toothpaste, and that brought her comfort. He was a clean man; he had tidy habits. So many men didn't. *Donny? The MasterCard? I'm so sorry. . . .*

"Sandy wants to take dance lessons," she blurted. She had cautioned Sandy not to get her hopes up, but the more Dora pondered the idea, the more she thought it was a good one.

"Dance? What kind of dance?"

And now Dora would have to tread carefully, because Tiny Dancer wasn't at Crossroads, and it didn't offer formal training, by any stretch of the imagination. It was the kind of place full of trophies and glittery tutus and pictures of giggling girls, and was located in a storefront beside the Lo-Buy grocery store. Sandy had peered in the window yesterday, glimpsed the sequins and feathers, and surprised Dora by asking to go inside.

"They do . . . recitals . . . and group things," Dora mumbled. "It would be good . . . exercise."

"How much?" Donny asked.

"I was thinking she could stop piano and take dance instead."

"She needs to stick to things," Donny said. "She's got to learn you don't up and quit when you get tired of something."

"But she really . . . *wants* to try dancing."

"She really wanted to play the piano, too, remember?"

Yes, she remembered. Sandy had once wanted to play tee ball, too, only she'd been terrified of the ball, and basketball—well, she'd never mastered dribbling; instead, she gripped the ball for dear life as if she were smuggling a melon through customs. She'd placed fourth in her second-grade spelling bee, which had been her first scrape with near-success, but on Awards Day two weeks ago, she'd been presented with a certificate, "The Student Most Likely to Improve," a dubious achievement, and in Dora's opinion, an "award" bordering on rudeness. Dora might have made a scene with that Miss Hotchkiss, Sandy's second-grade teacher, who didn't look old enough to vote, much less hold the fates of two dozen eight-year-olds in her hands, but Donny insisted Dora stop being so emotional. He didn't see the danger—he didn't know girls formed their groups early, and although Sandy was good-natured and oblivious of slights, that could turn. Girls got mean fast. It helped to have a talent, a little confidence. It was necessary to develop a passion. And Sandy's passion wasn't music; that was for sure. She had a tin ear. Jill Cuttler had done what she could, but as Kyle had pointed out, his sister couldn't carry a tune in a bucket.

"This is different," Dora said. "Dance lessons would be with a group of girls. She could make new friends over the summer."

"Life isn't just doing what you want. It's not just flitting from one thing to another. Sandy needs to learn that." And, as often was the case when her husband gave his frequent lectures on steadfastness and iron resolve, Dora pictured a plow horse, head down, trudging through the furrowed earth, row after row after row. Lately, the horse had acquired blinders and the sting of a lash.

"Maybe she could try it just for the summer," Dora said, "and go back to piano in the fall."

"We'll talk about it later," he said.

Dora seized upon the weary dismissal; it was as close as she'd get to an agreement. She would cancel piano lessons tomorrow. Jill would understand; surely she would.

Donny checked the clock radio's alarm setting again—he had a fear of oversleeping, especially on a "presentation" morning.

"Good night," she said. Sometimes they said a prayer together at night, but they hadn't done that for a while; she couldn't even remember the last time. *And Kyle—we have to talk about Kyle.*

Donny lay on his back beside her. Their spines were parallel as railroad tracks. Life was clattering along, Dora thought, to some distant destination. It went so fast. Donny had been happy to talk to her once, especially when she'd been a stranger. All those years ago, he'd come upon her standing in the housewares section of Kmart, holding a box of 60-watt lightbulbs, although she had no idea why. Wanda, her best friend from back in high school, who liked to talk about zodiacs, would have told her it was because Dora was in desperate need of new ideas—and lightbulbs—well, that wasn't even a subtle symbol. The cosmos had a bullhorn. But Wanda was gone by then. In fact, Dora had been, at that very moment, concentrating on wiping Wanda from her memory. Wiping out a lot of things. Standing there in sandals and cut-offs, unkempt and sunburned, cradling the carton of lightbulbs as if it were a kitten, Dora must have looked as lost as she felt. She'd just hitchhiked four hundred miles back to Palmetto that day and hadn't even had the courage to go home yet and tell her folks she was still alive. Then Donny appeared with a pamphlet in hand. (*Have you heard the Good News?*) His moss-green eyes on her were still warm then, in his soft, pink baby face, his conversation cocked and ready. A man with beliefs as sturdy and safe as a lifeboat. A friendly talk, which Dora had begun to believe she might never have again, since her polite, smiling self had atrophied into a weak, mewling thing deep inside her. "What if I told you all your problems, all your sins, all your burdens could be wiped away?" he'd asked. "What if I told you that you could be reborn into a new life?"

Donny was snoring softly now, but it was only eleven. In another hour, she would check on Kyle. Dora closed her eyes and saw the backs of heads, the entire Crossroads congregation, painted in miniature on the inside of her eyelids: gleaming pates; tresses curled, pinned, sprayed. The backs of heads. She'd arrived late again today to Sunday-night services and sat in the rear. Made Donny late, too. They'd hardly heard a word, either. The acoustics were awful back there.

Was that a thump? She tensed. *Oh, Lord, please,* please *don't let that be Kyle . . .* and Donny barely asleep. She held her breath, listened hard. Nothing. She'd just imagined it. She was just jumpy, was all. She was afraid to get up and check and find an empty bed again and sit there until three in the morning waiting for the window sash to slide open with the practiced smoothness of a thief and watch her son's face split open with shock. Even on a Sunday night.

And then—another thump, fainter this time.

Dora eased out of bed and tiptoed out of her bedroom, into the dark hall. Kyle's door was closed. Locked. She scratched a quiet knock. Nothing. She'd have to go outside in her gown and peer in the window like a robber. She'd left the flashlight and a Windbreaker in the coat closet for such occasions. She'd peek in from outside and make sure Kyle was in bed. *And so help me,* she thought. *So help me.* If he's done it again? This time she would tell Donny, and Kyle would be on his own.

ELEVEN

The waiting room at Dr. Babbitt's office on Monday morning was more crowded than usual. Still, Emma had long ago quit feeling put out by the overscheduled patient load. After all, she and Harold had taken Bobby to Dr. Babbitt since 1970. In all those years, the place had not changed. The green shag rug and orange molded chairs continued to clash, like ornery relatives picking the same fights. The algae-slimed fish tank burbled sadly in the corner, with its little treasure box flapping open and closed, releasing a sad burp of bubbles.

Yes, Dr. Babbitt was that rare breed of doctor who lacked ambition: expanding and updating were not to his taste. Mention the term *cutting edge* to Dr. Babbitt, and he'd turn the conversation to cheese graters or cutlery. For culinary art had always been Dr. Babbitt's passion. The practice of medicine, as he once explained to Emma, was the devil's bargain. He had to keep his considerable body and slight soul together somehow, until he managed to fund a retirement that would fulfill his passion. "The scapula for the spatula," he would say sometimes, sighing, writing out prescriptions for Bobby, winking at Emma. "How many years to go?"

In sixteen years, the prescriptions Dr. Babbitt wrote out for Bobby had changed little. "If it ain't broke, don't fix it," was a philosophy the doctor and Harold had shared and often voiced. Keeping Bobby manageable at home, as one of the pamphlets called it, was the major goal for their son, and Dr. Babbitt was more than happy to help. When it came to chemicals and medication, Dr. Babbitt was no slouch. You started heavy, tapering off as necessary.

"Bobby Hanley," the nurse called. Bobby and Emma rose obediently as choir members. "Right this way," the nurse, a new one, said, and bumped into the doorframe.

"Oh, it's been a long day," she said, rolling her eyes. It was not yet nine. They followed her down the hall. "I'm Suzelle, by the way" she said, with all the enthusiasm of a prison guard. She had a halo of platinum kinky hair, a portion of which had been caught and wrestled into a bristly puff that did not move, even when its owner did. A different nurse was a bit jarring, Emma had to admit. There were very few new things or people in Dr. Babbitt's office. Nurse Suzelle couldn't have known that Emma and Bobby had traversed this hallway numerous times and knew just where to go, for Dr. Babbitt practiced most of his medicine from behind a large glass-top desk in the faux-paneled room at the end of the hall. The door was ajar, and the nurse handed Dr. Babbitt a medical file. Emma and Bobby sat. Dr. Babbitt—fleshy, florid—closed the file and set it aside, as if it were a menu and his order was taken.

"Where's Miss Gail?" Bobby asked, beating Emma to the punch.

"Nurse Gail has . . . retired."

"Retired?" Emma said. Could Nurse Gail be that old? She pictured the nurse, with her spectacles on a chain, her pink scalp shining through the cottony hair and realized—yes, indeed—Nurse Gail could.

"Twenty years with me," Dr. Babbitt said. "I think she's earned it." He cleared his throat. "The real question, is how are you both doing since Mr. Hanley's . . . passing? You have my condolences."

"Yes, thank you," Emma said. She looked over at Bobby, who was staring intently at his shoe. "And thank you for calling and for sending the flowers," she added, wondering if Dr. Babbitt had been one of the lucky few who had received a thank-you note from her. She hadn't caught up yet. "The arrangement was lovely."

"Yes, I believe Miss Gail selected it."

"I'm sure you'll miss having her."

"Yes," he said, peering at her with his heavy-lidded eyes, touching his fingertips together. "I've been forced to hire a temporary nurse. Unfortunately." He shifted his gaze to Bobby, who still studied his shoe. "And what brings you in today?"

Emma opened her mouth to respond, her lips parting with a sticky pop.

"And how are we doing on the Haldol?" he asked without looking up, already writing on his prescription pad.

"Bobby?" she asked. "Talk to Dr. Babbitt. Tell him about your job."

"I am . . ." He stood. "I am ready to go."

Emma got right to the point. "I've tapered off the pills lately just a little," she said. "So he won't be so sleepy."

"Oh?"

"Bobby's been working some. It's with my grandson."

"Around the house?"

"On trucks," Bobby piped up. "In yards. Basically, on the planet when the clouds don't mess everything up. The Blooming Idiots. Heard of them?"

"Let's not taper off," Dr. Babbitt told Emma, rather pointedly. "And I don't think it's wise for Bobby to work. Not at all."

"Well, I just thought . . ." Something sank inside her, her stomach fluttered, as if she were riding on an elevator. Emma fixed her gaze on the red child-sized chair in the corner. Whenever Harold, Bobby, and she had arrived in Dr. Babbitt's office, it was that wooden wobbly child's chair where Emma had perched, between her husband and son, feeling peeved and silly. Now, in the large tweed chair, she'd never felt so alone.

"You've been through a lot, you two," the doctor said, handing the prescriptions over. "With Mr. Hanley's death."

"Yes . . . we have."

"What's that on your hands?"

"Oh," Emma said, rubbing her palms. "Just some little spots they took off the other day. At the dermatologist's office. Precancerous."

"I'm sure it's nothing."

"Yes." Why was it Emma got so close to confessing things here? She didn't even like Dr. Babbitt. "It seems I'm running to some doctor or the other all the time now," she found herself saying. "Since Harold—the way he—well, it just makes one feel—"

"Mortal," he said.

"Yes, I suppose. And I just—" She looked at her son. "I want the best for Bobby after . . . I thought he might be ready for—"

"Emma." Which alarmed her right away. The doctor had always called her Mrs. Hanley. "I'm retiring."

"Oh." She gasped. "Oh, no."

"You will be receiving a letter soon in the mail with all the details."

She was shocked. Absolutely shocked and perturbed. She should have seen it coming. A temp nurse, indeed.

"I will send you some appropriate doctors' names for referral," he said.

It occurred to Emma that in all these years, she'd only seen Dr. Babbitt sitting there, behind his desk. For all she knew, the doctor's legs were slippery spools of overcooked spaghetti. He could be wearing clown shoes. Or high heels.

"The doctors are in town?" Emma asked.

"Well, no. But their offices are no more than an hour away. Unless you want to go to the hospital program."

She shook her head.

"No," he said. "I didn't think so."

"That's something we"—she looked at Bobby—"that's what we never want."

"You'll want to attend to your son's new doctor immediately. You certainly don't want the state to come in and make those kinds of decisions about him, now, do you?" He looked at Bobby, then at Emma. Her mouth went dry. It was nerves, pure nerves. Dr. Babbitt always did that to her.

Then the phone buzzed behind him, and Dr. Babbitt, holding up a finger, answered it. She and Bobby stood to leave.

Emma would never see the doctor's feet after all.

Oh, Dora, I'm dead inside. Her husband had fled to his world of work, her summer-sleeping children were not yet stirring, but in the privacy of Dora's own bathroom, the postcard shook in her hands.

And those pictures. The worst was the group shot, at the surprise party for Will. Will looking . . . resigned. Duty-bound. Wanda looking back at him, doe-eyed. In love. You could just see trouble stalking them. And Dora herself, carrying on, telling whoever was taking the picture to—that was Jake. Yes, she remembered, Jake was taking the shot and she was telling him to . . . use the flashcube.

Oh, but that *postcard*, Wanda's scrawled words, that solitary line Dora had tried to forget. Only she hadn't forgotten. Not really. She'd buried it, and now the bones had been dug up and laid at her doorstep. Or not at her doorstep—much worse than that— in her house, *in her son's pockets.* What was he up to? That was what scared her to death. Why would Kyle want these things? *Where* he'd gotten them was clear. Her mother. *Oh, but why? Why? This was crazy. This was . . . hurtful. Yes, hurtful.*

She would get to the bottom of this. Just as soon as she had a shower and composed herself. She'd been so frantic last night, she didn't know what upset her more—discovering Kyle's empty bed or, after having crawled into his bedroom through the window and conducting a search, finding these old pictures and that motel postcard from Wanda in the pocket of his crumpled dirty jeans. By the time Kyle had come back in the wee hours, she'd been ready—concealed in the shadowy corner of his bedroom, patient as a vampire. When he saw her—shock registering dully in his glassy-eyed stare—he stammered in beery, panicked whiffs. "This is going to stop," she'd said, cutting him off. "This is the last time. You'll see." And then she'd turned and closed his door behind her with an air of menacing calm she'd somehow managed to conjure up, for she was anything but calm. She'd gotten back into her bed and pulled the covers up to her neck. Donny had not stirred as she lay rigid and trembling for the rest of the night, one hand on the photographs clutched in her pocket. Only when Donny arose and showered did she close her eyes, pretending to sleep.

Dora stepped into the shower now, turning the water as hot as she could stand. Her eyes burned from lack of sleep. *You'll look out for Wanda, right?* Will had asked. *She gets lonely. She's going to need you.* This was the morning after his farewell party, in the barn. He'd started picking up beer bottles with his fingers. He could pick up ten at once, even with his thumbs. He'd won bets. She'd waved him away. *Cleaning up after your own farewell party is pathetic.* He shrugged. *Can't sleep.* He looked out the open barn toward the darkened house. *I don't want to go in my room. I'll have to listen to Mom crying.*

Dora reached for the soap now, lathering furiously, foam clotting at her feet. She thought of the postcard again, remembered the motel room with its single paper-wrapped guest soap, a dingy place that reeked of cigarette smoke, with pillows that smelled like other people's heads. That first night, the three of them slept in a king-sized bed—all the rooms with doubles were taken—Wanda on one side, knocked out good with some pills the clinic gave her, Dora in the middle, listening to every breath Wanda took, and Jake beside her, his hand resting on Dora's hip.

By then, Wanda didn't look innocent anymore, or stupid with love—she didn't look at anyone with love. She was pale and shaky and hopeless. Ruined. Her words. *I'm ruined, Dora.*

Everyone back home thought they were at Myrtle Beach celebrating with all the other high school graduates. But they were in another country entirely. Later, Dora learned that they could have gone to New York, instead. It would have been easier. But who knew? It was a big mystery back then, how to arrange things. Jake's cousin had a sister-in-law who knew a nurse in Texas who told them where to go. So that's how they did it. Jake drove them there and back in his sorry Chevy—with that radiator leak—but he swore it would make it and it had. First to Eagle Pass, Texas, then across the border into Piedras Negras and there was a man there who took you to a *clean clinic*, a place for plenty of *American girls like you*. The three of them pooled their money, every cent. They were supposed to stay in the hotel a few days afterwards— just until Wanda got well enough to travel. Only, Wanda never really got well at all. She slept in the backseat most of the way home, rearing up in alarm at stoplights, or else sitting slumped over untouched plates of scrambled eggs, her freckled face wan and puffy in the cruel fluorescence of diners.

Then, just hours from home, at some truck stop in Georgia, while Jake was outside filling the tank and patching the radiator hose, Wanda's strangled confession: *I'm going to tell him.*

You're not. Dora reached across the table, squeezed Wanda's hand until her grip lost all warmth, until her nails pressed into the flesh of Wanda's hand like teeth. *Do you understand? You can't.*

I've got to.

It will kill him.

Dora turned off the shower when the water ran tepid. Faux-lilac lingered in the steam, but the fragrance sickened her. She did not feel refreshed or composed at all; she just felt tired. She sat, cloaked in towels, on the edge of the tub. When the doorbell rang, she couldn't even muster the curiosity to dress and answer it. Mormons or the Jehovah's Witnesses or Avon—sellers of salvation or hand cream.

Heavy knocks, then.

"Mom?" came a small voice outside the bathroom. Dora opened the door, peered at her daughter standing there in pajamas.

"Someone is at the door."

"Who, honey?" Dora asked.

"I don't know. I didn't answer it. Daddy said never—"

"Did you look out the window and see who it was?"

"I saw a stranger there. A man." Sandy shrugged. "He banged hard on the door. He was mad."

"Mad?" The neighborhood homeowners' association fee was late, but surely they didn't come knocking on your door? That was just rude. Donny had said he'd take care of it. The later the bills, the more peeved he got, which is why she hated telling him anymore. She just handed it all over to him so he could *take care of it*.

The knocks started again. Sandy jumped. "That man will go away," Dora said. "Don't worry, sweetie. Just ignore it."

"Okay."

"Come here," Dora said, kneeling down. She embraced her daughter.

"You need a hug?" Sandy asked, her breath warm on Dora's damp neck.

Dora nodded. She buried her face in Sandy's chestnut hair—breathed in bubble gum shampoo and playground dust. She was still a little girl. She would be nine soon, but they grew up so fast these days. And yes, at Tiny Dancer Sandy didn't have the easiest time learning the routines, but she hadn't complained. A girl needed confidence. A girl needed to be watched, too. A protector. Donny would see to that. He was a good father for a girl.

"It's quiet now," Sandy whispered. "That man went away."

"I knew he would." Dora stood, and found her chipper voice. "Wake up Kyle? Tell him to get ready. We're leaving in an hour."

"Okay," Sandy said, cheered by the prospect of giving her brother orders.

It wasn't until after they dropped Sandy off at Tiny Dancer—the less she knew about all this mess, the better—that Dora noticed someone following her. And he wasn't even being particularly smart about it. She angled the rearview mirror, squinting. Kyle, in the passenger seat beside her, was too sulky to notice, thinking he could wear her down with his tight-lipped obstinacy. Well, he wouldn't. He was shackled to her for the rest of the summer, no alone time for him! He was at her mercy, chafing already.

"Where did you say we were going?" Kyle asked, the first words he'd said to her all morning.

"I didn't."

And there it was—that truck again. Wasn't it? Now that she thought about it, when she'd backed out of the garage, the automatic door lurching up above them—Dora holding her breath, since it jammed half the time—that very same truck had been parked at the curb.

"Where are we going?" Kyle asked, his voice dripping with misery. "Mom, just tell me. Please."

There it was, all right. Two cars behind them now, in the other lane. Or was she imagining it? Her nerves were shot.

"You know where," she said.

She'd decided not to call first. It was easiest that way.

Lila Day was of the opinion that an outing was just the thing to lift Emma's spirits, and suggested the two of them drive over to Colonial Motor Lodge for the early bird two-for-one lunch. "My treat." She had phoned shortly after Emma and Bobby returned from Dr. Babbitt's to say so. Emma sighed. "Well, I'll just have to see." She told her friend about Dr. Babbitt's sudden retirement, and her worries about finding a new doctor in another town for Bobby.

"You do know they cleaned up Grady Bean?" Lila said. "It says right here in today's paper." For years in Palmetto, Grady Bean Hospital was a threatening term. A silly, cruel warning to mischievous children, angry employees, or eccentric neighbors. *Send you to Grady Bean.*

Emma clucked in disgust.

"They say it is different now, Emma. Look in section B if you don't believe me." There was the sound of newspaper pages rattling, and Emma knew Lila, who'd spent three decades as a librarian reading to wiggly children, was preparing to read aloud the article, whether Emma wanted to hear it or not. "Ah, here it is. Section B, page one. They call it a behavioral health center for inpatient and outpatient care—"

"Thank you, Lila, but I can read myself," Emma said, looking out the kitchen window, into the wavy heat of the day, where her own newspaper was still in its plastic sleeve in the driveway, warming in the sun. Neither she nor Bobby had bothered to bring it in and, in fact, had stepped right over it in the driveway that morning. Later, on her way out to fetch it, Emma forgot the newspaper again when she'd gotten sidetracked by her garden. There, the Secret Keepers appeared even more stunning today. She nearly mentioned them now to Lila, but stopped short when she thought of Bobby's warning. *Shhhh. It's a secret.* Perhaps she should hold off on confiding to Lila—the town crier—just yet.

"Lila, if one wanted to reach that speaker Dr. Burnside . . . how might one do so?"

"One wouldn't," Lila bristled, "if one had a shred of decency."

Emma sighed. "I only ask because I have a question I think he might be able to help me with."

But Lila was off on one of her tangents. Certain inquires had been made, she informed her friend. She'd heard the speaker—Lila refused to call him by his Christian name—had no permanent address.

"He said he's staying with family."

"And no job."

"He's retired."

"A man with too much time on his hands who just *walks the earth.*"

"He's a researcher."

"He's a transient," Lila said with a shudder.

"I'll take my chances," Emma said.

Emma wondered if she should turn on the sprinkler. Mr. Cary hadn't mentioned a watering schedule. She would ask him today. She would ask him about those things in her garden.

"I heard that speaker was going to do one of his slideshows at Monaghan," Lila said after a frosty silence. "I already warned Miss Gibble not to attend. For her own good. You know how Miss Gibble abhors vulgarity."

There was the distant crunch of gravel, and Emma moved the kitchen curtain aside to get a closer look. A cloud of dust arose at the end of her driveway.

"Lila," Emma said, "I have to go. I have company."

TWELVE

What is that?" Dora asked.

"A basketball," Kyle said. "Just a wild guess."

She turned off the ignition, put the minivan in PARK. "Don't," she said.

Kyle shrugged. Head averted, hands clasped in his lap in submission, as if he were handcuffed. Strong hands. Where did he suddenly get those big hands? Big feet, too. It just made his arms and legs look even thinner. But that's how boys grew sometimes—in sudden fits and starts, like balloon animals.

"Before we go in," she said. She reached into her purse and held up the pictures and postcard. "I found these last night."

He glanced at them, then looked away. "Ooohhh. Contraband. Mumsy groovin' at one of her barn bashes."

"I am trying to *help* you, Kyle."

"Yeah? I bet I'm the only kid around grounded for visiting his grandmother."

"You know what this is about. Sneaking out to parties at night is bad enough and—then to find out you come over here and lie about it? It's all gotten out of hand."

"I didn't lie. I just didn't mention it."

"Uh-huh. And why is that, Kyle?"

"Because it's no big deal. All I did was help Grandma clean out some stuff, okay? And sometimes I stayed with Uncle Bobby."

"Some*times*? Why did you come over here on these visits without telling your father or me?"

"You're going to have a cow over *that*?"

He was resigned to his fate, convinced that she'd already made up her mind about telling Donny everything—sneaking out at night at parties, and this, too. No need to curry favor with her: Kyle knew he was a goner. He did not suspect just how miserable Dora was with that burden.

They walked past the new basketball, still in the box, sitting right there at the foot of the rusty goalpost. The same spot where Will had spent his afternoons wearing away the grass, his rebounds crushing her mother's roses. And then all these years the goal stayed untouched, rusting, the net rotting off, because how could they ever remove something that Will had devoted himself to? And now—a bribe. To attract Kyle. A new basketball. An underhanded bribe.

"What a . . . surprise," Emma called out from the front porch, appearing not so much surprised as deflated. When she looked at Kyle, Dora sensed a signal passing between the two of them, like mirrors flashing a code from opposite shores.

Dora walked past her mother wordlessly. She headed for the kitchen and sat down at the table. Kyle and Emma followed— *were they whispering?*—and stood together by the sink like servants waiting for orders.

Bobby padded in.

"Sit down, Bobby," Emma said. "Talk to your sister."

But he didn't. As usual, Bobby stood against the counter, managing to appear both sphinxlike and fidgety.

"Tell Dora how much we've enjoyed having Kyle."

"Will Two," Bobby said. "He is magnificent. Truly."

"Will Two?" Dora asked.

"It's his nickname for Kyle."

"I like it when he calls me that," Kyle said.

"Bobby," Dora said, "Kyle is your nephew. You should call him *Kyle*."

"Dora, please," Emma said. "You're just going to stir things up—"

"He's Will Two because that's the nomenclature that has been decided upon," Bobby said. "There are lines of thought, got me? There are lines of thought with Will in the center, and Will Two and me have our orders."

"Bobby," Dora said. "I want you to sit down right here with me and have a normal conversation."

"Oh, for Pete's sake," Emma said. She turned to Kyle. "He's been looking forward to seeing you all day."

What hurt most was the conspiracy. Her son and her mother with their plans and their secrets. Kyle looked as if he was about to say something, but Dora shot him a warning look. "You can go watch TV with your uncle Bobby. I'll let you know when we're ready to leave."

Her mother sat down across from her and sighed.

"I need to know what's going on here," Dora said.

"I knew it would end up like this. With that poor boy in the hot seat for just wanting to help us."

"He's been coming here without permission, I know that much. But how and why—I can't imagine," Dora said with more venom than she felt. "He's going through a rebellious stage. And you're not helping matters."

"He wanted to spend time with us and make a little money. What's wrong with that for a boy, I'd like to know?"

"Make a little money? You *paid* him?"

"Well—I . . ." Emma's face shut down. "Why don't we get Kyle in here and sort this whole thing out. All of it. Let's get everything out in the open. Honestly, at my age, I just can't tolerate such foolishness anymore."

"All of it?" It was worse than Dora thought. Her mother was either naïve or—more likely—determined to ignore Kyle's mischievous intentions. *Helping out? Oh, please. And getting paid for it?*

"We had a fine time. He and Bobby watch television. They like that music station on cable."

"He's not allowed to watch that."

"And he helped me clean out the attic. He was the biggest help—"

Dora took out the photos and spread them on the table like a bad hand of cards. "These were in his pockets," Dora said.

"So he has some old pictures. Why not? He's interested in the family, in our past, his uncle and you—"

"Kyle doesn't need to know how awful we were back then."

"We?"

Dora thought of her mother's complaints: *Go to the barn with that noise.* Ignoring misbehavior was her mother's chief parenting strategy. And she didn't know the half of it. Let her mother think of Will as her golden boy, then, in love with perfect, pure Wanda. Let her remember Bobby as smart and cute and a teacher's darling. Let her forget that Dora was practically shacking up with her boyfriend in the barn.

"Maybe Kyle has questions," Emma whispered, leaning closer. "Why not be honest?"

"Questions about what? He knows I changed my life, that I was lost and—" Dora squeezed the bridge of her nose, willing herself not to tear up. "—that's all he needs to know."

"Dora, are you still furious about your daddy's funeral? Is that what this is all about?"

"What funeral? He didn't have one." Oh, she'd taken the bait. This was not about her daddy's funeral. For once. "This is about Kyle sneaking over here and you let him watch any old cable show and who knows what else he's up to—smoking with Bobby, maybe. When did he find time for these visits, that's what I'd like to know? And his . . . going through things, those pictures and letters—it just feeds his rebellion."

"Do you know I tried to give Kyle some of Will's things, but he wouldn't take them? I guess you and Donny would have sent out the cavalry if you'd found him with one those rock music albums you were always listening to in Will's room." Her mother got up and put on the kettle for tea. She was one of the few people Dora knew who made hot tea every day. It was left over from a phase her mother had gone through years ago, trying out all sorts of strange teas that no one else in the family would touch, especially her father, who never strayed from his cup of Sanka. For a while, she even had a tea ball, though where she'd managed to find tea leaves in this town was beyond Dora. "I tell you," her mother said, standing at the stove, her back to Dora. "It's time to thaw the ice between us, for goodness' sake."

Only with her mother, there was always a short thawing season. Something else would freeze them up.

"You can't just handle things from afar and send in Kyle with dinner or notes forever, you know."

"When did you two set up these secret visits?" Dora asked.

"Oh, for goodness' sake. I thought you people like forgiveness. I thought that's what you lived for."

"*You* people?"

"You know what I mean."

"Kyle is doing a lot of very sneaky things lately. It scares me to death. You don't know all the temptations and awful things out there for teenagers these days. On the television, the music lyrics, the crack. How can you *laugh?* This is not funny."

"We said the same things when you and the boys were coming up."

"Yes, and look what happened."

"What happened. What is that supposed to mean." Her mother said this with no inflection at all, as if she were reading ingredients on the back of a cereal box: zinc, iron, vitamin C.

"You don't know," Dora said slowly, "how wild we were. How bad. You don't know, Mama."

"Perhaps not. And I don't care to be apprised of the debauchery at this late date."

"You never did want to know."

"It sounded as if you were all having a fine time back there with your music and your friends. I would think there would be some happy memories, too."

"I was the kind of girl that needed a strict mother with strong rules."

"You were as headstrong then as you are now. If I'd tried to clamp down on you any more—well, I'm scared to think what you would have done."

"I am not headstrong."

"Ha."

"I am *not* headstrong!" Dora shouted.

Her mother turned her back to Dora and poured two cups of tea. She set them on the table, eyes downcast, with the faintest trace of a smirk.

Dora looked away. Oh, this kitchen, how it depressed her. It was piecemeal and shabby as it had been for decades, for as long as Dora remembered it. And the longer she was away from it, the more dreadful it seemed when she saw it again. The hideous Frigidaire in goldenrod, and the avocado green stove with the busted clock and cockeye burners. The dishwasher had to be at least twenty years old. Pudding brown, as if anyone would order an appliance in that color. But somebody had, of course. And changed their minds. And as usual it had ended up in the Hanley family kitchen. Customers had ordered appliances and then not picked them up, or else fell behind on the payments, and the things ended up in the Hanley family kitchen, a fact her mother harped on for years. *You would think I might at least have the best-appointed kitchen in Palmetto, but I have nothing but hand-me-downs. The tackiest kitchen! Why, no one would ever guess that I was married to an appliance man.* And on and on. *They work, don't they?* her father would shout back, goaded finally into a response. *You can cook on a green stove as well as white one, can't you?*

"When are you going to redo this kitchen?" Dora asked.

"Why, I haven't thought about it. Do you think it needs it?"

Dora looked at her mother. Just looked. "Mama, that's all we heard growing up. How you had a kitchen of hand-me-downs."

"It just doesn't seem very important anymore. I guess I'm finally used to it."

"You ought to do it in white," Dora said. "White kitchens are in." The thumps of a dribbling basketball began outside the kitchen window.

"Oh, I see they've found the basketball," Emma said.

Dora got up and set her cup in the sink. Outside, Bobby stood, arms at his side, while Kyle dribbled the ball, his back to her. *Like Will.* Dora's eyes filled.

"It's been good for Bobby to have Kyle around," Emma said from the table. "He perks up. And all those pictures and things— we had fun going through them."

Dora did not turn around. "Kyle reminds you of Will, doesn't he?" she asked.

"You make that sound like a bad thing."

"Bobby is confused. No wonder he calls Kyle 'Will Two.'"

"It's just . . . so nice to have a young man around the house again."

"It's not good for Kyle or Bobby to plunder around here and . . . drag out things."

"They're not dragging out things, Dora. I'm cleaning out the attic. The back hall is full. You wouldn't believe the junk we have—piles and piles! And when I'm dead, I'd rather not have my keepsakes sell for a quarter each at an estate sale, like what happened to poor Miss Briscow. Don't tell me you didn't know about that tag sale, either. Lila Day told me she saw you buy a boxload of her silver serving pieces and perfume bottles."

Dora got up from the table. She peered down the hall. Her mother was right—it was overflowing with boxes. There was the old silver-foil Christmas tree, and stacks of *National Geographics*, a pile of winter coats, and storm windows and—"Not my prom dress!"

"I've already called Goodwill," Emma said from behind her.

"But Sandy might want to wear it one day."

"Don't you remember? Girls never want to wear their mother's dresses—even the ones their mothers pick out."

"Oh, and my powder blue Easter suit with the pillbox hat, remember that? They are all in such good shape. Perfectly fine." Had she really worn these tiny jeans?

"What am I supposed to do with all that, Dora?" her mother said. "You can't wear them."

"I certainly can wear them!"

"I didn't mean you couldn't fit into them." She watched Dora hold up a dress. "They're probably rotting at the seams. They still smell musty," Emma said as she returned to the kitchen.

"They just need a little more airing is all," Dora muttered to herself. After a minute, when she joined her mother, Emma gasped.

"Oh, my stars," Emma said. Dora walked over to the kitchen table in wrinkled mint green crepe, smelling of cedar. "You did manage to—fit into it, didn't you?"

"It's a little snug, but I bet it shrank up there in the attic heat. It's just too bad it's this dreadful green. And the way it plunges in front—it's so immodest for a girl. Mama, what were you thinking? I can't believe you let me wear this dress out in public."

They took turns shooting baskets, and it was lame, but okay. Neither of them had his heart in it.

"Will Two, I'm ready for some TV."

"You don't want to go back in there," Kyle said. "Mom will just say it's time to leave and drag me the Pantyhose Warehouse or something." *Let me talk to her*, is what his grandmother had managed to whisper to him. She'd winked, but her face was grim.

His uncle took a granny shot, missed. Kyle chased down the ball.

"Hey, um, listen," Kyle said. "Come here." Kyle knew his mother was watching him; he could just feel it. He held the ball under his arm and motioned for his uncle to follow him to a spot beyond the shrubs, out of sight. "Uncle B, listen up. This is important. I'm not going to be able to work with Jake and them for a while."

He tossed over the ball, and his uncle hugged it to his chest, listening

"So I won't be able to come with you this week. But I think you should keep on, okay? It bites, I know, but I'm, like, under twenty-four-hour surveillance."

"Being watched?"

"Yeah." It was already driving his mother batty; at least there was that. No way would she last the summer dragging him everywhere. *Mom, do we really need another lampshade? How many candles do we have, anyway?* He'd be a regular Jiminy Cockroach. His mother was stuck with him, all right, just as much as Kyle was stuck with her. Only, she had him good this time. What could you say when you slipped back into your room after one of the better cemetery parties, thinking about that tiny daisy appliqué in the center of Julie's bra, and there on your bed, by the lump of pillows you'd fashioned to look like a slumbering skinny you—was your mother weeping by flashlight.

"We're busted," Kyle said, "you and me and Grandma."

"The jig is up."

"You said it."

"What's the prognosis?"

"Prognosis? You crack me up, Uncle B. Prognosis. Actually, not good."

Kyle had ceased feeling terrified sometime around dawn, and after a few hours of sleep, he'd awakened with a newfound sense of resolve. His anger flared, consuming him. He lay on his bed, his arms behind his head, staring at his cottage cheese ceiling, trying to work things out in his head. Yeah, his mother would spill it this time, and then his father would lose it, and there would be all kind of new rules, an iron grip. Forget the job. Somehow, he'd have to come clean about his Saving Souls "project." But if they sent him away to that military academy, he'd run away. Nothing to lose. If he ended up at Crossroads, he'd work around it. He wouldn't give Julie up. And nothing, *no one* was going to stop him from taking Julie to that concert—he was going to get the tickets this week. He had the cash. They could put bars on his window, for all he cared. They probably would. Now, the worst part was the waiting. Batten down the hatches. The shit storm would hit tonight, when his dad found out.

"Let's go see the Secret Keepers."

"The what?" Kyle asked.

"In the garden."

Kyle shrugged. He wasn't sure his uncle grasped the situation, and it troubled him. What would his uncle do with the Blooming Idiots now? Would he even go without Kyle?

He followed his uncle over to the spot where they'd helped the Blooming Idiots on Friday. Just three days ago, when all things were right with the world. Kyle's world, anyway. "Oh, I get it. Secret Keepers," Kyle said. Scarlet flowers had sprouted as big as his head. "They're freakin' humongous."

"They reveal things," his uncle said. "The Secret Keepers send messages right through here," he touched his nose. "Personal messages, and they enter the portal of the brain, here"—he pointed to his forehead—"and proceed to the amygdalae."

Kyle kneeled and reached for the nearest flower. It was downy, the stem thick and strong as a tendon. Kyle sniffed, and what he smelled there—in the cloying, kind, secretive center—knocked him to the ground. He looked back at the thing, stunned. "Oh, my God." He closed his eyes. Because the aroma was Julie. Not just her perfume. Julie's skin, her hair, her peppermint Lifesaver. Everything Julie. He didn't move, didn't dare, just sat savoring the memory, the feel of Julie's neck under his hand, and—he opened his eyes. They stung with tears. His uncle was studying him.

"That was . . . wild."

"Yes," his uncle said.

"You were right. About the power of . . . the smell. How did you know? I mean," Kyle chose his words carefully, "what happened when you smelled them?"

"Not today, thank you," he said. "You can't be greedy. They don't like that."

"Oh." Kyle cupped the flower over to him again, inhaled deeply. Nothing. Not a thing. A vegetable, prickly smell, like tomato vines. He sniffed another one. Nothing. "What happened? Why doesn't it work?"

"Presents like that are opened once a year, got me?"

"What? I mean, one little sniff and that's it? When will they work again?" But his uncle was already off on some other tangent, staring at something else. Kyle began snuffling each of the flowers like an addict or something. Pathetic, but another one of those things had to work. Julie, the closest he'd gotten to Julie in . . . hours.

"Uncle B?"

His uncle ignored him, was walking away, and Kyle stood up. "Where you going?" And then he saw a stranger walking across his grandmother's yard. Kyle stood beside his uncle. They watched the man who, without so much as a glance their way, walked up to his mother's minivan and opened the driver's door.

"Hey!" Kyle yelled. He walked toward the van and approached the passenger side. He peered in. "Excuse me, sir? Um, what are you doing?" He was a big man, bare-chested except for a leather vest. A wide leather belt, covered with keys, jingled merrily as the man fished out things—Kyle's things! his mother's things!—from under the seats. "I've never seen so much shit in my life," the man said, ignoring Kyle. Out came his mother's gym bag, his sister's Cabbage Patch doll, a curtain rod, a pencil case, a pair of Kyle's old tennis shoes, two paperbacks, three umbrellas—*thwack thwack thwack*—all of it landed in a heap at Kyle's feet.

"Sir?" Kyle asked, but the man began to fling faster. A box of Kleenex, a blanket, his mother's travel mug, his sister's juice boxes. It began to dawn on Kyle that this man was dangerous. He was a thief. Kyle stepped back. His uncle still stood at the edge of the drive, watching.

"Get lost," the man said. His shiny bullet-shaped head needed a shave, the black stubble there coarse as metal filings. And why, Kyle wondered calmly from somewhere deep inside himself, why bother with the vest?

"You can't just steal it," Kyle said in a small voice.

The front door opened, and his mother ran out—in some kind of long dress?—his grandmother right behind her.

"What's going on here?" his mother said. Her voice was too high, hysterical. Kyle felt his mouth go dry. "Kyle, get away from him!"

The man looked down at a paper he pulled from the back pocket of his jeans. "Are you Quattle—? Jesus, I can't read this crap—Quattlesomething."

"I'm Dora Quattlebaum."

"Close enough." The man's eyes fell on his mother and stayed there too long. Why was she wearing that dress? Kyle wondered. It was too tight, and it wasn't something a mother should wear. Especially not his mother. "I've got the paperwork here. I'm taking this vehicle in."

"You're *what*? This isn't your van."

"Yeah? Well, it ain't yours, either."

"I'm going to call the sheriff," his grandmother said.

"Help yourself," he said wearily. "The Notice of Cure was sent weeks ago."

Kyle saw that the truck parked at the curb, with its long bed in back, was for towing.

"You understand?" the man told his mother. "This is a repossession. Checked your VIN."

"A . . . repossession?"

"Yep. Collateral recovery. Been tailing you for a while today."

"I . . . don't understand."

"Call the car dealership. They'll give you an earful."

"I don't understand," his mother repeated.

Kyle's grandmother stood with Bobby now, who was pacing nervously. She said something to him and rubbed his arm.

His mother stepped behind the man, slammed the car door, and locked it. "You are not going to take my van," she said.

The man stepped close to his mother. His biceps were bigger than Kyle's legs. "Sweetheart," he said. "Just let me do my job, okay? I don't need your keys no way." And then he winked. The man with the hairy belly and ridiculous leather vest *winked* at his mother—the bad kind of wink, not the friendly kind. "So, don't play naughty with me, 'cause I got two more to pick up today."

"This is some kind of terrible mistake."

"I've heard all the sob stories, believe me."

"I don't appreciate your tone. If you think I'm just going to stand here and watch—someone like you drive off with our van— you're crazy." Kyle saw that his mother might cry, and he thought maybe that wasn't a bad idea, but she didn't.

"Someone like me?" The man laughed. Then he didn't. He fixed his squint on Kyle's mother. His voice dropped to a whisper. "Tell you what. Maybe you and me can work out an oral agreement." He stuck out his tongue and wiggled it at Kyle's mother, like a predator, a creature in a swamp.

Kyle was on him in a second, punching the massive belly. His fists bounced off harmlessly, like children on a trampoline. Kyle was powerless, weak, worse than weak. He smelled leather, sweat, smoke. He closed his eyes and kept hitting. His mother screamed, his grandmother called out his name, and then he was wet, Kyle was soaked, and there were hands on him, his shirt was tearing. He couldn't breathe. Something had him.

THIRTEEN

Monday began with such promise but went down fast and just kept getting crazier, until it ran off the rails completely. Jake started out the morning with his favorite kind of problem: a good one. A backlog of work, and a few more jobs as of yesterday. But when he'd arrived at Amaranth, Gordon and Terrell told him the four others they'd counted on to show up had been lured into town by a new plasma center that bought blood for cash.

"You just lay there, and get paid for it," Terrell said with a shrug. "Get free doughnuts and orange juice. How you gonna compete?"

"Probably be after lunch before they show up," Gordon said.

"That's all I need, blood-sucked workers fainting in the flower beds," Jake said.

The three of them headed out to the wholesale nursery supplier to pick up a new order of annuals and mulch. But just as Jake allowed himself a cheerful thought or two, the nursery manager told Jake his credit was overextended. There was no use arguing with this pig-eyed sour man, who was enjoying watching Jake squirm. Abby, the shy, sweet girl with a lazy eye and crooked teeth, who was there most days and giggled with a hand over her mouth when Jake kidded around with her, wasn't there today, and the manager said Jake's account was, "froze up till you pay up."

"Tomorrow," Jake said. "I promise."

"That girl shouldn't have gave you all those orders, no way," the man said, staring at his clipboard. "Must have been out of her head."

Well, he wouldn't beg, but this put Jake in a tight spot. He'd just bought a new mower on Saturday. Damned if he'd put up his truck and land for a credit line and turn around and lose it all. He'd sworn this would be a cash business.

"Nothing to load," Jake told Gordon and Terrell back at the truck. "Need to collect some cash and checks. We'll come back tomorrow." His face burned, a slow anger swelling in his chest. The best part of the morning had slipped by, and nothing much done.

He drove them over to a new customer to leave an estimate, heartened by the circular driveway in one of the better neighborhoods in town. An impressive yard as manicured and maintained as Ginger Welch herself, who, though she was older than he'd at first thought, a good deal older than Jake, judging from the honest noon sun overhead, kept herself well. She'd come right out as soon as they'd pulled up, fluttering out in a yellow silk wrap. But she did not seem the least bit interested in Jake's suggestions and estimate.

Right in the middle of his questions about her woody ornamentals, she laid a hand on his arm and lowered her voice. "Listen. I need a favor."

"A favor?"

"I saw you the other day trimming up the Verner place, and I just knew you were the one."

"Well, thank you. I think."

"You're hired. I pay cash. But—" She looked around, up and down the street, before turning her attention back to Jake. "—I need your help with something, you know, different. It'll be worth your time."

"Different?"

She nodded, squinted at him, shading her eyes with a hand. Her hair was more orange than red, the color of the drought-baked Carolina clay he shook off his boots at night.

"Is it . . . legal?" he joked. Or tried to.

"Yes, silly. It's perfectly legal. See, any minute now, he's going to come driving through here—"

"Who?"

"That private detective my husband hired. He'll come driving by in that awful midnight blue Chevrolet Cavalier with the radials."

Jake searched for an excuse to leave. This was developing into one of those "domestic situations that got out of hand" stories the evening news was always full of, and Jake didn't care to have his name—or body—listed in a report that involved "firearms" and "estranged husband."

"He's too cheap to hire a decent private eye and too stupid to know there's no way he's getting this house, because it's in my daddy's name. And so is my car. And so is every bond and fund and cent I have. So, he's not getting a piece of me, not one little piece. It just tears him up." For the first time, Ginger Welch looked happy. "So just be prepared. That detective might get some pictures of us."

"Of . . . us?"

"Do you think you could have your men take off their shirts? And I've got some baby oil to grease them up. It makes the pictures better."

"I don't get it," he said.

She gave a dramatic sigh. "Well, Jake. It's Jake, right? I don't know how much more plain I can be. I got this neighbor to agree to tip off my soon-to-be-ex whenever I have gentlemen callers. And then the private eye will come take pictures. He's going to think I'm having a high old time. Get him all crazy. Does that make sense?"

Not a lick. But scorned women usually didn't, at least not in Jake's experience. "I'll have to ask my crew," he said. "I can't speak for them. I'm not sure you want to have them strutting around here, shirtless, slicked up with oil anyway." He laughed and shook his head. "I don't think it would help your case any."

"Shhhh. Don't look! He's over there." She gripped Jake's arm. He looked. *"Don't,"* she rasped. "The private eye is parked three houses down under the willow." She hooked a finger under Jake's belt, pulled him flush against her, and suddenly she was kissing him, her white Chiclets teeth grinding against his, that eggplant-purple lipstick would be all over him. From the truck, behind them, arose howls and clapping, and Jake, eyes wide in surprise, tried to step away politely, but found himself anchored, one of Ginger's legs wrapped around him. When she finally pulled away, she glanced discreetly at the detective's car and said through clenched teeth, like a ventriloquist, "You and your boys schedule me in every Monday."

Back at the truck, Terrell and Gordon were worthless, floppy with laughter. "Man, she was on you like stripes on a barber pole," Terrell said after they pulled out of Ginger Welch's driveway.

"Just about to get out the hose on you two," Gordon told him.

"Yeah? Well, next time, she wants us all to take off our shirts when we work there," Jake said. "And oil up."

"What?" Gordon said. "How come we get dragged in this?"

"The price of business."

At the traffic light, Jake counted the cash in his pocket. At least there was enough to pay everyone at the end of the day. Just barely, but enough. Ginger Welch's perfume still lingered on the bills she'd slipped him. As shocking as it was, having her soft powdered body pressed against him reminded Jake just how long it had been since he'd had a woman's company.

"How long?" Gordon asked when Jake confessed.

"Godawful long. Weeks."

"Man, that's nothing. I've had dry spells for whole seasons," Terrell piped up from the backseat. "In the middle of one right now."

"Suits me fine," Jake said. "'Till I get this business going good. I don't need the distractions."

Unfortunately, he was beginning to realize that the swearing off was more distracting than the women. Carol Ann was still up in Pittsburg, along with her job and her kids. They talked on the phone sometimes, less often lately as she began to realize he wasn't coming back. She sounded surprised and a little sad that his business was working out after all. He missed her sometimes, her quiet, trusting voice. Carol Ann was like most of the women he'd taken up with in the last decade: soothing, sweet, and comforting—like custard. They liked to take on battered projects. The more clinks and chinks you had, the more eager they were. It just beat all. He had no money. A back wrecked from the war and screwed up worse in an accident, no children and no hope of producing any—thanks again to the war. If he was a car, he'd be in a used lot by now with a sign that said DAMAGED MERCHANDISE, BUYER BEWARE, and there'd be a crowd of those sweet, soft women around him, kicking his tires in their heels.

They headed over to the Hanley place to pick up Bobby and the boy. They were early, but with more help, maybe they could get some real work done and the day could be salvaged after all. Jake could only hope.

"Oh, Lord. That's Big Baby's truck," Gordon said.

"Who?" Jake asked.

"Greasy's boy. You know Greasy? Has that pawnshop?"

"Yeah . . . don't we all."

The tow truck blocked Emma Hanley's driveway, so Jake parked at the curb. "Big Baby is a repo man," Gordon said.

Jake considered leaving and coming back later, after the dust cleared, because Big Baby sure wasn't bringing good news. He wondered if Emma Hanley was having money problems, and felt a pang of guilt for taking her payments. He got out and stood there, considering.

He heard the commotion before he saw it.

Screams, not squeals. Nothing playful in this, even if Emma Hanley did have the hosepipe out blasting water at something behind a van. Jake broke into a run, faster than he should. The dog,

Sweet—agitated, thrilled—ran up ahead and barked. And there was Big Baby and the boy, clutched in an awful dance, soaking wet, both of them, and Emma Hanley still spraying Big Baby's face.

"Hey. Hey!" Jake said, and grabbed the boy from behind, shielding him, until he broke away, gasping, fists still moving. Everything stopped. The barking, the screaming, the water blasting.

Big Baby, clumsy with power, like King Kong battling planes, stood blinking with fury. He looked at Jake and yelled, "You better—" But his remaining response was lost when someone—a blur of a figure in a dress—swished by like an actor in a play, clobbered Big Baby on the head with a flowerpot, and disappeared.

"Owwwwww!"

"Holy shit," Jake whispered. He let go of Kyle. "Get behind me."

Big Baby really did look one—a bald, bad-tempered giant toddler, throwing a tantrum. Red geraniums and asparagus fern perched festively on his head and across his shoulders. He sputtered in rage, shaking off clumps of soil beaded with fertilizer.

Jake wondered about the gun. Every repo man had one.

He caught Emma Hanley's eye and mouthed, *Get back.*

Whoa, whoa. Big Baby fixed his poisonous stare on Jake. Probably thump his chest next. "Who the hell are you?"

"I'm the yardman," Jake said, stepping closer, offering his hand for a handshake, as if Big Baby hadn't just been brained. "Your daddy and me go back a ways. Unfortunately."

Big Baby ignored Jake's hand. "You know these crazies?"

"Yeah, I know them. Why? Is there a problem?"

"A *problem*? The problem is, I came over to do a simple repo. Real nice about it, too, and the whole bunch commences to attack me."

"Aw, you repo men were used to having folks riled up. What did you expect?"

"I didn't expect crazy-ass people! With hosepipes and flowerpots! And—" Big Baby ran a hand over his head, then peered down at the streak of blood on his palm. "Jesus, what happened to me?"

You just gave the term crackpot *new meaning*, Jake thought.

"Did you see what they did to me?" Big Baby demanded. "Did you see it?"

Kyle and the others huddled together under the big oak, like cattle in a storm. Still too close. Jake had two thoughts then, sharp and sobering as knives: He could not afford to take his eyes off Big Baby for a second. And that was *Dora* over there.

"Damn. I mean, *damn*. I'm going to need stitches, I just know it. I am going to call the law and press charges for assault."

"Yeah, I guess you could," Jake said, in a calm whisper. "Only the papers will get ahold of something like that, and the whole town will be laughing their heads off at a repo man scared off by a granny, a kid, and a dog. That wouldn't do good things for your business, now, would it?"

Big Baby took a bandanna out of his back pocket and pressed it to his head. He was bleeding, all right. And where was Gordon? Even Terrell might be some help. Jake couldn't take on Big Baby himself. "That's the last time I try to do something nice for people like this," Big Baby said.

"What you said to my mom wasn't nice," Kyle said from behind Jake. "It was an assault."

Good God, did this family have no common sense at all? These people knew nothing about the enemy, Jake thought with panic, whatever or whoever the enemy was. Could that boy not see that Jake's jabbing and teasing Big Baby wasn't an invitation for Kyle to jump in and rile him up all over again? And just when he'd nearly gotten Big Baby in his place, down a notch or two, so he'd at least listen to reason.

"That does it, you sorry little—"

"Okay, hold up," Jake said, and lay a hand on Big Baby's chest, which violated one of his basic rules of survival. Don't touch first. That Big Baby didn't haul off and slug him right now was a miracle. "Hey, let's me and you talk," Jake said, leaning into him hard now, because he had to get Big Baby away, fast, and there was only one way to do that. "Just hear me out," Jake said. "In private."

Big Baby stood still, considering his options, eyes narrowing, puzzlement grinding like gears. Only, in that primitive, dark mind, Jake mused, the wheel hadn't even been invented yet.

They stepped over behind the van, just out of sight from the others. "Most of you repo men are good ol' boys," Jake said, "and Lord I should know."

"Yeah? You done it, too?"

Jake smiled. "Nah. But I've been on the other side a time or two."

"Well, I'm reporting their asses," Big Baby said, "and I'm taking this vehicle in."

"I seem to recall something on the books about repo men having to stop if the vehicle owner asks them to. You know, something about how it's got to be peaceful."

Big Baby laughed. "Nobody pays attention to that, else we'd never get no work done."

"Tell you what." Jake took the cash out of his shirt pocket. "Let's pretend this whole thing never happened. Bet that's at least half your fee. Maybe more. So what would you say about holding off for a few days, just until the end of the week. Give them a few days, then they give it up peacefully. And you get your whole fee then, too, right?"

Big Baby took the cash, counted it, lips moving, brow furrowing. "Wait a minute," he said. "Why the payoff? You kin to them?"

"Are you kidding? Couple of them happen to work for me is all. And I'm a businessman, like you, and the day is wasting. Here's my card," Jake said, handing it over. "So you'll know how to reach me if you need to."

Big Baby stuffed the money in his pocket, but Jake knew better than to let his guard down. Only when Big Baby's truck roared away, spitting gravel, did Jake allow himself the luxury of pain. It was the running that started it, and breaking up the fight just made it worse.

Gordon appeared. "He gone for good?"

"Well, well. I was wondering where you disappeared to in my hour of need," Jake said.

"I went to get help," Gordon said, and held up a shovel.

"Was that to bury his carcass after I finished with him?"

"Knock him on the other side of the head."

"Where's Terrell?"

"Hiding. He owes Greasy."

Jake leaned against the back of the van, closed his eyes.

"You hurting," Gordon said. It wasn't a question.

"Naw. Just need a moment to get myself together."

But he didn't have a moment, because all of a sudden Emma Hanley was there. "Oh, Mr. Cary! Thank goodness you showed up when you did. I don't know what to say. I still can't fathom it. I don't know how to thank you—"

"All I did was get you a little more time."

"I don't ever want to see that horrible man again."

"You won't. Until Friday," Jake said. "He'll take that van then, unless you work something out. But at least you got a few days." They stepped back over to the driveway. Jake bit his bottom lip. Sometimes, it made the twinge back down.

"I'm just—shaking. Still," Emma Hanley said.

"It's all a big mistake," came the muffled, miserable reply from Dora, whose back was to them, who was hugging Kyle and not letting go. The broken zipper on her dress gaped like a wound.

"Mom? I'm okay. You can let go now," Kyle said.

"I just don't know what we would have done . . . ," Emma said, trailing off.

"You looked like you were doing just fine," Jake said.

"Why, we weren't, either. We were on the edge of something terrible, and you know it."

"Mom. Let go?" Kyle broke away from Dora.

She turned around, her glance skimmed smoothly past Jake, not snagged by his smile.

"Excuse me, miss?" Jake said with a grin. "Haven't we met before?"

She tugged at her waterlogged dress and did not look up. "This is all a terrible mix-up," she said, addressing everyone or no one.

"We're lucky Mr. Cary came by when he did," Emma said.

A sprig of fern fell from Dora's wet hair. She was drenched, mud-streaked, barefooted, one pale arm clutching the top of her ruined dress now, as if it were a bath towel. And then—did he think it or say it? Surely he didn't say it. But he must have, because Dora finally turned to him. Their eyes locked. She flushed, scarlet spilling across her cheeks, down her neck. *Dora Hanley, you haven't changed a bit.*

"Mr. Cary? Are you all right?" This was Emma Hanley now. "Would you like to sit down?"

And he tried to take a step, but for some reason, he couldn't. He couldn't move at all.

It's best we never speak again. In her slanted, tiny handwriting. That was all. She didn't even talk like that. It wasn't something she'd say. Not even—*Love.* Not even—*It's not easy.* Nothing. Oh, God. His back. He messed it up good is what he did, and there was so much to do, all that work, and now what? But Gordon was here, so it was okay. Gordon said, "Here, now, Jake, hold on," Gordon, whose eyes were too yellow, they would have to get Gordon to the VA, and he would just have to stop being so stubborn about it. Did Jake say that, too?

You did not fight pain; you did not take it on. You swam into the swell, you drifted with the tide, you kept your head up. His back his back his back. For some reason, his face was wet. The sun was gone, eclipsed, the day turned dark and quiet, the ground spun, grew closer. Someone said, "Oh, oh, oh, hold him," and Jake let go of the world for a minute to catch his breath.

"Mrs. Hanley, I seem to have ended up on your couch again," Jake said, looking up at her.

Emma forced a smile. "You just stretch out there as long as you need to."

"I'll be fine. Just need a few minutes."

"He's out of his head," one of the men said.

"I heard that," Jake said, eyes closed.

"You got something to take?" the other man asked. "Got you some pills?"

"Naw. I don't mess with that stuff anymore."

"Should we call your doctor?" Emma asked.

"No doctor," he said. "I'll be okay . . . really. This happens."

"Well, heavens. At least let me get you some water," Emma said. It had taken four of the men to move him. Kyle and Bobby and the two workers each with an assigned limb. They'd gathering speed up the porch steps, plummeting through the doorway—as if they were storming a castle door and Jake Cary was the log. She fretted he might have some permanent, paralyzing injury due to such rough handling. She returned from the kitchen with a glass of ice water, along with aspirin and an old bottle of pain pills left over from Mr. Hanley's root canal. Bobby, Kyle, and the two men stood around the couch, peering down at Jake. Dora, who still hadn't said a word, turned and fled down the hall. Emma was in a quandary about how to proceed.

The man named Gordon brought the glass of water over to Jake and held his hand out, two white pills in the center of his palm, like pinpricks of light.

"Here, man. Take these."

"What is it?"

The man looked at the bottle of pills Emma had handed him, squinted at the label. "Starts with a *V*." Jake tried to sit up. "Don't you know nothing?" his friend said. "Don't try to get up. You crazy?"

"We've got that whole apartment complex today," Jake said. "And three yards. Just mowing and edging today. Have to finish, get ready . . . for the bedding plants tomorrow."

"Yeah? You ain't going nowhere. It's funny you don't know that."

"Mr. Cary?" Emma said. "Please, just rest for a while. Is there anything at all I can do?"

She didn't think he'd heard her. He shut his eyes again. But after a minute, he said, "Mrs. Hanley, Gordon's in charge. If you could spare Bobby and Kyle, I'd appreciate it. We're a little short-handed."

"We are gonna be fine, Jake," his friend said. "Catch up in no time, you'll see. Ain't that right?" He looked up at the other man, then over at Bobby and Kyle.

"Uh . . ." Kyle looked at his grandmother.

"Of course," Emma said with a confidence she did not feel. "Don't you worry about a thing, Mr. Cary." She met Kyle's look of surprise with a reassuring nod and all the aplomb she could muster.

Emma knocked on the bathroom door.

"Dora?"

There was a furtive rustling, the whine of the bathroom sink faucet.

"You didn't tell me about him." The reply was barely a whisper. Better to have her head bitten off, Emma thought, than to hear this defeat.

"Him? You mean—"

"*Jake,*" came the whisper, fiercer now.

"Mr. Cary does my yard," Emma said. "And . . . this is what we need to discuss—he has been kind enough to offer to hire on Kyle and Bobby to help out. Open the door, please?"

Emma was relieved to see her daughter had gathered her wits about her and—though still damp-headed, puffy-eyed, and mascara-smudged—grimly pretty. She was wrapped in a bath towel, the grass-stained, sodden prom dress at her feet. No doubt she was mortified about bursting out of that ruined finery like a pupa. And nearly losing the van! Money trouble. Who would have guessed? Oh, but saving face was a most predictable trait in Dora. *Bless her heart, she gets that from me*, Emma thought. Out of that grab bag of genetic offerings, Dora had ended up with Emma's pride. Fallen arches or a weak chin, Emma mused, might have served her daughter in better stead.

"Now, I know you're angry about Kyle's visits and . . . everything," Emma said. She had decided the best approach was to swaddle the barbs of her confession in maternal firmness. "We have to sort through some things. You have every right to be upset, but the least you could do right now is let Kyle go along with Bobby and Mr. Cary's crew for the afternoon. They are shorthanded, and Mr. Cary can't even move. He's in awful shape. Just in torment. After what that poor man did for you out there—"

"I know," Dora said quietly.

Emma was speechless. She had prepared for a heated exchange, or a silent storming off. She had not expected this—Dora nodding sadly, her eyes filling.

"Why . . . Dora. My goodness." Emma felt the weight of pity settle on her, cool and functional as an X-ray apron. "Are you all right?"

Dora closed the bathroom door. The sink faucet screamed.

FOURTEEN

Though they appeared at first to be pitcher plants, with the thinnest pale membranes like skin, these things had grown into something sturdy and brave-looking, not delicate at all. Some of them spotted, some striped, a few of them big as a man's arm, reaching up from a boggy sludge. Ten yards over, in a stream of sunlight, a patch of blossoming wildness—sunflowers the size of hubcaps, with petals curled and looped, yellow as corn, the centers blue as autumn sky. A white trumpet creeper snaked up an oak, bonneted blooms glowing like lampshades. And there . . . there! A clump of flaxen buds in the corner—must have sprouted overnight—leaning toward him, stretching out their lavender throats, shining their ruby, sweet eyes, and sending that aching burst of perfume over to him, like a blown kiss. Like they were looking at *him*. Waiting for *him*.

"How's everyone getting on this afternoon?" Gordon asked.

Kyle nearly answered until he saw that Gordon was talking to a plant. "You the craziest bunch I ever seen," he said to a clutch of folded leaves at his feet.

Kyle's uncle walked over to a mossy stone. His knees popped as he knelt down. "The Secret Keepers," he said. "They have red faces. Red coats. The redcoats are coming. Ready or not."

"We gonna transplant," Gordon told Kyle. "We got to have things up there on the road ready to load by the time the truck gets back." Terrell had dropped off the three of them and then left to find the other crew members who were, Kyle learned, giving blood. Which was nice, but didn't they have work to do? Gordon handed Kyle and his uncle trowels. "But only what I say, hear? Don't go hog wild and dig up nothing unless I say."

"But is this—? I mean, aren't you afraid to dig up things—?" Kyle chose his words carefully. "Is this place yours?"

Gordon took a bottle out of his front pocket and took a swig. "I tend it."

Kyle nodded, biting his lip, and took a look around. A narrow footpath wound between rock-lined beds. Flowers and shrubs budded and bloomed, and the air was so sweet, it almost hurt to breathe.

"Remember what I said," Gordon said now, sounding almost stern. "About not telling a soul."

"Secret keepers," his uncle Bobby said.

"You got it, my man." Gordon said, and gave him a high five.

The thing was, Kyle thought, no one was about to stumble onto this place, because even if they got past the creepy run-down house, and through the kudzu and briars, they'd run into the wall of stink. The worst stench Kyle had ever encountered in his life, just fifty feet away. Like something had died. When he'd first smelled it, they were already halfway down the path with Gordon up ahead, and Kyle had frozen, as if he'd hit glass. He and his uncle nearly turned around, but Gordon, who'd tied his bandanna around his face like a bandit, motioned for them to follow. And so Kyle held his breath, continued down the path, and stumbled here, into the clearing, gulping in the honeyed air—finding it had turned just as suddenly sweet—as if he'd nearly drowned.

Kyle and Bobby spent the next hour digging up the things Gordon pointed out. They weren't allowed to take the ones that were blooming, only small plants with tender stems and fuzzy stalks. There seemed to be an order to things that only Gordon understood, and when he wasn't directing them, he was sitting down or leaning against the tree. He looked weary, dabbing at his wet face, batting away gnats, wilting in the afternoon heat. Once, he went to a pup tent under a tree at the far end of the garden and came back with candy bars and applesauce. "Keep your strength," he said, handing them out. Kyle and Bobby worked shoulder to shoulder, wrapping the plants with their plugs of soil in strips of newspaper until Gordon said, "That's it. We'll get us some more tomorrow."

Tomorrow. Kyle didn't know about tomorrow. The fact that he was able to work with the Blooming Idiots for the afternoon seemed to him a small miracle. *Run along*, his mother had told him behind the closed door of his grandmother's bathroom. The shower had been running.

He couldn't hear her well. He thought he'd misunderstood. "What?"

And then she'd said something about the van, *fixing the mix-up, picking up Sandy. You run along.* And so he'd been released by his mother. For a few hours. Which left him vastly relieved. Also confused and a little troubled. *Run along?*

The three of them sat down to rest on the border of smooth, cool rocks that encircled the garden. Kyle reminded his uncle to drink a can of Coke. He had to keep an eye on him; his uncle perspired a lot and grew red-faced, and he didn't drink enough water unless you reminded him. Kyle had somehow persuaded him to leave his cigarettes back at the truck.

"These here? Found them one night with my head," Gordon told them, patting the rock beside him. "All these noggin busters."

"You moved all these rocks yourself?"

"Naw, man. They was already here. Under leaf rot. I dug 'em out. One by one. Just like this—white and lined up, curved round like a mouthful of teeth. Figured something was about to eat me up, or else laughing at me." Gordon's chuckle turned into a dry hacking. His eyes watered, and he held a fist in front of his mouth.

"I've got dirty hands. Filthy hands," Bobby said, rubbing them together.

"Is there a place we could wash up?" Kyle asked.

Gordon sighed and shook his head. "Didn't you see them gloves up there in the truck?"

Kyle blushed. Were they being admonished?

But Gordon said, "Never mind. I ain't one to wear gloves, either. Come on over here and we'll get you all cleaned up."

They followed him until they came to a wooden bucket on a stump. Overhead, a vast network of large bamboo stalks tied to the trees. Gordon pulled a rope, and water trickled through some of them, dripping into the bucket. "Go on. Just stick your hands under there," Gordon said. When Kyle looked at him doubtfully, he said, "That's rainwater, the cleanest water you ever touched."

They washed their hands in the cool clear water, then wiped their hands dry on their pants legs. "Ever since I got the water going, I had visitors," Gordon said.

"I thought you said it was a secret place."

"Secret visitors, too. Had two deer come along this morning for a drink."

Kyle pictured the animals, black wet noses quivering, tottering on narrow hooves, as delicate as ladies.

"Raccoon, too," Gordon continued. "Owls. Pan-Sa."

"Pan who?"

"Never mind."

When it was time to go, they loaded up the plants on the wheelbarrow and braced themselves for the wall of stink ahead. Kyle took a last deep breath of the perfumed air, then raised his shirt to cover his mouth and nose and motioned for his uncle to do the same. The wheelbarrow was too full, and top-heavy. It wouldn't be easy to get back up the path to the road.

"Y'all crazy," Gordon said, laughing. He was talking to the plants again.

Jake opened his eyes to find Emma Hanley hovering over him.

"You look more pained than I am," he said.

"This is a delicate subject, Mr. Cary," she said. She stood nervously clutching her hands, before one broke free and flew to her collar, worrying the button there. "I was wondering if you needed—" Her voice dropped to a whisper. "—to use the . . . facilities?"

"I'm sorry?"

"Don't be. You are sofa-ridden."

"Oh. I gotcha. No thanks."

"I wouldn't want modesty to outweigh comfort."

"Not much danger of that, Mrs. Hanley." He looked at his watch. "Good Lord, it's late."

"I'm glad you got some rest."

"They'll be back directly. Gordon will help me up, and get me back home." At least, that's what Jake planned. It was why he wasn't moving a muscle until they got back. He had to reserve his strength. He had to heal enough to get back into his damn truck. And Dora? Where was she? He hadn't remembered seeing her with the others in the living room.

"Aspirin?"

Jake assured Emma that, no, he didn't need aspirin or water or a sandwich or television or a doctor. She nodded, but lingered still. "There's one more thing, Mr. Cary."

"I'm all ears."

"I've been meaning to ask you about those flowers in my garden. The ones you all planted last week. The red ones? Bobby calls them Secret Keepers, isn't that funny? What *are* they?"

" 'Secret Keepers' sounds good to me."

"They appear . . . old-fashioned. Like some kind of heirloom plant." She paused. "Actually, they resemble some sketches in my grandfather's diary. They are . . . extraordinary. I wanted to give you a proper thank-you."

"It was nothing." They were just a bunch of wacky plants, but Jake didn't say so, because Mrs. Hanley was clearly moved.

She pulled up a chair near him and sat down. She took off her glasses, polished them with the hem of her blouse, and put them back on. Even behind the lenses, her pale ice-blue eyes shone bright with intelligence. "A little while ago, I went out to the mailbox, and

I just happened to walk by the flower bed and I leaned down and smelled one of those . . . Secret Keepers. I tell you, Mr. Cary, I was back in time, holding my firstborn, smelling his head. Will, three days old. All of a sudden, I was standing"—her voice sped up—"right over at my bedroom window, and I had him wrapped in that yellow receiving blanket the hospital gave us, and I thought this is mine, this is my baby forever, and no one can ever take this moment away from me. It was the smell of my baby's head, that brand-new *tender* skin like *nothing else* in this world, and the barest whiff of mother's milk, and Ivory soap, and a smidge of the hospital antiseptic. It was a perfect bouquet of aromas. I can't explain it. Can you?" She watched his expression carefully.

"No, Mrs. Hanley. I'm afraid I can't . . . explain it. But I guess it doesn't matter if you—"

"Is that what they reminded you of, though? You and the others? A newborn baby?"

"I don't recall anyone mentioning that."

"Oh," she said, sitting back in the chair now. "Well, my mind is going."

Jake laughed gently. "I wouldn't say that."

"I suspected as much. Dementia. There have been signs."

"Maybe you just got yourself an extra-sharp sniffer."

"It's just . . . it was *uncanny*. I don't mind telling you . . . that aroma brought tears to my eyes." She stood up. "I'm just going to have to pick one of those Secret Keepers, Mr. Cary, and bring it in here so you can have a try."

Jake shut his eyes as her footsteps faded away. Sleep eluded him, however. The pills—whatever they were that Gordon had handed him—were wearing off. The hazy cloud of comfort began to thin and lift; the steely blades of pain approached, the iron bars of his worrisome predicament glinted. He began to fret about the backlog of work. Just how was he going to pay the Blooming Idiots for the rest of the week? Lines of numbers floated around in his head, but he couldn't get them to be still long enough to add up. And then he sensed someone was there again, hovering. He opened his eyes.

"I didn't mean to wake you," Dora said.

He tried to sit up—pure instinct—but the twinge was hiding in his spine, spiteful as a demon. He stifled his groan. "You didn't," he managed.

She had changed out of the torn wet dress and into a pale yellow blouse and a khaki skirt, perfectly respectable. Her hair was pulled back, her head down, and she gripped a purse under one arm, as if she were about to dash out into a downpour.

"Is it real bad? Your back?"

"It's better. Flares up fast, but heals quick." If only.

"I'm sorry you had to deal with that awful man." There was a deeper, richer timbre to her voice now, without its peal of girlishness. "I'm just sick about it."

"It was nothing."

She looked over at the large bay window and watched her mother stroll at the edge of the garden, holding a pair of scissors in one hand, moving from flower to flower, thrusting her face in each.

"How long have you been back in town?" she asked.

"Not long. Landed at my dad's old place for now. What's left of it."

"Mama said you do her yard now. I didn't know. . . ."

"That boy of yours didn't mention it?"

"He doesn't tell me anything." Dora's gaze followed her mother's progress around the garden. "No one tells me anything."

"Huh. Well, he's a nice kid."

"He gives me fits," she said. "You have children?"

"Nope. Never got around to it."

Her gaze moved briefly to his face, followed the length of him, to his feet. Someone had taken off his boots. The top of one toe peered out mischievously from a hole in his sock. Just his luck not to wear his good pair today.

"I figured you'd be mayor of this town by now," he said. The afternoon sun shone through the window, bathed his face. He squinted in the glare.

She moved to the window and angled the blinds, cutting the sunlight. He could not see her face.

"I mean, being as how you were president of the school and all," he said.

She stationed herself at the end of the couch again, serious as a sentinel. "Vice president, you mean," she said, "of the junior class."

"You sure were damn good at speeches."

"I guess my children would say I give them too many speeches," she said. "Not that they listen."

"Funny how things turn out. Remember career day? Some test they had us take? They told me I'd be a good forest ranger. I thought it was crazy, but you told me it would suit me." He laughed. "I guess that's just about what I've ended up doing."

The snipping sounds of scissors grew louder. Jake could tell Mrs. Hanley was directly outside the window now, cutting flowers and stems, oblivious of her audience.

"Jake," Dora said. It was the first time that whole afternoon she'd addressed him by name. She perched rigidly on the coffee table across from him and met his eyes. Something in him shifted, broke loose. "I called every day when they brought you back," she said. "Every day. You were on the fourth floor. I knew when they got you stabilized at the VA and then . . . when they discharged you. I prayed for you, for your healing. You don't know how hard. I wanted to tell you that for the longest time. But after Will . . . I just . . . ." Her voice drifted off. "You probably thought I didn't even care. . . . I'm sorry if it seemed like that."

He laughed. "Well, I accept your apology, Dee. Even if it is a few years late." Her eyes darkened, gray as damp slate. Was *apology* too strong a word? No. No—it was the nickname. That was it. *Dee* just slipped out. Maybe because he needed her to stop feeling sorry for him. To stop looking so damn sad. There were good times, too, before the bad at the end. Didn't she remember those? He'd taught her to drive a stick shift. Held a ladder for her once in the school cafeteria while she hung stars and streamers, his hand wrapped around her thin ankle. Listened to her rehearse her speech for student council. Drove her and Wanda to Mexico. Monday mornings, her skin would be red from a weekend of his unshaven caresses. Where did love like that go? It branded you, ruined you. Afterwards, the rest never really measured up. Love like that was harder to get rid of than you thought.

"I wrote you a lot of letters," he said. "While I was recuperating."

She looked away. "I never got them."

"I never sent them." He smiled, and a powerful need for some dignity clawed in him, feral and desperate. He decided right then he would sit up, because he just couldn't lie helpless and weak like this for one more minute. He inched up, slowly, slowly, but no. No! He winced. *Damn.*

"Don't," she said, standing. "Please don't, Jake."

And then there was the sound of Mrs. Hanley's footsteps on the porch, and the screech of the front door swinging open, and Dora bolted. Emma Hanley glided slowly in view, elegant as a swan, and stood in the hallway with her back to Jake while she murmured something to Dora. Jake groped for the pill bottle, and shook it. A lone Vicodin rattled like tooth. He swallowed it dry. And then the front door opened and closed and a car started up, and she was gone. Dora was gone.

Mrs. Hanley stood over him again. "I got carried away," she said. "What with the cosmos and daylilies, and everything else. You know how it is. You step out for a minute in the garden to pluck one thing, and suddenly time stops. . . ." She held the gathering of long-stemmed flowers in the crook of her arm like a beauty queen. She sighed, and looked at him with a tired smile. "It grieves me to report that I was wrong . . . about this." She held up a vibrant red flower. "The Secret Keepers don't smell like a newborn baby's head. They don't have an aroma at all."

"I'm sorry to hear that," he said, his voice thick with gloom. A couple of cold ones would kick-start that pill, but he doubted Mrs. Hanley had beer. He'd just look desperate and rude if he asked. And he wasn't rude. Desperate was another story.

She smelled each petal, inhaled deeply, and shrugged sadly. "Nothing." Jake took the flower from her and took a dismissive whiff. He wasn't prepared for the explosion. Aromatic sparks erupted in his brain, fluttering wild as bonfire embers. Baby oil. A trace of Breck shampoo. Vodka and grape Kool-Aid. A sun-warmed nylon cot. The barest whiff of reefer. Coconut sunblock. Sweet stickiness. The smell of Dee Hanley's neck.

FIFTEEN

He was irritated with her for dropping by unannounced. He was busy, he did not like surprises, she knew that, but she hadn't planned on coming until she found herself here, in the parking lot. Inside, she found Donny's corner office empty. No desk, no chairs, no lights. No family pictures. The receptionist shrugged—"I'm just a temp"—and went back to her phone lines. Dora, her heart in her throat, wandered through the office hallway—eerily quiet in the lunch hour—until she came to the last room, windowless and cramped, and there was Donny, hidden behind the Sports section of the newspaper. She recognized his loafers.

"Donny?"

The paper came down like a drawbridge. He looked back at her with alarm, then scrambled to his feet. "What's wrong?"

"Nothing's wrong." *Liar.*

She sat across from him in a dingy, armless chair that wobbled.

"You couldn't call first?" he asked. He sighed, folded the newspaper, and sat down hard behind his desk, looking flustered and put out.

"I was confused when I came in . . . your office is empty."

"This *is* my office."

"Oh." He hadn't bothered to tell her. "Why?"

"We're getting crowded in this building," he said. "As a matter of fact, I told Gus I didn't mind moving down the hall." He stretched and stifled a yawn, but the gestures were practiced ones, designed to convey reassurance, and she felt a wave of unease. "I'm mostly out meeting clients anyway. I stayed in today because everyone else is at a team lunch before a few holes of golf, but I'm here"—he slapped the desk—"to catch some leads"—then patted the phone affectionately.

"Maybe you should be at the lunch with everyone else," she said, and regretted it immediately. It was the kind of unguarded statement that drew his ire. "I mean," she said quickly, "it's a shame you have to stay here and work so hard and miss a business lunch that everyone else . . ." She swallowed and looked around the tiny cramped room. "Is it okay here, Donny? Working for Gus and all? Because if you—"

"Have you no faith in me?" His voice was smooth and low and angry. They'd had this conversation. His thoughts might as well have been scrolling across his forehead like a teleprompter. How easy it would be for him to give up his new career and go back to being a lowly manager of a hardware store again. How easy it would be to buckle under strife, to fail to succeed and reap riches, for *He chastens whom he loves. Hebrews 12.* He sacrificed for her, for the children; he had mouths to feed.

"The hardship I brought on us . . . is all my fault," she said. The sock sale at Penney's, and the new shower curtains, the vacuum, the Agape place settings. "For being greedy. For . . . all that . . . shopping."

He was pleased now. His face closed. He pursed his lips, reached across the desk, and squeezed her hand. *The wife is the manager of the home, but the husband is the manager of the wife,* Pastor Pete had instructed them last week during Model Marriage Mentor training. She and Donny were supposed to help couples just starting out—show them how to *build a firm foundation,* to *carve a bedrock* for a solid Christian marriage—as if newlyweds needed to arm themselves with little picks and axes. Dora thought young couples like that didn't need advice; they seemed so eager and all over each other. It was the mentors that needed a lifeline.

And now was the part she'd rehearsed. The envelope was concealed in her purse, and she fingered it like a talisman. "The van . . . ," was all she could manage. Her mind clouded with shame. "They said they would take it. Donny, they just . . ."

"Shhhh," he hissed. He got up to shut the door, a complicated task that involved moving a trash can and shoving a filing cabinet away from the doorframe. He brushed the dust off his hands. "When?" His voice held no surprise. He knew. Maybe Donny was even trying to teach her a lesson, to show her just how close her shopping had come to ruining the family.

Yesterday, but she couldn't very well say that. He'd want to know why she hadn't told him last night, after a family dinner so achingly tranquil—Kyle holding forth in his cheerful Good Son routine, but studying her with his sideways glances—that she hadn't had the stomach to spoil the evening. And then sometime around four in the morning, she decided she would tell Donny, but only after she found a way to fix the problem.

"He"—the memory of that horrid Big Baby man leapt up in her mind like a snarling dog—"*they* said we had until Friday. To pay." It took all her strength to say those words in a normal tone. "I didn't even know we were behind—"

"Don't worry," he said. "I'll take care of it. They just made a mistake is all." Relief flooded through her, pure habit, before she caught herself. For this was no mistake. She'd called the dealership finance company herself yesterday, and that wasn't all. This morning, she'd discovered their joint checking account balance— grocery money—was down to double digits. Most frightening of all were the bank statements she'd unearthed after some shameful digging through old papers and two trash bags at home—and despite the coffee grinds and oily stains, she could clearly see Donny's own checking account had ninety-eight dollars. Of course, since most of the accounts were in his name, she couldn't know for sure.

Maybe there were others. He had it all organized just so, and he worked so hard selling buildings or—whatever he sold—socking it all away. The home expense account—she thought she remembered Donny talking about that—had probably been tapped out from her shopping and that's why the van bill didn't get paid.

"I want to fix this mess," she said. "This hole I dug."

"I *said* I'd take care of it, Dora."

"But . . . how?" And now all her points flew from her head, escaping. She would not close her eyes; she would not. She would face up to this. "Mama offered to give me . . . us . . . enough to catch up. Just a little loan until—"

His blistering stare stopped her. "Your *mother?*"

She nodded. A poisonous silence followed. He drew himself up and glared back at her, hard and distant, furious as a stained-glass martyr. *Dad's getting all, like, Old Testament on my ass,* she'd once overheard Kyle say to someone on the phone.

"*You* asked for money from your *mother?*"

"I didn't exactly ask, Donny. She offered—"

"Don't You Think I Work Hard For You?" Each word like a nail pounding.

"I know you do," she said.

"Then why don't you work hard for *me?*"

"I was thinking . . . I could find a job somewhere. Just part-time to—"

"Work? *Work?* You're my *wife.* How would that look, Dora? I'll tell you how it would look. Like I can't earn enough for my family."

She nodded, discomfited again by the sight of the cramped room, which did not resemble an office so much as a storage space. There were some old real estate signs propped in the corner beside a coatrack, a doorless microwave on the floor. "Everyone is watching, Dora. All I ask is that you raise my children in the way of the Lord. That you keep a clean house and have food on the table. That's your work, Dora. Leave the rest to me."

The phone rang, startling her. Donny did not answer it so much as clobber the thing. He appeared to listen intently while

he doodled on his calendar. When she stood, he cradled the
phone, reached for his wallet, and handed her a ten. *Dry cleaning*,
he mouthed.

At Spring Daze Dry Cleaners, where she picked up Donny's suit,
Dora stood too long breathing in the steamy, sharp cleanness, in-
haling until people behind her in line began to clear their throats.
It wouldn't be half bad to work there, really. People dropped off
their smelly heaps of clothes, and later, you handed them back—
starched, pressed, folded elegantly over hangers, cloaked in the
whispery gossamer of cellophane. She didn't even mind the chem-
ical odor, the brutal steaminess that slightly burned her nostrils.
It felt . . . purifying.

She went by the bank and cashed her mother's check. Harold
and Emma Hanley. Her mother hadn't even gotten around to taking her father's name off the account. One thousand dollars. Part
of the Trip money no doubt, now Dora's mistake money. When
she drove to the car finance company and handed over the cash
through the little mouse hole in the window, they told her the
money would catch up late payments on the van. She'd hoped it
might pay off a good chunk of the balance.

How would she even broach the subject again with Donny?
When he discovered she'd accepted her mother's money, that they
were literally in her mother's debt, he would be beyond reasoning.
She couldn't even begin to tell him all the rest—about Kyle working at that outdoor job with Bobby, fibbing the whole time about
Saving Souls, and how her mother had hired Dora's old flame, a
man who just happened to be sleeping on her mother's sofa. Dora
wouldn't think about any of that right now, either.

She wouldn't think about taking Kyle over to her mother's that
morning for the second day of work *just for the week, Kyle, that's
it* and Jake in the living room, sitting in a careful, brittle way, sipping a mug of coffee. Just as he turned toward her, Dora had
stepped out of sight in the hall. Still, she felt his gaze follow her
through the walls and around corners and into the kitchen where

she stood at the window and watched the truck pull up. She felt
Jake's dark eyes on her even when the men got out and came to
the door, and helped him stand up and walked him over to truck,
her mother warning them *easy easy*, and Bobby nervously pacing
along, like a border collie. And after she watched Kyle jump up in
the truck bed with an easy confidence that startled her, and they
drove off, leaving mica-glinted clouds of dust, disappearing down
the white-dash-lined highway and through town, onto that narrow
back road, taking Jake into his sorry daddy's slapdash single-wide
trailer, which was probably half rust by now—even then, Dora
still felt Jake's steady gaze.

*Wanda weeping—Dora cradled her head, and Bobby . . . we can't
tell anyone, not a soul, you hear? You promise?*

She wouldn't think about that, either. It was hard sometimes
to remember all the things she shouldn't think about. After a
while, the brackish inky memories burbled up and spilled, pollut-
ing her thoughts, no matter what she shopped for, or how many
Firm Believers aerobics classes she taught, or what kind of fervent
prayers she offered up to Jesus. Just last night, she was shelling peas,
fighting tears, thinking about how she would tell Donny that a
repo man had been stalking them, and beseeching the Lord for
help, *please, Lord, just give me a sign,* when all of a sudden Sally
Struthers came on television, and Dora's living room was filled
with starving children with bloated stomachs and flies in their
eyes. Clearly, the Lord had more important things to tend to than
Dora's credit card debt.

SIXTEEN

There's a new medication we're trying these days, Bobby."
The doctor did not seem to include Emma in the conversation. He looked from Bobby to the file, bulging with
its years of misery, layered like filthy petticoats, contents spread
immodestly across the counter. "Hmmm. I wonder . . . ," he
said several times, ". . . why . . . didn't? . . . well . . . I've got an
idea." He was rather young, but already bald, this doctor. Or
perhaps he shaved his head, a fashion statement Emma found as
puzzling as his gold stud earring. Well, he was a homosexual,
then. It wasn't like Emma was naïve. She read the papers. She
watched the news with Tom Brokaw every night. The homosexuals weren't afraid about what people thought about them anymore. It was just the AIDS that scared them. Oh, but that must
make it so difficult to be a dandy these days. It turned you into a
skeleton with those awful hollowed-out eyes. She thought of all
the young handsome men who were dying of the AIDS every
day. And Rock Hudson. Rock Hudson, of all people, dead just
two years. She could still remember him in *Pillow Talk*—it was
one of the last pictures she and Harold had attended together in
a theater. After the children were born, it got harder and harder
to get out.

"It might give you some relief with such a loss of affect." The doctor wrote out a prescription and then glanced at Emma, and unfortunately, she hadn't bothered to pull herself together yet, thinking about Rock Hudson and Doris Day frolicking on the silver screen, and now both of them . . . gone. Oh, where had the years gone?

"Mrs. Hanley?"

"Yes?" She pulled a balled-up tissue from the sleeve of her cotton sweater and dabbed at her nose.

"We have a family group meeting here every week. It might be good for you. For both of you."

"Oh, no thank you."

"You can talk to the social worker—"

Social worker? She wouldn't repeat that mistake again.

"—she'll talk to you and set something up before you go."

"Oh, that's not necessary," she said, but the doctor darted out of the examining room, and before Emma could gather their things and herd Bobby out, there was a quick knock as a big blond woman burst in.

"Hello, there." The woman looked up at Emma and Bobby from her clipboard. "Why, I know you." She thrust out her hand to Bobby. "You work with Jake, right?"

Bobby allowed his hand to be shaken.

"So, Bobby," the woman asked. "What did you and Jake do to our garden?"

"We got things going there. Underneath," Bobby said.

"Yeah, you sure did. You tell Jake to come by and see me, okay? I've got to talk to him."

"Is something . . . wrong?" Emma asked.

"Yep. What's wrong is I can't get Lola out of the garden," she was addressing Bobby now. She was teasing. This big brash woman with the red triangle earrings. "Since you guys planted those—whatever they are—those gorgeous creations—Lola is outside all the time."

Lola must be the woman's daughter. Emma felt quite sure. "What kind of flowers?" she asked.

"Oh, my God, you should see them. They are these—I dunno they popped up—"

Emma thought of her own flower bed. Every morning, she was disappointed to find the Secret Keepers' aroma had not returned. Still, just in the last week, other flowers were blooming. Different ones that Jake's crew brought in.

The woman turned to Emma, extended her hand. "I'm Hannah Bradley, by the way. I'm your helper."

"Helper?" Emma asked, shaking the young woman's hand. Apparently, women shook hands now as if they were men. The young ones did, anyway. "But I thought you were a social worker."

"I prefer the term *helper*. That's what I do. Hmmm. Bobby, you've taken some great strides here, with the job, and I see Dr. V has you trying new meds. Let's set some other goals, shall we? Are you interested in housing? Your own place, I mean?"

"Bobby lives with me," Emma said. Honestly, did these people not read the files?

"Yep, I know," the woman said, still looking at Bobby. "You might be interested in Homes of Hope. We have one group home, real small, for adults. There's a waiting list, but you have a job, you'd probably qualify faster. Since Jake is your employer, we could ask him to fill out some paperwork." And now she turned to address Emma, chirpy as a tour guide. "And Mom, it would mean structure for Bobby. Meds, meals, friends, independence."

"You mean after . . . after I'm gone?" Emma asked.

She shrugged. "I mean soon. It's up to Bobby. You should talk about it. How about I arrange for the two of you to visit?"

"A group home, you said?" Emma asked.

"It's a real neat place. Over near Lavinia Avenue? Are you familiar with the area?"

"Quite."

"Meanwhile . . . hmmmm." The woman's fingers thrummed on the counter. "I think we should work on fun."

"Fun?" Emma asked.

"Yep. Some goals for fun. Let's start with that."

Fun. Yes, why not?

After they left the clinic, Emma dropped off Bobby to join Kyle at the appointed place, a new neighborhood the crew was landscaping called Sparrow Woods. The owner of such a place must have a wicked sense of irony in coming up with such a name, Emma thought, for there wasn't a sparrow or a tree in sight on the cleared lots. Not anymore. The Blooming Idiots certainly had their work cut out on this blank slate, Emma thought. She took a tube of sunblock out of her purse when Kyle spotted them and walked over. "Here," she said, handing it over. "The two of you need to reapply every half an hour. You don't want to get blistered."

"Okay," Kyle said, and handed Bobby work gloves. "Uncle B, we got weed duty."

It had been two weeks now. Two weeks since Dora had given her consent to Kyle's working with Jake's crew. Or not consent exactly, but a kind of prickly compliance that had morphed into guarded permission. Dora dropped Kyle off in the morning and picked him up in the afternoon. Who knew why exactly? Kyle was mum on the subject, and that was fine with Emma. It was best not to probe. With Dora you walked on eggshells; that was nothing new. Emma did not even ask her daughter about the family's money situation. She had, however, received the canceled check with Dora's signature on the back. The money was a gift as far as Emma was concerned, though Dora insisted she was going to pay it back. It didn't matter. What mattered was that Bobby and Kyle were working together, happy as beetles in dung.

"Where is Mr. Cary?" she asked Kyle.

"He's not here right now. He stays at his place and does paperwork in the afternoon sometimes."

"Oh. I see." Paperwork. That poor, poor man. He was no doubt still trying to recover from his injury, resting afternoons after mornings of labor. "I'm going to pay a quick visit to Miss Gibble on the way home. You'll be okay?"

"Fine, Grandma," Kyle called as he and Bobby joined two of the other men near the entrance.

As she pulled into a parking place at Monaghan, Emma sighed and looked warily at the entrance of the nursing home. She would go see her friend. It was only right. Oh, but the place did depress her so. No wonder Miss Gibble was such a curmudgeon. Who wouldn't be, in a place such as this?

Inside, at the receptionist desk, Emma was vastly relieved to be directed by a nurse to the courtyard outside. Away from the tan plastic trays of puddings, creamed corn, and Jell-Os stacked in the hall, the vacant or accusing stares, the sweet stench of aged humans slowly gummed to death in the maws of an institution. Out back, the courtyard glimmered green in the summer sun, a portal to paradise. Miss Gibble sat at a small cement patio table and smiled, as if she'd been expecting Emma's visit all along. She patted the seat beside her. "Come, my dear."

Emma sat. "You're looking quite . . . fine," she told her friend, and was struck by the truth of her own statement. Miss Gibble did look better than she had for quite some time. Clear-eyed with a hint of a smile. "My goodness," Emma said, looking around, "things are looking spruced up out here, aren't they?"

"The work of idiots," Miss Gibble said.

"Blooming Idiots. Yes."

"Excellent work."

Emma spied a clump of tiny blue flowers, a thatch of yellow blooms, two large lacy fronds, and several thick, ornate stalks of . . . something quite intriguing. No Secret Keepers, though, which was a disappointment.

Miss Gibble, pointing to the yellow flowers near her, leaned in closer to whisper, "They listen to me, Emma. They follow me with their eyes."

And indeed, the flowers, vibrant yellow, plumed, glossy bluish centers lashed with petals, seemed to stand in rapt attention, observing.

"Perhaps they're similar to touch-me-nots. Or prayer plant," Emma said. "They may respond to sound or touch—"

Miss Gibble clicked in disbelief. "Why, these are soul shines. I haven't seem them in years."

"Soul shines?"

"My goodness, Emma, if anyone should know about them, you should. You brought bouquets of them to me after I lost my Eric in the war. Surely you recall that spring. After the funeral and everyone was gone, you brought me soul shines every week. They sat on my kitchen table every day, awaiting my return from teaching those horrid guttersnipes."

"I do remember trying to cheer you."

"You brought them in a jelly jar. You got them from the yard at the rooming house."

"Amaranth?" Emma said, but Miss Gibble had turned back to the flowers, and her face softened, as if she were gazing down at a sleeping infant. Emma watched her friend pluck a shiny object from her pocket and hold it to her cheek. "Is that—?"

"My locket," Miss Gibble answered. "It was in the safe with the valuables, but I asked the nurse to bring it to me this morning. I plan to wear it always."

"Aren't you afraid—" Emma searched for the words, for she was mindful of the need to be tactful. Anything of value in a place such as Monaghan Nursing Home would surely be pilfered. "—that it might be lost or . . . stolen?"

"It's already good as gone if it sits locked up in an airless vault, Emma." Miss Gibble studied the locket in her palm as if it were a compass, then made a fist. "When it's next taken from me, it will be pried off my stiff, cold carcass."

"Oh, Miss Gibble, honestly." Emma stifled a laugh. "Here, let me to put it on you, then," she said, standing.

Her friend nodded firmly, dropped her head while Emma fastened the necklace. Miss Gibble then straightened and looked again at the flowers, turning this way and that, as if admiring her own reflection.

"Soul shines," Emma said, musing.

"*Animus mico*. From the Latin."

"Why, how did you know that?"

"The plant lover told me." Miss Gibble's eyes widened in exasperation. Or was it mischief?

"Oh," Emma said. Then, "Who?"

"A lifetime ago," Miss Gibble said with a sigh. "I thought I lost them . . . those pictures in my head." She smiled drowsily. "But they're back, aren't they, Emma?"

On her way to her car, Emma glimpsed a figure approaching in the wavy heat of the parking lot. As he drew closer, she saw it was Dr. Burnside. She was thankful for the sweltering heat on the asphalt, for it helped explain her reddening face. Only then did she admit to herself that running into Dr. Burnside was one of the reasons she happened to drop by that day to visit Miss Gibble. Friday was guest-speaker day at Monaghan; somehow she'd absorbed that fact along the way. And there he was, as if she'd conjured him up herself, smiling in recognition, bobbing along in his brittle, steady gait, holding a tray of slides with both arms in front of him, as if it were a cake.

"Why, Dr. Burnside. How nice to see you again." He wore the same blue suit he had for the Lunch and Learn. Perhaps he was a frugal man, or more likely, Emma mused, he was used to travel and packing lightly.

"Mrs. Hanley?"

She nodded with a smile. He remembered her name, and this pleased her.

"I hope you'll be attending my talk."

"Oh, well, I'd love to, but I just dropped in to visit a friend," she said. "I'm afraid I have to get home. My son will be off work

soon, and . . . I am so happy to run into you, Dr. Burnside, because I was hoping to talk with you about a question I have—"
She was rambling. She stopped and cleared her throat.

"Let's get out of this heat, shall we?" he said, and they headed
inside to the lobby. There, they sat on a worn sofa—Dr. Burnside
with his slides in his lap, Emma perched nervously beside him.

"Am I holding you up from your talk?" she asked.

"Oh . . . I doubt there's any rush," he said. He had a pleasant,
rich voice, without a trace of an accent. She wondered where he
was brought up. She'd heard that people with no accents were
usually from Florida. "I'll try to make it worth their wait," he said.

He took a small starched white handkerchief from his pocket
and dabbed his forehead. A man with a handkerchief was a wonderful thing, Emma thought, for it was a civilized habit, and she
brightened at the thought of telling so to Lila.

"I have the most unusual . . . plant in my garden," she said.

He trained his cobalt blue gaze on her. She realized he was
waiting for her to continue, and for a minute she grew flustered.
What was wrong with her? Had she lost the art of conversing
with strangers?

"The aroma is . . ." And here again she lost her footing. How
to describe the power of that first whiff—Will in her arms again,
milky sweet. "Breathtaking. Magical."

"Perhaps it's a hallucinogen," he mused.

"You mean," she said, horrified, "a drug?"

"It's easy to forget the hallucinatory properties of plants.
Opium from poppies. Mushrooms. There's a reason the common
morning glory is called heavenly blue," he said.

Just then the Activities Director bounded over, a big blond
woman wearing sweatpants and sporting a whistle. She introduced
herself and took the slides from Dr. Burnside. He stood to follow
her down the hall.

Emma rose as well. She was painfully aware it would be much
too forward to ask Dr. Burnside to take a look at the Secret
Keepers in her garden, and wished him well. He must have

sensed her quandary, for he said, "Mrs. Hanley, I'd be glad to help identify your specimen. May I call you?"

"Certainly. My number is in the phone book. Under Hanley. *Harold* Hanley. I'm a widow," she added, mortified she'd felt the need to clarify the issue. The statement sounded tawdry. What kind of thing was that to say?

"Soon, then," he said, and she met his blue gaze, glinting like bottle glass in the soft folds of his face. "Soon, before I depart. We'll get to the bottom of this."

"Depart?"

"I'm leaving. Heading out of the country next week."

"I see. Not settling, then?"

"Old habits die hard."

"They certainly do," she said with a grim smile.

Jake was in a boxing ring, and he couldn't get a good swing at his opponent. The referee kept ringing the bell. His father, young and shirtless, grinning and drunk, was about to belt him. Jake swung, but the bell rang again and he had fled to his corner and spit out blood. This time it was Will Hanley dancing around in the middle. *You banging my sister, man?* Jake swung and missed. The bell rang and rang and rang and then it was JJ there swinging at him, yelling *pick up pick up*.

"Goddamn it, Jake, pick up the phone. I know you're there. Pick up, man, because my blood is boiling."

Jake wasn't asleep exactly, but he was floating along just fine, thanks to his daily pain pill—a muscle relaxant he was weaning himself off of because he hated being woozy like this. He was on the lookout for a chiropractor who needed some landscaping done, barter himself a spinal alignment. The bell stopped ringing. Now there was just this angry voice nipping at him until it was silenced, mercifully, by a beep.

He opened his eyes, startled for a minute to find himself in his father's trailer. No, *his* trailer. No. He would never get used to the idea it was *his* trailer. He wasn't living here. He was just staying here. *Your daddy is the lonesomest man there ever was,* Jake's mother used to say, as if that excused things. She could never quit Tom Cary. Even when he came home drunk and mean, or just mean; even after he stopped coming home at all. He got himself this trailer while Jake and his mother still lived over in the two-bedroom rental on Second Avenue, and ended his life as solitary and poor as he'd lived it. *He's in my blood, I reckon. You can't pick who you love.*

He sat up too fast. The pain radiated from his back to his leg, bearable though, and better. He limped to the kitchen, peered into the refrigerator: mayonnaise, a block of cheese, a bag of apples, a six-pack. He made himself a sandwich and ate it over the sink.

At Palmetto Bank & Trust, the Blooming Idiots spread out on the grounds with the stealth and calm of soldiers. Gordon loaded the wheelbarrow—his job—only his. He didn't trust any of the others, because you needed gentle hands and a certain unhurried rhythm to untangle roots and settle in transplants. He bundled together four groups of the plants and handed them to Kyle and Bobby. The rest of the group dug holes.

"Where's Jake Cary?" a voice demanded. Only when Terrell stopped singing to answer did Gordon realize the music running through his head had been Terrell's song all along. If you didn't watch out, Gordon mused, you might think things were real when they were just vapors. It was easier than you thought.

"He'll be around directly," Gordon told his brother before Terrell could launch into one of his long-winded stories. JJ turned, startled to see Gordon standing there, his arm on a shovel. JJ looked Gordon up and down. His eyes narrowed when he spied the bottle in Gordon's shirt pocket.

"You tell Jake to come in right away and talk to me."

Gordon shrugged. "Might be tomorrow. Might be the next day."

"You telling me he left this crew—unsupervised? At my bank? With not a soul in charge?"

"I'm in charge," Gordon said. "Can't vouch for the soul. Maybe

I got one, maybe not." He looked his brother in the eye. "We finishing up."

"Finishing? What you call these humps of dirt everywhere? I want daisy-looking things. I want it looking good."

Gordon smiled into the sky. "You gonna get your flowers, my brother," he said.

The rest of the group lumbered over and stood around JJ in a circle. JJ looked over them, glanced at a customer coming out the bank, and shook his head.

Gordon said, "They don't see us."

"What you mean, don't see you? That the likker talking?"

"Your customers coming in and out, parking and leaving, don't none of them really see folks like us," Gordon said. "If that's what's got you worried."

"Well, I see just fine." JJ looked at Sweet, who sat panting in the shade. "Don't tell me you brought that dog here."

Gordon shrugged. "I'm not telling you nuthin'." He turned his back on his brother and knelt down to examine the soil.

"Oh, look how they love you, Gordon," Lay Down Sally squealed, pointing to the flowers. And it was true, the yellow blooms seemed to lean toward Gordon. His face was bathed in gold.

"The process is technically identifying energies from the mind, and translating them back," Bobby said, leaning in closer to Gordon. Terrell started singing "Build Me Up Buttercup." JJ muttered something about calling *that sorry-ass Jake*, then turned on his heel and strode back into the bank.

Kyle sighed in relief. Jake would handle it. As far as Kyle was concerned, it was nearly quitting time on a Friday, and the Blooming Idiots didn't need some kind of disagreement to get them waylaid. He and Bobby had to get back to his grandmother's soon. If they got there before his mother picked him up, Kyle would go in the back room and call Julie and tell her he had their concert tickets. He'd bought them with his own money today at lunch. One week from tomorrow. Van Halen. He and Julie would ride with Tee and the others. He'd need an alibi for the day, but he'd think of something. Things were easier now that his mother wasn't watching him like a freaking detective or something. He'd even been able to sneak out to the cemetery parties again. Yep, his mother had laid off him for a while, maybe because she had a se-cret, and Kyle knew her secret, and he'd promised not to tell.

He'd stumbled on her stash of job applications one day under her jacket in the driver's seat of the van—piles of applications from stores, furniture galleries, doctor and dentist's offices, dry cleaners—and she'd said, "I'm going to fill them out . . . soon. But promise you won't say anything to your daddy. It's a surprise." *Surprise* was just another word for "secret." Kyle knew that, too. Just like their unspoken agreement about Kyle working for the Blooming Idiots instead of Saving Souls. It worried Kyle at first— the surprises his father didn't know yet, but everyone seemed so much happier at home. He realized it was a tradeoff.

When they pulled into his grandmother's driveway, his mother's van wasn't there. She was late as usual. What did surprise Kyle was the red Triumph convertible partially hidden by the shrubbery, and by the time Gordon parked the truck and Kyle and Bobby hopped out, Kyle's heart pounded with a terrifying suspicion, confirmed by the sight of Pastor Pat-Rick—Bible and clipboard on his lap, iced tea in hand—sitting beside his grandmother on the porch, waiting for Kyle.

PART III

I bequeath myself to the dirt to grow from the grass I love,
If you want me again look for me under your bootsoles.
—Walt Whitman, *Leaves of Grass*

SEVENTEEN

Dawn brightened meekly, before the sun, brash as a starlet, claimed the day for her own. Drifts of strange flowers swayed in the faint breeze, petals thrown open like shutters. It was June in Palmetto, and the town was in bloom.

At Amaranth, precisely where Emma Hanley's grandfather had once planted his beloved *Animus mico* in full view of an appalled audience of dour businessmen in the drawing room, tender green buds now clasped in folds, shy as virgins. Fronds unfurled like geisha's fans, flashing lacy pleasures. On that day, William McCann had glanced only once at the window where the men in suits watched him, long enough to display a frightening passion blooming on his florid features. (On the rare occasions when the gentlemen silently observing McCann from the drawing room of Amaranth had allowed such vulgar expressions of unbridled ecstasy to cross their own countenances, it was during discreet visits to a House of Ill Repute in the next town, and even then, such ardor was loosed briefly, and in the dark, until satiation returned reason. McCann's passion never left his Scots-Irish sunburned skin.)

Across town, at Palmetto Bank & Trust, white, plump roots snaked out bravely, testing soil, plundering earth, running across stones and cement. In the courtyard of Monaghan Nursing Home,

the soul shines tittered in a hesitant breeze, the wooden arbor
groaned heavy with new vines—speckled leaves, petals pink as
tongues. The night shift was leaving. Nigel Johnson, nursing assistant, had had a particularly trying night, as one Miss Gibble
had been found hiding in the courtyard until the wee hours of the
morning and waited impatiently now in her bed, ramrod straight,
alert, demanding her morning airing.

Outside a modest brick ranch in town, Lola Dewberry, in-
somniac, walked out into the wet grass and pondered a trio of lu-
minous soul shines while sipping a steaming cup of Darjeeling
tea. She cocked her head at them. They cocked their moon-
bleached heads back at her.

In Emma Hanley's garden, fecundity was rife; the pine needles parted for more knobby-kneed lilies. Exotic knobs burst
forth from the ground, slick and innocent as newborns.

Inside her bedroom, Emma, in a fit of sleeplessness, had turned
to reading her grandfather's diary. *O such fever dreams I have! Visions of such fierce fecundity. I am surprised, upon awaking, to find
myself still among the living, so certain was I that I had passed into
the Next World, into such celestial, botanical brilliance.*

The ravings of a lunatic, perhaps, but such fervor moved
Emma. She began to read about the day her grandfather McCann
spent in the garden of Amaranth mortifying her grandmother,
Josephine, by ignoring his house full of mill operatives and business associates, who had come to call just that morning. He had
eschewed their torturous talk of capital and fled to the garden,
and while in full view of the drawing room window, had fallen on
his knees, digging with abandon at a place the colored man he'd
brought back with him from his latest venture, pointed to with a
stick.

How brave her grandmother had been on such occasions! For
as trapped as she was in the mannered, rigid society of her sex,
Josephine had clearly recovered from the shock of having married a gentleman who had thrown off the shackles of expectations
and tradition, whose hands had become callused as a farmer's,

whose skin stayed as sun-blistered as a common laborer's. Surely
Josephine's good heart thumped with anguish as it beat against
the whale-boned corset of convention, a heart that could not,
would not, separate William McCann from the travel and plant
hunting that brought such naked, terrible joy to his flushed features.

Just after dawn, Emma dreamed she was smothering beneath
a blanket of brittle leaves, squirming under a mound of soil, pale
and blind as a grub. She awoke gasping for breath, flinging off
her cotton duvet, scattering her grandfather's papers to the floor.

His answering machine filled up every day now.

"Jake, it's JJ. Where are you, man? 'Cause I'm sitting here in
my office looking out my window, and I'm seeing your Blooming
Idiots out there making a spectacle of themselves. I mean, that's
what they're calling themselves? I thought you were joking. My
brother looks like he's giving the orders, and he's nipping, you
hear me? My brother, at my bank, nipping. Not even hiding it,
man. Swigging from a bottle—" The beep cut JJ off.

"Jake, it's Lola Dewberry again. Oh, I love them . . . whatever
they are. I'm just—overcome. You know they just took off, and
are these some kind of . . . orchids? Should I water them?"

"Mr. Cary? It's Hank Wilson over on Blueridge Street? You
think I should stake these things? I've never seen anything like it."

"Mr. Jake Cary? This is Oleen Johnson. I'm the assistant director at Monaghan Nursing Home, and well, apparently one of the
residents ate one of those . . . flowers . . . y'all put out. Are they
poisonous? It was one of those vines that took off like kudzu. Only,
these are some pretty things, but we—none of us here—ever laid
eyes on them before, and of course, the residents are real excited
but then . . . Mr. Walt got so excited, he wandered out and ate
one. The whole blossom. Said he wanted to taste heaven. And
we have some of the residents . . . licking them. His mind was
already round the bend. I guess what we are wondering is what
in the world are these things?" *Beep.*

"Jake? JJ here. Man, what have you done? It's crazy up here. There's crazy stuff you all put out over here that's—I mean, people are starting to stare, and these things are staring right back. Damn things have about covered up the bank sign. You can hardly see the time or temperature. The interest rates are gonna be swallowed up next. And another thing. You better warn that ragtag crewman of yours to stop skulking around here after hours like he's casing the joint. Weird old guy with a pith helmet and a backpack. Crouches down in the flower beds, talking to himself, taking notes. Saw him yesterday when I was locking up, but by the time I walked over to him, he was gone. One look, and I knew he was one of your Blooming Idiots. Next time, I call the law."

All these calls, more and more customers, people wanting estimates left and right, and they were falling behind schedule, but Gordon wouldn't be rushed. In fact, he appeared to be slowing down. Slept under the stars at that place out on Lavinia, took hot showers, and washed weekly laundry loads at Jake's place. Came up late to meet Jake's truck, sometimes didn't come up at all. Camping, he said. Tending to things. That was Gordon. Try telling that to JJ, though, Jake thought. *My brother still flopping?*

This morning, when Gordon refused to come out, Jake left Bobby and Kyle to round him up, and dropped off Terrell and the others to finish up two yards across town. Meanwhile, he swung by Ginger Welch's place, hoping to edge the lawn in under ten minutes, but no sooner had he cut the engine, than she burst out her front door. She'd been lying in wait. He saw now how foolish he was to think he might get away with a quick job at Ginger Welch's place without incident. Apparently, she accepted no proxy. To quote Terrell: *That woman wants her bushes trimmed by Jake Cary, and Jake Cary alone.*

"Jake!" she called. "I wasn't here the other day. I must have missed you."

"Sorry about that."

It took him a minute to realize what was different about her.

She wasn't smiling. In fact, she looked downright pouty with her arms crossed and her high heel tapping on the sidewalk.

He turned off the edger. "Anything wrong?"

"How come you didn't see fit to fill my yard with those special flowers, is what I'd like to know."

"What . . . special flowers?"

"The ones you're doing for everyone else. Betty Pearle said she had the prettiest miniature lilies she's ever seen, and then I heard you did the apartments and old folks' home, too."

"Well, but you didn't say anything about wanting your beds done. Thought we agreed just to do the lawn . . . and . . . you know—" He looked up and down the street. "—put on the show."

"I guess you haven't seen today's paper."

"I'm lucky to keep up with yesterday's news," he said.

"Well, y'all are in it."

"Again?"

She strode over to the patio table and back, and held up the *Palmetto News*. There was a color picture of Palmetto Bank & Trust and with the heaps of showy blooms—speckled and trumpeting—it did look impressive. Lord, did it look good. There were people standing around, gawking. And right in the middle, wading through the sea of blossoms, was Terrell, grinning like a son of a bitch, in a lavender T-shirt. PALMETTO IN BLOOM the caption said. *Showy flowers with striking fragrance draws more than bees to area business. Blooming Idiots assistant manager Terrell Jameson checks on progress of plants recently set out at Palmetto Bank & Trust. The unusual flowers, which Jameson declined to name, have begun to draw crowds.*

"I don't believe it," Jake said. *"Assistant manager?"*

"Well? What have I got to do to get you fellas to plant some of those things in my bed?"

This struck Jake as the kind of question he best not answer.

"Uncle B? What's wrong?"

Bobby pointed.

"You saw . . . someone? You saw Gordon?"

"No," Bobby said.

"I think . . . we need to go down there, again. See if he's there."

"Who is there?"

"Gordon. You know. To see if Gordon is there, because Jake's gonna pick us all up."

When Will came back, Bobby would tell him about the strange man at the apartments yesterday. Bobby was watering, and the old man walked over and stood silently beside him and stared at the plant bed. Bobby was frightened and dropped the hose, but the man turned to him and said, "Smell this!" and held over a branch. "White chocolate. *Azara microphylla*. From Chile. Amazing, isn't it? Named after J. N. Azara, the eighteenth-century Spanish patron of science."

"Did you know him?" Bobby asked. The man laughed and laughed, and sat down at the curb. "I'm not that ancient, you know."

Microphylla. Micro, *meaning* "small." Phylla, *meaning* "leaf." The man read Bobby's mind and praised his excellent Latin. And then he reached into his backpack and pulled out a Polaroid camera. "I just bought this newfangled thing and haven't a clue how to use it."

Jake looked beyond the boy and Bobby Hanley, at the magnolias covered in crossvine and honeysuckle.

"He's still down there, and he's not coming up," Kyle told Jake. "He says he's waiting for someone."

"Waiting?"

Gordon could be waiting for anybody back there. Roselle, maybe. More likely Johnnie Walker or Jack Daniel. Oh, Lord, but Jake needed Gordon, especially today—to check on those crazy blooming creations he came up with, to supervise this crew he helped round up. Just how was he going to persuade Gordon to come out and join the living? Jake stared into the woods, considering. The bare outlines of a foot trail beckoned in the overgrowth.

"Well, boys. I guess I'm going in," he said. The truth was, Jake hadn't once been to Gordon's new hangout. To do so, he felt, would place him squarely in one of those conundrums he tried to avoid in life. He liked pleading ignorance about exactly where all these mysterious plants were coming from. Once he saw what Gordon had concocted down there, well—he became an accessory.

"Lead the way," Jake said. The boy nodded and lifted his shirt to cover his nose, and motioned for Bobby to do the same.

"What's the deal?" Jake asked, following along behind them, but found out soon enough when a sickening reek rose up and hit him like a mallet. He managed to hold his breath until they stumbled through the thicket and into the clearing.

"Thanks for the warning," he said.

"It's okay now. You can take a deep breath now."

"My . . . God," Jake said, looking around. It was all there— the buttery yellow blooms, the flowering vines, the blue-petaled beauties. Like they'd stepped into some museum exhibit. Gordon came out of his tent, carrying a water can and a sack.

"You have been one busy man," Jake said.

"Naw. It was just all waiting up in here for someone to let it loose."

"I just hope you didn't raid some rich lady's garden. Or some of those new fancy estates up there on the mountain."

"I don't thieve. I take only what I'm supposed to."

"What's that supposed to mean?"

"We did us some good work. Got all the planting done with you laid up. Just in time, too, before the rain, right at the edge of blooming. Got some shady, got some full sun."

"Yeah, you did good work, all right," Jake said. He watched Gordon spoon dark clumps of soil into a pair of pantyhose. "What in the hell are you doing?"

"Making tea," he said. He began dunking the dirt-filled stocking until the water grew dark. "Not for you, either."

"Well, that's a relief. Whose legs did you peel those things off of?"

Gordon laughed.

"Anybody I know?"

Gordon began watering the plants. "Compost tea," Gordon said. "See? They soaking it right up."

"Yeah, I see. You ready to go now? I need you out there to take a look at things," Jake said.

"Can't go yet," Gordon said. "The plant lover's round here somewhere."

"Oh, Jesus. Ghosts in the garden again? That I don't need."

"You ain't seen him yet?"

"I guess I'm the crazy one here," Jake said, "because I don't see things that aren't there or talk to spirits."

"I told him to hold up and talk to you."

"You got more in common with your brother than I thought," Jake said. "Seems he's been seeing one of your haints loitering around the bank, and he claims he's a Blooming Idiot."

Gordon smiled wryly and shrugged, as if he might indeed be considering the possibility. "This man followed me around when I was tending the Harlow place. Drawing pictures, too. I told him he should just get himself a camera."

"Ghosts have cameras now?"

"I didn't tell him nothing, if that's what you're worried about. He knew all about our planting anyway. Rattled off them fancy names of flowers like nobody's business."

"Uh-huh." Jake took off his cap, straightened the bill, put it back on. Bobby and the boy reclined across two large rocks. "So . . . you coming with us today?"

Gordon shrugged. "Told the plant lover I'd wait."

"See, the problem is, I have to act like I know a little something about all these flowers, since everyone is asking me about them. I don't know what to tell them. If they rot or look poorly, we're just going to have to tear all of it out and do everything again. I'll get an earful, believe me."

"Let things loose, you gonna get surprises." Gordon called Sweet over and disappeared in his tent.

"Oh, boy," Jake said. He rubbed his eyes.

From the far end of the garden, there was a rustle of leaves. Jake turned, suddenly alert. "Stay put," he whispered to Bobby and the boy. A figure, dappled in the morning light, stepped into sight. "Stop right there!" Jake yelled. "Whoever you are."

"Hello!" the man called. "May I approach?"

"If you're a flopper, you're off course," Jake said. "The house is up there." Jake tilted his head toward the house, but his eyes didn't move from the man's face.

"Oh, no. No." The man laughed. "No need to fret, I've spoken at length with your colleague. He mentioned we should speak."

"Colleague?" Jake asked. "Who the hell are you?"

The man shuffled closer, and Jake saw he was much older than he first appeared. He was carrying a small backpack. Sunlight glanced off his glasses, hid his eyes. He smiled broadly. Good teeth. Definitely not a flopper.

"I'm the plant lover," he said.

"We're heading to Walhalla," Lila Day announced as she took a seat in Emma's kitchen. She had arrived early and without warning at Emma's doorstep, a sure sign she was embarking on another of her missions—in this case, persuading Emma to accompany her on a day trip three weeks hence. Emma suspected that Lila's sudden enthusiasm for the annual day trip two counties over was due to panic, for Miss Gibble had refused to go along. Clearly, Lila needed a companion, and Emma proved a tempting target.

"You're going to love Walhalla," her friend said. Lila insisted on pronouncing the name with the Germanic V sound. *Valhalla.* The only other person Emma had heard do so was Miss Gibble, who had become downright dogmatic on the subject.

"You'll need to send in your fifty-dollar deposit by Friday," Lila said now. "I'd hurry if I were you. Silver Compass tours fill." That touring a town in Oconee County might actually quench Emma's lifelong thirst for travel seemed a tenuous theory at best, and Emma said as much. However, Lila remained impervious to excuses. After all, when was the last time Emma had explored her own backyard? There was plenty of the world to see right here in South Carolina, starting with a day in Walhalla.

"But I'd be gone most of the day, and . . . that would be quite an undertaking."

"Heavens, Emma. We'd be back by five o'clock. Bobby would be working until then, wouldn't he?"

"Yes. But . . . if we were late . . . I don't want to ask too much of Mr. Cary. He's done so much already."

Thank you, Emma told Jake every day now, for keeping her son on. Two words, two syllables, two hard stones of gratitude, worn smooth with use.

"Well, surely your grandboy could stay with his uncle a little late one day. He is still working with them, isn't he?"

Emma nodded. Yes, Kyle was still working with Jake's crew, thank goodness. With some help from the Blooming Idiots, she and Kyle had put on quite a show for the Saving Souls preacher who popped in to check on Kyle's "project." So convincing a performance, the preacher had overstayed his welcome, asking for glass after glass of iced tea and eating a plate of homemade lemon wafers Emma had planned to take to Miss Gibble. The preacher had, in fact, lingered past the point of rudeness, seeming to enjoy himself while having no inkling how his very presence tortured Kyle and her. It had been an afternoon of sheer agony. The irony of such an outcome was proof, in Emma's estimation, that the Creator had a sense of humor, and did not mind, on occasion, wielding it. Emma still smarted from the lash.

"There are antique stores," Lila said now, in her stubborn fashion. "And everyone has lunch at the Buffet Haus."

Emma sipped her tea to hide her frown. This, she thought, was what her dream of the Trip had come to: a busload of senior citizens pillaging antique malls, cafeteria lunches of soft food under heat lamps and sneeze shields.

"I'll think about it," Emma said.

Her friend nodded firmly but made no move to leave. She cast a disapproving gaze at Emma's newspaper, neatly bound and ignored, on the kitchen table between them. Lila believed reading the daily newspaper was not so much a pleasure as a duty, *the backbone of an informed citizenry*, as she once put it. By the time the sun rose, Lila's own newspaper had been thoroughly scoured—obituaries circled, coupons clipped, word jumble and crossword completed. Emma, who had for three decades received her daily news—the headlines and weather forecasts, anyway—when Harold read them aloud in his halting bursts, now eschewed the newspaper for travel magazines and novels. She hadn't gotten around to canceling her subscription. Her neglected yellowing newspapers, stacked like cordwood in the corner, were proof, her friend declared, that Emma was not in the Here and Now.

"That picture on One-B today will stir up more business for Mr. Cary," Lila said. "In color, no less."

"What . . . picture?" Emma asked, but was distracted by the familiar sound of Jake Cary's truck rumbling down the driveway. *Too early,* she thought as she peered out the kitchen window. *Something has happened.* She rushed to the front porch.

"Is everything all right?" she called.

Jake got out of his truck and nodded. "Just fine," he said. Kyle and Bobby emerged from the cab, and Emma sighed in relief.

"Why, Jake Cary," Lila said now from behind Emma. "I thought I heard your voice."

"Yes, ma'am."

"I hear your work is drawing crowds."

"Well, Miss Day, I have you to thank for spreading the word."

"Nonsense. A good, honest yardman is always in demand. It's a grassroots business." Lila tittered at her own joke, as was often her habit. It was the kind of quirk that might drive a companion batty, Emma reflected, especially if that companion was trapped on a Silver Compass tour bus heading to Walhalla.

Jake, distracted, glanced at the road, then back at Emma. Her heart sank. He had something to tell her.

A car turned in the driveway, and they all turned to watch it spray gravel and squeal to a stop.

"Who in the world?" Emma asked.

"Why, it's the authorities," Lila said. "Only the authorities drive like that."

"Damn rentals." A man got out of the car and looked at it with suspicion. "They switch around the gas and the brake pedals to fool old men like me." He carried a back sack, an army green shabby thing. He wore sandals and socks, and a large floppy hat.

"Dr. Burnside?" Emma said. He peered steadily at her from behind wire-rimmed glasses.

Jake watched him with cool curiosity. "You've met?" Jake asked.

"I promised Mrs. Hanley I'd help identify a specimen in her garden," he said, then looked at Emma. "But now I understand you know something about that marvelous place on Lavinia Avenue."

"You mean . . . Amaranth?" Emma asked.

"I didn't really connect you with the place, Mrs. Hanley," Jake said. "Until the plant lover here told me."

"Oh?" Emma looked at Dr. Burnside.

"On several occasions, I had the pleasure of talking to a Miss Gibble at Monaghan Nursing," he said. "She was good enough to tell me a little about Amaranth, and . . . she said you once lived there."

Lila gasped outrage. "Miss Gibble? Her mind *has* gone around the bend."

"My family—," Emma said. "My grandfather once owned it."

Jake nodded, then glanced at Dr. Burnside before meeting her eyes. "See, it's where our plants came from," he said. "There's this garden out back. Hidden. That's where we met up here with the plant doctor here."

"Amaranth?" Lila said. "With those . . . drifters? Why, that's a dangerous, *filthy* place."

Emma turned to Jake. "You mean the bedding plants at the bank and . . . the nursing home . . . and here in my own yard . . . the Secret Keepers . . . and all the rest . . . are from Amaranth?"

He nodded. "Transplanted."

"I don't believe it," Lila said. "I can't imagine how anything survived back there in that neglect."

"Oh, this man's colleague is a plantsman of remarkable talent," the plant lover said before Jake could utter a word. "To have rediscovered, indeed *rescued,* such a swallowed-up garden, and then to oversee the transplanting around your town. That's quite a feat."

"Gordon," Jake said with a shrug.

"Why, he's a Blooming Idiot," Emma said. The plant lover laughed heartily. "No," she said, flustered. "I mean, the Blooming Idiots are what they call themselves. My son is one. My grandson, too." She looked at Jake for assurance, but he was rubbing his eyes wearily.

"Yes, I know. I've followed their work." Dr. Burnside fumbled around in his shirt pocket and held up a stack of Polaroid snapshots. He lamented the fact that his favorite camera had been misplaced some weeks ago, and he'd been forced to buy this contraption on the cheap. No fuss, but no focus, either. "A crude tool, but serviceable, I suppose," he said. "But I'd really love to get slides, of course. Before I leave."

"Yep," Jake said, gazing at the pictures, "that's our work, all right."

"The microclimates at that place," Dr. Burnside said, shaking his head. "Incredible. Boggy with pitcher plants. Bright heat in the clearing with the indigenous rocks and—I couldn't believe my eyes—some kind of rare succulent. And Oconee bells! Do you have any idea how rare it is to find them out of their habitat? Native plants among the exotics. How it all stayed a secret is beyond me."

"Well, I know how. That rank smell stops most people from poking around back there," Jake said. "Stopped me in my tracks."

"Dragon arum, you mean?" the plant lover said. "Yes. What foresight! Brilliant."

"Brilliant?" Kyle asked. "It's painful."

"Dragon arum—*Dracunculus vulgaris*—smells like rotten meat to attract flies. I've only seen that carnivorous plant in the Mediterranean. I imagine its stench at the borders of Amaranth has kept many a wayward stranger from trespassing."

"I never imagined . . . ," Emma said, sifting through the pictures. "I haven't stepped onto the grounds for . . . years."

"Do you mean," Dr. Burnside asked Emma, "you haven't seen that enchanted garden for yourself?"

Lila gave the man a withering stare. "Why, it's not safe over there for a woman." She looked at Jake. "For anyone."

"This one," Emma said, holding up a photograph of a tall yellow flower. "I remember looking at a sketch of this one. I painted it."

"You're an artist?" the plant lover asked.

"Oh, no. I'm no artist. I just painted a little. Once. On dishes. Poor attempts, as Miss Day will tell you." She looked over at her friend, hoping to share the joke, but there was no trace of mirth in Lila's stern, suspicious expression.

"In this town," Lila said, "we don't make a habit of poking around other people's business."

"In this town, we already know it," Emma told her.

"We don't go around stirring up trouble," Lila continued, "and . . . *unearthing* things."

Emma knew her friend suspected Dr. Burnside was sweet-talking Emma to find out more about Amaranth for his own selfish purposes. Lila had always maintained Emma had no radar for scalawags.

"Good," Dr. Burnside said, unfazed. "Every half-ass money-hungry plantsman will be out here soon, digging up samples from the beds, working on hybrids and cultivars. You ought to hold out as long as you can. I've been downright sneaky myself."

He picked up the Polaroids again, shuffled through them, and handed them to Emma. "Plants don't forget, Mrs. Hanley. They lie in wait."

Relief opened gently in Emma. Perhaps he *was* authentic. Surely he would be genuinely interested in the McCann saga.

"Shall we go inside?" she asked.

EIGHTEEN

Jake met up with another photographer over at the bank, this one from *Southern Living* magazine. And then a newspaper reporter, a young man with a wisp of a goatee and beady, cynical eyes, followed him and Gordon around for a couple of hours, taking pictures and asking them questions, then jabbing a little tape recorder in Jake's face, which made him forget what he was going to say anyway.

"How did you all get wind of us anyway?" Jake asked the reporter. "Not like Palmetto is the center of the world or anything."

"Story gets on the wire—everyone knows."

"The wire?"

"AP picked it up. You got good visuals. We got a slow news cycle."

When they went to the nursing home courtyard, Gordon took off his cap, as if he'd just stepped into a cathedral. A few of the residents clustered around the honeyed plumped blooming thing there, whatever it was, that draped languorously over the arbor.

"What are they doing?" whispered the reporter. One of the residents, still in pajamas, licked a flower.

"I guess they're enjoying themselves," Jake said.

The reporter cupped a speckled bloom. "And what did you say these are called?"

Jake exchanged a weary look with Gordon. "I didn't."

"Looks like it's tired out, this ol' vine, probably from bolting so quick," Gordon said. "Resting here, like a snake that swallowed something. Nothing to do but bloom."

The reporter scratched on his pad.

"Have you talked with a specialist to identify these?"

"We have a . . . consultant . . . working on it," Jake said.

The man studied Jake, his eyes narrowing. He tapped his pen on his pad. "You're rather reticent about the subject, aren't you?"

"If that means tired of gabbing about it, yeah."

The reported shrugged.

"Look, we aren't hiding anything, if that's what you're thinking," Jake said, watching the man eye the vine again. "Do I look like a rich smuggler or something? Do we look like smart science types to you?"

It occurred to Jake that he should be insulted by the reporter's swift agreement.

JJ prided himself on spotting panic in the eyes of a loan applicant. The kind of disguised desperation, like unexploded ordnance, that called for delicate handling. It was his job to send such customers back through the door with a pat on the back and no hard feelings. Which was exactly what he planned to do with the gentleman sitting across from him now, whose loan application was flapping more red flags than a day at the races. The messes people got themselves in—well, you just wouldn't believe it, as JJ told his wife, Marla, every night. You could take opportunities in life and hold on, or you could watch them slip right out of your hands like a bar of soap. Like JJ's own brother, Gordon, who lived like a bum. Like Jake Cary, who told JJ yesterday he was *getting too many customers.* As if such a thing were possible.

"You understand an unsecured loan has a higher risk, sir?" JJ asked the applicant. He hadn't seen the credit report yet, but he had no doubt it was a stinker.

"Yes, I know." The customer wore a nice suit, and that was a good sign—the man knew the value of an impression, which indicated pride and a willingness to pay back.

"I see you're married," JJ said, fishing around for other income. Just maybe the wife was the one bringing home the bacon, and the husband here didn't want to admit it. That happened more and more.

"This loan will be individual."

"I see." The fax machine beeped. JJ excused himself and took a look at the credit report. Worse than he thought. Late payments. Second mortgage. Hell of a mess. And where was the income? *Commercial real estate broker*, the customer had written under occupation. *Broker is right*, JJ thought. This man can't even afford to pay attention.

"I'm waiting on my commission, but they don't always come in . . . regular."

"Mr. Quattlebaum?" He doesn't have to say it. A flush rises from the man's collar to the roots of his thinning blond hair. "There's a ratio of debt and assets we use, a credit score . . . I'm sure you know what I'm talking about." JJ tried to smile. He didn't want to patronize the man. He wanted to tell him to loosen his green tie. "I know you want a fast answer, but in . . . complicated cases . . . like yours, I'm required to . . . run it through some channels."

JJ glanced up through his window to see Jake's truck pull in the parking lot. Jake must have finally checked his phone messages. Hallelujah.

The customer cleared his throat. He stared at JJ, his jaw working. When they sensed they'd be turned down for a loan, the men got mean and the women cried. Unless you were Queen Heywood who came in here last Thursday wanting a loan for some home-based makeup business. "I about raised you up, boy," she'd said, leaping up from her chair in that purple suit. "Might as well say I'm kin, the way I helped out your mama. So I know you are not gonna sit up here in this office behind this big-ass desk and try to tell me you can't make some calls and get me some funds." But yes, that's exactly what he tried to tell her, right before she swung the big purple purse toward his head, much to the amusement of several of his colleagues, who witnessed the scene from outside the glassed-in walls of JJ's office. All this glass just made him feel like he was in a gold fishbowl with the cat watching. But it was for safety, he supposed. Safety, so some pissed-off man like Mr. Quattlebaum here did not swing at him with something heavier than a purple crushed-velvet pocketbook.

Just then, Bubber Anderson stuck his head in JJ's office, a big no-no. JJ didn't barge into Bubber's office when he was with a customer, did he?

"Donny! I was at lunch," Bubber said. "I'm sorry I missed you."

"No problem at all," the customer said. "Just a little thing to take care of. Didn't want to bother you."

"You're in good hands," Bubber said, winking at JJ, who nodded back. *Yeah, I get it,* JJ thought. *A buddy. Golf buddy or . . .*

"We go to Crossroads," the customer said after Bubber left.

Crossroads. Uh-huh. That explained some things. Those people were chummy as hell. JJ's gut glowed like a charcoal: It was no accident the customer had missed Bubber. *This man doesn't like asking for money from me, a stranger,* JJ thought, *but he doesn't like asking money from his Crossroads buddy even worse.*

"When will I know?" the customer said, rising.

"I'd say we could have an answer for you in three business days, Mr. Quattlebaum."

"That's not good enough."

"I understand your frustration."

"No, I don't think you do."

JJ sighed. He'd take it to Bubber, anyway. Let *him* check off his buddy's loan. He was always pulling rank on JJ anyway. "Give us a call later today," JJ said. Yeah, let Bubber Anderson put *his* ass on the line for this customer, because JJ wasn't. He had enough to worry about. Like all these people coming to the bank just to see the flowers after that photo ran in the paper. His own brother was probably out there drunk on the job. That dog of his was probably pissing all over the parking lot. And now—JJ absently shook hands with the customer but couldn't resist looking out the window beyond him—that skinny guy was holding a shovel like a microphone, singing and carrying on, drawing a crowd. How was that going to look on camera? This bunch of fools out there, at his bank—JJ couldn't believe the sight. And judging now from the growing shock on his face, neither could the customer.

JJ scanned Jake like a machine—from cap and T-shirt to grass-stained Levi's and mud-caked boots. "You gotta get ready."

"Well, hello to you, too," Jake said.

"You got my message, didn't you?"

"Which one? You left me a passel of them."

"Damn, man. A businessman like yourself needs to check his messages."

"I'm no businessman. I'm just a man who digs and plants and rakes and drives around with, as you put it, a bunch of idiots."

"You're going to be on camera. The TV news people called," JJ said. "They're coming to do a story on these flowers."

"And?"

"*And?* You gotta be ready."

"I reckon I'm as ready as I'll ever be."

"You got to be kidding."

"Naw, man. I'm not wearing fancy anything out here. That's nuts."

"Too late for a haircut. How about I call Marla to bring over a nice ironed shirt—what size?"

"No idea."

"Look, this can be . . . real, real good," JJ said. "For you, for me, for all parties concerned. You could expand. All over the state, cover the South." He slowed down his words, the way he did when he was especially frustrated. "You can leverage this *opportunity*, Jake. But you got to *look* like—"

"I'm not a banker, man. I work in soil."

"I got a call from corporate headquarters after that newspaper piece. The bank looks good in all this, unless people see we got a bunch of weirdos"—he looked over at Pedro—"and some illegals. Better make sure your papers are in order."

"Okay, I got it. If it's good—you want credit; if it's bad—you don't know me," Jake said. "No problem. Now, why don't you go inside and count money?"

Jake looked around. A clutch of customers had gathered around the flower beds. Gordon was weeding. Terrell was watching Lay Down Sally pinch off spent blooms. Bobby stood by the truck, his head to the side, as if he were listening hard to some muted thing. The dog sniffed the crotch of a man in a suit who appeared to be trying to ask Terrell a question. Pedro was around back, and the boy—where was Kyle? Must be around back, too.

Jake walked over to Gordon and crouched down. "What we got?" he asked. "The TV people are coming, and they're gonna ask me. Or maybe you'd like to tell them."

"Naw."

"That's what I thought you'd say."

"These here are different from the others," Gordon said. He cupped a hand under one of the blossoms. Yellow, as wide as his hand. Gordon's face glowed as if he held a candle in the dark. "Shiny things."

"Terrell," Jake said, sensing the customers watching them, "would it be too much to ask you to do a little work?"

"What you want us to do? No more weeds I can see."

"At least try to *look* busy. You're an expert at that."

Terrell put his hands on his hips and glared at Jake. "Uh-huh. Who got that picture in the paper, bossman?"

"That's right. I almost forgot, my *Assistant Manager*," Jake said. "By the way, did that man in the blue suit talk to you? What did he want?"

"Wouldn't you like to know?"

JJ, jumpy as a groom, paced nearby.

"Oh, Lord, here he comes," Gordon said as JJ strode toward them.

"Would it kill you to say hello?" Jake asked. "Running interference with you two tires me out."

Was it Jake's imagination, or did the petals widen, the velvet brown eyes glisten? A nearly imperceptible angling toward Gordon's face, which was glowing even more than usual, basking in that topaz glow. *Jesus,* Jake thought, *I've been out in the sun too long.*

When JJ approached, Gordon nodded and walked away. Well, at least a nod was something.

"Don't you have money to make?" Jake asked JJ. "People to swindle?"

"I'm gonna get Marla to bring over that shirt," JJ said.

"You're hurting my plants," Jake said. The flower petals had shriveled, hadn't they? Jake looked up to see the man in the suit and lavatory green tie emerge from around the back of the building. He was heading straight for JJ and him.

"Why don't you come inside and wait for the TV people," JJ said, "so you can think about what you want to say."

"I avoid thinking when I can," Jake said. "And you want me to *think* about *talking*? That makes me want to run for the hills."

"Jake—"

"You don't have to worry about it anymore, man. Looks like they're here."

The television truck turned in the parking lot.

It wasn't until his father finally left the bank parking lot that Kyle realized he'd made a mistake. Hiding was the worst thing he could have done. He just panicked. One minute he was helping Bobby thread a weeder, and the next his father was emerging from the bank heading right for him. His eyes had locked on Kyle like a ray gun, and Kyle had frozen. Then Kyle had ducked behind some cars and crawled over to Jake's truck. He'd managed to get Terrell's attention. "I'm not here," he whispered, which was all it took. The Blooming Idiots were experts at slippery quick disappearances, no questions asked.

Even Bobby, who'd stood talking to Kyle's father, or not really talking but mumbling and shrugging, and then walking off, hadn't breathed a word about Kyle. "Will Two," he kept saying, which his father, thank goodness, had no clue about. His uncle had acted like he didn't even recognize Kyle's father, which made his father even more angry. And all the time Kyle huddled under Jake's truck, watching his father's new black dress shoes—the left one squeaked—circle the bank grounds and parking lot. By the time Terrell told him the coast was clear, and Kyle stood and watched his father's car pull out, it began to dawn on him: He'd screwed up royally. What timing! Tonight he just had to see Julie. He just had to slip out and hit the cemetery party because . . . something was up with her, he didn't know, but he was trying not to lose his mind over it, and he didn't need a blow-up at home, to wreck his plans . . . to wreck everything. Why couldn't he have just played it cool, and told his dad . . . what? What could he have possibly told his father that would make him understand how he didn't want to lose his first job . . . or his first girlfriend . . . or get in hot water with Pastor Pat-Rick?

Everyone was clustered around the television truck now, but Kyle hung back. He couldn't take a chance on getting caught; that was for sure. Right now, his father was probably calling his mother, or even Pastor Pat-Rick. Forget sneaking out to the party tonight, forget his job, forget everything. Kyle's life was basically in shambles. Unless . . . Kyle watched the cameraman head to the flower beds. The talking head was interviewing Jake. Terrell and Gordon and even his uncle Bobby clustered around, listening. More people came out from the bank to watch. The afternoon was shot. They'd be tied up here forever.

His father's office was three blocks away. Kyle could run there and back in no time. He could . . . explain. He didn't need to get his mom involved. He was old enough to take care of his own business. He would fix this.

For the first time in her life, Emma allowed her travel trunk to be plundered. Indeed, Dr. Burnside, who had spent several afternoons in Emma's kitchen, was headfirst in the trunk now. Emma was relieved that, for once, Lila Day wasn't here, too, sitting ramrod straight, wary as a chaperone. Lila found Dr. Burnside's exuberance uncouth. Emma thought it odd Lila had not taken to their research at all, but remained convinced Dr. Burnside was an interloper—*a carpetbagger, mark my words.* Who *was* this man, and what was he doing here in Emma's house rifling through her precious things? Lila's expression seemed to declare. Poring over all those private documents and Emma's own recounting of her family history—with its madness, scandal, and ruin—what good was that? *A man like that wants something,* Lila had insisted.

But wanted . . . what? Emma countered. There was nothing to be had. Emma had done a title search and discovered the Amaranth property now belonged to the Billy Peake, who owned half the gas stations in town and a bingo parlor, and plenty of weed-swallowed lots and tumbledown eyesores. All Emma had to offer the plant lover were these notes and sketches, this story.

"Ah . . . a mottlecah eucalyptus," Dr. Burnside said now. He turned from the trunk and held up a sketch. "Just last year, I was Down Under and happened upon one myself. It lures the Australian honey possum, you know."

"The honey . . . possum?" Emma asked.

"One of two mammal species that live only on nectar and pollen."

It was just the kind of statement that provoked Lila's ire. She considered the man a braggart, and didn't mind saying so—after he left, of course. Emma's retort—"It ain't bragging if you done it"—an old saying of Harold's she'd formerly found crude, was, Emma discovered, an apt response, chiefly because it silenced Lila.

"It was a sight I won't forget," he said.

Dr. Burnside put down the sketch and joined Emma at the kitchen table, where she had made them two cups of tea. He cleared his throat. "I found my good camera," he said.

"Oh, you must be relieved. Where was it?"

"At my niece's. In a spare room. Behind a dollhouse."

Dr. Burnside admitted his convalescence from his hip surgery at his niece's—with her husband, three children, and two dogs—had been far from peaceful. He had, he said, forgotten just how noisy families were.

"Do you have children of your own?" she asked, her voice gone soft, as if a whisper could make the question less pointed.

"I don't." He stirred his tea. "I had one . . . just one."

The answer hung in the silent air—the single word *had* dense with sadness, and they did not speak for some minutes.

"You must be ready to leave this place," she said finally. "My goodness—on Monday, is it? To Costa Rica, you said?"

"Yes, I'm off. I have a former student there kind enough to invite me. His wife is an ornithologist."

"How long will you visit?"

He laughed and shook his head. "I couldn't say. I never know where my visits will take me."

Emma cleared her throat. "I want to thank you for your expertise." She looked at the trunk. "You've gone to a lot of trouble combing through all this."

"The pleasure is mine."

Dr. Burnside looked down at his hands, and it occurred to Emma she'd never seen him shy. They'd been too caught up in sifting through the contents of her trunk. There were the sketches, the maps, the letters—but now there was just the two of them, sitting across from each other. He met her eyes and smiled, and she saw a glimmer of youth in his sapphire wink, the skinny, brash boy he must once have been.

"I was thinking we might go tomorrow to Amaranth," he said. "Now that I have my camera."

Emma had visited the periphery of the place, but still hadn't had the heart to go in the back, and see the garden proper. She blamed her reluctance to revisit Amaranth on the need to keep quiet and not attract attention to the place until Jake decided how to proceed with his plants, but she suspected tromping through the grounds of Amaranth would only rekindle her sense of loss and her family's heartbreaking past, and leave her with a bad case of melancholy.

"The morning offers the best light," he said.

Emma opened her grandfather's diary there beside her teacup, flipping through its yellowed pages, casting about for a new topic of discussion, but the passionate words leapt from the pages like sparks, burning her. *"I must, I must . . . it blooms even now . . . wild and unencumbered!"*

"Of course, I'd be happy to drive over and pick you up," he said.

Dr. Burnside looked at her expectantly. It was his imminent departure, his leaving, that emboldened her. He would be gone in two days, disappearing as if she'd never known him, as if he'd never given his talk at the Lunch and Learn, as if he weren't right here sitting at her kitchen table. If Emma did not agree to go to Amaranth with him, with the plant lover, she would never go at all.

"Around ten, tomorrow?"

"I'll pack us a lunch," she said.

NINETEEN

I t surprised us, too," Jake said.

"Not really," Bobby said. "There are no surprises here."
Bobby turned up the volume on the television and sat back
down.

"And then the next thing we knew—," Jake was saying now to
the lady standing there in a red suit. Red! A clue. A red lady talking to Jake about the red Secret Keepers. Talking and talking and
talking. A surprise. A secret. *Our secret, okay?*

"Bobby? Turn it down, please?" his mother said from the hall.

The red lady again: "Jake Cary said his crew has managed
to—"

"Good Lord, is she talking to *Jake?*" his mother asked.

"—and it's drawing crowds. Take a look at these—"

"I can't believe it! Bobby, it's Jake on the news. Why didn't
you tell me?"

"What's your secret, Mr. Cary?" the microphone hovered
now in front of Jake.

"Gordon," Jake said. Terrell waved. And there was Sweet. But
Gordon wouldn't talk. Gordon kept secrets.

"As you can see, a blooming business has taken root in this
town. Kayla Karl, News Center Four. Now back to you, Lorna."

"Soul shines," Emma said, standing up suddenly, as if rooting for a team. "Those were soul shines."

Dora was setting the table when she happened to look up and see Jake.

There he was, taking off his cap, gesturing at something behind him. Raking a hand through his blue-black hair, then saying . . . what? Saying what? The television, at the far end of the den, was angled just enough so she could watch it from the kitchen sink. She made it over in three steps, fumbled for the volume.

Jake nodded at the perky coiffed woman in red in front of him. Jake, sunburned as usual, sable eyebrows raised, hand rubbing his chin. Nervous, but covering it up.

"Oh . . . ," she said into the empty room.

She was alone. Thankfully, alone. Sandy and Kyle were at the pool. Donny was on his way home.

Jake was nodding. Smiling at her. With—Bobby, now. Dora's knees went weak. A spoon fell from her hands, clattered to the floor.

And then—the garage door's battered screech, like a rickety, mechanical pterodactyl at an amusement park. The purring engine of Donny's car, the door opening. Jake was talking about . . . beauty? Beautiful secrets. Mysterious blooming. The woman smiled up at him, small beside Jake, who hunched down a little to answer her.

Donny stepped into the kitchen, and Jake disappeared. A commercial for bathtub cleaner blasted. Scrubbing bubbles, mustached, googly eyes floating down a drain.

"Where are the kids?"

"The pool." She did not look at him.

"Dora, do you have something to tell me?"

Dora turned to her husband. His question crept cool as a reptile into the bright, hot kitchen. Donny looked weary standing there in his rumpled suit, and she did not like when he looked weary. She had married a confident man, sure in his convictions, and this was what she'd done to him. She ruined people.

He tossed his keys and a pile of mail on the counter, and sat down at the kitchen table. He saw her black heart. He always had.

"I—," she said. "I don't—," she managed, then sat down across from him. Her mouth was dry. This was what it was like. To wreck her family. To face what a shitty wife she was.

"I had a good week. Commission came in," he said. She nodded. He leaned back in the chair and loosened his tie in three raspy jerks. "Dora?" he sighed. "Did you think I wouldn't notice?" And now she met his moist green eyes, opaque as olives. "Did you think I wouldn't care? Or that I was dumb as a fence post?"

She shook her head. "Oh, Donny I—"

"The shame of it. The shame I felt! For both of us."

Something like relief washed over her—she would confess everything!—followed by new waves of guilt and dread. Which deed was she being chastised for? It didn't matter. It was all . . . connected. A web of lies. Where could she possibly start? How could she begin to explain?

"I was weak—," she said, which was what she always said.

He held up his hand to quiet her. He licked his lips, and then pursed them slightly before he continued. "I paid the usual expenses, and lo and behold, I'm sure you can guess what happened next. I just happened to find that the van has a thousand dollars paid toward it. You did that, didn't you? Behind my back."

Silence. She waited. This was . . . it? The realization began to dawn on her: not Kyle's lies, not her own covering up for Kyle, not her own secret fat cache of job applications, not the fact their son worked for Dora's old flame. *It wasn't Jake.* It was her mother's money.

"But . . . Donny. They tried to take the van. I told you. I had no choice."

Poor Kyle was still unsettled by that repossession scuffle. Traumatized! On the way back from her mother's the other day, he'd sworn to her he'd seen a stranger lingering around the places he and Bobby worked. He was just sure some repo man would pop up again any moment.

"You always have a choice, Dora." Donny sighed. "I myself—had a moment of weakness. When the Lord saw fit to stop my sales commissions last month, I began to . . . wonder why. Just like that." He snapped his fingers. "All of a sudden, money dried up like a famine on the land. Clients, well, they didn't call back . . . and nothing—not one property sold. But then I knew it was a test. A test of my faith." He looked at her, his hands folded on the table in front of him. "Dora, don't you have faith in me? To lead this family? Because I'm having to be strong for both of us."

She nodded. "Of course I—"

"I'll take care of us," he said now. He was, she saw, flushed with something like pleasure, confident again now that money had come in. He leaned over and kissed her cheek. Forgiveness was a cornerstone of marriage, as any Marriage Mentor knew. She would have to tell him everything. All of it. One day.

"Dinner's on the stove," she said. She'd thawed out the last steak for him. The kids would have fish sticks. She didn't get the grocery money for another two days.

"Kyle and Sandy should be back anytime."

"Has Kyle been home all day?"

"Why? Is something wrong?"

He shrugged, on the cusp of another pronouncement, Dora could tell. "No reason."

"There's a salad in the fridge," she said. She'd found the last cucumber in the crisper, frozen solid. But there was lettuce and half a tomato. There were croutons. Seven of them.

"I have to leave now," she said, "before I'm late."

"Leave?"

"LPC," she said. "Remember?"

Yes, he said, he remembered now, and his face brightened. He was apparently far happier about the fact she was heading to Ladies' Prayer Circle at Barb's than Dora herself was.

"Donny?" she said as he turned to leave the kitchen. "I signed up to bring paper plates and napkins." And now it was he who avoided her eyes. "I need to buy them . . . on the way there."

He sighed, and handed her five dollars.

She drove around aimlessly, pondering how awful it would be to arrive late again, picturing eye-rolling Barb secretly pleased to prove what a flake Dora was. By then—it really was too late. A car behind her honked furiously. She'd been too busy blubbering to notice. Yes, for some reason she was crying. She pictured Jake again, on television, remembered an afternoon half a lifetime ago when he'd pressed his face against the back of her neck.

She proceeded through the four-way stop, on down the highway in the right lane—too slow, as it turned out, because another rude driver blew his horn and passed her. She gave him the finger. It felt good. She groped for a tissue and found a balled-up napkin on the dashboard reeking of ketchup. She dabbed at her eyes and drove up and down Main Street, lost in thought, until she took a left on Washington Avenue and headed south, and somehow ended up at Jake's place.

While he was at the cesspool with Sandy, Kyle called Julie. That was the only good thing about their neighborhood swimming pool—the pay phone. He himself never planned to stick one toe into a body of water filled with pee-happy little kids.

He called Julie twice more, but the line was busy. And then it was ringing, ringing forever. Her little sister finally answered and said—surprise—Julie was babysitting. *Again.* And no, she didn't know when she'd get home. He hesitated, wondering if Julie's sister could be trusted to pass on a secret message about meeting up at the cemetery party later that night. *I'll be waiting for you with the general tonight.* Something mysterious and thrilling like that. "I gotta go," the little brat said, and hung up before Kyle could say a word.

"Sand," Kyle called. "It's six." His sister was holding on to the side of the pool, doing kicks. Practicing for dance, she said.

"Five more minutes? Pleeeease?"

A horn honked, and Kyle's mother drove by, waving at them as she left. Which meant his father was home. Waiting. Kyle's stomach tightened. His mother still didn't know. No way could she know and still go to her meeting at the Hendersons' tonight. She'd be bawling her eyes out if she knew.

"C'mon," Kyle told his sister now.

"I'm not finished with my kicks."

"Storm's coming." One of those tricks he learned from his mother when she wanted Sandy to get out of the water pronto.

Sandy looked up in the cloudless sky and narrowed her eyes. She was getting harder to fool. "There's no *storm*."

"Yeah, there is." A big shit storm was brewing. He could just feel it.

His father sat at the kitchen table, lying in wait. Kyle noted the crappy dinner—fish sticks and salad—end-of-the-grocery-week dinner. His appetite was gone, anyway. Sandy went to change out of her wet swimsuit, and Kyle felt the room change.

"I saw you with those roughnecks," his father said, as if they were continuing a conversation.

"Roughnecks?"

"Bobby, too. At the bank."

Kyle swallowed and looked down at his hands in his lap. "It's this program I'm helping out with," he said, too rushed, all wrong. "You can ask Mom."

"I don't know anything about a program like that."

Kyle fell silent. "I was going to tell you. I wanted to, you know . . . explain." He spotted a new blister on his thumb and began to pick it. "I went to your office," he said finally, looking up.

That afternoon, the receptionist at his father's office had peered at Kyle with a look of pure pity when he'd asked to see his dad. Kyle thought at first she felt sorry for him because he was sweaty and out of breath after running all the way there from the bank. "Honey, your daddy . . . ," she said. Kyle stood there looking stupid until she figured out he didn't have the faintest idea what she was talking about. "He doesn't work here anymore," she whispered.

"Doesn't work here anymore," Kyle had repeated, like an android.

She nodded. "Let go."

"*Let go.*"

"Yes."

"When?"

"Last week."

"Last *week?*" For some reason, he began to back away, toward the door, moving in reverse. As if the horrible moment could be rewound, undone.

"Oh, honey," she called, as he left, "are y'all . . . okay?"

Are we okay? That's what he wanted to ask his father right now. Because he was pretty sure they weren't.

"The lady there," Kyle said now, "she told me—"

"You were checking up on me?" his father said, his face gone bloodless. "Your mother sent you—"

"Mom doesn't know anything about it," he said. There was fear in his father's eyes now, a new fear—beyond shame or anger. His father was worried his mother would find out.

"I won't tell," he said.

"No," his father agreed.

"She'd worry."

His father nodded. "She lacks faith in me. In . . . us."

But . . . where was his father going every day, all dressed up?

"I have irons in the fire," his father said, as if reading Kyle's mind. "I go to seminars." And then he began to talk about how lonely it was in the dark, dark valley of his life with all his heavy burdens. Kyle knew he himself was one of them.

"Maybe . . . you can find a better job."

His father looked as if he'd been slapped. "You don't ever give up when your faith is being tested, Kyle. Don't you ever forget it." He began to tell Kyle, excitement mounting in his voice, that no matter how many deals fell through, no matter what they'd said at the office about how he couldn't move property, no matter how many clients they claimed he lost—and he didn't believe that for a minute! He had the gift of gab, always had—he would not grow discouraged. "Doubt is a tool of the devil," his father said. "Don't forget that, either."

"But maybe the plan is for you . . . to do something else. I mean," he said, racing to head off his father's glower, "like the sermon last week from Pastor Pat-Rick. About a guy in a flood?" He began to repeat the speech verbatim, realizing he'd somehow adopted Pastor Pat-Rick's cheerful intonations and hand gestures, as well. "And so this man in a flood was stuck on the roof of his house and a truck came by to rescue him, and he told the driver to go on, because the Lord would rescue him, and the next day a boat came by, but the man waved the crew away because the Lord would save him, and then, the waters rose higher, and a helicopter came, and the man still clung to his roof and told them to go away because he was waiting for the Lord to save him. Well, he drowned. When he got to heaven, the man wanted to know why he was left to die, and the Lord said, 'What do you mean? I sent you a truck, a boat, and a helicopter!'"

"That's not Scripture," his father said with such seriousness Kyle's stomach clenched all over again. "That's just a story someone made up. That's a . . . *joke*. An old joke. Pastor Pat-Rick shouldn't be saying something like that to the youth of Crossroads."

There would be bill collectors calling again, Kyle knew now. And even though his mother hadn't gone on one of her sprees in ages, there would be repo men galore. He fingered two twenties in his pocket. Maybe he should save them for bread and milk.

Sandy came back in, sat down, and his father stopped talking. Kyle had never been so glad in his life to see his sister.

"When's Mom coming home?" she asked.

Kyle met his father's eyes, looked away.

"Little later, pumpkin," his father said.

"I'm not really hungry," Kyle said. Brave, maybe, but stupid. Mealtime was not something you blew off at their house.

"All right," his father said, not even looking up from cutting his steak. Kyle, astonished but pleased, stood up and fled to his room, and lay on his bed, and counted down the hours until he could sneak out to the cemetery party. He began to understand just how powerful holding a secret could be.

"There's something I have to tell you," she said when he answered the door.

Jake blinked at her, cast a quick glance over her shoulder.

"It's just me," she said, appalled at how sneaky the statement sounded.

"Come in."

"No, I better not. I just—dropped by."

He laughed. "You'd rather stand out here on this half-rotten deck?"

And, yes, the gray boards were splintered, the lattice dingy and warped. Three cement blocks served as steps. Not that the place had seen better days. Jake's daddy was no count, and from what she remembered, his trailer on this swallowed-up slice of farmland always did look hardscrabble as the man himself.

"It's good to see you're feeling better," she said. There was a dab of shaving cream on his neck. His hair was damp. It occurred to her he was expecting company. A woman. How foolish of Dora to just come by. How awkward. How typical of her, to want to unburden herself.

"I'm on the mend."

"I'm real glad to hear that." She cleared her throat. "I saw you . . . on the news."

"Oh. That. Well, it turned out to be more trouble than it was worth. I wasn't too prepared."

"I thought you did . . . just fine."

A silence fell between them.

He crossed his arms and peered at her, curious and amused and patient. He always was patient. Waiting for her in the hot sticky vinyl seat of his car, or outside of class, or after she got lost at that crazy demonstration in Columbia, and once, in a hotel room. Patience was a virtue. She had so little of it herself.

"I don't know what I was thinking of," she said, "coming around like this . . . you're probably worn out from working all day." She looked back at where she'd parked the van in the grass, and half turned to leave. "Maybe I should—"

"Dee? C'mon now." He raked his hand through his hair. There were worry lines on his forehead. "You're gonna make a man stand here hurting?" He opened the door behind him again, wider this time. "Come on in."

She did.

"You keep a neat house," she said. The room was narrow and dark, which she'd expected, but it was sparsely furnished and clean, too, which she hadn't.

"I keep an empty place, you mean," he said. A glass-topped wagon wheel coffee table and a sagging tweed sofa sat in the center of the room. "That's his stuff," Jake said from behind her. "You won't believe the junk I already threw out. And I'm not even near finished."

"I guess you'll want to move your own things in."

He laughed. "I don't have things. Anyway, I'm not staying in this tin can long. I aim to get my own place one of these days. When I get the Blooming Idiots going."

She sat down on one end of the sofa. He moved to the kitchen. He opened the refrigerator and looked at her over the door. "Can I get you a beer?"

She closed her eyes and shook her head.

"What's so funny?"

Was she smiling? "Nothing. It's just—I don't drink anymore."

"No kidding? I'm sorry to hear that." He peered back inside the refrigerator. "Got nothing much here for teetotalers, Dee."

His teasing tone chilled her. The sound of the past again. A record needle had skipped, and was resuming, crackling the same tinny song. "Love Her Madly."

"Water is fine. I just want to get this over with."

His steps were tentative and careful; pain brought him a kind of grace. He eased down on the sofa beside her and handed her the glass of water. She took a sip. He took a long swallow from his beer, then rubbed his chin with his thumb, a nervous habit. She'd nearly forgotten how he did that. His T-shirt strained across his chest. He wore a black-strapped digital watch. Otherwise he was nearly the same: blue-black hair covered his ears, beltless faded jeans, sunburned arms.

"You ever been married?" she asked.

"Nope."

"Why not?"

"Just lucky, I guess."

"What have you been up to all these years?"

If he was puzzled at her chitchat, he didn't let on. This was up to her. He played along. "GI Bill, two semesters of community college. That was a disaster. Except I ended up registering for a course in landscaping by mistake, and figured out I liked it. When my mother died, I moved away because I could. Worked forklifts, meat plants, baggage handler for a while, trained to be a lineman. Then I turned three-oh and I finally grew up. I ended up with this place and the bright idea to start my own business . . . and so . . . here I am, back in Palmetto." He took another drink of his beer. "Lord, who would've thunk it."

"Did you kill anyone over there?"

"Over there?"

"The war."

"That was the idea," he said, but his smile vanished when he looked at her. "Lucky for the enemy, I had pretty piss-poor aim. I try not to think about it."

Her eyes filled. *Here it comes,* she thought. It wasn't too late to leave. She could just . . . make her excuses and walk out the door and he would understand. She shouldn't dredge up the past. She couldn't just unload here.

"I killed him, Jake," she said. And unloaded.

The day her brother died, Dora had been obsessing about her overdue paper on the Hungarian Revolution for Western Civ, and squabbling with her roommate about Jiffy Pop. It was November 3, 1970. She was three months into her freshman year at the University of South Carolina. She'd been in the dorm kitchen burning the popcorn when someone barged in and told her she had a phone call. It was her father. She could hear tragedy in his intake of breath, even before he said a word.

And then, at the funeral, at the heartbreaking, crowded, endless funeral—Wanda went missing. Where was Wanda? That's what everyone wanted to know. Will's own sweetheart not showing up? Heads shook; tongues wagged.

Wanda. Infuriating. Goody-goody. Sad sack. Pining for Will. Hard to believe she'd once been a fun best friend for Dora, the kind who read your palm, or helped you glue on false eyelashes, or laughed when you shoplifted *True Confessions* magazines under your shirt. But then she was Will's sweetheart, and they were going to get married, so Dora had her orders. *Keep Wanda company.* Will wrote it in every letter. *There are monkeys here, we have a pet. The lieutenant comes from Charleston. Keep Wanda company.*

When Wanda came by Dora's, she always went right to Will's room and put on a record, the same record. The Byrds sang "Turn! Turn! Turn!" while she wallowed on Will's bed. "It still smells like him a little." She wore Will's heavy class ring on a chain around her neck. She ran her hands over Will's trophies, hordes of metal athletes frozen in acts of catching or throwing or running or jumping—an eternal frenzy of competition on the bureau. A few months were left of high school, the days ticked by, the same days Will was counting off, too, in a jungle on the other side of the world. Only, with Will gone, so were the parties.

The fun ones, anyway. And now it was Wanda who was a third wheel—a squeaky sad little wheel. When Jake got off work, there Dora would be waiting, and Wanda, too. And then came the April night when Dora insisted they throw a barn bash. "Oh, I don't know . . . ," Wanda said as she lay on Will's bed, swinging his class ring on its chain in lazy circles like a hypnotist.

Dora bought Cokes and spiked them with rum. Wanda was buzzing in no time, her eyes bright and clever. A few people in the barn swelled to a few dozen—strangers, too, which broke Will's cardinal rule: Nobody we don't know gets in. The second rule was Dora's—unless they bring great stuff to share. Beer, vodka, weed, records.

Jake started clearing out the place at midnight. Dora woke up later, shivering on the cot. Jake covered her with a tablecloth and crawled in beside her. Then Bobby appeared. He stood looking in the doorway at Dora. He held a cat. One of the neighbor's pets. "Daddy said it's late. Party's over."

The cat was making the worst sounds, like screaming, like . . .

"Bobby, for God's sake put that cat down," Dora said.

But it wasn't the cat, it was a horrible shriek, otherworldly, agonized . . .

"Where's Wanda?" Dora sat up, already groping for her jeans.

They found her crying, half-naked, lying on the tarp in the dirt in the back of the barn, the smell of oil and mowers and wet soil hanging in the air, and something else, something metallic and sharp as blood. Dora dropped to her knees and held her. Wanda's teeth chattered in her ear. Jake brought the tablecloth, and she draped it around Wanda's shoulders. "What happened?"

"Don't tell anyone," Wanda said.

"I thought you got a ride," Dora said numbly. "I thought you were home."

But Wanda never made it home that night. She never left the barn. She was in the back, with the old tractor, on a tarp on the floor, with two boys taking turns. *Maybe I let them*, she said later. *I don't remember, so I guess it's the same.*

"Wanda. Oh, Wanda," Dora said, pressing her face against Wanda's limp, dank hair. But she was thinking *Will Will Will.* "We need to call . . . someone." The police. The hospital. Sirens. Notepads. White coats. Cameras. Oh, God.

"No! No, promise me. Don't tell."

"Who?" Jake asked, squatting down closer. Not what, but who. "Who was out here with you?"

She shrugged. "Strangers. I don't know their names."

"What should I tell Dad?" Bobby asked. Dora turned around to look at her brother. He held the cat, ears flattened, petting it with desperate strokes.

"It's a secret, Bobby. Don't tell anyone anything."

Dora thought that was the worst, that night, but it wasn't. Two months later, they headed to the clinic in Mexico, and then Wanda took off and didn't even come back for Will's funeral, but that wasn't the worst, either. The worst was the letter Dora got from Will just days before he died. She thought of the letter with its venomous message, a message that still stung her now, every day. *Dora, you had to go and ruin her. This is going to kill me.*

"He went to his death—," Dora said, before her voice ran high and broke. "On *purpose.*" She buried her face in her hands. "He wanted to go in that spider hole and get himself blown up. He knew exactly what he was doing."

Jake put a hand on her arm. They waited until her tears stopped. "So Wanda wrote and told him," Jake said finally. "God, how stupid was that."

"I begged her not to." Dora paused. "I didn't think she would. But you know how she was." *Oh, Dora, I'm dead inside.* Postmarked from California. Wanda's aunt. "I took off trying to find her after the funeral. Her mother wouldn't tell me anything, and then she just upped and moved away. I bought a bus ticket and went looking for Wanda just to find out why. Just to hear her tell me what she wrote Will. I needed to know. I don't even know why. I was crazy with grief. I never found her. Her old maid aunt wouldn't tell me a thing. Wanda's life was ruined. And now, I still think about how they could've been this happy family—they could have been married and had kids if it weren't for . . . that night."

"Good God, Dee. You can't think that way. You'll go crazy. Living in the past like that."

"That night ruined everything. Will and Wanda—for all I know she's dead, too—then Bobby turned crazy, and you got drafted and nearly killed, too. Don't you see?"

"Will died because it was his turn to go into that tunnel," Jake said slowly. "That's how it worked. You were lookout, you went in tunnels, you just did what you had to do. And Wanda? She went wild on the wrong night with the wrong people. Bobby's mind was already going, you know that. And me—I'm no warrior, I'm just lucky I came back at all. Those are the facts. Shit happens, Dee. Sometimes bad shit happens. So stop torturing yourself."

"It's worse when you have children. You'll see when you have kids of your own. I thought I was okay again and I could forget things, but when my children were born, it all came back. The worst kind of fear . . . when you're a mother, it's a constant black worry. I can't explain it. You remember what evil and dangerous things are out there. And . . . then it gets worse and worse." She sighed. "Kyle looks so much like . . . him. Like Will."

"Yeah."

"You noticed? You see it, too?"

"There's a resemblance, sure, but you got your mind tuned that way, Dee. You got your antenna up, flashing you certain pictures. You need to change the channel. That's my theory. You see what you want to see."

"Listen to you. Like it's that easy."

"I didn't say it was easy. But don't you think your brother would want you to be happy? He was mighty protective of you. I've got the scars to prove it."

She wiped her eyes and smiled.

"He'd be pissed to see you still miserable about what happened all those years ago. Don't you think?"

She shrugged.

"That's what I mean about changing the channel, Dee."

She nodded and after a minute stood and asked to use the restroom.

"Twelve feet north, you can't miss it."

She splashed cold water on her face, blotting with the solitary thin white towel, shower-damp and smelling of soap. She came back in the living room, picked up her glass, and took it to the sink. "Don't worry about that," he said, but she washed it anyway.

She sat back down beside him on the sofa. "I burned Will's letter," she said. "No one else knows about it." She found his eyes. "Not even my mother."

"No one needs to. Let it go, Dee."

"I'm sorry about . . . coming here and dumping all this on you," she said. "Like you don't have enough troubles." She felt lighter, emptied out. *Everyone needs a good cry*, her mother used to tell Dora all those years ago, back when Dora didn't cry much at all.

He sighed. "You're not safe here, Dee." She looked at him, and he brushed her hair aside with a finger. "You might think you are. Married lady like you. And me, laid up with a bum back. You might think you're safe, but . . . you should leave," he said, his voice turning stern. But his hand on her knee was warm and strong, and she closed her eyes, and did not move.

TWENTY

Emma had spent the morning assembling a picnic for the two of them, but you wouldn't know it from the way she dashed around her kitchen now, adding extra napkins, salt and pepper, a jar of homemade pickles to the basket on the counter. This was not a bad thing, she thought, as she felt Dr. Burnside's eyes follow her, for she didn't want him to know just how much she'd agonized over this lunch of theirs. Let him think she just threw it together slapdash, and not pored over potato salad recipes. It was silly, is what it was, this ripple of nervousness, a sign of just how empty her days must be. Was she more nervous about seeing Amaranth up close again, or strolling across the grounds with this man . . . this plant lover?

"You know, I happened to remember my grandmother used to have one of my grandfather's plant carriers," Emma said.

"Made of glass?"

She nodded. "A sort of terrarium."

"A Wardian case, probably. Used to transport plants."

"I don't know what could have happened to it. When I was a little girl, I used to keep lightning bugs in it at night and pretend they were fairies. I probably left it in the woods."

"No telling what we might find out there," he said.

A man like that wants something. Lila's warning rang out in her mind, but Emma was determined to ignore it.

"More coffee?" she asked.

"No thanks. I'm good." His hat rested on his knees, his backpack was at his feet, but Dr. Burnside appeared perfectly at ease.

"I don't know what's keeping Mr. Cary."

"I'm in no hurry," he said.

She nodded. As soon as Jake arrived to pick up Bobby, who waited outside now on the porch, she and Dr. Burnside could be on their way. "He should be here any minute."

"We have all day," he added with a smile. Emma felt her cheeks grow warm. Had the statement sprung from brazen friendliness or gentle patience? She sat down at the table across from him, her own cup of coffee grown cold. The two of them did not speak, but sat in shared silence, and she began to feel calm.

She really needed to get ahold of herself, Dora reminded herself now, as she nearly burned a second batch of oatmeal. She could hardly function. Ten hours since she'd left Jake's place, and time had dragged by inexorably, without mercy. And now, with her children sleeping, her husband dressing, the milk jug sweating on the table, the coffeepot puffing steam, the oatmeal burning, Dora was determined to get ahold of herself. Only, it wasn't getting any easier.

No good would come from this kind of longing. She knew that much.

"Can I have Count Chocula?" Sandy sat down at the table.

"Good morning . . . and no you may not, sweetie. We're having oatmeal, okay?"

Her daughter's eyes gazed sadly at the pantry where the box of cereal she'd begged Dora to buy was still stashed. Sandy nodded. "Okay."

Dora kissed the top of her head. What a good child. How . . . easy. Compared with her brother.

"You don't need that sugary stuff anyway," Dora said. "Not

before your rehearsal today. You need fuel for all that hard work."
Sandy's face brightened at the mention of her dance rehearsal at
Tiny Dancer. Dora had picked up Sandy's costume yesterday and
spirited it away to Sandy's closet, where she planned to keep it
until the last possible moment, as if it were a stowaway. Donny
did not need to see the thing until the actual recital. Once he saw
the performance, with their own Sandy, more graceful and confident in her prepubescent, pudgy body than Dora ever thought
possible, he would see the value of dancing lessons. And yes, it
was a flashy thing, with its sequins and streamers, but when the
girls lined up for the group photo, with their little hats askew,
their flesh-colored tights and batons, their white gloves, stifling
their giggles, Sandy had looked so . . . happy. Her daughter was
finally blossoming, she thought now. And she was still *good*. A
pleaser. Unlike Kyle and Dora herself.

She could feel Jake *waiting* for her in that empty old trailer,
waiting for her to call. She wouldn't. Ever.

"Mom? Are you listening?"

"What . . . was that?"

"Are we going to Tiny Dancer early for warm-ups?" Sandy
asked.

"Warm-ups?"

"Yeah, you know—" Sandy hopped out of her chair and
stretched to demonstrate, and Dora was struck again at the innocent confidence of her daughter's moves, even in the straining,
elastic-band pajamas. Would Sandy feel that unself-conscious
about her body at thirteen? Sixteen? A girl's self-image seemed so
fragile to Dora now, something to be guarded.

"We'll go early," Dora said.

"Daddy!" Sandy said as Donny entered the kitchen. She was
still at the age when greeting parents in the morning was a delight, and hugged her father as if he'd just returned from a journey. Donny embraced her, his face turning, for a moment, soft
with love. Dora's eyes filled, and she turned away.

She would not see Jake again. She would not even talk to him.

That much she had decided. Barb Henderson would have a field day if she even suspected. And how terrible for Sandy and Kyle . . . to hear such gossip. Yes, there was nothing to do but stay away from Jake, the only person on earth who knew all her secrets. Who *was* her secret. She wondered what Jake might say if she told him she had a dozen different job applications filled out, but for some reason, hadn't worked up the courage to turn in any of them. What would he advise about the absent way she was dishing out oatmeal, slicing bananas, and in a monotonous, distant drone, reminding Sandy that one heaping spoon of brown sugar was enough? And what of the vacant manner in which she was moving from sink to table to refrigerator, as efficient and brisk as a servant, and all the while the secret of him—of Jake!—flickered steadily inside her, blue-bright as a pilot light. How could she purge him from her heart? That's what she would have liked to ask Jake, because she could ask him anything on earth. She was in an awful state, and the only person who might understand was the person causing it.

"Kyle?" she called. "Breakfast."

"Maybe he needs the sleep," Donny said. She looked at her husband with astonishment. That he was not, at this instant, demanding Kyle join them at the kitchen table was not only shocking but a little disconcerting, as well.

"You mean . . . you think we should let him sleep late?" she asked, and then wondered, incredulously, if the two of them—father and son—had managed to do some bonding the night before. Dora felt herself soften. "And miss breakfast?"

But her husband had stopped listening and was intently reading a brochure: *The Nuts and Bolts of Nailing Down the Christian Customer.* He wore a shirt and tie, and she remembered he had a Saturday sales seminar at Crossroads that morning.

"I guess he is going through a growth spurt," she said.

"Mom, can I try on my costume?" Sandy asked now.

"Only if you stay in your room," Dora whispered. "We want to keep it a surprise, remember?" Sandy ran to her room. Donny was, Dora saw with relief, still studying his brochure with the intense glower he reserved for overdue bills and Revelations.

Dora headed to Kyle's bedroom, but all manner of knocking and cajoling wouldn't bring out her obstinate son. Oh, that boy was going through a growth spurt, all right—he'd sprouted one dangerous stubborn streak.

"What's going on?" Donny called from the kitchen. "Where is everyone?"

"Kyle?" Dora said, louder.

Silence.

"Kyle?" she called. "Open up."

And now the silence was filled with the sounds of Dora's own heart pounding. Something was wrong.

"Kyle?" Her voice broke high in fear. And then she was barging in, not bothering to knock, because *something was wrong.* Even from the doorway, she could tell that wasn't Kyle there in his bed. That wasn't her son. Not those pillows, awkwardly arranged to resemble a slothful kid who should be sleeping late, and burrowing in the covers, crabbing at her to leave him alone. Oh, no, that wasn't . . . The window was still wedged open with a ballpoint pen, the screen propped carelessly outside.

He had sneaked out. He had not come back. He was gone.

And then Donny was there because Dora was sobbing. Something terrible had happened and it was her fault. Something horrible. Something was wrong. She'd brought this on; she'd missed the signs. She'd been so caught up in her own daze of transgression, she hadn't seen Kyle chafing and plotting. She hadn't checked his room at night all week, and now he was in harm's way. Now he was . . . gone.

"Daddy? What's wrong?" Sandy asked from the door. She was wearing her costume, her small face sober in the festive garb.

"What kind of getup is that?" Donny asked his daughter.

"It's for my dance recital. It's a surprise," she said, crossing her arms and hunching, as if she weren't clothed at all.

"Well, honey, you're not wearing that thing outside of this house."

"But—"

"I've got to call my mother," Dora gasped, running past them, down the hall to the phone. Her hands shook so badly, she could hardly dial. But when she called, her mother hadn't heard from Kyle, and sounded alarmed, though she tried to hide it. She couldn't.

"Call the police," Dora told her husband when she got off the phone, and returned to Kyle's room. Sandy burst into tears.

"The police?" Donny said. "We'll handle this my way. No use brewing a scandal."

"Scandal? *Scandal?* I don't care about scandal, Donny. I just want my son back." She collapsed on the bed beside Sandy, and buried her face in Kyle's pillow.

"Get ahold of yourself, Dora. You don't want to let him see you like this—give him the upper hand."

"But something *terrible* has happened," she shrieked. "Don't you see? He always came back before."

"Sandy, go on to your room and wait," Donny said.

Sandy, bewildered, looked at her father with a forlorn face, but plodded out, costume tingling merrily.

"Before?" Donny asked after she left. *"Before?"*

"The other times," Dora said, quieter, sniffling. "He always came back . . . by the middle of the night. Never like this."

"Other times? What do you mean, other times? You didn't tell me? You lied to *protect* him?"

No, she hadn't protected him. Not at all. She hadn't been watching him closely anymore. She was not vigilant. She was too busy with her own temptation. Now, she was paying for it . . . *her son* was paying. She thought of car accidents, mangled bodies by the roadsides, drug overdoses and . . . it took only a moment of stupidity, an instant of weakness, one wild night to wreck a life. She closed her eyes and thought of the photograph of Wanda and Will she'd found jammed in Kyle's pocket, as if it were a sign. A warning.

Watch him. But she hadn't. She hugged Kyle's pillow tighter. "I want him back safe. Oh please, please, please safe," she said, in an utterance so intensely private, Donny was stunned into silence.

His eyes burned from lack of sleep; his throat was raw. He struggled not to retch. He'd thrown up hours ago—silent, productive heaves. Oh, God, where was he? The blue tarp above him sagged from the night's rain; rivulets ran like tears. Living wild wasn't hard if you knew how to do it, Gordon had told him. Living wild. Kyle sat up. His head felt like a freaking medicine ball.

Where was Gordon? His tent was empty. Sweet was gone, too. Kyle stood up slowly. His tennis shoes were ruined, the soles of his feet burned. He needed to take a leak. Where was *that* supposed to happen? He tried to remember what Gordon had told him. Something about a key to the Hot Spot restroom . . . or the house up there? . . . or something. He rubbed his eyes. The memories of the night began their assault: sneaking out of his bedroom past midnight. His mother had gotten home late, after his father had already gone to bed, and the house had fallen mercifully silent. He'd run like the rabbits he'd seen in the truck headlights, running for dear life, heading for underbrush and thatches of trees to the cemetery. And then . . . he didn't want to think about it. He couldn't.

Sweet Sweet Sweet, somebody was calling, nearer now.

Kyle turned around and gasped. Jake stood there. Too late, Kyle reminded himself to play it cool. "I didn't see you."

"No kidding. What in the hell are you doing here?"

Kyle shrugged. "Maybe I wanted to get an early start."

"Uh-huh."

"Where's Gordon?"

"I don't know. He was gone when I woke—when I got here." It had been Sweet that greeted Kyle up on the street in the moonless night and led him down to Gordon's tent. Gordon seemed happy to see Kyle, and fixed him a plate of beans. Shared the whiskey, too.

Jake rubbed his chin, looked around, then just looked lost in thought.

Kyle sat down on a rock. He felt Jake's eyes on him.

"So, is this about that girl you love?"

Love. Not a crush. Not puppy love. The girl he *loved*, the girl he ached for so badly right now. The girl he just got his ass in hot water for. The girl he loved. Jake understood.

He nodded. "Julie."

"Your first love is the worst. The best, too. Like kindling. Flares up high and fast, leaves you hurting. The other ones won't be as bad. Or as good."

"I wish you were my dad," he said.

"You don't mean that," Jake said.

"Yeah, I do."

Jake managed a dry laugh. "You don't know me too good to say something like that."

Kyle was silent.

"It's nothing against you," Jake said. He looked away. "I'd be proud if you were kin to me."

There was a rustling sound as Gordon stepped into the clearing, Sweet behind him. He didn't appear surprised to see Jake. He took out a biscuit from the paper bag he was carrying and threw it to the dog. He handed the bag to Kyle. "Breakfast," he said.

"Thanks," he said, "but I'm not hungry." The smell of sausage drifted up to him, and his stomach curdled. There was nothing left to throw up.

Gordon laughed. "You got the dry heaves?"

"Good," Jake told Kyle. "I hope you puke your guts out. Maybe you'll think twice next time before you get shit-faced."

Kyle wiped his mouth with his shirt.

"You been here all night, haven't you?" he asked Kyle. "Better let your mama know you're all right."

"I want to see Julie first."

Jake crossed his arms and studied Kyle. "Well, I can't let you stay here. How about I take you to your grandmother's?"

Kyle was silent, considering. It was all beginning to seem hopeless. Any moment now, if she hadn't already, his mother would discover the fake-out pillows in Kyle's bed weren't really Kyle. His ass was grass, and Julie might not even want to see him now after the things he'd said to her last night. But he had to try to talk to Julie today. It was all too much—crashing the cemetery party and finding her with that prep boy . . . Worth. And then she was all, *I'm sorry, okay?* begging Kyle not to be angry about her going out with Worth, who would demand his pound of flesh. No wonder Kyle got wasted and said those things to Julie. Could she blame him? *First love is the worst,* Jake said. Yeah, you got that right.

"No offense, but you stink to high heaven," Jake told him, stepping away. Kyle shrugged.

"Sor-*ry.*"

"I got a good mind to hose you off," Jake said. "You smell like a sorry-ass drunk, and we can't have your grandmother see you— smell you—like that."

TWENTY-ONE

K yle, swallowed up in Bobby's ill-fitting black sweatpants and a green T-shirt, sat stewing on Emma's living room sofa, hugging a pillow. Emma had called Dora. The scene wouldn't be pretty. Kyle looked up at Emma with a hopeless look.

"Well, that was a quick shower," Emma said. "I hope you feel better."

Emma sat down across from her grandson. Dr. Burnside spread his photographs and her grandfather's diary on the coffee table. "Young fellow? You want to help me match these up?" he asked.

Relief crossed Kyle's face. "They have to be polite in front of company, right?" he asked Emma.

Emma saw at once the wisdom in Kyle's strategy. Surely Dora's pride would outweigh an emotional outburst in the presence of a perfect stranger. Dignity might at least put up a struggle. One could only hope.

Emma stood up. "I better check on your uncle," she told Kyle. "I don't know where he got off to."

She didn't have to go far. Bobby and Jake were sitting in the backyard.

"Why, Mr. Cary. I had no idea you smoked," she said.

"I don't," he said, stubbing out a cigarette. "But Bobby wanted some company." Jake rubbed his chin nervously. "I was thinking since we're here, we oughta go ahead and mow your yard."

"Grandma," Kyle said from behind her. "They're here."

Emma followed Kyle back into the living room. She barely had time to steel herself for the onslaught before the front door swung open and Dora burst into the room.

"Kyle!" she said. "Oh, Kyle." He sat back down, burrowing deeply and defensively into the sofa cushions, like a tick in flesh.

Dora threw her arms around Kyle. She drew back after a moment, peered at him carefully.

"What *happened*?" she asked. "Where were you . . . all night?"

"Son?" Donny said. "Get your things. We're going." He thrust a furious look in Emma's direction.

"I don't have any things," Kyle said.

"I'd like you both to meet my guest, Win Burnside," Emma said.

When Dr. Burnside stood and extended his hand, Emma was not sure Donny would shake it. Her son-in-law was seething, no doubt about that, and clearly flummoxed.

But it was not the presence of Emma's guest Donny found baffling, it was the disconcerting sight of the urn containing Harold Hanley's ashes on Emma's fireplace mantel. Clearly, Emma was determined to keep her husband on a short leash, even in the hereafter. That Kyle had fled to his grandmother's did not surprise Donny, though it did alarm him. You could feel the pull of waywardness in this place. And Donny, an expert at finding the plots of the devil in everyday life, would not have Kyle lost in the wilderness of sin here, as Dora had been—lost in fornication, and drink, and all the rest. How easy it would be to give in to the pull of Satan, for he was a trickster, an accuser, and Donny was fighting that one's wickedness and wantonness every day. He'd been chosen to. For the Lord saw fit for Donny to choose a wife who was a lightning rod for trouble, and who bore him a son whose soul was clouded by the worst temptations. No one save the Lord knew what a struggle it was to be married to a woman with such *appetites*, such enormous wants and endless needs, a woman who responded only to periods of deprivation—financial, emotional, and physical. There had been times when she'd nearly sabotaged his resolve with immodest nightgowns and melon-scented slippery goo that did not, he was certain, come from Agape or any other Crossroads shop, but lately it appeared she'd learned her lesson. She'd stopped crying about having no money of her own, or enough for groceries, and ceased her accusations that he didn't love her. He didn't love her; it was true. It was too much work. But Dora was his wife. She was his cross to bear.

"You ready, honey?" Dora murmured. She squeezed Kyle's hand.

"Dora," Donny said. "We talked about this." She would baby Kyle to death if Donny let her. The very idea! Letting Kyle sneak out nights. Maybe now she would learn her lesson. No wonder Donny couldn't concentrate on closing deals and property lists. No wonder, with this kind of tomfoolery under his roof. And that's exactly what he would tell Dora. For there was *Iniquity of the fathers in the bosom of their children after them.* And the mothers, too. Especially the mothers.

At times like these, Donny allowed himself a smidgen of regret. For he'd once planned on being a missionary, and how different his life would have been had he finished Holmes Bible College and not let his fear of parasites stop him. What a different life he would be leading had he not seen Luther Henderson's slide show about his year as a missionary in darkest Africa. Luther had stood at the front of the classroom with a missionary doctor, clicking through a noisy carousel of slides, and told about the mission they'd started over there, but then he got to the part about parasites. Worms. White, blind, ribbons of them, squirming, filthy worms. People died from them, *they exuded from every orifice*, the doctor said in a pleased tone. Donny had left the lecture early and vomited in the men's room. No missionary work for him. After all, you could save people and lead them to the Lord right here in

Palmetto, just as he had a week later, when he'd found Dora's lost soul in Kmart.

Kyle sighed, closed his eyes, sat back, and put his head on Emma's shoulder.

"Let's go," Donny said. He looked at his watch. Dora had agreed they would stay no longer than ten minutes, and there would be no dramatic outbursts. He could still make the seminar if they left now. "Your sister's waiting." He'd ordered Sandy to stay outside, and not enter the portals of this place, and he'd been forced to cloak her in his suit jacket to cover an outfit no eight-year-old daughter of his should ever wear in public.

"I imagine he's exhausted," Emma said.

"*He's* exhausted?" Donny said quietly.

Emma thought how truly ominous such a seething anger could be. Harold always walked away in the middle of arguments, infuriating Emma, or else claimed he wasn't mad in the least, and she theorized now on the effectiveness of avoidance and denial in the heat of anger. Her own marriage managed to survive, hadn't it?

"Let's calm down, shall we?" Emma said. Dr. Burnside did not appear fazed in the least by the family theatrics. He sat back in his chair with an amused expression.

Dora stood, and tugged at Kyle's hand, but the boy was all limp stubbornness and refused to budge.

"I'm not going." Kyle said. "I'm going to live here with Grandma."

"*What?*" Donny said.

"Mama!" Dora said, "Please just stay out of this. Don't make matters worse."

"I—didn't say a word," Emma said, flustered. Kyle's statement was, in fact, news to her.

"This is no place for you to spend unsupervised time," Donny told his son. "Your mother and I agree."

"Oh, really?" Emma said, catching Dora's eye.

Emma knew she wore a tight, hard smile, the kind you might

see stitched on a doll's face. She felt removed from her own people—from this raving idiot in her living room, from the sad sack, weak daughter, the rebellious grandson who would take more energy than Emma had to offer. She sighed quietly, not out of exasperation, but an eerie sense of calm. Across from her, Dr. Burnside, removed from the squabble, unrolled the sketch of soul shines, examining it.

"I don't care to spend another moment listening to this twaddle," Emma said.

And then the sound of a clearing throat. "Sorry to interrupt," Jake said, standing there looking miffed, Emma thought. More than miffed. The man looked tormented. His back must be giving out on him again, as if he could hide it. Well, he couldn't. He wore a searching, sad look that wrung Emma's heart for no good reason.

Jake was suffering, all right, but his back wasn't the cause. Seeing the Husband with Dora hurt worse than he'd thought. Worse than what Dora had told him last night before she left, when she swore she could never see him or talk to him again. *I'm going to try to be good.* He shouldn't even come into Emma Hanley's living room, he should have stayed outside or left, he knew it. At least his brain knew it. Other parts of him were less accommodating. He just couldn't bring himself to go, and when he went out to his truck, in an agony of indecision, pacing worse than Bobby Hanley, he discovered he couldn't have left anyway. He was blocked in by Dora's van. And that, he realized now, was fine with him.

Jake forced himself to look at the Husband. "Excuse me, but I'm about finished up with Mrs. Hanley's yard, so could you move your van out there? It's blocking my truck."

"We're going," Dora said, two red spots on her cheeks, not looking up.

"Jake, you walked right into a hornet's nest," Emma said.

"Yeah, I'm good at that." Jake shrugged, good-natured again, but his eyes were on Dora. The Husband wasn't likely to leave her alone, and Dora wasn't helping matters. And that made him even more determined to stay. He had to talk to her; he had to *see* her.

Dora was relieved that Donny was too angry at Kyle and her mother to notice how difficult it was for her not to look at Jake. Impossible. Ever since she saw his truck parked in her mother's driveway and knew he was nearby, her concentration was shot. She wanted to flee, to run, but she was, at this instant, glowing in his smitten stare. It was hard enough to be good when Jake was in the same town, much less the same room. Didn't he know that? Didn't he *see* what effort it took for Dora to go back to her life of . . . what? What kind of life was she leading? Or, not leading, but *enduring*, because she had to keep the children . . . safe. And now, well, she'd nearly lost Kyle. He would act out even worse when he heard Donny was taking him out of Palmetto High and—next time where would he run? What would he do? Her own son, taking refuge with Dora's mother, as if this were a safe house, and it wasn't, it wasn't. And poor Sandy, out on the porch now, sweltering in her father's suit jacket, which she still dutifully wore to hide her costume. She'd been forbidden by her father to enter her own grandmother's house, and pressed her wet face to the window now as if she were the family dog.

Safe? They weren't safe!

Her children were *besieged* with troubles, and she and Donny were just making things worse. Dora's throat tightened. She would not cry here. She would not cry, despite the fact that she had failed—yes, *failed!*—Kyle and Sandy, by fumbling through their young lives like a sleepwalker. *What has happened to me?* Years and years of this *ether*, this dark fear, this remorse, this reined-in will, this stifled frustration, hunkering down as if she could protect her children from . . . the world. She couldn't even save herself. Her prayers were nothing but desperate bargaining. *Please, God, keep him safe and I promise I'll . . .* Oh, she was broken. Dora was broken. And Donny was saying something now in a terse tone, trying to herd Kyle out the door. How could she go back to this life of hers? Dora reached for her purse, rising to her feet like a marionette.

Dora's unguarded gaze wasn't lost on Kyle, who, with narrowed eyes, began to connect the dots. No *wonder* she'd kept mum about his working with Jake! No wonder she'd let him fudge about Saving Souls! The better to hide her secrets! And to think Kyle felt a twinge of guilt minutes ago when his mother hugged him, when she was skittish and weepy, and he knew she still didn't have a clue his dad had been sacked. Kyle hated when she got like that—all beholden and shit. Letting his father run all over her for a while—until she did something to piss him off again. But then Jake had come in the room—and look at the way Jake was staring at her—at Kyle's mother! Jake with his love advice. *Mr. First-love-burns-hottest.* This had happened right under Kyle's nose. And his father was clueless, even now, staring at the fireplace mantel, his jaw working, thinking about a sales seminar or . . . something . . . while ten feet away *his own wife* was moony-eyed over her *first love.* Did no one else see? Were they blind? And now that annoying old guy was chattering again to his grandmother like a biology teacher on a field trip. Kyle's head throbbed.

"We need to leave," Dora told Kyle. Poor Dora looked stung, her face pink with shame. Emma did not envy her daughter. She had her hands full.

"Don't leave, Dee," Jake said.

Dora looked at him. "Please," she said. "Don't."

Dee? Emma thought. *Don't leave, Dee?* What was happening here? Emma sat up straight. Why, Jake was . . . besotted. And Dora—*Dee!*—radiant, but trying her best to hide it. *Jake Cary loves Dora!* Still loved her after all these years. Had not *stopped* loving her! How could Emma have missed such a thing? Why, just look at the naked adoration on Jake's face. Dora's downcast eyes. All the signs, and Emma had failed to see them.

"All right, now," Donny said, looking again at his watch, the only face in the room, Emma noted with relief, that he actually appeared interested in. Donny pointed to Kyle. "Let's go."

"Tea," Emma managed to utter. "Would anyone like a glass of tea or—?" Silence fell in the room. Palpable tension, or was she imagining it? No one wanted refreshments, or perhaps she just hadn't heard them. She was too shocked! Her ears were ringing, as if she'd been struck. *He loves her.* Finally, there was the sound of crinkling parchment as Dr. Burnside gingerly rolled up sketches, in a gentle way that touched Emma. His hand moved to his chest, fingering something there hidden beneath his shirt. Something sacred. Like the Catholics did.

"Dr. Burnside, would you care to see the Secret Keepers out back?" Emma found herself asking. "They're in fine form today."

He cocked his head at her in surprise, then rose to his feet. "I would, Mrs. Hanley. I certainly would."

"Are we finished here?" Emma announced. "My guest and I are adjourning to the backyard." She did not wait for a response. She and Dr. Burnside threaded their way through the snarl of confused souls and headed to the kitchen, and just before she opened the back door, while her hand was, in fact, on the doorknob, the thought hit her again—Jake Cary loves my Dora!—and she halted midstep, causing Dr. Burnside to bump into her. Emma was too overcome to apologize. They ventured out into the backyard, where a new clump of Secret Keepers waited, eager, she thought, for an audience.

Bobby still sat at the picnic table in the backyard. He did not look up at his mother. He drew circles with his finger on the table, and thought of the time he and Will had helped their father build a picnic table. The pine planks were hard and white, and smelled like sawdust. Not like these planks. This table was gray and rough, and gave you splinters. But Bobby could see the pine tree here in the wood anyway. The pine tree was hiding in the table, you could tell—the knots like eyes. Surely Will would want to know. Bobby would tell him. But Will had not appeared for days. There were just echoes of Will's words sometimes. Whispers.

Emma called to her son, but he did not answer. He was staring at some miniscule thing in front of him, some creature perhaps only he could see. From a distance, Emma reflected, her son looked like a normal man with an extraordinary mind. That is how she vowed to think of him.

"I can see them from here. Oh, my." Dr. Burnside took out his camera and broke into a trot with Emma following, patting her chest, a little winded, though he showed no signs of fatigue. He kneeled to examine them, then looked back at her in awe. "Amazing specimens."

What will happen to them?

"That's what I don't know. The microclimate is extraordinary, but whether they will survive in this zone—"

Emma, startled, realized she'd spoken aloud. "No," she said, with a sad laugh. "No, I mean—I can't imagine—" *What will happen to them?* She pictured Jake, and her heart squeezed with pain. And he not even kin. You'd think she had enough worrying to do over her own family, but no, no, she had adopted another into her fold. And—Dora would need a place to stay. She and Kyle and Sandy? No. Dora would never—Emma rubbed her collar absently. She felt breathless, squeezed.

"Mrs. Hanley, are you all right?" Dr. Burnside asked. She watched the eagerness on his face fade, replaced by concern. Did she appear that weak? Was she so very feeble already?

"This heat," she said, looking back again at the house.

Dr. Burnside studied Emma Hanley and felt a pang of nostalgia. He'd once stolen Xi Ling, his own beloved wife, from missionaries in China. He had, in the course of events, witnessed her sorrowful extrication and resulting liberation from the clutches of a greedy assembly. Xi Ling, pale and fragrant as a lily, had loved the plant lover enough to flee with him while he was still a graduate student, with little money and few prospects. They had traveled for nearly five decades, rarely stopping for more than a few seasons, and she bore him one child, a puckered bean of an infant, who lived only three days. In the end, it did not matter; Xi Ling was all he needed. He was even more rootless now since she had succumbed four springs ago to a voracious cancer, a fiery blight that devoured her in great gulps. In a small glass vial, on a braided necklace of hemp from the valley of Quillota, Chile, the plant lover kept a pinch of Xi Ling's silvery ashes, and moved his hand there now, to his chest, as he was wont to do in moments of reflection. Emma Hanley watched him, her eyes the extraordinary blue of the starflower *Borago officinalis* he'd once admired in Syria.

"Perhaps it would be helpful to get out of the sun?" he asked.

"No, really. I'm fine, thank you," she said. "Splendid."

Oh, but her heart, how it was thumping! Leaping, pirouetting, hurting. She gulped in air. She was having an event, as the doctors called it. A heart attack. *What will happen to them?* But no, this wasn't pain exactly, it was . . . an unbinding. A letting go.

"I was thinking . . . ," she said slowly, her voice growing thin as a filament. Dr. Burnside stepped closer to listen. "We should go see the garden at Amaranth now. If your offer still stands?"

"Why, of course," he said.

"I'm . . . seventy-two," Emma said, as if that explained things.

She turned to look at Bobby, smoking. No one had emerged from the house, not one of them. What were they doing in there? *What will they do?*

Dr. Burnside put the camera into his backpack and offered his arm. "Shall we?" he asked.

Emma nodded.

Dora, having escaped to her mother's bathroom, stood by the window and peered through the blinds. The view of the backyard—the familiar swath of lawn, the ragged kitchen garden, the ivy-scaled pines and oaks in the distance—calmed her. In fact, she began to feel disembodied, detached from the morning's snarl of events, as if they hadn't happened, as if she hadn't just turned and left Donny and Jake standing there in the living room.

It was like being dead, Dora supposed—this remove, this watching her family scatter and gather outside without her. Bobby sat quietly at the picnic table, while Emma and that man—her *guest*—stood together at the edge of the garden, apparently deep in conversation. And now Sandy appeared, running through the side yard to Emma, who turned and dropped the man's arm to hug her granddaughter and admire her dance costume. Kyle now—his voice first, then his back, as he headed over to his uncle, his hands jammed in his pockets. Yes, there was something final about the scene out there, some shift, something funereal.

Her mother's companion smiled, and Emma turned to take his arm again. It was a tender gesture, startling in its intimacy. Had there been even one instance of such casual affection between her parents? Dora could not recall. Except—except for Will's funeral, when her mother clutched her father's elbow for hours, but that was a kind of grasping, Dora thought now, borne of desperation and black grief, not this . . . tenderness.

And now her mother appeared to be going somewhere with her guest. Leaving? *You can't go. You can't leave me like this, holed up in here. I don't know what to do.* Emma was calling out something to Kyle, who nodded, sat back down with Bobby and, surely not, Dora thought. *Leaving me like this? With this?* Her mother drew closer, passed the window, heading to the side yard, arm in arm with a stranger.

Dora could not remember her mother's face like that—glowing with pleasure—and felt a wave of empathy. Her mother had managed to spend years in a troubled marriage, and Dora was just beginning to understand the kind of resolve that took.

PART IV

Compared with the leaf, the flower is a dying organ. This dying, however, is of a kind we may aptly call "a dying into being." Life in its mere vegetative form is here seen withdrawing in order that a higher manifestation of the spirit may take place.
—ERNST LEHRS, MAN OR MATTER

TWENTY-TWO

Mornings were Bobby's favorite time. Nights came on hard and dark, and by then he wanted to be left alone in his room, the new room with the wide clean window and the small bare desk, and the narrow white bed that he made up every morning. You got up, you made up your bed, you showered, you put on your pants and your T-shirt and your white socks and your shoes, you went to breakfast downstairs and talked to Chino or Bill, or whoever was on duty, and you swallowed the blue pills nestled in the small pleated paper cup like tiny robin eggs in a nest. And then you sat out on the front porch and waited, and before long the truck came, trailing dust like a tail, the happy dog head sticking out the window like a puppet.

"You can't be serious. She just up and ran off with him?"

"She certainly did," Lila Day said.

"Well, pinch me," Betty Snodgrass said. "I would've never believed it. She don't seem the type."

"I tried to tell her she was going to ruin herself by running off with a perfect stranger."

"You didn't."

"I did. And you know what she said?"

"There's no telling."

"She said, 'Yes, he *is* pretty near perfect isn't he?'"

"Well, Emma Hanley's lost it all right," Betty said. "Leaving her family behind. Who knows? That fellow could be an axe murderer."

"I heard he was once married to an Oriental," Lila said.

"And sticking that poor boy in a home," Betty said. "It just makes you wonder if poor Hal fell in that retention pond or if he was pushed."

"Oh, I don't know about that now," Lila said, flicking off an imaginary speck of lint from her lapel. Indulging in a rare spurt of gossip with Betty in the pharmacy line was one thing, but accusations of homicide were another. It *was* Betty Snodgrass here, after all, one of Hal's Gals. Lila was of the opinion that Emma's taking off to live in sin with a man—at her age! In another hemisphere!—was bad enough without murder tacked on. Indeed, she remained astonished at Emma's fate: widowed in spring, and by summer's end taking off to the ends of the earth with a suitor. And to think that just weeks before Emma set off to parts unknown, Lila had practically begged her homebound friend to accompany her on a day trip. Instead, Lila had been forced to bring along Miss Gibble to Walhalla, a venture that had proved most vexing. Miss Gibble had not only berated the bus tour guide for repeatedly mispronouncing the name of his native town—*it's Valhalla young man!*—but also derided the poor man for claiming Walhalla meant "Garden of the Gods" when anyone with any sense of history—she didn't care *what* the Walhalla Chamber of Commerce said—any fool knew the name was, in fact, of Nordic origin, and meant "Hall of the Slain." At the end of the day, despite Lila's frantic attempts to distract her companion, sharp-eyed Miss Gibble had spied the billboard THANK YOU FOR VISITING WALHALLA: GARDEN OF THE GODS. Y'ALL COME BACK, and flew in a rage all over again.

"Poor Dora," Betty said now.

"She certainly seemed beside herself."

"I reckon so if your mama runs off with a man like that," Betty said. "I saw her last week, her eyes so swallowed up and red, I thought she took sick." She shook her head in disgust. "The cremation and then this . . ."

Actually, what Dora had said, was, *Mama, no, you're not serious. You're not running off with a man you hardly know.*

Emma stifled a smile and swallowed a comment. For a woman juggling a husband and a love interest, Dora seemed confident about expressing her misgivings regarding Emma's plans.

"How well do you know this man?"

"Well enough."

"After just . . . weeks?"

"Two months. He canceled his trip to Costa Rica just to stay here longer with me."

"Where are you staying on this . . . this trip?"

"No itinerary. Tents and hostels and modest hotels, I suspect."

"Tents? At your age? Tents. Isn't that . . . dangerous? How will you sleep?"

"Very well," Emma said.

"In . . . *one* tent? Mama, what will people think? What will I *tell* people?"

"Nothing at all. It will be much more fun to let them tell you."

"But . . . why not plan something for next summer? It's so *sudden.*"

"Oh, Dora, it's been the slowest thing in the world, this thing I'm doing. Traveling with a passport and little else, you don't know how long I've waited. I think, sometimes, it's fate. A plan. I never thought such things, but I'm keeping an open mind. Perhaps it's the hand of the Creator in this. Doesn't that make you feel better? At my age, you don't agonize over decisions. You make them."

And Dora had nodded.

"Besides," Emma said. "I've grown very fond of him. I love him."

Her daughter's eyes filled. "Yes. Go, then."

"By the way, I've got all the papers in order," Emma said, sliding a folder across the kitchen table.

"What's . . . this?"

"The deed. To this house."

"For me? But . . ."

"You know why," Emma said.

And then, later that day, Emma had gone, the jet scratching the sky.

Sometimes, Dora lay awake in her old bedroom at her mother's house, thinking about all the women at Crossroads who would make Donny a better wife. Allison Knight, for example. She was a young widow whose husband had worked for the power company and died up in a cherry picker. Everyone knew Allison was looking for a quick replacement; for months, she'd scanned the congregation, one eyebrow arched like a hook, snagging any man's casual glance. And then there was Meryl Granger, who was still single and had money, thanks to her daddy's mayonnaise company. Both of them devout Christian ladies whose faces had always lighted up when Donny passed the offering plate or greeted them with all the charm he reserved for strangers and acquaintances.

But, Donny. Well. Even though Dora hadn't set foot in Crossroads for weeks, she had no doubt her husband remained oblivious of Meryl and Allison. A man who still didn't admit he'd been fired from his last job wasn't about to acknowledge his marriage was in trouble. He remained confident Dora really was preparing her mother's house to sell, and that her job at the Office Warehouse couldn't last. Donny was certain they'd settle right back into their old life in no time. Sometimes, Dora almost believed him. That kind of dogged insistence was hard to argue with. In fact, she and Donny didn't argue. They didn't discuss anything much at all. He'd found some kind of temporary sales position at another one-horse real estate office in town, and even though Dora and the kids now practically lived here at her mother's house, they all still had dinner together most nights with Donny at the other house.

Two households, two worlds. Dora had a foot planted in each.

When her mother had deeded the house over to Dora, Emma's point had been obvious. Move out slowly, to save face, if that's what she wanted. Or sell it to climb out of a hole of debt. Her mother left Dora with more choices—one choice, anyway. And it was just about to kill her.

One thing about the dead heat of summer's end—it brought a respite, however brief, for a yardman. "Everything is tuckered out," Gordon said before he disappeared.

Well, of course everything was tuckered out. The heat beat you down, beat everything down—grass, vines, flowers—the wild party was over. The plant lover—the old guy who ran off with Emma Hanley—had warned Jake about that. Could be a short blooming season, he'd said. The price of fireworks was brevity. The more captivating, the briefer the stay. Beauty flickered, then vanished. Exploded, Jake thought, left you with your ears ringing and your dick in your hand.

There was nothing much to do but water the scorched vines and bushes, deadhead the spent blooms, soak the sad lawns. Jake and Bobby Hanley and Terrell worked early mornings, just watering mostly, waiting for planting season.

Gordon had been gone two weeks before he called Jake. Three in the morning. A train whistling low and long in the background, and if there was a lonelier sound on earth, Jake didn't know of one. "That you?" Jake asked, instantly awake.

"Yeah," Gordon said.

"It's ours. Official. Emma Hanley paid the back taxes, got it quiet-like." He did not tell Gordon the details. Too many plans, too much structure, and Gordon might sense a trap. And it wasn't a trap—it was a safety hatch. At this point, Gordon just needed to know he had a place to stay, and that his place at Amaranth was safe after all. Emma was leasing Amaranth to Homes of Hope—the group home outfit where Bobby lived—for next to nothing so they could expand on down Lavinia Avenue, with the stipulation that Gordon be the gardener there in perpetuity. "The deal is, we look after the grounds there," Jake said. "Just like you were doing. Only official, now."

The train whistle again.

"You gonna be here for fall planting?" Jake asked. "Already got more jobs than I can handle."

"Maybe. Me and Sweet."

"Starts tomorrow," Jake said.

"Fall planting already?"

"Pre-planting. It's all in the planning, man."

"That don't sound right."

"When," Jake asked, "have we ever done anything right?"

There was a special end-of-summer ceremony today at Crossroads. Pastor Pat-Rick stood at the podium in a new gray suit, looking older, more serious, and rather ecstatic to be addressing the entire congregation, instead of the youth group. After a summer of Saving Souls, it was time for an accounting.

Kyle sat on a folding chair that creaked if you didn't sit just right. If he concentrated on not making the chair squeak, he didn't have to think about Pastor Pat-Rick up there, who cleared his throat and began to launch into how important Crossroads kids were. How youth was the lifeblood of the church here, and how the youth program was growing like kudzu, praise the Lord. Saving Souls was . . . Kyle stared at his shoes and silently counted to one hundred in Spanish. If that didn't help, he'd grip the black-zippered Bible in his lap and recite to himself the Shakespeare sonnet Miss Dewberry made them memorize in English last year. His father would think he was praying. Of course, Kyle couldn't pray here, because he'd be praying not to get caught, and that just wasn't right. He'd dodged a bullet, as far as he was concerned, and all he wanted to do now was get through this long torturous service, get the hell out of here, and avoid the eyes of Pastor Pat-Rick.

Kyle resumed his silent counting and got all the way to *ochentay seis*, but he was still hyperaware of his father's movements, how he recrossed his legs. From the corner of he eye, Kyle could see his father's stodgy black dress shoe. He hated that shoe.

". . . And in Mission Possible . . . these kids were out in the heat . . . drywalling . . . ," Pastor Pat-Rick droned on.

Kyle's sister was yawning and wiggling, so he handed her a Lifesaver and gave her a look, just as his mother would do.

". . . and I've given a lot of thought to this, and it wasn't easy. But the award for Saving Souls goes to . . . Kyle Quattlebaum. . . ."

Huh? Kyle said the word aloud. "HUH?" And then there were faces turning around and smiling, and Mrs. Mann beside him nudging him with her bony hand, asking him what he was waiting for.

Kyle found himself standing behind the podium, sandwiched between Pastor Pete and Pastor Pat-Rick. He couldn't make himself look out at all those faces—all those smiles!—for fear his vision would snag on a very scowling face. His father. He couldn't see him, but he didn't have to. Oh, he would pay dearly for this. Oh man, he would pay.

"Now, Kyle, you had what is called an Individualized Project," Pastor Pat-Rick said, his hand thumping on Kyle's back. His words echoed out into the shopping center corridors, buzzing and shorting on the crappy sound system. Was it a question? Kyle trembled so hard, he appeared to be nodding. But now Pastor Pat-Rick turned and addressed the audience, teetering a little on the balls of his feet. "Folks, I want to tell you a little about Kyle's project. I showed up one day out of the clear blue and observed him and the people he chose to work with. And I mean work. Because you won't believe the changes he has brought to these people by bringing them the Good News." There was a clatter of applause, until Pastor Pat-Rick held up a hand. "I talked to a widow woman who said she hadn't darkened the door of a church in years." And here Pastor Pat-Rick took out a folded piece of paper from his suit pocket and glanced at it. "I quote, 'This boy has opened my heart at a time in my life when I had hardened myself. Until this young man reminded me of the joy in life and . . . ' '" Pastor Pat-Rick squinted at the paper, his lips moving silently. He looked up, " 'and I have no doubt she is near to accepting Christ as her savior." There was more clapping and Kyle's every muscle went rigid. *Please please please don't say their names.*

"And I talked to a man tormented by devilish thoughts. I saw it myself, how this poor fella talks to things that ain't there, and drops down to the dirt and stares and whispers. It's a sad thing, but Kyle had a special way with him. He told this poor man that I was from a big church and I was a preacher and then he told him not to worry and to listen a minute. And then I commenced to talk to the man and ask him if he'd heard that the Lord Jesus Christ had died for his sins, and let me tell you he got really interested fast. I told him how Jesus rose from the dead and ascended into heaven and sits at the right hand of the Father and then this man looked up like he was watching a movie up in the clouds, and asked me if I had seen Saint Paul lately, and told me how he saw an angel just the other day, in the Dollar Daze parking lot. And who are we to question that?"

Pastor Pat-Rick looked out at the spellbound crowd. Kyle swallowed. "There are angels among us." There were murmurs of agreement. "Well, this lady told me all about how Kyle had helped them, keeping them company and doing yard work and cleaning out the attic. And then, if that wasn't enough to keep the frogs hopping, like my daddy used to say, well, then I commenced to speak to a truckload of the most downtrodden souls you have ever seen. They drove up and parked in this lady's driveway, and lo and behold, she went over and talked to them for a minute. I talked to the tormented man first, like I said, and then the rest of them came over to say they'd be glad to testify how Kyle has been so good to them and turned them all back into Christians. Looked like they did odd jobs and yard work. Of course, I knew this wasn't a real business. No one would hire that kind of riffraff, but Kyle had given them hope, you see, by witnessing to them, by not judging them, by sharing the Good News. One of the black fellows said he was even thinking of stopping his drinking. And then another one said he had quit women and then started singing gospel—'Amazing Grace'—that brought tears to my eyes. I told him he had a voice from heaven, and he said, yes, his mama always said so. I said, 'You ought to sing in a choir with that voice,' and he said he liked singing in shows at a place up in Charlotte. I said, 'How do you know every word of "Amazing Grace"?' And he said he never heard it before in his life. The songs and words just popped in his head. Well," Pastor Pat-Rick sighed dramatically and gazed out into the congregation. "Well, I tell you. That's when I knew I had just seen a miracle transpire before my eyes." There was more clapping. "I can't even explain it, I can't find the words. So you see why I am presenting Kyle Quattlebaum with the Saving Souls award. This boy got through the hardest hearts, the most pathetic bunch of people you've ever seen, and I don't think it would be wrong to say—he penetrated a criminal element—all to save their souls. Yes, he has saved a passel of souls this summer. Half a dozen people born again, by my count. Why, just think what this boy can do in a year. He's got talent." He turned to Kyle and handed him a pin. "Wear this with pride, Kyle, and you should consider a career as a missionary." There was laughing and applause that lasted an eternity, and all the time Kyle thought, *This is not real. This can't be happening.* Too late, he remembered not to look at the congregation, too late, because when he did, his eyes instantly found his father, who sat erect, shoulders back, his face shining with pride.

After the service, Kyle found his father sitting behind the soundboard, beside Joe Henley, and when he spotted Kyle and waved him over, his father looked so eager to please him, Kyle was appalled. Worse, he felt hobbled with pity for his father. Kyle walked over and stood there in his good white shirt and khakis, a black, narrow knit tie, the kind his father always complained about, and felt his father's hand on his shoulder.

"It's a shame your mother . . . couldn't be here to see you honored."

"She said she was going to the other church."

His father tried to look as if he weren't frustrated by his wife's going back to the little Baptist church near an hour away where she was baptized, where the two of them started, but he failed miserably. His father's mouth tightened and his eyes widened to cut off the sadness. Kyle's mother had taken a job at an office-supply store last week, and Kyle was pretty sure his father didn't approve of that, either. Lately, his mother was acting distracted, but in a good way. In the last couple of weeks, she hummed while she did dishes, or smiled into space, and she'd started cleaning the house from top to bottom, and this was the weirdest thing—she'd started emptying closets and clearing off shelves, and cleaning out the garage and taking loads of things every day to charity. There was air and space in the house; they could *breathe*.

"Well, come on over here and sit by Mr. Henley, Kyle. He's going to teach you everything you wanted to know about sound systems."

His father actually thought working on the sound system at Crossroads would interest Kyle. An award. In lieu of guitar lessons or rock music. Pathetic. But Kyle forced a smile. He'd learned to tune out all his dad's Blood of the Lamb talk and how God watches you all the time and knows exactly what you're up to—like a CIA Santa Claus for adults—all that paranoid, tight-laced shit got tiring, but Kyle still prayed every day, mostly to complain to Jesus about his crazy-ass parents. His father beamed at him as Kyle pretended to listen to Mr. Henley talk about microphone quality. Something else Kyle would have to get through, like any unpleasant situation—his sister's dance recital, for example. Kyle had discovered the value in just getting through things. It was a skill that sure came in handy.

Yes, Emma Hanley had surprised him—leaving the homestead where she raised her family, leaving the town. Running off with the plantsman. She surprised him, but he understood. Love did strange things to people. By now, Jake had expected to find a place of his own somewhere, a small house, a bungalow, something that wasn't on wheels. It just didn't seem right to get rid of the trailer, though. His daddy's trailer—a piece of shit, but he couldn't sell it or scrap it to save his life. Just physically couldn't bring himself to shed it.

The place was no longer empty. The counter and kitchen table were crowded with appliances—a toaster oven, a blender, a coffeemaker. Stacks of plates. *I worry about you alone in this empty place*, Dora had said, so she brought him things. Place mats, canisters, cutting boards, cutlery, a lamp. Filling up, filling in. Pots and pans, a clock, mixing bowls, soap dishes—shiny objects, scraps, leftovers, *a few extra things*, she called them. She was planning on donating it all to Homes of Hope, but she wanted him to take whatever he needed first. The truth was, he did not need any of it, but it didn't matter, because all these things brought her here.

First love was a wildflower, Jake thought. A regular weed. You reaped it for years. They'd had no barriers all those years ago when they were kids, but nowadays, they were hemmed in by rock—blooming, impossibly, in a cranny in the wall. All those years ago, he'd had free rein over the lengths and curves of her, he could have mapped every crevice of the land of Dora, which she'd not only offered to him, but in fact demanded he explore. But now? She did not give herself to him; she did not share but these little bits of herself: memories, long tortured embraces that ended too soon, and all these . . . things. These gleaming, burnished objects. These thick cushions and soft towels. These candle-less candlesticks, these fuzzy bathmats, this Crock-Pot, these milk-glass vases, this magazine rack. He really needed to load it all up today and take it on down to Homes of Hope. Because all this stuff jammed in his cabinets and on tables and bed stands and across counters just reminded him of Dee, and every dish and glass and coaster made him miss her more after she was gone, and the more it all piled up, the more empty he felt, and god-awful lonely.

Just as Dora's feet hit the floor, a water pipe screeched. Good. Kyle was up. Today was her long day. A double shift.

It helped to stay busy. Looking in on Bobby at Homes of Hope, taking care of Kyle and Sandy, working full-time at a place where *inventory* was a verb—Dora was busier now than she'd ever been in her life.

She pulled on cut-offs and an old shirt, and tiptoed past Sandy, who was still asleep. In the kitchen, she measured out coffee. She heard the truck in the driveway.

"Kyle?" she called.

"Coming."

She stood in the shadows at the kitchen window, out of sight, her mother's ancient percolator tut-tutting and tsk-tsking steamy puffs behind her. Jake got out. He stood, trying not to look like he was waiting. But he was. Dora poured a cup of coffee.

Dora Hanley, you haven't changed a bit, Jake had told her that day in June, and he was thinking it still, she knew, even today, as she opened the front door and walked out on the porch. When he took the mug of coffee she offered, he met her eyes, and she longed to tell him, *You don't know me, Jake. I'm not Dee. I don't know who I am. But I'm trying real hard to find out.*

So Gordon returned and they started up their routine: Jake picked up Gordon and the dog, swung by the home for Bobby. Saturdays they picked up the boy at Emma's place, where Dora and her kids were staying. These days, there were two kinds of mornings: disappointing ones and wonderful ones, and Jake couldn't tell today which one today was. Not a soul was out there at first, so it looked to be a disappointing one, but then the screen door opened and out stepped Dora and the morning turned wonderful. She had on cut-offs and a big T-shirt that must have been Bobby's. She was barefooted and had her hair pulled back in a ponytail.

She handed him a cup of coffee. "You got Bobby back there?" she asked.

"Course I do," Jake said, trying to sound casual.

"Bobby?" she walked to the truck and Bobby looked out.

"Mama called last night. She wanted me to tell you. She's mailing you another letter soon. It has a dried-up bug in it. Some kind of beetle."

"Good," Bobby said, looking unsurprised, as if the news were secondhand.

"She's in Costa Rica," Dora added. She patted Kyle on the back as he walked past and got in the truck. "Be careful now."

And then there was just the two of them, Jake standing by his open truck door, pushing his sunglasses on his head, Dora there in the driveway, hand shielding her eyes. The briefest of smiles crossed her face, but he could not bear to take encouragement from it.

He took an envelope from his pocket, handed it to her. "I found out Wanda's living in a little pink house in California," he said.

"Wanda is . . ."

"With a husband and kids and a cat. The works."

"She has a . . . family?"

He nodded. She opened the envelope—there was Wanda's married name, her address, even some photocopied pictures from her family Christmas newsletter. Turned out the private eye that Ginger Welch jerked around was cheap, all right, but thorough enough. With the barest of details, the man had found Wanda Wilson's whereabouts.

"Dee, look. I don't know how you feel about that, but . . . I thought you should know."

"I thought for sure . . . she was . . ." Dora stared down at a smiling Wanda, flanked by her children.

Wanda made her own choices, Jake wanted to say, but didn't. *Wanda has moved on. You can't blame yourself anymore.*

Two weeks ago, Jake had made the hardest promise of his life. He'd sworn to leave Dora alone. He'd vowed not to interfere in her decision about changing her life. He couldn't bear to think what she'd decided, if she had decided. She was at a crossroads, all right, and he waited on down the path. He would wait for her to take the fork. He wouldn't beckon to her. He wasn't the type. She had to find her own way. All he could do was wait. And he was mighty good at that.

The plane nosed up now, pressing Emma back into her seat. Her stomach fluttered.

"Em, this is gorgeous," Win said from beside her. He was admiring her sketch of *Phragmipedium caudatum,* with its remarkable pendulant petals, though she hadn't done it justice.

"Oh, goodness. It isn't, either. It's the barest resemblance. Interesting, perhaps."

"Well, I'll take interesting over gorgeous anytime. But it sure is nice when you have both."

The plane shuddered slightly, tilting, and Emma caught sight of the verdant green of Costa Rica below. She always got the window seat. He insisted. She sighed. "Oh, it's so lovely, isn't it?"

"Just wait until we get to Madagascar."

"I know . . . but still. I hate to leave." How terribly easy it was to settle, Emma thought. Before you knew it, you found yourself rooted to a place. But as Win Burnside reminded her daily, you dare not linger, not when there was so much more to see.

He pressed his warm whiskered lips against her palm.

"In Madagascar, the traveler's tree has gargantuan flowers to support the weight of the ruffled lemur," he said. "That's a ten-pound primate."

"The . . . traveler's tree?"

"Page eighty-six of William McCann's splendid account. Figure forty-four." He winked and tipped back his seat, pulled his hat over his eyes. "You're going to love it, Em."

The captain's greeting crackled now in the cabin, the flight attendants' strange pantomime began. How different the world looked from above, Emma thought. When they'd left Palmetto, the town had appeared parceled, more square and orderly than Emma ever thought possible. And now she was floating away again, tethered to nothing but Win's hand on the armrest beside her. Below them, the clouds, clots of spun silk, left shadows on the land. Somewhere on that shrinking skin of earth were Bobby and Dora, Kyle and Sandy. Emma had only to close her eyes to imagine them, to see their upturned faces.